ALL PROFITS WILL BE DONATED TO THE LITERACY PARTNERS, A NATIONAL ORGANIZATION PROMOTING READING AMONG ADULTS.

THE GREATEST ROMANCE STORIES EVER TOLD BY ELEVEN OF THE MOST POPULAR ROMANCE AUTHORS IN THE WORLD!

MADELINE BAKER, MARY BALOGH, ELAINE BARBIERI, LORI COPELAND, CASSIE EDWARDS, HEATHER GRAHAM, CATHERINE HART, VIRGINIA HENLEY, PENELOPE NERI, DIANA PALMER, JANELLE TAYLOR

From the Middle Ages to the present day, these stories follow the men and women whose lives are forever changed by a special book—a cherished volume that teaches the love of learning and the learning of love!

SO DO YOU WANT TO KNOW WHO WROTE THE BOOK OF LOVE?
READ ON AND FIND OUT...

MADELINE BAKER

"To Love Again"

Madeline Baker is the author of eighteen romances for Leisure. Her novels have consistently appeared on the Walden and B. Dalton bestseller lists, and she is the winner of the *Romantic Times* Reviewers' Choice Award. Her newest historical romance is *Lakota Renegade* (Leisure; September 1995).

MARY BALOGH

"The Betrothal Ball"

With more than forty romances to her credit, Mary Balogh is the winner of two *Romantic Times* Career Achievement Awards. She has been praised by *Publishers Weekly* for writing an "epic love story...absorbing reading right up until the end!" Her latest historical romance is *Heartless* (Berkley; October 1995).

ELAINE BARBIERI

"Loving Charity"

The author of twenty-five romances for Jove, Zebra, Harlequin, and Leisure, Elaine Barbieri has been called "an absolute master of her craft" by *Romantic Times*. She is the winner of several *Romantic Times* Reviewers' Choice Awards, including those for Storyteller Of The Year and Lifetime Achievement; and her historical romance *Wings Of The Dove* was a Doubleday Book Club selection. Her most recent title is *Dance Of The Flame* (Leisure; June 1995).

LORI COPELAND

"Kindred Hearts"

Lori Copeland is the author of more than forty romances for Harlequin, Bantam, Dell, Fawcett, and Love Spell. Her novels have consistently appeared on the Walden, B. Dalton, and *USA Today* bestseller lists. Her newest historical romance is *Someone To Love* (Fawcett; May 1995).

CASSIE EDWARDS

"Savage Fantasy"

The author of fifty romances for Jove, Zebra, Harlequin, NAL Topaz, and Leisure, Cassie Edwards has been called "a shining talent" by *Romantic Times*. She is the winner of the *Romantic Times* Lifetime Achievement Award for Best Indian Romance Series. Her most recent title is *Savage Secrets* (Leisure; June 1995).

HEATHER GRAHAM

"Fairy Tale"

The author of more than seventy novels for Dell, Harlequin, Silhouette, Avon, and Pinnacle, Heather Graham also publishes under the pseudonyms Heather Graham Pozzessere and Shannon Drake. She has been celebrated as "an incredible storyteller" by the *Los Angeles Times*. Her romances have been featured by the Doubleday Book Club and the Literary Guild; she has also had several titles on the *New York Times* bestseller list. Writing as Shannon Drake, she recently published *Branded Hearts* (Avon; February 1995).

CATHERINE HART

"Golden Treasures"

Catherine Hart is the author of fifteen historical romances for Leisure and Avon. Her novels have consistently appeared on the Walden and B. Dalton bestseller lists. Her newest historical romance is *Mischief* (Avon; September 1995).

VIRGINIA HENLEY

"Letter Of Love"

The author of eleven titles for Avon and Dell, Virginia Henley has been awarded the *Affaire de Coeur* Silver Pen Award. Two of her historical romances—*Seduced* and *Desired*—have appeared on the *USA Today*, *Publishers Weekly*, and *New York Times* bestseller lists. Her latest historical romance is *Desired* (Dell Island; February 1995).

PENELOPE NERI

"Hidden Treasures"

Penelope Neri is the author of eighteen historical romances for Zebra. She is the winner of the *Romantic Times* Storyteller Of The Year Award and *Affaire de Coeur's* Golden Certificate Award. Her most recent title is *This Stolen Moment* (Zebra; October 1994).

DIANA PALMER

"Annabelle's Legacy"

With more than eighty novels to her credit, Diana Palmer has published with Fawcett, Warner, Silhouette, and Dell. Among her numerous writing awards are seven Walden Romance Bestseller Awards and four B. Dalton Bestseller Awards. Her latest romance is *That Burke Man* (Silhouette Desire; March 1995).

JANELLE TAYLOR

"Winds Of Change"

The author of thirty-four books, Janelle Taylor has had seven titles on the *New York Times* bestseller list, and eight of her novels have sold over a million copies each. Ms. Taylor has received much acclaim for her writing, including being induced into the *Romantic Times* Writers Hall Of Fame. Her newest historical romance is *Destiny Mine* (Zebra; January 1995).

Love's Legacy

EDITED BY KATHRYN FALK

MADELINE BAKER

MARY BALOGH

ELAINE BARBIERI

LORI COPELAND

CASSIE EDWARDS

HEATHER GRAHAM

CATHERINE HART

VIRGINIA HENLEY

PENELOPE NERI

DIANA PALMER

JANELLE TAYLOR

LEISURE BOOKS  NEW YORK CITY

A LEISURE BOOK®

January 1996

Published by

Dorchester Publishing Co., Inc.
276 Fifth Avenue
New York, NY 10001

Printed in the United States of America.

Love's Legacy

FAIRY TALE

HEATHER GRAHAM

Fairy Tale

"Another book? Alas, my lady! All that reading will cause your eyes to squint if you do not take care!"

Genevieve swung around, nearly stumbling off the small stool she stood upon to reach the high shelf in the library and the beautifully bound book that had been tempting her day after day. It was a unique book, she had discovered: ancient, exquisitely bound in doeskin, gilded in gold, painstakingly written by hand. The author was anonymous, but had created pictures of great beauty with her words alone. The tale which Genevieve had just begun was a love story, a beautiful story to appeal to the romantic in anyone—other than a jaded knight such as Lord Robert, Earl of Betancourt, who stared at her now from the library doorway.

It was extraordinary that she hadn't heard him enter before he spoke in the deep, rich, taunting voice. He was dressed in full armor. Not battle armor—she had seen his battle armor. He had ordered it created by the finest German smiths, painted black, and ornamented little because it was functional wear. In battle, he wore his tunic atop it with his coat of arms emblazoned in startling yellow-gold and cobalt blue. They had obviously waged a triumphant battle in France, for he had returned to his home handsomely clad in his parade armor of silver mesh and plate. His tunic was a rich sky blue; his helmet had been shed when he arrived at Betancourt Castle.

Genevieve's heart seemed to quiver within her chest, and for several moments she found herself silently thanking God for his return, for in the service of Edward III, he was constantly waging war. But then, war was his game, his life. From the time he had been a child, he had been taught to fight. Prowess in the saddle, with the sword, leading men to battle, those were his talents, and he had learned them well. He sometimes had little patience for anything else, yet part of the reason he had intrigued her so when they had first met had been his ability to listen.

And perhaps that was a lie, she admitted, for he had intrigued her from the moment she had first seen him on a night when she had entertained at Edward's court. Edward had heard that the French king had been fascinated with the poetess and balladeer from Brittany, and so had been determined to have her in his own court. She had been glad of the invitation, for kings paid well, and she dreamed of being financially independent and secure one day.

Once, when very young, she had been married—to a young man from a merchant family much like her own, a boy who had dreamed of riches and grandeur. Henry had been knighted on the field by the King of England. But Henry had fallen on the field, too, and she had been left with the debts he owed for his horses, his armor, his page, and all those accoutrements that had allowed him his moments of grandeur. There had been days then when she had been desperate. Rich men had made her offers—for her favors. Men with wives who had longed for an intriguing mistress. Her marriage to Henry had been arranged, but they had cared for one another, and no matter how desperate she felt, she had been determined not to become the mistress of a rich man, no longer free. She had spent a night on the floor of the chapel in the small manor where she had lived with Henry, and she had looked up continually at a statue of the Virgin Mary and prayed through the night.

The next day, she had started writing, setting her thoughts and feelings down on paper. She added music to her words the following day, strumming upon her lute. She played first in the house of a widowed noblewoman who had long been her friend; then she had crossed the Channel, and played across Europe. Soon, her roots had been forgotten, and she was welcomed wherever she went as one of the most talented artists of her time.

She feared the day, however, when she would no longer be hailed as a great talent and beauty, for though kings and queens and nobles were wont to vie for her time now, it might not always be so. She meant to be financially secure when that time came, and never to depend on the whims of the nobility—or to become nothing more than a well-dressed and well-educated plaything for a rich man. With such goals in mind, she had determinedly avoided the advances of the rich and noble men she came across—managing to dodge the kings of both England and France with her serene and icy demeanor and blunt refusals to their propositions.

Then she had seen Robert.

He had been sitting at the king's table that night, newly returned from some campaign. He had come into the hall in battle armor, and when he first strode in, he had seemed almost unreal, far larger than life, a knight out of a legend. His page had followed swiftly behind him, and even as he spoke with the king about the battle under way, he had shed pieces of armor. Even in a coat of mail and overtunic in colorful blue and gold, he had still seemed larger than life, taller than the king, with coal black hair, rich and thick, falling upon his forehead, startling yellow-green eyes, bronze skin, and handsome, cleanly chiseled features.

Genevieve had noted him from her place far down the table, where she had been seated with the lesser gentry and some of the clergy, but he had not noted her—not until she had been called upon to sing. Then, for the first time in her life, she had felt as if she had been actually touched by a man's eyes. His gaze seemed to wash over her with a liquid yellow fire. It warmed her, touched her. The very thought of *desire* for a man had been buried along with Henry, not that they had been together long enough for her to discover much about passion. But even as she sang, even as she kept her own gaze upon others, she could feel him watching her. Feel things awaken inside of her. She had always loved fairy tales and legends. He was like a knight out of such a legend, taller, fiercer, faster than others, more striking, more courageous . . .

A nobleman. Distant kin to the king. Out of her

reach. A man from the same station in life as all those who had propositioned her before, those who wanted to have her, rule her, perhaps even love her—in their way. As a mistress.

She tried to forget him. Tried to forget his eyes.

Later that night, she was summoned to his chambers by his page, a young man named Alex. She refused to go. Alex pleaded, begged, threatened. She still refused. She hadn't cared how rich or wonderful the Earl of Betancourt might be. She didn't want the pain of knowing him. Of wanting what she couldn't have.

But she had just settled into her small chamber for the night when Lord Robert suddenly burst in on her. Fear, outrage, and panic seized her. She forced herself to stand very still in her bare feet and simple white gown and stare up at him with complete contempt.

"How dare you, sir—"

"Are you daft? Do you know who I am?"

"Were you a knight with any sense of chivalry, sir, you would have knocked upon my door and awaited my bidding before entering. Better yet, were you a man with the manners of one I would bid enter my room, you would have heeded my refusal to see you!"

"I am the Earl of Betancourt, my lady, and I am not accustomed to being rudely ignored by servants."

"But I am no man's servant. I am my own mistress."

He ignored her again. "I have a proposition for you."

"My lord!" she enunciated regally. "I assure you, I am not interested. For all of your arrogance, I have turned down *propositions* from better men than you!"

He arched a brow. Suddenly his lips curved, and though his arrogance remained—his chin high and shoulders so very broad and set—there was suddenly something much more touchable, human, about the man. "Better men?" he inquired. "Ah, my lady! There are richer men, and men with higher titles, but no *better* men, I assure you."

"But there must be more humble men, my lord."

"Ah, but humility does not keep one's opponent at bay, my lady. Still, I do admit to the great desire to tease and taunt you, for never have I met a woman quite so stubborn. And though I am not certain what their propositions were, I rather doubt that you are aware of what my 'proposition,' which you are so very eager to turn down, will be. It is not indecent, I assure you."

"Indeed?" she queried, her eyes narrowing warily.

"I am rearing a younger sister, Lavinia. My proposition, my lady, is only that you come and entertain at my family home. I'm afraid that our father passed on when I was reaching my majority, and though she has learned much about war and campaigns, she is woefully ignorant—or so she tells me—of the gentler arts. She wishes to read and write, to create music. I have no patience for such leisurely pursuits myself."

"Surely, my lord, your wife—"

"I was once wed, as my father desired, to the Earl of Claiborne's daughter. Alas, she was a victim of the plague that so fiercely ravished us all."

Genevieve didn't know why she was intrigued by him, perhaps because he seemed so amused by her. He was brash and arrogant, but blunt and honest as well, and there was something about his eyes . . .

Dangerous, she thought.

"I—I am presently engaged—"

"But 'presently' will end, my lady. I will pay you in gold, richly, I promise."

"But—"

"You needn't fear me, my lady." Again he smiled, crossing his arms over his chest.

"Oh?"

"I've no interest in buying, er, special favors. Perhaps this will amaze you, but I don't need great riches, promises, or bribes to find companionship, and it is my belief that neither love nor good carnal entertainment should be bought. Both are such gifts as must come willingly from each partner."

He was laughing at her, she thought. Or perhaps he was telling her that he would never need to pay for certain services from her. If he desired her, she would simply succumb to his good looks, strength, and arrogance.

"You may rest assured, my lord, I will only bed the man I wed."

"Alas! I shall die brokenhearted!" he mocked, and she blushed with fury, despite herself. But his voice went on, softer, deeper, richer, and somehow more taunting still. "But I will respect your wishes, my lady. Will you come to my home? I will pay you well."

He offered her a staggering price, but she refused to betray her relief at the sum. Aye, it would be enough. Enough to buy freedom to the end of her days, as long as she was careful.

So she had come to Betancourt Castle. He had not been there when she arrived. Lavinia had given her a large, beautiful room that overlooked the gardens, and she had quickly grown fond of Robert's lovely young sister, just as she grew very fond of the castle. Parts of it were ancient, built from Roman ruins, while other areas were newer. There was a great hall with beautifully paned glass windows, exquisite carpets, thick upholstered chairs, and window seats. Her bedroom was captivating, huge, with a massive carved marble fireplace and a balcony that led to parapets overlooking the river.

And there was the library, between her room and the master's chambers, Robert of Betancourt's rooms. She had come here frequently, as well she should, for she had taught Lavinia how to read.

Robert had come home upon occasion. As he had promised, he asked nothing of her. Once a week, he requested her presence in the library so that she might report on her work with Lavinia.

He rode away to war, on the king's business.

He never touched her.

But more and more . . .

She could *feel* him.

Ah, yes, feel his eyes. The deep, rich tenor of his voice could evoke a trail of dancing heat down her spine. She tried so very hard to speak evenly with him. To keep her distance.

But today, even as he taunted her, he seemed weary. He leaned within the doorframe, and she cried out suddenly, dropping the book as she came from her stool to stride toward him. She moved swiftly, then stopped dead as his eyes touched upon hers. "You're bleeding, my lord."

"A small wound, nothing more."

"The smallest wound can kill, my lord, if not treated properly."

"And you can treat it properly?"

"I can, my lord."

"And you are willing to do so?" he inquired again, his lips curling into an inquisitive smile. "And I had thought you disliked me so, Genevieve."

"You are an arrogant boor, at times, Lord Robert," she said smoothly, "but arrogance is not a crime that should be punished by death."

"Indeed," he teased, "it is a virtue."

She sighed with deep exasperation. "Mock me, sir, and you may well die."

"Are you a sorceress then, with a golden voice like a siren of old, to tempt men to their doom? A witch perhaps to poison and torment me?"

"I'm not a witch."

"But you know about potions."

"I know how to read!" she exclaimed, her patience wearing thin. "Have it as you will, my brave, noble, arrogant sir. Do you fear my touch?"

"Ah, that I do," he said very softly. "But the shoulder pains me. Fine, lady, have it as you will!"

He called for his page, and between the strong young boy, Robert, and herself, they stripped him of his fine mantle, overtunic, plates, and mail. Genevieve called one of the young kitchen maids and ordered the herbs she wanted soaked together to treat Robert's wound. He sat before the fire in the library, and she set a number of stitches into the wound; then her salve was finished and she applied it to the wound, and bandaged it carefully.

"Aye, but what a bargain I acquired! A poetess and alchemist/physician as well—since you are not a witch," he teased, looking up at her.

She tried not to notice the ripple of bare muscle beneath her fingers, the heat of his flesh, the scent of him. She didn't look into his eyes, but replied curtly, "I told you, my lord. I read. And I have learned a great deal from books."

He didn't reply, but the smile she saw upon his lips was skeptical. "Books! They are for dreamers."

"Your arm will be well soon. You'll see. And by no magic or mystery, simply because I learned from those who have come before me."

"So you read only to learn?" he asked her.

His eyes seemed very dark. Intense. Her fingers still lay upon his flesh, and she almost snatched them away.

"No, my lord," she said, and stepped back from him. "I read to learn, to gain what is offered. And I read to dream, to see the lives of others, to fly, to soar."

"Dreams can only be realized with sweat and blood upon a battlefield."

"Perhaps. But no man can taste and touch and feel all that life has to give. Yet in a book, my lord . . . in a book, all things are possible."

"Perhaps I will allow you to teach me."

"Perhaps I will be good enough to do so," she said serenely.

Ah, but she should have known him! The challenge was what had brought him to her, she realized quickly.

"You will teach me," he said firmly.

"Perhaps later—"

"Perhaps now."

"Then perhaps we had best renegotiate my contract—"

"Perhaps you should get a book!"

"We will renegotiate!" she said haughtily, but since he was so close and so towering, and she was so very afraid that he would touch her, she reached for a book.

The afternoon turned to evening, and it seemed

that no time had passed at all. He knew the basics; he had been taught before. He had just never read. She started him out with a manual on crossbows. Their heads bent low, they studied it together, and the time seemed to sweep by.

Eventually, he stood, ready to replace the book. It was then he found the ancient volume she had reached for when he had come, fallen upon the floor. He picked it up, and Genevieve gasped, rushing forward to take it from his hands and study it carefully, hoping she hadn't damaged it. He laughed as she took it from his hands. "Ah, Genevieve! And I had thought you cared about the condition of my flesh. You are far more tender with this book."

"It is far more fragile than your flesh," she assured him.

"And what is this book?"

"I don't really know," she said softly. "It is very old, beautifully crafted, and a story—"

"A story . . . ?"

"A love story, as beautifully told as penned," she finished. "I think it was written in the first few centuries after Christ, and this particular version of it was copied in Latin by a talented monk."

"A love story by a monk?"

"Monks are craftsmen still," she reminded him, refusing to blush. "But I do not believe the monk was the original author. I believe this tale was woven by a woman, a woman of great sensitivity and feeling."

"Such as warriors often lack?"

She shrugged. "You would know the answer to that, my lord."

"Perhaps we should read it."

She started to protest, but the book was in his

hands, open to the first page. His fingers were long. Despite their power and the size and strength of his hands, he held the book carefully, and turned each page so that the fragile paper would not tear.

"I will begin."

And so he did. But she soon found the book in her own hands, and she was reading aloud to him. She was absorbed in the story, and he was silent, watching her all the while. The fire crackled behind them. Warm, inviting. She fell deeper into the tale of lost love, of two hearts and souls striving to be together, of evil forces keeping them apart. The hero, Damon, striving to be noble, described his love:

" 'For the scent of her was like a field of flowers, the taste of her flesh was honey and life. To be—' "

She broke off. He took the book.

" 'To be embraced deep within her sweet fire, a part of her, was anguish and ecstasy, like dying just to live again. To love, to soar . . . ' "

He broke off himself. Genevieve looked up to discover that Lavinia had come to the door. At twelve, she was almost a lady, but with a sweetness of spirit that made her seem very young and innocent still.

"Robert!" She kissed and hugged her brother, taking care with his wound. "I just heard you were home. You hadn't even come to see me!"

"His shoulder needed bandaging," Genevieve said quickly.

"She seduced me—into reading," Robert corrected.

Lavinia giggled happily. "She's very good at that."

"Indeed, she is," Robert agreed, watching Genevieve.

"Since you are here, my lord brother," Lavinia said firmly, "you must come to dinner. Now. It is very late, and I am very hungry."

"Come then, dinner is served," Robert told Genevieve, reaching a hand down to her.

Since she had come to the castle, she had taken her meals with Lavinia, except for when Robert had been in residence. She had kept to her room then, maintaining her distance from him unless she had been called down to entertain.

"Forgive me. I am tired—"

"I'll not forgive you. You must eat, and the meal is ready below." He hesitated, bowing low, offering her his hand. "Please, my lady, you will accompany us?"

And her hand touched his . . .

It was that night when things began to change. She came to dinner each night; she read with him upon occasion. She watched him as he worked with his sword and lance in the courtyard below, regaining his strength. By the end of the week, his injury was all but healed. She took out the tiny stitches she had sewn. He made her laugh and smile upon occasion. When they read one afternoon, she learned about his past. "This story of yours is nothing but a child's tale," he told her impatiently. "These two falling in love. Life is not so enchanted."

"Your life is enchanted," she commented.

He rose, walking to the window, his mantle drifting behind him, his hands clasped at his back. "Enchanted? Madame, I came off the battlefield at the age of sixteen to find that a young girl of thirteen whom I had never even seen was waiting in the chapel to be my wife. She brought me very rich lands in Poitiers, and she was of very noble birth, and so she was deemed perfect for me."

"But?" Genevieve whispered.

He shrugged. "But she was timid and more fragile than your book. I pitied her, and spared her my presence as much as possible. After two years of marriage, she nearly died in childbed and we lost our newborn son. She was never strong, and I swore then that I'd not come near her again, but to little avail, for she cried over the babe's grave, and blamed herself for failing as a wife. It was a match made in hell, not that we hated one another, but that we cared—but not enough to love. You'll understand why I tire upon occasion of this fairy tale of yours!"

"Life is what we make it," she told him fiercely.

"Is it?"

"I have made my life, and I am happy with it."

"Happy?" he demanded, and he smiled bitterly. "Genevieve, there you stand! You still have youth, and God blessed you—or cursed you—with incredible beauty. Violet eyes, golden hair, flesh like marble. To what avail? You've damned yourself to grow old and lonely. I pray, lady, that your books will keep you warm when the years have passed and you think of the love you may have passed by!"

"The love?" she whispered. "I have been offered townhouses, country estates, clothing, and jewels. Never love, my lord."

"And what if you were offered love? To you, my lady, it comes only with a wedding band."

"It comes with a commitment!" she cried in turn. "It comes with caring, with needing, with—"

"With a wedding band," he said wearily. He

swung on her. "By law, lady, I cannot wed without the king's permission—"

"I've never suggested that you should wed me! I have merely told you that I cannot . . ."

"Cannot what?"

"I cannot . . . care about a man who is destined to wed another heiress, and have sons with her while I sit and wait in a London townhouse or country estate."

"I would rather have loneliness and this anguish."

"I would rather have freedom and dignity."

"At the price of love?"

"I keep my soul!" she cried.

He turned then, slammed a fist against the wall, and the whole of the castle seemed to shudder. He didn't look back at her, but strode from the room. The door slammed in his wake.

That night she could not sleep. Hair free, restless, dressed in her bare feet and white nightgown, she bolted up when a gust of wind opened the shutter doors that led to the balcony and parapets. She rose and wandered out, and saw that a storm was coming. Lightning split the sky with a jagged streak of gold, and the wind rose, becoming a tempest that blew her hair in soft silken sheets around her and lifted and played with the hem of her skirt. She didn't know what alerted her to his presence; she heard nothing, but some instinct warned her to turn.

He, too, had come outside. The width of the library stretched between them, for he had come through shutter doors as well, and stood in the wind. He wore a cobalt velvet robe, and nothing more. His hair was caught by the wind and flung around his rugged features. His feet were bare, his muscled calves were visible as the wind whipped the robe around his towering form.

She could have changed things. Could have turned and walked back into her room, closed the shutters to the wind and tempest. But she didn't move. She felt the wind roaring around her, as if beckoning. It was a cold wind, but it seemed as if the lightning had streaked inside her. He was walking toward her, staring at her, not yet touching her. Then he was shouting to her: "I cannot marry you! The king will never allow it. I am an earl, kin to Edward. You are a commoner."

Still, she didn't move. He hadn't needed to tell her such a thing; she knew it all too well.

Now! Run from the wind, from the man . . .

She closed her eyes. Still, he didn't touch her. "For the love of God!" he cried out, and her eyes flew open. His hands were clenched at his sides. He was so very close. She could feel the heat that emanated from his body, see the tension that corded his throat, that caused a vein to tick out a furious pulse.

"Go!" he told her. "Go back inside, save your soul, your dignity, your pride, your freedom."

Yes, that was what she should do. But she couldn't move. Lightning struck the sky again, vivid, blinding. The wind tore viciously around them both.

Then the rain started. Pelting down in huge drops, molding her gown almost instantly to her body. He swore, crying out almost as if in anguish to some ancient gods; then he swept her off her feet and raced down the parapets.

To his own room.

The bed was huge, canopied, curtained in rich black and red damask. A fire burned in the hearth, hot and high, warm against the wet chill of the rain. It cast all of the room except for a few mystic shadows into a realm of gold. Her hand lay against his heart. She could hear the thunder of its beat, see the wild, reckless tension in his eyes. He laid her down upon the damask bed, spreading her hair out over the pillows, gazing down at her. She stared up at him, amazed that she could find no words now when she needed them so desperately.

He was the one to find speech . . .

" 'For the scent of her was like a field of flowers, the taste of her flesh was like honey and life. To be embraced deep within her sweet fire, a part of her, was anguish and ecstasy, like dying just to live again.' "

He leaned close to her, just touching her lips with his own. Then he looked into her eyes again. " 'To love, to soar, to reach the glory of heaven upon the very earth . . . ' "

His voice trailed away. He straightened up again. "For the love of God, my lady, leave me now. Run. Run from me, and keep your soul!"

And still she couldn't move; she could only feel the gold heat of the fire, the closeness of the man. Savor the texture and strength and rugged beauty of his features. She longed to reach out . . .

"Go! For the love of God—"

"For the love of God! Must you be so noble, and make me give everything?" she cried out. "Fight, my lord, for what you desire. Do not release it so very quickly! Make me stay here. Leave me some pride!"

She was suddenly in his arms, held in a grip so fierce she could scarcely breathe. "By God, lady, I pray that your words are the truth of your heart, for you shall never leave me now . . ."

This time his mouth crushed down upon hers. His tongue filled it with sweeping hunger. His hands were upon her, stroking, and his fevered kiss ravaged her mouth. Damp fabric slipped from her shoulders, and his lips descended upon bare flesh there, and then moved lower. Over the sheer wet fabric his mouth closed upon her breast, teeth grazing the nipple, tongue teasing there. The feel was like the lightning that had split the sky, hot, jagged, filling her with heat just as the lightning had filled the night sky with light. She cried out, arms clasping around him at last, the whole of her trembling with the warmth and spiraling ecstasy of being held so, loved so, wanted so . . .

Wanting in return.

He tried to ease her gown down further; it would not come. With an oath of impatience, he ripped away the fabric. His robe fell open, and she felt the searing brush of his body against hers, a knight's body, hard and taut, rugged, bronzed. So very strong and demanding, so giving.

His touch, his kiss, his caress . . . In a whirl of golden mist and pleasure, she felt them all. So intimate, creating liquid, shimmering desire. He could move her as he wished, touch her at will. She had never known desire like this, aching, hunger like starving. And each sweet caress seemed to make her soar, fly, leave her very flesh, and yet feel the earth with every fiber of her being. Then he was one with her . . .

And it was like dying, and touching heaven, agony and ecstasy, such sweet pleasure . . .

His cry came like thunder in the night. He held her in a rigid clasp, as if he'd never let her go. She was alive, slowly releasing her hold upon heaven, coming down to earth with him. And earth itself remained heaven, for he held her still, and the firelight bathed them gently then, even as his arms remained fierce.

She had done what she had sworn she would not do. She was a mistress now. She had cast aside her pride and her dignity.

And her soul . . .

But it did not matter so very much, she realized. Even the pain that would come did not matter so much.

Because she loved him.

"What do we do now?" she whispered suddenly.

"We live."

"But—"

"And love." He rolled to her, arms fiercely now on either side of her. "Sweet Jesu, I do love you! From the moment I saw you . . . I was such a fool! I thought myself above the love of just one woman. I thought that I could watch you as a man might gaze upon a beautiful piece of art, cold art, a sculpture of stone, perhaps. I never meant to hurt you, never meant to have you. But before God, Genevieve, I do love you!"

She almost wept. She bit into her lower lip, keeping her tears at bay. "And I . . ."

"Aye, lady!"

"Dear God, I love you as well!"

There was nothing more to say then. Nothing, for the touch of his lips, the hunger of his embrace, said it all.

Their days fell into a pattern. She worked with Lavinia, and wrote poems and ballads in her room. He exercised with his men, held small mock jousts in the courtyard below. Sometimes she would watch him and he would see her. On one such occasion, he smiled, left his men behind, and came to her room. "A token, my lady. A scarf." He bowed to her deeply. "A knight must wear his lady's colors into the joust, you know."

She smiled, but a sudden sadness filled her. "Alas, my lord, you should carry the colors of a noble lady who might one day be your wife."

He gazed at her intently. "Alas! You forget the rules of chivalry and the joust, Genevieve. You are the poetess, the great reader. A knight wears the colors of any maiden he admires from afar, any lady he would set upon a pedestal and adore. Surely, such things came about since so many a knight is saddled with a rich countess who sports her own mustache!"

He didn't smile, and she knew he was in dead earnest, and she was sorry she had spoken. She lowered her head suddenly. "Forgive me. I know that you love me. . . ."

"And it isn't enough."

"It is enough!" she vowed heatedly.

It was not. Not for either of them. But she did love him deeply, and so the days passed on.

Then he was called upon to serve the king once again and he rode out with his men-at-arms. She whiled away the days, waiting for his return, praying that he would come home safely to her.

At long last, he did. A servant came to tell her that he was in the great hall, and she rushed to meet him there, heedless of the men who would fill the hall along with him. Her eyes were afire as they touched upon him. His were dark, somber, anguished.

Though she longed just to touch his cheek, he didn't come near her. He knew her heart, and had never betrayed their relationship before any of his men. She thought she would die, waiting for the day to end, for him to come to her.

But when she was talking with Reginald of Poitiers in the hall, he raised a glass to her and commented on Lord Robert's good fortune.

"I am afraid I'm at a loss. What good fortune is that, Reginald?"

"Well, 'tis not fact as yet, but it seems that the king has been negotiating a new marriage for the Earl of Betancourt. It's to be announced after the king's tournament next Thursday. He is to be wed to Blanche, Countess of Durham, cousin to the King of Norway. It will be a splendid match. She is sixteen years old, a great beauty, and incredibly wealthy." Reginald lifted his silver wine chalice in the air. "To our lord, Robert of Betancourt!"

She nodded; she smiled. She felt ill, as if she wanted to die.

She fled from the hall and hurried to her chamber. She sat on the floor before the fire, hugging her knees to her chest, fighting the sting of tears. In time, she heard a tapping on the door, which she had bolted. "Genevieve!" His voice was rich, deep, creating a stir of longing within her.

"Go away, Earl of Betancourt!" she said curtly.

The knocking did not come again, and she wanted to cry out in deeper anguish. He hadn't even tried!

But then she leapt to her feet, aware that he had come in through the shuttered door to the parapets. Swift, determined footsteps brought him to her. She gasped out furiously, slamming her fists against his chest, trying to free herself from his hold. He would not let her go. His lips were on hers, and she could not twist away from them. His hands were upon her, and it seemed that clothing melted from her body. "Little idiot! I love you!" he told her. She tried to fight him still, but she lost the battle with her own heart and soul and limbs. He wrenched the covers from her bed and laid her upon the cool sheets, ravished her with his most tender kisses and caresses, made love to her with a passion and fever that bordered on violence.

"She isn't to be a hag with a mustache," Genevieve said flatly when the fury was spent and they lay together. "Sixteen, beautiful, cousin to the King of Norway, rich as might be imagined. She will help you create quite a dynasty, I imagine."

"Genevieve—"

"No!" She spun away from him, dragging the sheets with her to cover her nakedness. "I'm glad for you, truly. It wouldn't make things better for me if she were old and ugly and horrible. Don't you see it wouldn't change anything? And it had to come to this. I knew it had to come to this! I was always afraid, because I knew—"

"Genevieve!" He leapt out of bed, naked as well, like a great cat, determined to stop her. She backed away from him, one hand up.

"Please!" she whispered. "For the love of God—"

"Aye! For the love of God!" he said, and she was trapped, caught by the door, by his massive strength. She laid her head against his shoulder. She could fight them no more—the tears came.

"Please let me go!" she whispered. "Somewhere far away, I beg you . . ."

"Please, lady, grant me this!" he implored. "Grant me time! Grant me until the deed is done, and I swear, I will see you safely wherever you wish to go!"

"You'll never touch me again, never seek to find me? Never see me, swear it!"

"Give me the time, Genevieve. Give me that, and I will swear what you wish! Damn you, Genevieve. I am not married yet, and perhaps—"

"The king has negotiated this!"

"Genevieve, give me time."

"I can't—"

"You must!"

She hated herself, hated him. But she slept in his arms that night, and she could not really hate either of them then. Because she loved him.

He stood in the library, Lavinia at his side. She was babbling.

"I should love to go to Norway," Lavinia was saying dreamily. "Perhaps I could meet and marry a Viking. They were so fierce—"

"Lavinia, hush!" Robert thundered. Then he looked at his young sister, who wore a crushed expression. He was so accustomed to leading men, to shouting out orders. "I don't read very well," he admitted gruffly. "And I am searching for something."

"For what?" Lavinia demanded.

"A story. My tutor read it to me once. Years ago. I had not thought about it until . . ."

"Until?"

Robert of Betancourt looked at his sister. She was growing into a beauty with rich dark hair, glittering green eyes, and a slim, lithe figure. Once, he'd had her future planned for her. She might even make a good wife for one of the king's many sons. But his own life had been changed. Ever since he had heard a melodious voice singing in a great hall, a voice that touched the heart, the soul . . .

Genevieve. With her golden hair and violet blue

eyes, with the absolute beauty and perfection of her face, smooth as marble, soft as silk. Aye, she was beautiful, more beautiful in person even than by reputation, and more intriguing still. Her beauty had arrested him, but he was not a fool. Many women were beautiful. It hadn't been her outer beauty that had made him lose himself to her. What lay inside of Genevieve had caused him to fall in love: her enchantment with words and music, her elegance, her spirit.

She had made him long to read!

Coming home, he had been in despair. He had sworn he would not touch her again.

Then he had seen her, and had known that he would die if he did not.

But he couldn't bear her anguish, and it had been while holding her through the night that he had remembered the story. All that he had to do was find what he wanted now.

He cried out suddenly, his finger running down the page as he read the words over and over again. He threw the book down and laughed, gripped Lavinia by the shoulders, and danced her around the room.

"I've got it!" he cried. He kissed her on the cheek. "I've got it!"

"What?" Lavinia demanded.

He shook his head. "Never mind. Now listen well. I am going to the king's court. Tell Genevieve she is not to leave here now. If she does, I will hunt her down to the ends of the earth and never give her a moment's peace. If all goes well, I will be home on Friday."

"But—" Lavinia began.

"Do as I say!" Robert commanded.

Then he was gone.

* * *

He had left, and without saying a word to her. Life seemed to be void of meaning. She had to look to her music again, to her words. To books, to dreams . . .

Ah, but this once, reading had betrayed her! She had been seduced by the very words written in the book she had caused him to read.

She wanted to leave; he had said that she must not. And now it was especially important to play by his rules. If she waited until he returned, he would let her leave without following her; it was imperative that it come about that way. For she was expecting his child.

It shouldn't have been much of a shock, and perhaps it wasn't. She had fallen so deeply and completely in love that she hadn't thought beyond her emotions. She wasn't dismayed; she was almost glad. She wouldn't be the old, lonely woman he had once warned her she might be. One day, when she was old and still living with the memories of her one great love, her grandchildren would sit at her knee, and she would create stories for them.

Stories, books. She would set all her magical fairy tales down on paper, and she would tell her granddaughters that sometimes knights in shining armor did exist, that happiness could be grasped and held, if only fleetingly.

But she couldn't let him know. He would hurt for her, want to help her, want to hold on to their child. He would have his Norwegian countess, and a lifetime would stretch before the two of them. If she was to survive, she would have to do so alone now, holding fast to the dream they had once shared, and to this child of theirs.

She had determined to stay; to see him once

again. But early the following morning, Lavinia burst in on her.

"We're to go to the tournament!" she cried.

"No! I can't. I—"

"The queen herself has summoned us!" Lavinia said.

"But—"

Dear God. She would die if she had to sit through announcements regarding Robert's marriage. Worse still, what if the girl was to be there, to meet her future lord?

"I can't—"

"If we don't arrive the morning of the tournament, Robert has warned that he will come himself. Why is he so afraid that you're going to run away?" she asked Genevieve.

"I . . ."

"He will come after you. And he will find you. Oh, Genevieve! I'd love to see a tournament!"

Their rooms in the massive palace were small, but then, London was crowded with the families of knights and noblemen home from the wars in France. Monks, priests, nuns, scholars, and pilgrims lined the streets, and sought audiences with the king.

Edward loved pageantry. There were stands decked out with banners, a mass array of tents in a multitude of colors for the knights and squires and horses and equipment. There was to be a battle between the gray and white knights, and Robert was to fight for the gray, along with the king's younger sons. Then there would be individual jousts, and at the end, the knight who had won the day would select a lady from the stands, and they would be crowned king and queen of the joust by the King and Queen of England.

Genevieve had thought that they would be given seats far to the rear, but when she approached the stands with Lavinia, she found herself summoned to the queen's side. She was very fond of Philippa, a good lady who had given her husband a multitude of children and traveled with him on a good many campaigns as well. Philippa lived ostentatiously, had given her all to the trades and the people. She loved the arts and artists, and had always been exceptionally kind to Genevieve.

"Ah, Genevieve!" the queen said happily. "And young Lady Lavinia. Welcome."

They bowed low before Philippa, who waved a hand and indicated two chairs at her side. "Here you will see the tournament very well, my dears."

Edward appeared then, arching a brow at his wife, but smiling at Genevieve. "Welcome to the joust, Genevieve. I had not known we would see you."

"Sire, I apologize if I intrude—"

"Nay, lady! You perfectly grace such a chivalrous occasion as this! Perhaps you will sing for us this evening."

"As Your Grace commands," she murmured. She longed to see Robert. To slap his face, to shake him. Sweet Jesu, what had he done to her? Was she now going to have to sing as he was betrothed before her?

A trumpet sounded, announcing the beginning of the games. The knights rode before them, one after another, as they were announced. The queen gave her scarf to a visitor from her own Haunaiult. Other ladies offered favors to the men as they were requested.

Then Robert was before her. She could see nothing of his face, for his helmet and visor were in place and he carried his blunted lance against the rest on his left side. He suddenly stretched the lance out to her.

She didn't move.

Philippa leaned forward. "The earl has requested a favor, Genevieve. You must give him something."

Ah, but I have given him my heart already. I wear it on my own sleeve at times! she thought. But she dared not draw too much attention to herself and so she ripped a swatch of silk from her headdress and tied it to the end of his lance. His head lowered to her; then he rode back into the lines.

Once upon a time, he had told her that no man was better than he, and he proved it that day in battle. His side fought a hard battle and won the first of the games. Then, one by one, the knights began to meet on horseback. Riding from opposite sides, lances aimed, they rode hard upon one another. At the moment of impact, they were actually blind, for their joust helmets were designed with eye holes that gave them visibility only when they were hunched over to ride hard at their opponents. When they straightened up, they could no longer see. The helmets had been designed to keep them from being blinded by shards of wood or direct hits in the eyes. Still, just thinking that each man was blinded at the awful moment of shuddering impact caused her to sit forward upon her bench, her heart in her throat. Again and again, Robert came forward to meet a new opponent.

Again and again, he bested the man.

Until he came down the line for his last battle. She screamed, hand and heart at her throat as she leapt to her feet.

Robert was down. But his opponent rode on, getting his sword from his squire. Robert rose quickly to his feet, and raced to meet his squire in the field to procure his own sword.

The knights then met upon the ground, swords clashing, flying, meeting, swinging, clashing again.

Then, with a mighty slash, Robert caught his opponent's weapon, and it sailed into the sky, landing straight down into the earth about ten feet before the stands. The crowd roared; the spectators all leapt to their feet.

No one was better . . .

Genevieve felt a terrible pain close to her heart as Robert marched forward in his armor, stripping his helmet from his head as he did so. He stood before the king in mail and tunic blazing with his colors.

"Sire! I have bested the last man."

"Indeed, Robert, you have done us proud in joust as in battle, and you are duly crowned king of the joust. You may now choose your lady, and command your prize."

He could claim gold, land, whatever riches the king had to offer. But he could claim something else as well; he had discovered that in his book.

"Sire, I choose my lady and prize as one." He pointed to Genevieve, and wondering what game he played, she felt the blood drain from her face.

"Stand!" Philippa hissed to her.

She wasn't certain that she could do so.

"What is this?" the king demanded in a bellow.

"Sire, in the order of today's joust, tradition and law have it that the knight champion may choose whatever treasure he desires that the king has power to give. I don't wish gold or fields or jewels of the typical kind, my lord. I request that you grant me a dispensation to wed Genevieve. It is within your power."

"Why, you unruly whelp—" Edward began, but Philippa was quickly at his side, and quickly working upon his love of pageantry and show.

"What a beautiful, noble, chivalric gesture, fair knight!" she cried out loudly.

Edward, still disgruntled, looked down upon his wife. "I'd had other plans—"

"And you have other subjects!" Robert reminded him very softly and very politely.

For a moment, it still seemed as if Edward would explode. But then the king started to laugh. He was bested, and he knew it. He prided himself on his laws and his sense of chivalry. If the rules of the game granted the winner his choice of reward, then the rules must be followed.

Someone was tugging upon Genevieve's arm. She got to her feet slowly at last. Robert came through the stands and plucked her up. Together they stood before the king and queen, and were crowned with wreaths of flowers. Men and women, noble and common, screamed and cheered.

Genevieve noted that the queen winked to Robert, and she thought that Philippa had been in on this game from the beginning.

Genevieve and Robert were separated then. Lavinia hopped up and down and kissed her. With a rush of other ladies Genevieve found herself returning to the court, sipping wine in the hall—still too dazed to believe that her good fortune could be true.

But very soon, Robert appeared, stripped of mail, handsomely decked in hose and a blue-and-gold short tunic. Her heart fluttered when he entered the room. She stood her ground, waiting for him to come to her. He did. Before everyone there, he tilted her head and kissed her lips. Then his eyes were upon hers and he whispered softly, "Did you hear it? I just got much more thunderous applause for a kiss than I did for unseating ten men in a row!"

She smiled. " 'Tis a nobler thing, a kiss."

"Always?"

"When shared in love. Oh, Robert!" she cried softly. "How did you do this? I cannot believe what you have done for me—"

"For you? I am the one in love head over heels, milady! And you did this anyway."

"I?"

"Umm. You never finished your book, did you?"

"My book?"

"Aye, the beautiful, ancient piece, the love story."

"No," she admitted.

"Well, let me tell you how it ends."

"How?"

"Happily ever after."

"But still—"

"You opened my eyes. Dreams lie in books. So does knowledge. I remember long ago my tutor reading a story about this particular tournament of the kings. Men being men, the prize is usually a fabulous jewel, a title, land. But my tutor had read me a story about a knight asking for the hand of his lady love, and the king could not turn him down."

"But the king had you all but betrothed—"

"Yes, well, there were no guarantees. It was a risk. Life is a risk. But it is what we make it. A very wise, stubborn, but beautiful poetess told me that once."

She smiled, and then started to laugh, and she still couldn't believe . . .

She sang that night. She played her lute and sang a love song, a very beautiful, sad one, and they told her later that even the king had tears in his eyes when it was done. Edward had been furious with Robert, and ready to douse her in the river, no doubt. But he was a man who could be gracious in defeat, and it seemed now that, though he wouldn't forget what had happened today, he just might forgive them both.

The evening came to an end. Robert disappeared when the last of the entertainment was over and the king's guests began to disperse to their rooms within the court. She was nearly the last one in the great hall when she suddenly heard Robert shout her name. She turned. He leapt down from a stairway to stand before her. Then he dramatically fell upon a knee before her.

"Will you marry me, Genevieve?"

"Get up! Quit acting like a fool! You know that I'll marry you."

He stood. "Ah, just making sure, my love. Then come."

"Come?"

Before she knew it, he had ushered her down a hallway and into a tiny chapel. A priest stood at the altar, yawning. To Genevieve's amazement, the king and queen were there as well.

"He thinks he's hoodwinked me," Edward growled, referring to Robert with a nod of his head. "But still, best get this done before I decide to send him on a three-year mission to the East!"

"We're going to be married—now?" Genevieve said.

"Any objection?" Robert demanded, arching a brow.

She shook her head. "So quickly, will it be legal?"

Edward cleared his throat. "I am still the king, madam, no matter how rudely you two have behaved! Can we get on with this? How did they do this to me?"

"He read about another knight having done this—in a book," Philippa said.

"A book?" Edward said indignantly. "I have been bested by a book?"

"By a man who read a book," Philippa said serenely. "Now, do come along. We must be quick. The king can be fierce and change his mind upon occasion. So let's hurry!"

The priest, a common man himself and delighted with his task, began the ceremony.

The dawn had just broken when the last words had been said, the last papers signed. The king and queen witnessed the ceremony, then retired—Edward still grumbling that he had been taken in by a book.

The priest wished Robert and Genevieve God's blessing, and then they were alone again.

They went to Robert's quarters, for his were far grander than hers. And when they stood together at last, she found herself shaking again, staring at him.

"I still can't believe this," she whispered.

"I always told you that I love you," he returned. Then she was swept into his arms, ravaged by his kiss. "I love you, my *wife!*" he told her huskily. "Aye, my lady *wife*!"

"Oh, Robert, I do so adore you."

"Ah, sweet Genevieve! You came into my arms, and into my heart, when I could give no promises."

"But you were so brave and strong to test the king—"

"You were my strength. You gave me my weapons, and they weren't swords or armor or lances, but words."

"I will love you into eternity," she promised him.

"I will demand it," he assured her. And he lay upon the bed with her, cupping her cheek. " 'For the scent of her was like a field of flowers!' " he whispered. " 'The taste of her was like honey and life . . ."

He made love to her tenderly, passionately, his wife, upon their wedding night.

They had been married a month when he found her in the library, busily working away with quill, parchment, and ink. She was so absorbed in her task that she didn't hear him. In fact, he cleared his throat twice before she looked up, smiling at him, her beautiful smile even lovelier now, for her face was touched with the radiance of her happiness.

"What are you doing?"

"Copying the book."

"The book?"

"Our book."

He walked into the room, pausing behind her, a frown upon his face.

"But why? We will never give it away. It's a treasure to be kept forever."

"Precisely. But I want our son to have a copy."

"Our son?"

"Or daughter. Either shall be taught to read—"

The ink spilled as he drew her up and into his arms. He kissed her tenderly and long, then drew back from her.

"A son or daughter? You're sure?"

"That it will be one or the other? Of course."

"No. That—"

She laughed delightedly, arms around him. "Yes, I'm sure. I've known, but I waited to be absolutely certain to tell you. In fact, I had planned to disappear . . . but you married me before I could do so."

"Disappear?" He seemed to growl the word.

"It's over now!"

"I would have found you."

She shook her head. "You had promised me that you would leave me be," she whispered.

"I would have known. I would have found you. I—"

"You would have defied God and kings for me!" she teased with deepest affection.

"Hmmf! And you meant to run away."

She clung to him. "Never now, my love. Never now."

He lifted her chin and kissed her lips tenderly. "Perhaps you had best make several copies of the book," he said.

"Several?"

"Well, I do love you so very much. We're both relatively young. And each child we have is going to need his or her own copy of such a wonderful creation . . ."

"Ah, several copies!" she agreed. "And I will add my own notation to each: Great risks reap great rewards! Perhaps I should get back to work then."

He swept her up into his arms. "Later!"

"Later?"

"Much later!" he said softly, carrying her from the room.

A breeze stirred the delicate pages of the book,

and dried the fresh ink. Genevieve laid her head upon her knight's chest, and smiled.

To soar, to love . . .

Indeed, each child of hers would have a copy. Each would learn to fly and dream—and live!—through the magic of words.

But as he had said . . .

Later!

LETTER OF LOVE

VIRGINIA HENLEY

Letter of Love

"Your mother was a willful little jade," the queen said, thumping her fist upon the magnificently carved desk. "Some maggot in her brain made her throw away her position of maid of honor by making that disastrous marriage with a common spy, rather than accept the union I had arranged for her with the Earl of Devon. Even the flamboyant name she chose for you flouted convention."

Burgundy Bedford stood silently before Elizabeth, thinking the queen looked like a corpse that had been resurrected. How she hated this bitch of a woman! Well, if Bess thought her mother had been willful, she would soon learn that Burgundy Bedford was even more headstrong and unbiddable!

Elizabeth's red wig screamed its falseness to the world, making Burgundy wonder if her own abundant wine-colored tresses had triggered this tirade against her mother. The queen was overdressed in silver gauze, slashed with red taffeta. Pearls and rubies studded the lining of the high-collared gown. In contrast, Burgundy wore one of the queen's castoffs in dark green velvet.

"Before you follow in your mother's footsteps, I have made arrangements for you to marry into that same noble family." The queen's expression altered for the worse as she smiled. "The husband I have chosen for you is Lord Nicholas Mountjoy. So you see, I hold no grudge against your mother, who was, after all, my dear friend at one time."

So the rumor Burgundy had heard was true! Elizabeth was marrying off her profligate favorite before he scattered any more bastards about her realm. Well, she'd be damned if she'd have the queen's leavings! Burgundy lowered her lashes so that the shrewd Elizabeth would not see the rebellion in her eyes. She curtsied. "Thank you, Your Majesty," she said sweetly, trying not to recoil as Elizabeth presented her beringed, bony fingers for Burgundy's kiss of homage and gratitude.

"Lord Mountjoy is without. I think it is time you two met each other."

Burgundy's lashes flew up to reveal shocked surprise in her violet eyes. As if by magic the anteroom door swung open to admit the broad-shouldered Earl of Devon. She was trapped!

His black eyes swept her from head to toe before he gave his complete attention to the queen. "Nicholas!" Elizabeth greeted him intimately. Her voice was the only thing still beautiful about her.

He was one of the Queen's Gentlemen, an elite corps of royal bodyguards, and clearly in the inner ring of the court's charmed circle. "Your Majesty

. . . Bess," he replied in a tone equally as intimate as hers.

Burgundy watched the byplay between the aging monarch and her arrogant courtier with distaste. With both hands Elizabeth opened the front of her gown as if she were too hot, so that the whole of her bosom was visible! Finally the queen tore her eyes from the powerful male before her.

"Mistress Bedford, I present Lord Nicholas Mountjoy, Earl of Devon, who has graciously agreed to become your husband. I hope you realize the enormous honor he does you, for though your grandfather is a baron, his estate is much diminished and your mother's marriage to a commoner made you plain Mistress Bedford."

Burgundy's chin went up.

"Mistress Bedford could never be 'plain,' Your Majesty," Mountjoy asserted.

"Pish, sirrah! Continue your wooing in yon garden, not in my presence, you rogue!"

"Glorianna's radiance can never be eclipsed." He bestowed a passionate kiss upon his sovereign's hand.

The queen's fan tapped Burgundy on the breast in a signal of dismissal and perhaps envy. "This marriage will unite two great shipping families, which will benefit not only yourselves, but England. I trust you are mindful of this great honor, mistress."

Burgundy curtsied once more, then withdrew from the Queen's Presence Chamber, her back as stiff as a ramrod.

Nicholas Mountjoy's lips twitched with secret amusement as he followed the curvaceous beauty out into the formal gardens of Hampton Court Palace. "A stroll in the maze, perhaps?" the deep voice behind her suggested.

Burgundy spun about, hands on hips. "My lord, I beg you not to sacrifice yourself upon a commoner." Her voice dripped with sweet sarcasm.

"Your blood is good enough, I warrant," he drawled lazily.

"I have no doubt of it," she said coldly, "but since a Mountjoy wasn't good enough for my mother, a Mountjoy certainly isn't good enough for me, sir!"

His dark brows drew together and his jaw clenched as he suppressed his anger at the insult. Like mother, like daughter. Lady Jane had spurned his father, so Burgundy would refuse him. "Your mother caused a fine scandal when she flouted the queen's wishes. Surely you are not so reckless, Mistress Bedford?"

"That is the last insult I shall ever suffer from you about my mother!" she flared. "Must she be condemned forever?"

"I am happy she did not wed my father . . . that would make us brother and sister and tempt me to incest."

Burgundy said coldly, "You may be an earl, sir, but you are certainly no gentleman!"

"My reputation precedes me," he mocked.

She nodded stiffly. "And your presence offends me. I prithee, begone."

"I don't dismiss so easily," he said, taking her wrist in a viselike grip before she could escape. "Stop this nonsense, mistress. The queen wishes this match and has arranged for the marriage to take place while I am on leave from Ireland."

"Remove your hand from my person, sir, before I stab it with my bodkin." Her voice almost froze him.

Before Nicholas Mountjoy had come into the garden, he had been indifferent about Elizabeth's choice of bride for him; that it pleased the queen was enough. He was indifferent no longer. The wench was an instant challenge. He decided to have the little bitch at any price.

"You are an ice queen in need of a damn good thawing." He pulled her into his arms and kissed her. Thoroughly.

Burgundy forced herself to remain passive until he loosened his hold; then she drew back her hand and slapped him full in the face. "You arrogant swine!" she hissed.

Nicholas was amused again. It was the first time he'd ever been slapped before he had his hand beneath a lady's skirts.

She fought back a retort that she would not marry him because she wanted another. No one must learn of Anthony Russell, a fellow spy of her father's who had been wooing her for almost a year. Her mind darted about like quicksilver. She must contact Tony; they would have to elope. He'd been pressing her to it for months, and now she wished she had listened to him.

The autumn wind suddenly rustled the fallen leaves amidst the Michaelmas daisies. Burgundy's lashes swept to her cheeks. She shuddered. "Let me go, my lord. I'm cold."

"So I've discovered," he taunted.

Her lashes lifted, and he felt the full impact of blazing violet. His mouth curved. "Burgundy should be warmed by the hands before being tasted," he said softly, freeing her wrist, but enjoying the flush upon her cheek before she fled.

* * *

"Whatever's amiss, my lamb?" asked Burgundy's waiting woman.

"Oh, Nan, the queen has finally tallied the bill for my education."

"And the price is marriage, as we suspected?"

"Aye. She is determined to wed me to Mountjoy, just as she planned for my mother."

"Only this time she won't be thwarted," warned Nan.

"Aye, but she will!" Burgundy vowed. "Tomorrow we will go into the city. I have a notion to see a play."

Every fortnight they went into London to John Bedford's townhouse. Her father was usually off on Walsingham's business, but the house was convenient for shopping and visiting the Globe Theatre. It was at her father's London residence that Burgundy had met Anthony Russell, and Nan knew they often attended the playhouse together.

Burgundy penned a note and summoned a page to dispatch it. Nan fervently hoped she wasn't planning anything foolish.

Nan was thankful Burgundy had chosen a warm cloak for the wherry ride on the Thames. Winter was just around the corner.

When they arrived at the townhouse, Burgundy donned her mask and went off to see a performance of *The Merry Wives of Windsor*. A deliciously ironic choice, under the circumstances!

When Anthony Russell slid into the seat beside her in the gallery, Burgundy slipped her hand into his. When he squeezed it, her mouth curved sweetly beneath the mask, and she let out a sigh of relief that Tony was in London. Her attention was all taken up by his whispers and the players' antics, so it was not until the interval between acts that she looked across the gallery to see Nicholas Mountjoy. She stiffened, then, remembering she wore a mask, forced herself to relax.

The Earl of Devon was squiring Dorothy Devereux, whose scandalous reputation forbade her attendance at court. The voluptuous blonde, though heavily painted and patched, was incredibly attractive and rumored most wanton by nature. Beneath her mask, Burgundy's mouth turned prim. It was women like that who gave playhouses a bad name and caused the Puritans to call them little better than brothels exhibiting bawdy fables. *I thought the wages of sin were supposed to be death, but judging by yon whore they are expensive jewels!*

The profligate earl's marriage would obviously not interfere with his mistresses, Burgundy thought with distaste. When she realized she had missed most of the last act, Burgundy whispered to Anthony, "I want you to come back with me for dinner. I have something most urgent to discuss."

Nan was not surprised when Anthony Russell escorted Burgundy home, but she was disturbed. That her mistress had brought him back to sup did not bother her; it was the plans that might be hatched that worried Nan. Against her better judgment she allowed her charge her privacy, hoping Burgundy would confide in her before she committed any folly.

She thought perhaps the time had come when she should give Burgundy the legacy that her mother had entrusted to her. As the hour grew late, Nan entered the firelit chamber to see the young couple cuddling and whispering together and she was convinced the time was at hand.

Nan climbed to the attic with her candlestick and lifted the lid of Lady Jane's trunk. With reverent hands she withdrew the book she had kept for twenty years. It was centuries old, and though Nan could not read, she appreciated the beauty of the handwritten pages, now yellow with age. She rewrapped the treasure in the cloth of purple velvet and took it down to her bedchamber.

Before the embers of the fire died low, Burgundy and Anthony Russell had made plans for their secret marriage. She hadn't told him to whom the queen planned to marry her, only that the wedding was imminent and that there was a need for great haste. Anthony promised to take care of the license and find a willing priest who would make it legal.

"I've been looking at a house in Surrey, in the country. Would you like that, sweeting?"

"Can you afford it, Tony?" she asked with concern.

He laughed. "I have money aplenty, Burgundy. I sell information, and it brings a high price in Elizabeth's England."

"I hate her!" Burgundy said with passion.

"Softly, my sweet. Walls have ears. We could end up in the Fleet for what we plan, or worse, the Tower."

Burgundy shuddered. "I care not. A few months of prison is preferable to a life sentence in a loveless marriage!"

They lingered long over their good-night kisses. Anthony fervently wished Nan Greenwood wasn't in the house or he would persuade Burgundy to let him stay all night. She, too, was tempted to spend the night in Tony's arms, but knew that one more week would melt away as swiftly as snow in summer, and then they would be married.

* * *

Upon her return to Hampton Court, Burgundy was again summoned by the queen, but this time she was serene in the knowledge of her secret plans.

"Mistress Bedford," Elizabeth said in a voice that carried to the other ladies in the chamber, "it seems that Lord Mountjoy is well pleased with my choice of bride."

Burgundy felt the women's glances as they looked at her with speculation.

"Well, mistress, what do you have to say to me?" Elizabeth demanded archly, tapping her foot on the parquet floor.

Burgundy immediately went down before the queen in a gracious curtsy. "I thank Your Majesty with all my heart. I am unworthy of the honor you do me."

"Tush, child, I shall have my reward when I see Lady Jane's daughter the Countess of Devon." Elizabeth's lips twitched as she heard her ladies gasp. "I am giving a private dinner in the Presence Chamber this evening to celebrate your betrothal." The queen's imperative hand summoned her Mistress of the Wardrobe. "Mistress Bedford is to wed in a sennight. See that she is fitted with a gown worthy of a countess."

That evening when Burgundy entered the Queen's Presence Chamber, she had rehearsed her role as if she were an actor on the stage of the playhouse. No more sparks must fly between herself and Nicholas Mountjoy. She must be all sweet submission. Burgundy swallowed hard as he came to meet her; sweet submission was probably beyond her.

His dark glance swept over the violet taffeta that

matched her eyes, moved up to her throat with its snowy ruff, and came to rest upon her earbobs. "Good even, Burgundy," he said low. "Pearls are for tears. I think I shall gift you with amethysts." His voice was as rich as his apparel. His doublet was wine velvet, his monogram pricked out in garnets, or were they rubies? Yes, rubies, she decided when she saw his earring. Nothing so paltry as garnets for the arrogant earl!

Tonight the chamber was lit by hundreds of candles, bathing the strolling musicians with their lutes in a romantic glow. Burgundy clung sweetly to Mountjoy's hand as he led her forward to make her curtsy to the queen, then seated her beside him in the place of honor.

Nicholas noted immediately that the light of challenge was gone from her eyes, replaced by a look of deference. The little bitch was a consummate actress!

She caught a look of secret amusement on Mountjoy's dark face, as if he knew something she did not. It made her slightly uneasy. She ran the tip of her tongue across her full bottom lip and flushed as his eyes followed it.

"My lord, I fear the queen exaggerates when she refers to the Lyntons as a great shipping family. They were great once, but, alas, their fortunes and their fleet have dwindled over the years."

"I could be instrumental in restoring the Lyntons' fortunes," he replied smoothly.

Burgundy shook her head. He watched the play of light and shadow on her silken tresses and longed to bind himself in them. A half-smile of apology curved her soft mouth. "My lord, I am afraid Her Majesty is trying to fob me off on you.

The Lyntons cast out my mother when she wed John Bedford."

A muscle ticked in his jaw. "They will doubtless welcome you to their bosom once you are wed to me, mistress."

They can go to hell and you with them, thought Burgundy. Instead she said, "Perhaps, perhaps not. I must warn you the queen always likes to get the best out of any bargain."

"Elizabeth's shrewd all right. Shrewd enough to use your grandfather's vessels to help transport my reinforcements to Ireland in exchange for this union," he said, grinning.

So that was her attraction . . . her grandfather's ships! The situation got better and better. Elizabeth, Devon, and the bloody Lyntons deserved each other! What sweet revenge when they all learned the poor little pigeon had flown the coop.

Nan Greenwood stood gazing through the leaded panes into the darkness with unseeing eyes. The picture she saw so clearly was in her mind's eye, as she relived the night Burgundy's mother died.

The pain was as sharp as if it had happened yesterday. The lump in Nan's throat almost choked her. Behind her, the fire crackled and she turned to gaze into its flames, remembering . . . remembering:

Sleet dashed against the windowpane of the bedchamber as Nan tried to poke up the meager fire.

"Don't cry, Nan. I brought it all upon myself and I am resigned to my fate."

"Jane, my lamb, you mustn't say such things. You have the babe to live for now."

Jane smiled poignantly and shook her head. "It's all right, Nan. It is very important that we don't pretend anymore. There are things you must promise to do for me. I have no one else."

Nan was almost overcome. If only the Lord in his mercy would take her instead.

"Bring me a quill and parchment. I must write a letter to the queen begging her forgiveness. I am going to ask her to see to my child's education. I must find words that will pull on Elizabeth's heartstrings."

"She has no heart, Jane. She flew into a fury and dismissed you because you flouted her authority."

Jane shook her head again, then brushed the burgundy tendrils from her baby's temples. "The queen will do what is right, as I should have done."

Lady Jane Lynton, maid of honor to Elizabeth Tudor, had fallen in love with John Bedford, a secret agent of Walsingham's. The intrigue had been exciting until she suspected she was with child. Rather than marry the man her family and the queen had chosen for her, she eloped with her lover and turned her back upon her duty to others. And as the legend of the ancient book foretold, disaster had followed.

Jane had been dismissed from court amid a scandal. Her parents had disowned her. Trouble had not drawn her and her new husband closer, but had caused bitter feelings. John Bedford was away much of the time in France and Holland, leaving Jane in poor lodgings in London with only her devoted Nan for company.

Then ill luck befell the Lyntons. Their merchant ships sank in storms, their precious cargoes were lost at sea, two sons drowned, and then the queen had withdrawn her patronage and bestowed it elsewhere. Now, Jane lay dying, her lifeblood ebbing away in childbed, leaving her babe motherless.

When Nan took the queen's letter from her, Jane clung to the quill. "One more letter . . . this one for my daughter. Promise me you will keep this book safe for her. It has been in my family for generations, lovingly passed down from mother to daughter through the centuries."

Nan's heart constricted as she heard her lady's voice growing weaker. "Do not give it to her until she is old enough to comprehend the legend. This ancient book is her legacy. I hope she is wise enough to see that 'With Honor Comes Glory.' "

* * *

When Burgundy came from the dinner party she found Nan sitting with the book in her lap. She unfastened her ruff and kicked off her slippers. "Nan, it was kind of you to wait up for me. Please take that worried look off your face; I want to share my plans with you."

"I know you are about to take a big step in your life, my lamb, but before you tell me your decision, I must keep a promise I made to your mother after you were born."

"Nan, what are you talking about?"

"This book. Your mother asked me to keep it for you. She said it was a legacy, handed down for generations from mother to daughter."

"But why did you wait until now?" Burgundy asked, taking the book.

"Because I feel in my heart the time is right."

Burgundy carried the book into her chamber, lit the candles, and lifted the cover. It was old, ancient perhaps, and a thing of great beauty. Obviously it had been treasured and lovingly preserved down the centuries. The capital letters were illuminated so that the T's were broadswords, the V's kite-shaped shields, and the S's fiery dragons.

Burgundy felt great awe as she traced an inscription by a woman named Genevieve Betancourt, dated over two centuries ago. As Burgundy began to read, deciphering the Latin with ease, she realized the tale was a legend and also a great love story. It was fanciful and romantic, as all legends ought to be. Burgundy was swept away to another time and another place, totally caught up in the story as she turned page after page.

Between the sheets of parchment, she discovered a letter. It bore her name! Her hand trembled as she picked it up and realized it was written to her by her mother.

My precious Burgundy:

How do I convey what is in my heart in one short letter? I want you to know that from the moment I conceived you, you became the most important thing in my life. I hope you will forgive me. Because of the choices I made, you must suffer.

From the beginning I realized that you would need a special guardian angel and have prayed for months that God would not turn his face from me.

Though we will never see one another, I have passed on the only legacy I have. I am entrusting this book to Nan Greenwood for when you are old enough to understand its powerful message. When the time comes, you too must pass it on.

I have written to Her Majesty, Queen Elizabeth, begging her to educate you, knowing you will receive the finest education in the world. I hope she forgives me, I hope my parents forgive me, and also the Mountjoys, but most of all, I hope you forgive me.

I beg you not to grieve over my death. I am content because God has answered my prayer to give you a special guardian angel. He has chosen me. Know that I shall love you forever.

Jane Lynton Bedford

The words blurred together as Burgundy wiped the tears streaming down her cheeks. Her mother's presence in the chamber was a tangible thing, as if she reached out to put loving arms about her. She read and reread the letter, tracing the words with her fingertips, so grateful to have her mother's last precious thoughts.

Burgundy tucked it beneath her pillow and readied herself for bed. Then she again took up the book, reading with new insight. Gradually, as time melted away, she began to feel as one with all the women who had gone before. She turned the page and read:

The Quest
You alone decide your Destiny.
At the crossroads, choose wisely.
One path is cursed, the other blessed.
Life is a double-edged sword.
You have free will to carve out the rock!
Will you rise or fall, succeed or fail,
Taste ambrosia or bitter aloes?
To find the key, ask what is neverending,
everlasting;
What is noble and sacred, selfless and eternal?
The answer is Love.
Love is the greatest power on earth.

Pass on the gift of Love.
With Honor Comes Glory!

* * *

The next morning as the wardrobe mistress fitted her with a gown for her wedding, the tale was still with Burgundy. It had caught her imagination, filled her senses, and touched her heart.

Womanlike, she stroked the heavy satin of the dress, delighting in the crystals scattered across the square-necked bodice. It was such a beautiful wedding gown, she decided not to waste it, but would wear it when she wed Anthony. Of course, no one would see it save the bridegroom, but that would be enough. Burgundy hugged her secret to herself, silently counting the days that remained until Saturday.

Phrases from the ancient book floated through her mind as she went about her daily routine, and she found she had memorized the letter. On her deathbed, her mother had written to the queen, begging her to educate Burgundy. And Elizabeth had given her the finest education in the world. For the first time she appreciated the queen's generosity. Without it, her life would have been unendurable.

A page brought Burgundy a note from Nicholas Mountjoy, asking her to ride out with him in the afternoon. She sent a gracious reply, accepting the invitation.

The first frost made the ground hard beneath her palfrey's hooves as she trotted from the stables beside the earl. Her habit was peacock velvet; her gloves and feathered hat matched perfectly. She realized they had been presents from the queen.

Mountjoy's dark eyes licked over her like a candle flame. He was in a black doublet and high black boots today, and his short black cape, lined with crimson, made him look as dangerous as Lucifer.

"The ceremony is arranged for Sunday in the chapel, an' it please you, Burgundy." His voice was as smooth as the black velvet he wore.

"Is that as close as you can come to a proposal, my lord?" she asked, playing a game of cat and mouse.

"You want a proposal? Then how's this? I propose you deal honestly with me. I propose you play me no tricks. I propose you make me a dutiful wife, and in return I promise to make you the best damned husband in the realm!"

Burgundy's guilt made her blush. He spoke as if he knew her secret, but that was impossible, unless he were in league with the Devil. She cast him a pretty, sideways glance to divert him. "What do you mean by dutiful, my lord?"

"The qualities I demand in a wife are chastity, loyalty, honor . . . I would add obedience, but I fear that is asking the impossible of you," he said with a wicked glint in his eye.

"You are most perceptive, Lord Mountjoy."

"Call me Nicholas." It sounded like an order. An order she would ignore.

"What else do you deem dutiful?"

"You will have to leave court. I must return to Ireland almost immediately. The day after the wedding, we leave for Dunster Castle."

"Dunster is in Devon," she said, startled.

"Certes it is. I am the Earl of Devon."

"As if you'd let me forget," she mocked. Silently she thought, The damned knave would pack me off to Dunster, alone all winter, while he's off playing war! "Surely you would allow your wife to stay at court for the Christmas festivities?"

"Absolutely not. The court's festivities are designed for flirtation and intrigue. You will await my return at Dunster. Your grandparents are less than twenty miles away in Lynton."

She almost gasped. He expected her to visit her grandparents. "They want naught to do with me."

"Strange, then, that they entrusted me with this letter." He took the sealed packet from his doublet and handed it to her.

Burgundy drew rein while she broke the seal and scanned the lines:

Dearest Burgundy,

We are so proud and happy that you are about to become the Countess of Devon. I am sending this letter by Nicholas Mountjoy so that you will receive it. I suspect all the letters I sent through your father never reached you.

I beg you will come to see me when you arrive in Devon, if you can spare the time. Having you back will ease our heartbreaking loss of Jane.

Sarah Lynton

Burgundy tucked the letter in her bosom, her thoughts in disarray. "I'm freezing! I'll race you to yon copse," she challenged, digging in her heels, leaving him standing.

Nicholas took off after her, determined to win. He knew she would lead him a merry chase if he allowed it, but he made up his mind that he would not. In this marriage, he would lead and she would follow. And by God's wounds, she would learn to love it!

When a triumphant Nicholas looked over his

shoulder to see by how much he had won, he discovered she had cheated him of his victory. She had turned her mount the moment he passed her and headed for the stables.

"Devious little bitch!" he swore. Then he decided to go about the business as he would a military campaign. Since he had no time to lay siege, he would have to storm her walls. Nicholas Mountjoy was determined to win this battle. She would go down in defeat. He would accept nothing less than unconditional surrender!

He was after her in a flash. He overtook and captured her in minutes, dismounted and lifted her down in a heartbeat. Then in full view of the leaded windows of Hampton Court Palace, he mastered her with his mouth. When he let her go, she was panting. Fascinated, he watched her breath float from her lips and turn frosty in the freezing air.

Violet eyes blazing, she lifted her hand to strike him. He seized her hand before it made contact and gave her a small foretaste of his physical strength. When she stilled, fear threatening to replace her anger, Nicholas Mountjoy deliberately stripped the glove from her hand and lifted her palm to his lips. When he traced a pattern upon her flesh with the tip of his tongue, the gesture was so intimate and erotic, Burgundy blushed hotly.

"Four more days," he murmured.

Three, she thought silently, wishing Saturday were already here.

Before he released her captive hand, he said, "Go and pack for Dunster."

"Yes, I shall pack today," she said breathlessly, then added silently, But I shall pack for Surrey, not Dunster, you arrogant swine!

And Burgundy did begin to pack.

"Nan, I should have told you sooner, but you have probably guessed. I don't intend to marry the man Elizabeth has chosen for me, any more than my mother did. Anthony Russell and I are being wed on Saturday."

Nan did not scold her, but Burgundy could tell that the news saddened her. All she said was, "Jane came to regret her decision deeply."

"Nan, I'm in love! We're going to live in the country, in Surrey. You will come with me, won't you?"

"Of course I will, my lamb."

When Burgundy undressed, the letter from her grandmother fell to the carpet. She called to Nan, "I forgot to tell you; I received a letter from Sarah Lynton today."

Nan asked stiffly, "After all this time, what did *she* have to say?"

"She said she had written before, but suspected my father destroyed her letters."

Nan sagged visibly. "Ah, God, I wondered why she never tried to contact Jane. Sarah Lynton was a good woman. Perhaps she did write, but your mother never received the letters."

"Why would my father destroy them?" Burgundy demanded.

"Ah, child, you have no idea the bitterness that dishonorable union caused."

There it was again. It seemed everyone spoke of honor and dishonor. Burgundy retired, but when she was in bed, she took up the book once more. Its lure was irresistible. Now that she examined it more closely, she saw that most of the women whose hands it had passed through had added inscriptions to the book. Some had lost love, but those who had striven against all odds with honor had found their soul mates. Some of the descriptions of love were rapturous. The last words she read before she slept were, "With Honor Comes Glory."

The next two days were reflective ones for Burgundy, as she considered carefully the step she was about to take. When finally she examined her conscience, she was troubled to realize it was not clear. Again and again she went over the reasons for making the choice she had, until it came to her that the sticking point was the word "honor." She wavered, first leaning one way and then the other. When Saturday dawned, she decided she would compromise her honor for love's sake.

She donned the lovely wedding gown, then carefully concealed it beneath her best velvet cloak. Resolutely, the faithful Nan wrapped herself up warmly and followed her charge down to the waterstairs. Each carried a small trunk with the personal belongings she would need until the rest of their luggage could be sent for.

When they arrived at the London townhouse, Anthony Russell was there before her. His face looked pinched; Burgundy had no idea how long he had waited in the freezing cold.

"Oh, Anthony, come upstairs and get warm. My own hands are like ice."

"Just for a minute then. It won't matter if we are a bit late. I'll just slip the priest an extra five pounds."

His words jarred Burgundy's nerves. It secretly appalled her that a man of God could be bribed.

Nan bustled off to see to some hot tea, leaving the young couple so they could be private.

Burgundy turned from the fire to face Anthony and said the strangest thing. "I cannot marry you."

"What did you say?"

"I'm sorry if I hurt you, Anthony, but I cannot marry you."

"Why not?" he demanded.

"I don't know. I only know I cannot do this thing," she said wretchedly.

Russell laughed cynically. "Shall I tell you why? You have decided to go to the highest bidder! A title and a castle are too tempting to refuse."

"My God, that's not the reason!" she cried out, appalled at his accusation.

"Then answer me this: Are you in love with Nicholas Mountjoy?"

"No! I don't even like him!"

"Then if you are not marrying for love, it must be for money."

"That's not true, Tony. I'm doing it for honor's sake."

He laughed. The sound wasn't pleasant. "If this is some misguided attempt to right the wrongs your mother committed, you are sacrificing yourself for a hopeless cause. Grow up, Burgundy. There is no such thing as honor!"

As Burgundy stood in the chapel on Sunday morning, she fervently hoped that Anthony Russell was wrong. She clung to the hope that there was indeed such a thing as honor. Why had she changed her mind at the last minute? Was it because of the book, because of the letter? Both those things and more. It was as if someone were guiding her to choose this path.

Beside her, the Earl of Devon silently overwhelmed her with his powerful presence. His dark eyes had searched her face with an intense look as she came to stand with him at the altar. Apprehension curled inside her belly.

Queen Elizabeth, garbed in silver and white, failed to detract from the exquisite bride. The queen wore a self-satisfied look that plainly said, without her fine hand at the rudder, this perfect union would never have been launched.

A dropped pin could have been heard upon the frosty air as the priest asked, "Do you, Burgundy, take this man to be your lawful wedded husband?"

"Yes, I do, yes," Burgundy replied quickly before she could change her mind. The rest was a blur—the ring, the kiss, the congratulations, the rice. The thing was done quickly and irrevocably. *Wed as long as we both shall live!* Burgundy realized with a sense of impending doom.

Her groom spoke urgently with Elizabeth, then came striding toward her. "I'm sorry. There is a need for haste. We leave on the next tide. Did my man pick up your trunks?"

"Yes. Excuse me. I too must speak with the queen."

Nan never left her mistress's side. "I am pleased you have done your duty, child," she whispered as Burgundy approached the queen.

"Your Majesty, I want to thank you."

Elizabeth bent toward her intimately. "Lord Mountjoy is a fine prize. The name says it all!"

"Nay," Burgundy said, her cheeks as rosy as the dawn had been. "He would have been my last choice! I came to thank you for all you have done for me. The education you gave me was a priceless gift."

"How could I have done otherwise, child, with your mother's spirit hovering to make sure I did my duty? Devon awaits you, and patience isn't one of his virtues."

* * *

Aboard ship, Nicholas took her belowdecks. He assigned Nan a small cabin, then took Burgundy into a larger one, next to Nan's. "This is ours. It's rather spartan, and not very conducive to romance, but with any luck and a strong wind, you'll only have to spend one night aboard. We should reach Devon before midnight tomorrow."

Burgundy's throat ached with unshed tears. She had done this thing so that she wouldn't feel guilt over acting without honor, but now she felt a crushing guilt for what she had done to Anthony Russell. How would she endure Mountjoy's dominant presence in this small cabin? They would be caged together like two wild beasts.

When he left, her legs felt like water. She sank to the bunk, wondering how she would get through the rest of the day, let alone the night and all day tomorrow. Then that thought was replaced by a bleaker one. How would she get through the rest of her life?

She thought of all the women in the book, all the women who had gone before her, and drew strength from them. She decided to go up on deck. She had only sailed on the Thames; this should be an adventure. She stood at the rail until the vessel reached the open sea. The bitter cold wind penetrated through her clothes.

Suddenly, Nicholas was beside her, wrapping her in a sable cloak with a hood of soft gray fox. "My wedding gift."

She was angry that he was giving her something so costly. "Think you it will thaw an ice queen?" she challenged.

His dark eyes held hers. "One way or another, I *will* make you hot for me, Burgundy."

She wanted to fling the fur into the sea, but the bitter wind made her cling to it possessively. She turned her face from him, but already he was walking away.

The moment the ship headed south into the Strait of Dover, nausea swept over her like one of the waves beneath her in the pewter sea. "Some bloody adventure," she muttered through tightly clenched teeth. She went back to her cabin, where she found Nan in a similar state.

"Oh, my lamb, I hope you don't feel as poorly as I do."

"Go and lie down, Nan, and I'll do the same. What can't be cured must be endured. Isn't that what you've always told me?"

"All we can do is pray," Nan advised, going to her own cabin.

Burgundy wrapped her arms about her churning belly. "Pray for death," she muttered irreverently.

All afternoon and evening she rolled about the bunk in the living nightmare that was mal de mer. Finally, unable to bear the heaving cabin longer, she staggered up on deck. The seas were high; Burgundy lost her footing as she was thrown against the ropes.

A curse dropped from Mountjoy's lips as he saw her floundering. He turned the wheel over to his captain and sprinted to his wife's side. "What in hellfire are you doing up here? It isn't safe!"

"I'm sick . . . dying . . . I needed fresh air . . ."

He grabbed her up into his arms before she was swept overboard, and carried her down to their cabin. He tossed aside her sable, set her down upon the bunk, and began to unbutton her wedding gown. She clutched the dress to her bosom, moaning. He forcefully loosened her fingers from the fabric. "Your misplaced modesty is ridiculous. I've undressed a woman before."

He was too forceful, like a tempest, sweeping her clothes from her, tossing them aside, flinging a nightgown over her nakedness. He propped her against the pillows while he poured her wine.

"Drink this. It will settle the queasiness. God's wounds, wench, are you sure you're descended from a long line of seafarers?"

For answer she vomited most indelicately into his lap. "My wedding present," she gasped.

His eyes blazed black fury; then his sense of humor came to his rescue. "Touché, Burgundy. I swear you did it a-purpose."

She shook her head, feeling slightly better. "No, but I wish I'd thought of it. I enjoyed spewing on you!"

Mountjoy made himself scarce the rest of the voyage. Meals were sent to her at regular intervals, but food was the last thing either she or Nan needed. They nursed each other as best they could, and by the evening of the second day, finally got their sea legs. Even so, they were grateful to set foot on terra firma two hours earlier than Mountjoy had predicted.

Dunster must have had a watch out for their ship, for before they dropped anchor in the bay, the lights in the castle atop the cliff were blazing in welcome.

They were met at the entrance by a man of middle years with a square build and an air of calm competence.

"This is Mr. Burke, my steward. He will take care of any problem you may have, no matter how difficult," Nicholas said warmly. "This is my countess, Mr. Burke. I was married at court."

The steward's eyebrows rose ever so slightly at the news.

Nicholas watched his face intently. "Her name is Burgundy . . . Burgundy Bedford . . . Burgundy *Lynton* Bedford."

She saw the light dawn upon Mr. Burke's countenance. She was relieved to see that he was neither shocked nor disapproving. Actually, he seemed pleased.

"Welcome to Dunster, Lady Mountjoy."

"Thank you, Mr. Burke. This is Nan Greenwood, who has been with me all my life. She's had a rough voyage and should go straight to bed."

"Welcome to Dunster, Mrs. Greenwood." He smiled at Burgundy. "Come, my lady. Let me show you to your chamber."

Burgundy didn't even glance at Nicholas for his approval; she simply followed Mr. Burke, instinctively knowing she was in very capable hands.

The master bedchamber was huge. A fireplace was built into one of the granite walls, and the other three were hung with tapestries. A deep-piled carpet covered the floor, and the bed was hung with emerald curtains.

In no time at all, Mr. Burke set the servants to building a fire, hanging her clothes in the wardrobe, and carrying in a bath for her. "Thank you, Mr. Burke. Could you see that Nan is provided with a bath? Seasickness leaves a horrid miasma."

"I have already seen to it, my lady. The master has asked that supper be served up here. He asks permission to join you."

The corners of Burgundy's mouth twitched with amusement as she studied him. "Mountjoy doesn't ask permission for aught. Those are your own words, Mr. Burke."

He neither confirmed nor denied. "I wish you joy on your first night in Dunster, my lady."

After her bath, Burgundy put on a nightgown, then added a lavender-colored bedrobe for good measure. She was brushing her hair when Nicholas came in without knocking. A sharp rebuke was on her lips, but before the sparks flew, two servants brought in supper trays.

The food was delicious, far better prepared than the meals at court. Burgundy ate sparingly, however, not wanting to repeat her indelicate performance. Mountjoy's dark eyes roamed over her, missing no detail. She'd be damned if she'd avert her eyes and play the shy maiden. Instead, she boldly surveyed her new husband. His velvet bedgown was black and gold. She guessed he wore nothing beneath it; even his feet were bare.

"I hope you like Dunster, Burgundy."

"I imagine daylight will confirm my suspicion that it's a forbidding fortress on a windswept coast. I warrant the only way I'll survive the winter is in front of a roaring fire."

"The winters are somewhat cold," he acknowledged, "but Devon's waters and climate are generally mild. Spring arrives early, and then Devon becomes incredibly beautiful."

"When do you leave for Ireland, my lord?"

"Tomorrow." He rose from the table and held out his hand. "We only have till dawn."

Burgundy was vastly relieved. All she had to do was get through the next few hours. Nicholas moved straight to the bed and turned back the fur covers. Burgundy was agitated; the gesture set her teeth on edge. When Mountjoy removed his robe, she was annoyed with herself to find she averted her eyes and played the shy maiden after all.

She had no choice but to remove her own bedrobe. She did so quickly and slipped between the sheets, shivering with apprehension at the ordeal awaiting her.

He found her breath stoppingly lovely, but prickly as a bloody thistle. His hands were strong, firm and insistent as they reached for her.

Burgundy stiffened as she was implacably drawn to his hard body. When he tried to kiss her, she averted her face. When his hand roamed to intimate places, she recoiled.

Nicholas schooled himself to patience, but finally realized she was determined that he would not woo her into a giving mood. She left him no choice. He intended to consummate this union tonight, whether his bride was willing or no. He managed to perform the hymeneal right without her cooperation, yet without her actual refusal.

Burgundy lay absolutely still; her husband's harsh breathing was the only sound in the room. There had been pain, but the ordeal had not been as devastating as she had expected. The worst part was the guilt she felt over Tony.

When Mountjoy saw the tears upon her cheeks, he flung himself from the bed. Burgundy wiped away the tears, sighing heavily.

"If those sighs are for your lost love, madam, they are wasted."

Burgundy sat up quickly, her dark violet eyes liquid with tears.

Jealousy rode him relentlessly. "Anthony Russell took my bribe not to go through with the marriage."

She sprang from the bed like a tigress. "That's

not true, you lying bastard! It was I who withdrew—for honor's sake." She laughed and cried at the same time. "I sacrificed myself for honor's sake, if you can credit such naiveté!"

"Sacrifice?" he thundered, his black eyes glittering with suppressed violence. "The penniless Mistress Bedford sacrificed herself to become the wealthy Countess of Devon!"

"I hate you! Get out!"

Nicholas Mountjoy bowed with arrogant contempt. "I am thankful I am on my way to Ireland."

"I hope you never return from the barbarous, ill-fated place!" she flung at him as he departed, crashing the door upon its trembling hinges.

Within the week, Burgundy received a visit from her grandmother. Sarah Lynton had her own shade of hair, gray now at the temples. Her care-worn face had once been as beautiful as Burgundy's. "My dear, I have waited twenty years for this day."

"I never received your letters, and Nan swears my mother received none either, though she watched for them so hopefully."

Lady Lynton took Nan's hand eagerly. "How can I ever thank you for staying with Jane through all her suffering and taking the responsibility of her child upon your shoulders?"

"It was a labor of love, my lady. I only wish Jane could have known that you forgave her before . . ." Nan began to cry.

"Oh, my dear." Lady Lynton said, gathering Nan in her arms, "no tears, I beg you. This is a time for rejoicing. To be united with our granddaughter brings us such joy. And another wonderful thing has just happened. Her Majesty has renewed our export licenses."

Mr. Burke served them refreshments so that Burgundy and Sarah Lynton could become better acquainted.

"Tell me, my dear. I gave Jane an ancient, treasured book when she was very young. Was the book ever passed on to you?"

"Yes, it was my mother's last wish that Nan keep it safe for me." Burgundy hesitated, then confessed, " 'Tis because of the book that I agreed to marry the Earl of Devon."

"Your mother refused Nicholas's father, but now you have set everything right."

"Well, perhaps not everything, but I am happy that we are now close to each other, Grandmother."

Before Sarah departed, she extended the hospitality of Lynton Hall, and Burgundy promised to come to meet her grandfather and her one remaining uncle.

The following week she was surprised by a visit from her father. She expected him to be angry with her for marrying the Earl of Devon. Not so much because Anthony Russell was a friend of his, but because her mother had been contracted to wed a Mountjoy. John Bedford, however, seemed resigned to it.

"Somehow it seems inevitable. Jane missed out on being a countess, but her clever daughter did not."

Burgundy was stung. Though father and daughter had never been overly affectionate, they had always been able to speak their minds to each other.

"You think me clever, Father? Apparently not

clever enough to guess you destroyed my grandmother's letters."

"Sarah Lynton more than disapproved of me; she loathed me. There was much bitterness over the marriage. When you were born and your mother died, I didn't want it all dragged up again, and by that time the Lyntons had other troubles to occupy them."

"Sarah has been to see me. We are going to try to close the chasm."

John Bedford nodded. "I suppose that is as it should be. I only came to see if you were happy with your choice of husband."

Burgundy laughed shortly. "We do not deal well together, I'm afraid. Mountjoy probably regrets the union by now. My parting words were rather venomous. I wished he'd never return from Ireland."

"You very well may get your wish."

"What do you mean?" she asked bluntly.

It was privileged information, but after a slight hesitation, he told her, "Five thousand Spaniards are on their way to Kinsale, to aid Tyrone in his rebellion."

Dear God, it couldn't be true. Yet who would know better than one of Walsingham's spies?

When her father departed, she went straight to Mr. Burke. "You must somehow get a message to Nicholas. Can it be done quickly?"

"I'll have a ship and a captain within the hour. Will you write the letter, my lady?"

"Yes," she said quickly, before she could change her mind.

My Lord Mountjoy:

I have word on the best authority that Spain has sent 5,000 men to aid Tyrone. As your wife,

I am honor-bound to inform you immediately. I regret my parting words to you. They were most undutiful and now taste like ashes in my mouth. B.

* * *

As the weeks went by, she heard nothing from Ireland. To pass the hours of the short winter days with their long evenings, Burgundy decided to teach Nan Greenwood to read. At first Nan protested. "Oh, my lamb, I have all the knowledge I'll ever need. I'm too old to learn."

"Age has absolutely nothing to do with it, and you don't need to read for knowledge. There is no sin in reading for pure pleasure! Don't refuse, Nan. It is a gift of love. How else can I repay you?"

Nan agreed because Burgundy wished it. The lessons were so successful that Burgundy called the housemaids together and offered to teach reading to anyone interested.

The housekeeper protested, "I don't think it a good idea, my lady. It will put notions into their heads. What if their new learning prompts them to look for higher stations in life?"

"I should be delighted!" Lady Mountjoy asserted, to the secret amusement of Mr. Burke.

Gradually, Burgundy came to realize that the message of the ancient book had been right. She had acted with honor and she was most content with her life. Her grandparents' shipping business now thrived, and they gave her love and also a sense of her heritage, something she had never known she lacked. One of their ships returning from Ireland brought the news that Kinsale had fallen, the Spaniards had been sent packing, and Tyrone put to flight back to Ulster. Burgundy realized her husband would soon return to England, and she dreaded the reunion.

Spring arrived, bringing with it Nicholas Mountjoy. He was taken off the ship on a litter, but, refusing to be carried feet first into his own castle, he called for his favorite horse.

When Burgundy saw his dark head appear in the courtyard below, he looked even more arrogant and blood-proud than she remembered. But when she saw Mr. Burke go to his side to help him dismount and half-carry him into the castle, her heart was in her mouth. He had received a bad sword wound to the thigh which refused to heal. Black eyes sought violet. "I'm sorry," was all he said.

Her heart turned over in her breast. Why was he apologizing to her? Was he going to die? Was he going to be a cripple for the rest of his days? Not if she could help it, she vowed!

"Bring him upstairs," she bade Mr. Burke.

When Nicholas was on the bed, she picked up her scissors and advanced upon him, intending to cut off his hose and bandage. Nicholas appealed desperately to Burke. "You can see to it. Burgundy, it isn't pretty!"

"Nothing about you is pretty, Mountjoy. I received a fine education from the queen's own tutors. Herbs and the care of wounds was taught by Elizabeth's physicians. Why do you not wish me to look at your leg? I know it is not from modesty; you have none."

His lips twitched with amusement despite the pain. She was exactly as he remembered her. An instant challenge to his manhood, and he knew he would have her no other way.

"Burke is no slouch at caring for wounds. Surely you don't wish to slight him? But if you wish to fight each other over me, go to it."

Burgundy began to laugh. "You damned rogue. Two dogs slavering over a bone would amuse you, so we shall desist." She nodded her head to Mr. Burke. "You may have the pleasure of stripping him."

Her humor covered her apprehension. When the long, puckered wound was uncovered she was furious. "Bloody hell, who stitched this?"

"A field surgeon. Conditions weren't exactly ideal."

She saw that he was gray about the mouth. She knew she must act decisively; womanish hand-wringing and tears would avail him nothing. "I'll cleanse it, if your hand is steady enough to restitch it, Mr. Burke." Burgundy knew hers was not. Before she went for herbs and hot water, she poured Nicholas a goblet of brandywine.

Please God it deadens the agony.

After he was bathed and bandaged, he wouldn't eat, but dozed occasionally between bouts of restless tossing. Burgundy sat with him, quietly reading her precious book, so that she could monitor his condition.

About midnight, something awoke her.

"Burgundy . . . I'm so damn cold."

She moved to the bed and put a hand to his forehead, expecting him to be fevered. His skin was icy. She tucked the furs about him, put extra coal on the fire, then slowly undressed.

In the big bed she moved carefully to his side. His body was just as hard as she remembered, but it was considerably colder. She wrapped her arms about him and pressed her warm flesh to his. Gradually, his restlessness subsided, and finally she knew that he slept. His words floated through her memory: *"One way or another I will make you hot for me, Burgundy."*

Before dawn he cried out in his sleep and thrashed wildly. He was not burning hot; she doubted he was delirious. "Nicholas, wake up. It's all right, it's just a nightmare," she soothed.

He opened his eyes and thanked God he lay in his own castle, in his wife's arms.

"It was a nightmare," he said low. "Ireland."

A lump came into her throat. She could never imagine the nightmare that it must have been. He and his brave men had won against all odds. He had done his duty for Queen and Crown. It would have been catastrophic if Spain had seized Ireland to launch an attack on England.

"It's over, Nicholas. It's over." She feathered kisses across his temple, and he closed his eyes to savor her tender concern.

In a few days, dispatches came from the queen, thanking him and offering her congratulations on his victory. The only thing Elizabeth regretted was that he had spared the lives of the Spaniards and sent them home. She thought the enemy should have been put to the sword.

Nicholas flung the letters across the chamber.

Burgundy picked them up and read. Then she smiled at him. "I am proud of you. You acted with honor."

"You understand," he said with wonder.

Nicholas Mountjoy gradually regained his strength with the care his steward and his wife administered. He still couldn't walk far, but he and Burgundy rode to strengthen his leg. They rode along the sand, splashing through the waves that grew warmer each day.

Rhododendrons and azaleas filled the castle gardens with their brilliant blooms, and the scent of roses and lilacs wafted in through the open windows. Whenever Burgundy came close, desire flared in him.

Desire had awakened in Burgundy, too, and she found excuses to be with him, to talk, to touch. His thigh no longer needed a dressing, and she was almost regretful. The sexual tension between them became a living, breathing thing. Burgundy knew she would scream if he touched her.

She would scream if he did not!

One night Nicholas pulled her to him and kissed her deeply. Ah, sweet heaven, the taste of her was intoxicating. With frenzied hands he bared her silken flesh for his avid gaze, his fingers, his mouth.

She pushed off his robe so that she could indulge the fantasies she'd had about his hard body.

Nicholas moaned with pleasure as he caressed her full, soft breasts, and then his hand sought her heat below.

Burgundy gasped as he slid his finger inside her. The pleasure was exquisite. Her sugared sheath contracted upon him, and he rejoiced that she was so passionately responsive. He came full over her then, she opened for him, and he plunged down into Paradise.

They were drunk with love. She arched against him blindly; he thrust, scalding himself in her heat. He was big and hard and everything she had ever imagined he would be.

She was so tight and hot, Nicholas thought he might die from pure pleasure. The tremors seized them at the same exquisite moment. She clung and shivered and cried his name.

Later, as she lay in his arms, he cupped her

cheek tenderly. "Do you love me, Burgundy?"

"Yes, I do," she answered quickly. She knew she would never change her mind. "I've been thinking . . . perhaps swimming would strengthen your leg. What think you, m'lord?"

"Mmm, if we swim by moonlight, if we swim naked, I think it would strengthen me considerably." He stood up and pulled her by the hand. "Let's try it."

Much later, after they had dried before the fire, he lay abed watching her write in a book. "What are you doing, my love?"

"Perhaps I'll show you someday." She smiled as she looked down at what she had written:

WITH HONOR CAME GLORY!
Burgundy Mountjoy, Countess of Devon, 1602.

THE BETROTHAL BALL

MARY BALOGH

The Betrothal Ball

She was trapped at the very top of the library steps. In her nightgown. With her hair loose down her back. The candlestick, with its hastily blown-out candle, was still clutched in her left hand, while her right hand held the book she had taken from a shelf just below the ceiling but had not had time to open. Three minutes more—even two minutes —and she might have been down the ladder, out of the library, and back upstairs in her room. Safe.

Instead of which, she was trapped at the top of the movable steps and might be there for the rest of the night for all she knew. She looked down gingerly at her bare feet and wondered if it would be possible to move down one step and sit down without either falling or making a noise. Heights had always made her dizzy, and this was a high-ceilinged room. She would feel safer if she did not have to rely upon her knees to hold her up.

She felt foolish. And alarmed.

Very alarmed. When she was finally free to move again, the room would be in darkness—unless it was after dawn—and she had no means with which to relight her candle. She would have to feel her way down the steps and across the room to the door. She glanced down again. The steps looked alarmingly steep.

How stupid she had been. How very stupid to have forgotten that there had been one essential change in the house during the day. How foolish to have forgotten that he had come home. Not that she had forgotten exactly. How could she forget? It was the very fact of his return that had kept her awake thinking about her first encounter with him, when she should have been sleeping. It was her wakefulness that had brought her down to the library in search of a book. She had done it before several times. And having discovered that the whole household retired early, she had learned that there was never any need to be furtive. Or to dress and put up her hair beneath a decent cap.

She had become bold and careless.

Although she had not forgotten that he had come home, she had neglected to consider the possibility that he might not follow the habits of his household, that he might not himself retire early.

And there he was in the library below her, seated in a large leather chair close to the fireplace, though there was no fire, it being a warm summer night. From where she stood, only the top of his dark hair was visible over the high back of the chair—and well-shaped, long legs encased in tight pantaloons stretched out comfortably on the hearth in front of him.

He had been dressed immaculately when he had appeared unexpectedly in the schoolroom late in the morning. He had worn shining, white-tasseled Hessian boots over buff-colored pantaloons, and a form-fitting green tailed coat over a paler green waistcoat and gleaming white frilled shirt and neckcloth. He had looked as she imagined a London gentleman would look, only finer. But then, of course, he *was* a London gentleman, who rarely put in an appearance at the country home and estate he had inherited, along with his title, a little over a year ago on the death of his elder brother.

When he had opened the schoolroom door and stood in the doorway, Bea had squealed and gone hurtling across the room and into his arms.

"Uncle Bram!" she had shrieked. "You have come home."

"As you see, child," he had said, hugging her briefly before setting her firmly at arm's length. "You are growing remarkably pretty. But your manners make me shudder. Young ladies—or older ones, for that matter—do not shriek or yell or rush, Beatrice. And they most certainly do not hurl themselves into gentlemen's arms, much as gentlemen may regret the fact. Have you not been taught these things?"

"What did you bring me from London?" Bea had asked, uncowed by the scolding, taking one of his well-manicured, heavily ringed hands in hers and lifting it to her cheek. "You brought me a gift, Uncle Bram?"

He had grimaced. "Wait and see," he had said, "greedy imp. You have a new companion? And have kept her longer than usual, I hear?"

"Oh, Miss Melfort," Bea had said carelessly. "How long must I wait? Don't tease, Uncle Bram. Is it a bonnet? A parasol?"

But Bramwell Lattrell, Earl of Dearborne, had turned his attention to Bea's governess—she deeply resented being referred to as a companion. Bea was not very teachable, but nevertheless Laura Melfort was a teacher. She was trying every method she knew of to teach Bea to read. It was not easy when Bea was fifteen years old and had a brain made entirely of feathers—or so Laura believed in her less charitable moments.

But companion or governess, she was without any doubt a servant, a paid employee of the Earl of Dearborne. She had been made fully aware of that as he had looked her over unhurriedly from head to toe with pale blue eyes. She had looked steadily back at him, resisting the foolish urge to glance down at herself to make sure that she was clothed. His eyes had made her feel as if she were not.

He had nodded coolly to her before turning away to address a few more remarks to his niece. He had flicked one long, careless finger beneath Bea's chin before telling her that she might dine with him in the evening if she was very good and promised not to squeal even once.

Bea's response had been a squeal and clapped hands.

The invitation had not been extended to Bea's governess.

Now he was not nearly so formally dressed. He wore leather slippers with his dark pantaloons, and his lace-trimmed white shirt, his only other garment, was open at the neck. Indeed, it was open almost to the waist. Laura had seen that when he had come into the room, carrying a full branch of candles. She had extinguished her own candle as soon as she had heard the doorknob turning.

She had assumed—oh, how foolish of her—that he had come in merely for a few moments, to retrieve a letter from the desk, perhaps, or to pick up a book. She had expected him to be gone without delay and had held her breath, praying with frantic fervency that he would not look up into the shadows and see her there, where she had no business being. In his library.

And in embarrassing dishabille.

But he had not come for just a brief while. Even as she had watched, frozen and horrified, he had picked a book from a lower shelf and sat down with it in the leather chair. And if there had been any doubt about his intent, it had fled when his valet followed him into the room after a few minutes, bringing a full decanter and a glass on a tray. He had poured liquor into the glass after setting down the tray at the earl's elbow.

It had been too late after the valet's withdrawal to make her presence known. If she had been going to do that, she should have done so immediately. She should have kept her candle burning, descended the steps with as much dignity as she could muster, murmured an apology, and left the Earl of Dearborne to his leather chair and his book and his brandy.

Oh, how she wished now that she had done just that.

It took her perhaps ten minutes—it felt more like an hour—to set her candlestick silently down on a shelf and to lower herself into a sitting position on the library steps. She sat there, hardly daring to move a muscle, for what seemed hours longer, though perhaps it was only another ten or fifteen minutes. No, surely it was longer than that. The edge of the step was digging awkwardly into the top of her legs, causing increased pain until she was almost screaming with it. But she dared not move. She clutched the unopened book with both hands to her bosom.

She wanted to cough. There was dust floating in the air close to the ceiling, dust that perhaps she had dislodged with the exploration of the books on the top shelf—why, oh why had the top shelf always fascinated her when she could as easily have found something readable at ground level? She swallowed three times in succession, ruthlessly suppressing the urge to cough.

And then she jumped and was almost dislodged from her precarious position at the sound of a voice. A man's voice, speaking quietly and conversationally. *His* voice, though there was no one else in the room to answer him.

Except her.

"It would probably be the wise thing to do," his voice said, "to come down from there. It must be a rather uncomfortable perch."

It was obvious, as soon as she had fully digested his words, that they had been addressed to her.

He knew!

He had known all along.

She rose slowly to her feet and descended the steps with care. But her nostrils flared with anger. He had been toying with her. How he must have been enjoying her predicament.

But when her bare feet finally made contact with the warm safety of the carpet on the floor, anger fled and humiliation took its place. She was in her nightclothes, without even a dressing gown for decency. And she had been hiding on top of the steps for goodness knew how long, believing herself unobserved.

"Are you down?" the voice asked, sounding faintly bored. "Come and stand where I can see you."

She circled to the side of the chair, keeping to the shadows, keeping as much distance between his chair and her person as she was able. He was looking down at his book, apparently reading it. She wondered if he would come in pursuit of her if she kept going toward the door. Doubtless she would be relieved of her employment in the morning. But then her employment was probably forfeit anyway.

"Closer," he said, his eyes still on his book. "Much closer. Within the circle of light cast by the candles."

The light of the candles really did not radiate very far at all. She was forced to move within three feet of his chair. She stood slightly to the front and side of it. She resisted the urge to hang her head, though she doubted that she had ever in her life felt so embarrassed. She looked steadily at his bowed head until at last, after several minutes, he closed the book quietly and unhurriedly, set it on the tray next to the decanter, and looked up at her.

She had to make a conscious effort to stop herself from taking a step back. Those pale, rather heavy-lidded eyes seemed to penetrate straight through hers to the back of her skull. Or rather, they seemed to peer straight into her soul.

It became quickly apparent—had it not already been so—that he was a man accustomed to having and to wielding authority. He said nothing for so long that she could almost feel herself shrinking in size, and she wondered foolishly if she was expected to say something or perhaps to go down on her knees and beg for mercy. She had to remind herself that she was a gentlewoman, even if Papa was impoverished and she was forced to earn her own living. Her chin lifted a fraction.

"Ah," he said at last, still sounding rather bored, "I wondered if you came equipped with a temper. It would be strange if you did not."

He was referring, of course, to her hair, dark in shade but still unmistakably red. Every strand of it was visible to his eye, from root to tip. What awful humiliation. She would not let her mind stray to her nightgown and bare feet.

"Might I be permitted to ask what you are doing wandering about my home in a state of such, ah, inviting dishabille?" he asked, and his eyes slid down her body and back up again, peeling away garments as they did so, much as they had done in the schoolroom earlier. She could feel her toes clenching into the carpet. "In pursuit of willing footmen?"

She felt her nostrils flare again. "If that were my intention, my lord," she said, "I would hardly be searching in the library and at the top of the steps, would I? Unless I was determined on a lonely night," she added outrageously. She listened to the echo of her own words, scarcely believing that she had spoken them.

"A good point," he said, raising arrogant eyebrows. "But you would be well advised to put your claws away, Miss—Melfort? You would not enjoy the consequences of digging them into me." He leaned forward suddenly and reached out to take the book she held clasped to her bosom. She felt his fingers, bare now of rings, against one breast and relinquished the unknown volume in some haste.

He sat back in his chair and looked at the cover and spine of the book before opening it and turning the pages with some care.

"You enjoy romance?" he asked her.

Her steady gaze became a glare at his lowered head. "My lord," she said, "I would remind you that even though I am in your employ, I am a lady."

Blue ice from his eyes impaled her. "If that was what I was asking of you, Miss Melfort," he said, "I would not be calling it romance. I would call it something altogether more earthy. I was inquiring about your reading tastes."

If the library floor had just opened up at her feet to reveal a yawning cavern, she would gladly have jumped in, even if she had spotted demons and pitchforks down there. She had misunderstood him. How wretchedly mortifying!

She licked her lips and watched his eyes follow the gesture.

"This is something of a family heirloom," he said, indicating the book he held in one hand. "It was handed down from my mother to my sister. Although I am a reader, I have never cared much for this sort of thing. It is some sort of romance, I believe. Is that why you chose it?"

She had not chosen it at all. It just happened to be the book she had had in her hand when she heard him at the door.

"Yes," she said. "I wanted something to put me to sleep."

His eyes strayed downward again, pausing at her breasts, whose rather generous fullness she had been hoping in vain the cotton of her nightgown would conceal. She wished she could bite out her tongue. Though there would be no use in doing so now. The words had been spoken.

"You might have been better served," he said, "by seeking out that footman."

She drew a deep breath and saw that his eyes were on her breasts again.

"Here." He held out the volume. "Take it to bed with you, Miss Melfort. Let an imaginary lover put you to sleep. His name is Damon, I believe. You must let me know if he lives up to his name. It suggests a certain—virility, does it not?"

She took the book from him, careful not to touch his hand as she did so. He was sneering at her. Sneering at the idea of reading about love and romance. So typical of men. She had a wide variety of reading tastes, but that was not the point.

"Perhaps I read romance," she said, looking deliberately into his eyes, knowing that she was being goaded to say what she should not even dream of saying, "not in order to find an imaginary lover to warm my lonely maiden bed, but in order to recall the more lovely aspects of life, those in which love and commitment and relationships give joy and meaning to an existence that is so often wasted in self-gratification and basic unhappiness."

To her surprise and annoyance he looked amused. He got to his feet and she was aware, as she had been earlier in the day, of his superior height, though he was no longer wearing boots. Even though she was not short, the top of her head barely reached his mouth. She was also very aware of his half-bared chest with its noticeable dusting of dark hair.

He set a hand beneath her chin, though she had not tried to dip her head, and touched the pad of his thumb to her lips for a brief, electrifying moment, during which she almost lost her knees.

"A worthy maidenly speech, Miss Melfort," he said. "But you really should try self-gratification one of these days. It is a wonderful way of wasting a meaningless existence. You have done well with Beatrice. Despite this morning's alarming display of enthusiasm, she has pleasing manners and can converse agreeably on a wide variety of topics, ranging from the weather to bonnets to fans. She is, of course, fulfilling the promise of beauty she has given since childhood. In two or three years' time I should be able to marry her off very creditably indeed. Does she dance?" He had removed his hand, though he continued to stand in front of her, his hands clasped behind him. Laura would have been more comfortable if she could have taken a step or two back, but she stood her ground.

"Very gracefully," she said, "including the new waltz, which pleases her greatly. But she is not doing well, my lord. She will not be a great prize as any man's wife unless somehow over the next couple of years she can learn to read and acquire some knowledge of literature and books."

"Good Lord," he said, his eyebrows raised arrogantly again, "you are never a bluestocking, are you, Miss Melfort? Do you think all the young bucks who will crowd around Beatrice in a few years' time will care that much"—he snapped a finger and thumb of one hand—"for the fact that she is a ninnyhammer? She will be prized for her beauty and her dowry and her youth and her ability to breed heirs."

"And her accomplished conversation," Laura added.

"That too," he agreed. "Why do you think men hunt and shoot and fish and frequent their clubs?

It is to escape hearing more than necessary about the weather and bonnets and fans."

"And so they lived happily ever after," she said tartly. "Would it not be better if a man could converse with his wife? Really converse?"

"Ah, but you see," he said, "a really stupid man might be shown up by a wife of superior intelligence. It would not do at all. He would be unmanned. Better far if she is a mere ornament. No, don't try the impossible, Miss Melfort—even if it seems to you to be merely the improbable. Leave Beatrice in happy ignorance. My brother never saw the need of teaching her anything but feminine accomplishments. It is too late now to imagine that she might read and learn to love books and all the knowledge they contain. She has very little aptitude, I believe."

"I would say it is interest she lacks rather than aptitude," Laura said. "I live in hope of arousing her interest, my lord."

"And making of her a sharp-tongued, bold-eyed spinster like yourself?" he asked. "I think not, Miss Melfort. I had you employed as a companion for my niece more than as a governess."

She was stung. More deeply than she would care to admit.

"I have none of Lady Beatrice's attributes," she said. "But that is hardly the point. It is your niece of whom we speak, not me."

"Is it?" he asked. He sounded bored again, though his eyes regarded her keenly enough. "Which attributes do you lack, Miss Melfort? The large dowry, no doubt. You have the beauty. You are not young—five- or six-and-twenty, at a guess—but doubtless not so old that you cannot breed. You can converse on numerous topics, I do not doubt. Do you dance?"

"Yes," she said curtly. "Of course I dance."

"You do lack one other important attribute, though," he said.

She lifted her chin, hurt again and thoroughly despising herself for being so.

"Straw," he said.

She frowned her incomprehension. "Straw?"

He took his hands from behind his back and framed her face with them. She froze into immobility. "In here," he said, tightening his hold of her head. "You have a brain instead. It can be a severe handicap."

"I would rather be a spinster with a brain," she said defiantly, "than a married lady with straw." She was not at all sure that she spoke the truth. Her spinsterhood had weighed heavily on her for years, ever since she had admitted to herself that governesses rarely married because they were caught between the world of servants and that of masters, belonging to neither.

"Ah," he said, apparently reading her mind, "you tell the blackest of lies without blinking an eyelid, Miss Melfort."

"I suppose," she said, hearing bitterness in her voice and trying to quell it, "you think it impossible for a woman to live in contentment without a man."

"As impossible as it is for a man to live contentedly without a woman," he said. "I wonder if having a brain instead of straw makes a mouth less kissable. I have a mind to put the matter to the test."

Although he continued to gaze into her eyes for a few moments, she did not grasp the meaning of his words fast enough to escape. Perhaps escape would have been impossible anyway. Perhaps he would not have allowed her to escape. Or perhaps she would not have fought hard enough—or at all—to effect escape.

His mouth was warm and firm against hers. She could smell brandy and cologne, a heady combination that had her losing her knees for sure this time. The thighs and body she swayed against were firmly muscled and quite distinctively masculine. And then she could taste the brandy. His lips had parted over hers, so that she felt heat and moistness, and the tip of his tongue was brushing over her mouth and pressing lightly across the seam so that it appeared she had no choice but to part her lips and allow him access to the sensitive flesh beyond. She was gripping something—two things. Her right hand clutched the book; her left hand held a fistful of shirt. The back of her hand was against chest hair and chest.

"No," he said, "it does not. Interesting."

She stared blankly up into his blue eyes, drowning, totally disoriented. The fact that she had a brain did not make her mouth less kissable. That was what he was talking about. She was curiously pleased.

She thought too late that a glare of outraged indignation and a "How dare you!" and perhaps even a crack across the face would have been far more in order than her blank, mindless, besotted stare. Belatedly she withdrew her hand from halfway inside his shirt and released her hold on its fine fabric.

"Go to bed, Miss Melfort," the Earl of Dearborne said. "With Damon for company. He is not likely to do you great harm as he will have his lady with him. You will discover her name within the pages of your book. If you remain here, I will be seducing you and breeding you. I make it a habit never to seduce my servants—or ladies who happen to be in my employ."

She stared at him for a moment longer before turning to make her escape. But his voice stayed her when she had a hand on the doorknob.

"Miss Melfort," he said, "I will not forbid you the library, but I must ask that in future you dress yourself with more propriety beyond the bounds of your own bedchamber. I will have a houseful of guests here within the week."

It would have been mortifying in the extreme to have anyone tell her such a thing. But the Earl of Dearborne himself . . . She turned cold, remembering her appearance.

"Besides," he said, and it sounded as if he had walked closer, though she did not turn her head to look, "I am not made of iron, Miss Melfort. You will never know what a superhuman effort it has cost me tonight to keep to my usual habits."

Laura turned the knob, jerked the door open, and fled.

It was certainly not a good time to be thinking of setting up a mistress. Or the time to be contemplating changing the habit of years—if "habit" was the right word. As a young boy he had been aware of his older brother taking dairymaids and chambermaids and laborers' daughters with about as much frequency and carelessness as he would pluck apples from the orchard in the autumn. The present Earl of Dearborne was still honoring his dead brother's obligations to two bastard children in the neighborhood—the two who had been begotten after his marriage. The others were all grown up and independent.

He himself had remained determinedly celibate through his boyhood. He had certainly made up for those years since, but only with women whose profession it was to give men all the pleasure they were willing to pay for.

It was not the time to be dreaming about what he would like to do to and with his niece's governess. No time would be the right time, but now was the worst time of all.

He had decided to take a bride.

The Honorable Miss Alice Hopkins, daughter of Viscount Gleam. Someone of his own rank and background. Someone who had been out in Society for three years—she was one-and-twenty, ten years his junior—and knew the rules of polite living. She was pretty, accomplished, charming. She would suit him admirably. She would be a perfect hostess, an amiable companion, a suitable mother for his children. She would understand that he would want most of his life to himself—as she would want most of hers to herself.

And so they lived happily ever after. He wished he had not heard those words, spoken in the scornful voice of Beatrice's governess, every time he congratulated himself on his choice.

He had invited Miss Hopkins and her parents and a number of other guests to spend a few weeks at Dearborne, his country home. Although he had made his choice, he had not made it so obvious that he could not honorably withdraw his attentions. He had not yet made an offer for her or even spoken with her father about his interest in her. Marriage was for life. It was not to be entered into lightly. He would see how they felt about each other in country surroundings, he had decided.

But his decision was made. Unless something quite unexpected happened, he would speak with Gleam before his guests left. He would marry Gleam's daughter before Christmas.

He certainly did not want to be distracted by a prim bluestocking of a governess who just happened to have the most glorious red hair he had ever seen and who happened to look almost irresistibly beddable in a long, unadorned cotton nightgown and bare feet. And whose hand happened to feel like a firebrand when the back of it was set against his bare chest.

Damnation, he did not want to be distracted. And he would not be if the woman had not been cavorting about the house at midnight in a shocking state of undress. He had thought when he first opened the library door and caught a glimpse of her white-clad figure apparently floating up below the ceiling that she was some sort of ghost or angel. He had decided to tease and punish her for making him feel such a prize idiot, pretending not to notice her, keeping her trapped where she was for forty-five minutes—he had intended to make it a full hour, but had relented.

He should have barked at her as soon as he spotted her and sent her scurrying on her way.

But the damage was done. He had seen her on that first morning in the schoolroom as a youngish, prettyish, quiet, disciplined sort of woman—the typical governess, if there were such a thing. She looked exactly the same whenever he saw her after that night in the library. No one to upset his equilibrium.

Except that he had seen her hair loose down her back. Except that he had seen her clothed for bed. Except that he had kissed her and held the slim shapeliness of her body against his own. Except that the back of her hand had branded his chest somewhere in the region of his heart.

Except that he wanted her more than he could remember wanting a woman for a long time. Probably because he could not have her, he told himself firmly. She was forbidden fruit.

He had always been fond of Beatrice. He used to feel sorry for her, abandoned as a very young infant by her mother, who had run off with a lover, and largely ignored by her father. He himself used to spend a good deal of time in the nursery, playing with her, listening with amused indulgence to her chatter, sometimes taking her riding in the park about the house. She had always adored him.

So it was only right, he told himself during the days following his return home and even after the arrival of his guests, that he visit the schoolroom frequently to observe for himself the progress his niece was making toward becoming a young lady worthy of Society and the husband of high rank he would find for her when she was eighteen or so.

He was given the impression that Beatrice showed off for his benefit whenever he was there. Certainly she smiled and chattered excitedly, played the pianoforte and sang for him all her favorite songs, displayed her best stitches and her best sketches for his admiration, begged to be allowed to dine with his guests and join them on picnics and other outings, and generally, he guessed, was a severe trial to Miss Melfort. Miss *Laura* Melfort—he had discovered her given name.

Miss Laura Melfort, he also discovered, did not once smile during his frequent visits to the schoolroom, or once raise her eyes to his, or once show any awareness that he was in the same room or the same universe as she.

He wondered if she was as much obsessed by him as he was by her. He wondered if she wanted to go to bed with him as badly as he wanted to go with her. If the truth were known, he found her very quietness and primness almost unbearably arousing.

She had no choice one afternoon but to raise her eyes to his and acknowledge his presence. He was out walking with Miss Hopkins and her married sister and a few of his other guests. They were strolling among the trees to the east of the house, along beside the river that would lead them to the lake. Beatrice and Laura Melfort were seated on the bank of the river—until Beatrice spotted their approach and jumped to her feet. She remembered, he was pleased to note, not to race toward him, shrieking his name. She smiled brightly instead and blushed and curtsied and looked altogether the pretty, budding young woman that she was. He smiled affectionately back at her.

She had been permitted to take tea with his guests a few days earlier and had behaved quite prettily. Miss Hopkins and her sister made much of her now and invited her to walk with them. She glanced bright-eyed, first at her governess, who had risen quietly to her feet and stood in the shadow of an old oak tree, and then at him. They both nodded to her, and she stifled a squeal and allowed Miss Hopkins to take her arm on one side and Mrs. Crawford the other and walk off with her. His other guests followed after them, a merry party.

Miss Laura Melfort, the Earl of Dearborne decided, was good at melting into the background.

He doubted that Miss Hopkins or any of the others had even been aware of her presence. She was a servant, of course. Servants were meant to be invisible. He stood where he was, watching his chosen bride and his other guests move out of sight and out of earshot.

The contrast was enormous. Alice Hopkins, blond and petite and smiling, was dressed in fine muslin, her clothes, from bonnet to slippers, in the very latest mode. Miss Melfort, hidden in the shade of the oak tree, was dressed unfashionably and inexpensively in cotton. He would like to clothe her in silks and satins and muslins, he thought, not looking at her. He would like to deck her out in jewels. He would also like to unclothe her. He turned his head to look at her. She was calmly observing the grass at her feet.

Waiting for him to be gone so that she could slip away.

"For a moment," he said, "I thought Beatrice must be desperately ill. She looked so absorbed in what she and you were doing that I thought she was not going to notice us. That is definitely abnormal."

She looked up at him, and for a moment he was jolted by the directness of her gaze and remembered how it had gradually stripped him of sense in the library.

"Tell me," he said. "I am convinced I must have been mistaken—a touch of sunstroke, no doubt. Was it a *book* that was so absorbing my niece's attention?"

She almost smiled, and there was a hint of smugness in the expression. "Yes," she said. "She wants to read it for herself. She is frustrated that she cannot do so with any degree of fluency, but she is making every effort to improve herself."

"Good Lord," he said. "Talking of sunstroke . . . And how have you effected this alarming transformation, Miss Melfort? By putting her on a ration of bread and water? By administering the birch twice a day after meals?"

This time the smile and the smugness were unmistakable. "By introducing her to a story that she desperately wants to read for herself," she said. "Hearing it told in my voice is not good enough. She wants to hear it in the voice of her own mind, though she has not expressed her wish in quite those terms."

"Let me guess," he said, trying not to remember how those slim thighs had felt pressed to his own and how her mouth had softened and opened under the persuasion of his. "Plato?"

"No." She was looking triumphant, wretched woman.

"Ah, Milton?"

"No." She was almost laughing. He wanted to continue the game until she did. A dangerous thought.

He grimaced. "Never tell me," he said, "that she wants to listen to the virile and romantic Damon whisper to her in the voice of her own mind."

She laughed. God! He did not want her to laugh. Or rather, he did. He wanted to catch her up in his arms and twirl her about and laugh with her.

"That is the book. I have made an English translation for her from the Latin," she said. "It is a love story, you see. It has caught her imagination and she wishes to read it for herself, even though I have read it to her. I have even hinted to her that there are numerous other books she would find as satisfying."

"Love stories?" he said.

She nodded.

"My niece," he said, "is to learn to read so that she may entertain herself with sentimental drivel?" He tried to feel the disgust his intellect was dictating he should feel.

"Love is sentimental?" she said. "Love is drivel? Then give me sentimental drivel, my lord. Give me love."

There was an arrested look on her face. He had seen it there once or twice in the library. He guessed that Miss Melfort sometimes got so caught up in an argument that she did not pause to choose her words with care. On this occasion she appeared to have opened wide her mouth and thrust her pretty foot firmly inside. And she had just realized it.

"That," he said quietly, "is quite an invitation, Miss Melfort. You will forgive me if I do not take you up on it."

Her eyes were directed downward to the grass again. For all the plainness of her clothing and hairstyle, he thought treacherously, she was many times more lovely than Alice Hopkins. *Give me love*. Oh, yes, quite an invitation.

"What is her name?" he asked. "Damon's lady?"

"Angeline," she said quietly, though she did look up at him again. "She might have chosen another man, one more like herself in every way. Damon was not from her own world."

"Do you disapprove, then?" he asked. "Do you admit that the story that seems to have affected both you and my niece rather powerfully would not stand up to the test of reality?"

"Perhaps it would not," she said. "Certainly it ought not to work, that kind of union. But perhaps it would for the very reason that it ought to fail. Perhaps differences between two people make them work harder at the relationship. Perhaps they take nothing for granted as they might if they were of the same world."

Like him and Miss Hopkins. Laura was of a different world. Oh, not quite, perhaps. She was a lady. But she was not really of his world, for all that. In his world ladies did not have to work for a living or wear cheap, serviceable clothes. In his world ladies did not have to exert their minds in any way.

"You are an incurable romantic, Miss Melfort," he said, "even though we established on a former occasion, I believe, that your head houses a brain instead of straw. You are doing well with Beatrice. I am pleased."

Her lips parted and her eyes widened somewhat. "Thank you," she said so quietly that he read her lips rather than heard the words.

"I suppose," he said rather grudgingly, "that being able to read, whether for pleasure or information, can be of some value even for a woman. How it is learned is of little significance. Perhaps I should read about Damon and Angeline for myself. Perhaps you would win a convert." He glanced down at the book, which she held in one hand.

"Yes," she said.

He wanted more than anything else in the world at that moment to step closer to her and kiss her again. She was becoming rather like an addiction. He wondered how long it would last if he were free to take her and use her at will. He had the strange feeling that perhaps it would never go away.

Because he had the even stranger feeling that the attraction was not just sexual.

An alarming thought.

"I shall leave you to an hour of leisure, Miss Melfort," he said, "while I go in pursuit of my guests. I am sure privacy during the daytime is a rare luxury for you."

It was only after he had walked determinedly away, leaving her standing beneath the oak tree, that he realized he had made her his most elegant bow.

His niece's governess. His servant!

Everyone knew why the guests had been invited. Servants always did know such things. They had known even before their master returned home. Perhaps, Laura sometimes thought fancifully, they had known even before he did.

Mrs. Batters, the housekeeper with whom Laura sometimes took tea in the evening, had told her that the Earl of Dearborne was to entertain his prospective bride and her family and other selected guests.

The Honorable Miss Alice Hopkins was to be his bride. And she was pretty and vivacious and fashionable. The servants all approved of her, especially as she ignored them totally and generally behaved as a very grand lady ought.

"Soon we will have a mistress in the house again," Mrs. Batters had said. "It is about time. The last one did not stay for much longer than five minutes and has been gone a long time. There will be children in the nursery within the next few years, you may be sure, my dear Miss Melfort. Perhaps you will be kept on for them after Lady Bea has left the schoolroom."

It had been a comforting thought. Had been. It no longer was.

She waited each day with some dread for his visits to the schoolroom and prayed inwardly that he would not come. And yet on the rare days when he did not, she found herself dejected. It seemed that some light was missing from the day. She dreaded feeling his eyes on her when he should be concentrating his attention on Bea, and yet when he did not look at her, she felt like a worthless nonentity.

She dreamed about him at night. Oh, that was not strictly accurate. She did not often dream about him when asleep. But she lay awake when she should have been sleeping, remembering the look of him, remembering the curiously compelling paleness of his blue eyes, remembering things he had said to her, remembering his kiss, the feel of his body against hers.

Give me love. She remembered with deep mortification saying those words to him. She remembered the arrested look on his face and his answer. *Give me love.* She wondered what he would feel like . . .

She despised herself. Poor lovelorn, lonely, frustrated spinster. Dreaming romantic and even lascivious dreams of her employer. Of a peer of the realm, no less. Hating the very pretty and quite blameless Miss Hopkins merely because he was going to marry her. Hating the thought of his and Miss Hopkins's children in the nursery, perhaps under her care.

No, never!

She hated herself. And so she threw herself into her work, insisting that Bea practice her pianoforte playing and singing more than usual because she was growing up and would soon need to use her accomplishments in company. And shamelessly enticing the girl to read by giving her stories to feed her romantic imagination and tender heart. Bea, who had had the skills for reading for some time but no inclination to use them, improved remarkably in just a few days. The ancient book from the library worked its magic on her—and on Laura. It was possible for a man and a woman from entirely different worlds to come together . . .

No! It was not possible. He had been right to question the idea. It would not work. Not in reality. Within the pages of a romance perhaps. But not in real life.

Not that the matter would be put to the test anyway, of course.

Bea was a great favorite with the ladies. Despite her pleas and wheedling, her uncle would not allow her to join the company for either dinner or the evening entertainments. She was far too young, he told her firmly. Her time would come soon enough. But sometimes, as on that afternoon beside the river, the ladies asked her to join them in some daytime activity.

One afternoon Miss Hopkins and Mrs. Crawford, her sister, came to the schoolroom. They did not knock but just walked in, talking and laughing. They both hugged Bea and admired the watercolor she was painting before inviting her to take the air with them. They completely ignored Laura, who rose quietly from her own painting and started to clear away. She nodded when Bea looked at her with eager inquiry, and the girl rushed from the room to fetch a bonnet.

One day perhaps Bea would learn that ladies did not rush everywhere. One day perhaps she would lose the eagerness of youth. Laura sighed inwardly. Why did she and everyone else responsible for

Bea's upbringing work so relentlessly toward that day? Why did youth and eagerness have to be lost?

"She is tiresomely gauche," Miss Hopkins said.

"But it is necessary that you dote on her," Mrs. Crawford said, looking at Bea's painting again and smiling disdainfully. "Dearborne is fond of her."

"Perhaps," Miss Hopkins said, "she can be sent away to school for a couple of years. I am not sure I will enjoy sharing even this large mansion with a bouncing niece."

Mrs. Crawford, glancing across the room to where Laura was cleaning brushes, coughed delicately. "Have a care, love," she said. "I do believe there are ears open."

"Oh." Miss Hopkins followed the direction of her glance, and for a moment her eyes raked over the governess with some contempt. "Servants who wish to keep their employment and to be given a character when they are dismissed must learn when it is expedient to keep their mouths shut."

Bea came bursting back into the room at that moment, all bright-eyed and flushed and smiling. "I am ready," she said. "This is the new straw bonnet Uncle Bram brought me from town."

"And very handsome it is too, my dear," Mrs. Crawford said. "Quite in the latest mode, I do assure you. But then one would expect nothing less if Dearborne chose it."

"I do declare I am quite jealous," Miss Hopkins said. "You are ten times prettier than I, dear Beatrice. We had to persuade you to come along to brighten our walk, did we not, Clara? I do not know when I have taken to anyone with as deep an affection as I feel for you."

"So prettily behaved," Clara Crawford murmured as the three of them left the schoolroom, leaving the door open behind them.

Laura continued to tidy the room. Poor Bea. She was not a particularly intelligent girl or particularly skilled at any of the accomplishments expected of a lady. But she was a sweet and affectionate girl. With the right handling and the right companions she could develop into a warm and loving woman and could expect a happy life.

Bea would not enjoy school. And having been deserted at an early age by her mother and made anxious about whether she was lovable or not, she did not need an aunt who disliked and despised her—and was jealous of her. The Honorable Miss Alice Hopkins had spoken the truth there.

And it was Miss Hopkins he was going to marry.

It did not matter. It really did not matter whom he married.

And then she looked up sharply. He was standing in the open doorway, one shoulder propped against the frame, watching her. She did not know how long he had been there.

"Beatrice is gone?" he asked.

"Miss Hopkins and Mrs. Crawford came to invite her to go walking with them," she said.

"Ah." He continued to watch as she straightened papers that did not need straightening. "I knew it, of course. I saw them walking away together. My other guests are all busy about various pursuits. I excused myself on the grounds that I had business to attend to for a few hours."

She clasped her hands in front of her, refusing to fidget further in his presence. "It is happening already?" she said. "You feel the need to escape the boredom?"

"Miss Melfort." His eyes bored into hers from across the room. "You are impertinent."

Yes. She really could not imagine how she had said those words aloud. Perhaps she had felt the need to strike back a little for the humiliation she had just suffered at the hands of his future bride and her sister.

He pushed his shoulder away from the door-frame and strolled into the room and across to the window. He stood staring down at the formal gardens below. "And quite correct, of course, damn you," he said.

"In the rectory where I grew up," she said, "we were not allowed to use profane language and no one was allowed to use it in our hearing."

His head turned and he regarded her coolly. She could not decide if his blank eyes hid anger or amusement. "My apologies," he said.

She swallowed.

"My guests bore me," he said, "when I must suffer them throughout the daylight hours and beyond. And so I must plot occasional escape. I have come to you, Miss Prim and Proper. Entertain me."

She wondered if he realized that his words were provocative. And she wondered if she had become very depraved to notice. "I don't know how," she said.

He was still looking at her over his shoulder. "And yet we are both thinking with great clarity of one way, are we not?" he said. "It would be inappropriate, Miss Melfort. I do not know if I will ever be able to forgive you for showing yourself to me as a woman on one very memorable night. Or forgive myself for kissing you. Talk to me. About something other than the weather or bonnets or fans."

He was not flirting with her. He had made that very clear. And yet he had made her suffocatingly aware of him as a man. His fashionable form-fitting coat and his pantaloons and Hessian boots molded themselves to his powerful frame. His face was achingly handsome.

"Never tell me," he said, "that you have no conversation except on those topics. I expected better of you. Come." He stood back from the window. "Sit on the window seat and make yourself comfortable instead of standing there in the shadows like a statue."

She approached him hesitantly and seated herself on the padded window seat in front of him, arranging her cotton skirts carefully about her. He continued to stand, though he lifted one booted foot and set it on the seat beside her. He rested one arm across his raised leg, so that his face was on a level with her own and a little too close for comfort.

"The rectory," he said. "Tell me about it. Tell me about your childhood and girlhood."

"It would make very dull telling, my lord," she said, feeling a sharp stab of homesickness. She always tried not to think about her girlhood.

"Let me be the judge of that," he said. "Tell me about your father and mother and about your brothers and sisters if you have any. Tell me about Laura Melfort and who she is."

"I had a happy childhood." She was almost whispering. "So very happy. There were eleven of us, including Mama and Papa."

And as poor as church mice. Made poorer by the fact that Papa gave away money that his own family desperately needed and Mama gave away food that her own children would have devoured with great enthusiasm. But they were never hungry or cold for all that, and were never dressed in rags.

And they were rich beyond dreams in love and happiness. They were never lonely. There was always a brother or a sister or more often several of each to play with and occasionally fight with. And they were never bored. There were always chores to be done and lessons to be learned and parishioners to be visited and family social or musical or literary evenings to be participated in and enjoyed.

It had been an idyll, her girlhood. Unfortunately, she had not realized it or appreciated it fully at the time. Or perhaps it was not unfortunate. Perhaps happiness such as that had to be unconscious. Perhaps happiness would be marred if one tried to clutch it greedily to oneself.

Perhaps, as Papa had always said, the moment was a fleeting thing and had to be lived to the full and then relinquished so that the next moment was not wasted.

And there was always memory. Memory was one of God's most precious gifts to man—and woman.

"I had only one brother and one sister," the Earl of Dearborne said. "My brother was twelve years older than I. I never particularly admired him, and he found me a nuisance. My sister LeAnne married when I was just a child and went to Barbados with her husband. I was not allowed to play with other children of the neighborhood. They were too far beneath me socially. And I rarely saw my parents. They spent most of their time in London. They died before I reached manhood. I had everything I could possibly need, and everything I did not need too. I envy your memories, Miss Melfort."

She gazed back into his eyes. She felt absurdly like crying. Memories, even good memories—*especially* good memories—could be painful. They could make the present seem so very barren, so very empty.

"Who educated you?" he asked. "Your father?"

She nodded. "He taught us all," she said.

"Sons and daughters indiscriminately?" he said. "I suppose he taught you Latin and mathematics and everything else that is usually reserved for a boy's education?"

"Yes," she said, "and Greek."

He smiled fleetingly. "A bluestocking indeed," he said. "No man can be expected to take you on, you know. Any man would be terrified of you."

"I don't care," she said. "I am able to reach out to a world beyond my physical being. With my mind and with books I can transcend the frequent dullness and boredom of everyday living."

"Miss Melfort." He leaned a little closer to her, and she resisted the urge to press her head back against the glass of the window. "Was that meant to be a reproach? Were you being impertinent again?"

No. Her mouth formed the word, but no sound came out. She cleared her throat awkwardly. "No, my lord."

"Is the lure of living romance vicariously still inducing Beatrice to read?" he asked.

"Yes," she said. "I believe she has finally penetrated the mystery of linking letters and sounds together and making sense of what is written on a page."

He looked at her in silence for what seemed like a long while, his eyes roaming over her face. He looked directly into her eyes at last and smiled. "Thank you," he said softly. "Thank you, Laura Melfort. She is an important person in my life. Not just because I am her guardian. I am fond of her."

"You love her," she said, "as if she were your own daughter."

"Yes." He lowered his foot to the floor at last and straightened up. "I am glad I lied shamelessly and avoided my guests for a short while. I feel restored. I am going to have to keep you in my household in some capacity, Miss Melfort, after Beatrice has flown from the nest. You may very well save me from death by boredom at some future date."

"How absurd," she said tartly. "You should marry someone who can give you companionship, my lord."

He impaled her with his blue gaze again, and she realized the impertinence of her words. "Indeed?" he said softly. "Are you applying for the position?"

She shut her eyes tightly and could feel herself flush.

"You deserve your embarrassment," he said. "I think I may be trusted to choose my own bride and order my own life without your advice, Miss Melfort, learned and wise as I am sure it is."

There were a few moments of unbearable silence before she heard his booted feet crossing the room. Then she heard the door close quietly.

When she opened her eyes, he was gone.

The house party was to culminate in a ball on the last evening. Neighbors had been invited from miles around to fill the ballroom. The house and the neighborhood were abuzz with preparations. There had been no full-scale ball held at Dearborne for years and years.

He felt somewhat guilty. He knew that everyone, from his lowliest servant to his most distant neighbor, expected it to be a betrothal ball. Although he had not breathed a word to anyone about his intentions, they nevertheless seemed to be common knowledge. And he knew that Viscount Gleam was expecting to be taken aside to discuss a marriage settlement, and that Miss Hopkins herself was expecting a declaration.

But he was curiously hesitant to make it. The visit had been a success. She was everything he had hoped she would be. Yet now that the time had come, he could not bring himself to take the final and irrevocable step. And of course he really had not committed himself in any way. He was not honor bound to make the offer, despite the general expectation that he would.

He did not have to marry Miss Hopkins. But he did not know why he hesitated. He felt that it was time to marry. He needed and wanted children. She was the perfect choice in every way.

You should marry someone who could give you companionship, my lord.

Laura Melfort was an impertinent, outspoken woman for a governess. She had dared to reprimand him for using the mildest of profanities in her hearing, the prude. Not that it had been a gentlemanly thing to do, of course—he ought to have known better. She had studied Latin and Greek, for the love of God! And mathematics! And she had eyes that terrified him because they did not flutter before his but gazed directly into them and beyond them into the very depths of his being.

He would have to keep her in his household in some capacity after Beatrice left the schoolroom, he had told her. Was he mad? If she was in his house, he would never come home. Even now he vowed to leave soon after his guests, and not come back until Beatrice no longer needed a governess.

He could not live under the same roof with such temptation.

He had given in to Beatrice's pleadings against his better judgment and agreed to allow her to attend the ball for a short while—for three sets. She could continue to watch from the old minstrels' gallery until supper, at which time she was to go to bed. And if she did not, he would want to know the reason why, he had added while she pulled a face at him and called him an old ogre and then hugged him and thanked him for allowing her to attend at all.

He had chosen her partners with care—two young men from the neighborhood for the first and second sets, and himself for the third. On no account was he going to allow any of his town guests to get their hands on her.

She danced very prettily. The dancing master who had spent a month at the house during the winter had done his job well. And Miss Hopkins danced very elegantly—as he knew from having danced with her on several occasions in London. She also looked at him a little—anxiously? And everyone else all evening had been looking at him with an air of expectation.

But he was largely unaware of it all—the splendor of the flower-decked ballroom his servants had prepared, the elegance of his guests, the richness of the music, the excitement of Beatrice, the anxiety of Miss Hopkins, the expectations of everyone else. It was all like something that was happening around him but did not concern him.

All his attention, though he rarely glanced in her direction, was on Beatrice's chaperon, dressed neatly and unfashionably in gray silk, her hair in a simple knot at her neck. As was to be expected, she somehow found a shadowed corner in the ballroom and sat there, a part of the furniture. Invisible.

Except to him. To him she might as well have been seated on a high dais surrounded by banks of lit candles. He could see no one else.

And after she had withdrawn following the third set with Beatrice, who gazed at him first imploringly and then reproachfully, it seemed to him again that she was some kind of angel hovering over him from the gallery, where she stood with his niece, much as she had in the library that night.

He blessed the coming of supper. Perhaps for the rest of the evening he would be free of her and able to concentrate his attention on his guests. Not that he particularly wished to do that. He felt uncomfortably guilty. Expectations were almost as powerful as facts, it seemed. He felt almost honor bound to make the offer he was more and more reluctant to make.

He felt a flashing of anger when he returned from the supper room, the Viscountess Gleam on his arm. It seemed Beatrice had defied him. He would have sharp words for her in the morning and cold words for her governess. She was to be in bed by now, not still watching proceedings from the gallery.

And yet when he looked up, he found that there was no one there. He looked away again, relieved, and engaged the viscountess and another lady in conversation.

But *she* was there. He knew she was there.

When the music began again, he made sure that all the ladies had partners before slipping from the ballroom and climbing the stairs to the wide landing that held the door leading out onto the minstrels' gallery. He turned the knob and drew the door toward him very quietly.

She was in the alcove where the minstrels used to sit, in shadow as was to be expected. She was gazing down onto the ballroom, a look of naked wistfulness on her face. She was alone.

And then something must have alerted her. She turned her head sharply, and her eyes met his. His heart turned over and his knees felt unsteady. Her eyes were very bright. With unshed tears, he realized in some shock.

"It is a waltz," he said quietly. "Do you waltz?"

She continued to stare at him as if she had not heard him.

"Come." He held out a hand toward her. "We have our own private ballroom out here. Come and waltz with me."

She shook her head quickly, but he stood unmoving, his hand reaching out for hers until she looked down at it and came slowly toward him. She paused for a long while just beyond the reach of his hand before lifting her own from her side and setting it slowly in his. It was cold.

"Come," he said again, closing his hand about hers and drawing her out onto the landing, dimly lit with only two widely spaced branches of candles.

She stood rather stiffly as he slipped his palm to the back of her waist and took her hand with his, but then she raised her free hand to his shoulder and her eyes to his. Her gaze was still bright with tears.

And he knew the truth with such stunning force that it amazed him he had blocked it so effectively from his consciousness for almost three weeks.

"You see?" he said. "We can hear the music quite clearly from here."

"It is not right," she said. "You should not be dancing with me, my lord. You should be dancing with—with your future bride."

He smiled at her and they danced. She waltzed gracefully. She felt like a mere feather in his arms, her spine arched beneath his hand. She moved perfectly to his lead. They danced silently for many minutes, their eyes on each other's. A footman, coming upstairs on some errand, paused, hesitated, and then scurried downward again.

"I always imagined," the earl said, "that a bluestocking would have two left feet."

But she had no answer. She looked as if she danced in a dream. She looked incredibly beautiful.

"Laura." He had not even realized that his arm had tightened about her until he felt the shock of her breasts touching his coat.

Her lips parted and he was lost. He stopped dancing, drew her all the way against him, and lowered his mouth to hers. He kissed her deeply, opening her mouth with his own, thrusting his tongue deep inside, straining her supple body to his own as if he would take her into himself.

"Laura. My love," he murmured, his eyes still closed, his lips still touching hers.

It was then he noticed that her arms were about his neck. Her eyes were tightly closed, he saw when he opened his own, and on her face was an expression of agony.

And he knew at the same moment what he would do, what he must do. What he wanted more than anything else in this world to do.

"Come," he said, pausing to kiss her lips warmly

again. "Come with me." The music was drawing to a close, he could hear.

She opened her eyes and gazed at him with perfect calmness. Her tears had disappeared.

"Yes," she said, and when he lifted his arm, she set her hand on it. Her eyes, he saw when he looked into her face, were directed at the floor ahead of them.

She knew that in a more rational moment—tomorrow morning—she would not be able to believe the meekness with which she was going with him. Or the meekness with which she would give herself to him when they reached his bedchamber or wherever else he was planning to take her. She was about to lose her virtue without even a token struggle.

Because she wanted it.

Because she wanted him.

Because she loved him.

Because it was one of those moments in time to be lived to the full and because she would never again have this chance and because it would be one of her cherished memories. She knew it would, even if she must also remember with shame and with guilt.

"Yes," she had said. She would go with him wherever he cared to lead her and she would do with him whatever he wanted. She would receive him into her body and give him herself.

She knew it was sordid. Correction—tomorrow she would know it was sordid. Tonight she knew only that it was beautiful, what was happening between them. Tonight she did not care about tomorrow.

But when they reached the staircase, he turned

to go down, not up. She moved at his side, but she looked inquiringly into his face. He was looking steadily back.

"Where are we going?" she asked.

"Into the ballroom," he said.

She tried to draw back then. She would follow him into ruin and disgrace but not into the ballroom. But his free hand came across to hold her arm in place along his.

"Where did you think I was taking you?" he asked. His eyes were smiling at her. "To bed, Laura?"

"Yes," she said.

"And you would have gone there with me?" he said. "Ah, my love."

The terror of walking into his bedchamber with him would have been nothing to what she was feeling now. She was invisible no longer—because she was at his side, her arm along his. She knew that everyone saw her. Really saw her. There was an almost perceptible pause in the buzz of conversation when he led her into the ballroom and across to the platform on which the orchestra sat.

"Another waltz, if you please," he instructed the leader, who leaned toward him.

And then he turned to bow to her and take her hand in his and raise it to his lips.

"Will you do me the honor, Laura?" he asked.

She knew then how Cinderella had felt. Except that she had no glass slipper to lose when she left eventually. She would not think of having to leave.

She knew that everyone was watching curiously as the Earl of Dearborne treated his niece's governess like a princess.

"Yes," she said.

The music began and he led her into the dance,

beneath the candelabra with their hundreds of candles, amongst the flowers whose combined perfumes made her almost dizzy with their sweetness. And he was Prince Charming with his ice-blue satin evening coat and knee breeches, with his silver embroidered waistcoat and gleaming white linen. She had felt almost sick with admiration and love for him while Beatrice danced and she sat unnoticed in a corner. And now she was dancing with him herself.

"And where may I find the rector, your father?" he asked. "How far away?"

"Thirty miles," she said.

"Tomorrow," he said, "I must see my guests on their way. I will ride to the rectory the day after."

She dared not understand his meaning.

"But it is a mere courtesy," he said. "You are of age, are you not, Laura? Am I being offensive to assume that you have passed your twenty-first birthday?"

"I am six-and-twenty," she said.

"We do not need his consent, then," he said. "We can make the announcement tonight if we wish. I would like to make it tonight. After this waltz. Shall I?"

"What announcement?" She could not be understanding correctly, though his meaning seemed as plain as the nose on her face.

"For some reason," he said, "it seems that people are expecting me to announce my betrothal tonight. I want to do so. But I need a bride. Will you oblige me, Laura?"

"How absurd," she said.

"Somehow," he said, "I expected you to say something like that. Shall I go down on my knees to you in front of all these people? I will if you want."

She was suddenly aware of all those people, politely dancing and conversing, covertly and curiously watching them.

"No," she said hastily. "Don't be silly."

He laughed, and she lost her knees and stumbled. His hand tightened at her waist, steadying her.

"I love you," he said softly. "I don't believe I can live with any degree of happiness if you will not agree to share my life with me. Will you? Please?"

"You are an earl," she said. "I am a rector's daughter. A governess."

"Ah," he said, "but you speak Latin and Greek and that makes all the difference. And you read about other people's romances too. It is time you had one of your own. Will you have one with me? Just for a lifetime and perhaps an eternity too? After that you may go free if you wish."

"I think, my lord," she said, hope painfully soaring, a dream becoming reality before her very eyes, "you are mad."

"Bram," he said, smiling. " 'I think, Bram, you are mad.' "

"Yes, him too," she said.

"Name him, then." His smile had turned to a grin.

"Bram," she said. "Bram, you are mad."

"Do you love me?" he asked.

She bit her lip then, and felt the tears come back. He must be playing with her. Surely he must. "Yes, Bram," she said.

"And will you marry me?" His head was shockingly close to hers.

"If you are sure," she said, her fingers curling

about the dream, beginning to grasp it. "If you are quite, quite sure."

She was being twirled then—recklessly, exhilaratingly. Twirled about and about so that flowers and candles and fellow dancers blurred into a kaleidoscope of light and color.

"After this waltz is finished," he said. "Up on the platform. Both of us. You by my side. And yes, I am indeed going to take you to bed, my love. As soon as the banns have been read and our marriage solemnized. Three weeks. An eternity, dammit."

"Bram," she said, "at the rectory . . ."

"Yes, I know, my love," he said. "My humblest apologies. I said it deliberately, you know, to see if you were paying attention."

She looked up into his laughing eyes and bit hard on her lower lip to convince herself that she was not indeed dreaming.

"Are you going to keep my life from boredom by quoting Horace every breakfast time and Homer every dinnertime, my redheaded bluestocking?" he asked.

"And I shall tell you a little of Damon and Angeline's story every bedtime to whet your appetite," she said outrageously, and blushed rosily as he threw back his head and laughed.

Guests and neighbors stared in amazement and growing wonder even before the music came to an end and the Earl of Dearborne led his niece's governess up onto the orchestra platform.

This was, after all, then, a betrothal ball.

GOLDEN TREASURES

CATHERINE HART

Golden Treasures

Atlantic Ocean, August 1814

The sea surged beneath the storm-tossed ship, pitching it furiously from side to side. Inside her small, dank cabin, where she was trying to dress by the dim morning light, Angela Aston gave a startled shriek as she and her maid both lost their footing and slid helplessly across the slippery plank floor. They landed in a tangle of limbs and clothing.

"We'ze gonna die, Miz Angie," the dusky-skinned maid wailed, her large black eyes rolling in fright.

"Stop that, Dinah!" Angela snapped, her tone abnormally sharp as she fought down her own fear. "Surely the storm can't last much longer."

"Longer dan dis rickety old tub yore papa sent to fetch us back to Barbados, I warrant," Dinah argued. "Dat man shore is in a powerful hurry to get ya home, to hab us sail in hurricane season, and da middle o' dis war 'tween England and da States. Could be he's hopin' somepin' bad gonna happen to us, and seems to me he gonna get dat wish."

"Hush such talk, and help me finish dressing," Angela demanded, levering herself to her feet, where she struggled to gain her balance.

Dinah did likewise, grumbling all the while. "Why ya gotta hab clothes on jus' to drown? Don't make no sense, nohow. Nobody gonna take notice but da fishes."

"We are not going to drown, I tell you," Angela insisted, praying that she was voicing the truth.

Yet she, too, had to wonder why her father had insisted she return to Barbados now, when sea travel was so perilous. Surely this war which had kept her in England for two years would soon end. Her visit with Cousin Beatrice, her mother Le-Anne's niece, had been wonderful, and Angela would not have minded staying longer—perhaps indefinitely. She didn't relish going home to face her father and stepmother, for she was certain they would not be pleased that she'd failed to acquire a husband in all this time, as had been their primary intent in sending her to England.

Not that she hadn't had her pick of suitors, but none of them had "tripped her trigger" as Dinah had put it, and Angela didn't want to settle for less. Of course, now she'd most likely have little say in the matter. Her father, tired of waiting for her to make a suitable marriage, had probably taken matters into his own hands and would have her future husband and the preacher waiting on the dock when she landed.

Angela cringed at the thought. She wanted to

make her own choice, whether it be marriage or spinsterhood. She wanted to marry for love, not for title or wealth or prestige. And now that she'd read the book Cousin Beatrice had given her, the book LeAnne had bequeathed to her young daughter, Angela yearned all the more for a love such as Angeline and Damon had shared in that heartwarming story. A love so strong, so abiding, that it would stand firm against all trials, all odds, all attempts against it—even against death itself, if need be.

Truth be told, she was thoroughly enchanted with the ancient tale of star-crossed lovers. Probably she was more fascinated than most would be, since the heroine bore a name so similar to her own. It had been so easy for Angela to imagine herself back in time, in Angeline's place—to feel what the other woman felt, to experience all the wonders and woes as though they were her own, to become just as enamored of Damon as Angeline had obviously been. Indeed, even now, Angela was half in love with the man—even knowing he was but a fantasy, a character who might or might not actually have lived many centuries ago.

As the ship gave another mighty lurch, Angela had to wonder if Dinah was right, if she and her maid would be fortunate enough to live much longer themselves. On the heels of that dreadful thought came a loud, ominous cracking, followed by a tremendous thud that shook the sailing vessel violently. Though the thud was similar to a sharp clap of thunder, Angela was sure the noise she'd heard just now had been louder, more menacing somehow.

Wide, frightened blue eyes met those of black. "Oh, dear Lord! What was that?"

"De Debil, maybe," Dinah replied in a horrified whisper. "I wasn't gonna tell ya, but I 'spose it don't make no difference now if I do or don't. I dreamed of da raven bird las' night, Miz Angie, an' if dat don't be bad juju, I don' know what is. We'ze bound to die. Dat raven comin' for us, for sure, with death in his eyes."

"You . . . you know that's just superstitious nonsense, Dinah," Angela said, trying hard to convince herself as well as Dinah. "You've heard Pastor Jones preach often enough to know that there's no real power in black magic. Just stones and bones and foolishness."

"You b'lieve what you want, an' I'll b'lieve what I has to," the young black woman countered shakily. "My mama was a voodoo priestess, an' her mama b'fore her, an' I knows what I knows. There's things can't be explained in this world. Strange things, dat can't be reasoned away by some preacher man or all his fine words. Signs. Omens. Visions."

As if to reinforce Dinah's claim, shouts sounded in the passageway outside their cabin, accompanied by the sound of swiftly running footsteps. "Abandon ship! Abandon ship! We're sinking! Man the jolly boats!"

"Merciful heaven!" Angela cried out, grabbing Dinah by the arm. "Oh, Dinah! We've got to hurry! We've got to get away before the ship goes down with us on it!"

Dinah nodded mutely, and turned to pull a traveling bag from beneath one of the bunks.

"No! There's no time to pack!" Angela told her. Then, contrary to her own command, she grabbed an oilcloth bag from a hook on the wall and stuffed her precious book into it, wrapping the volume securely in the waterproof covering. "Let's go!"

Dinah snatched up her red cloth juju bag from the bed, tucking the charm deep inside the bodice of her dress. "Got to have my juju, Miz Angie. Maybe keep da Debil off my back till I gets to Hebin."

To Angela's horror, when they tried to open the door, it wouldn't budge. Even now, seawater was seeping in beneath it, wetting the thin soles of her shoes. "It's stuck!" she wailed, suddenly believing that she might truly die this day.

"Jammed, mos' likely," Dinah agreed in an oddly resigned voice, as if reconciled to the fate she knew was coming.

Angela grabbed Dinah by the shoulders and shook her until the girl's teeth rattled. "Don't you dare give up so easily! Just because you think it's your time to die doesn't mean I have to go with you! Now help me with this bloody door!"

Together they tugged on the stubborn door, beating at it and screaming for help that never came. Finally, they managed to pry it open, just enough for the two of them to squeeze through.

Angela wiggled into the narrow, swiftly flooding passageway and made a mad dash for the crude stairs that led to the upper deck. Three steps up, her foot slipped on the wet wood, and she fell, knocking Dinah down with her. Her breath coming in quick, frightened pants, Angela yanked at the sodden ribbons that secured her slippers, ignoring the way the ties cut into her ankles as she ripped them off and went charging back up the ladder with Dinah fast behind her.

The deck was slick and listing perilously. Already, water lapped over the edge as the ship heaved with the crashing waves. The last of the sailors were leaping into the bobbing longboats.

"Wait!" Angela shrieked against the howling wind and pounding rain. "Wait for us!"

One seaman turned and shook his head. "Fend for yerself," he shouted back. "And take your island witch to hell with ye! We warned Cap'n Lewis not to bring women aboard! 'Twas the two of ye brought this ill fortune down on us!" With that, the boat cast off, leaving the two women stunned and abandoned.

"Oh, my God!" Angela cried in frantic disbelief, sweeping her rain-drenched hair from her face. "They've deserted us, as if we were nothing more than refuse to be tossed into the street! They can't do this! They can't!"

"I hope da sharks strip dey bones clean!"

As the ever-encroaching waves lapped eagerly at her skirts, Angela instinctively sought higher ground. Looping the drawstring of the oilcloth bag around her neck, she headed for the bridge, which along with the weaving masts was now the only part of the vessel still above the waterline. Slipping and sliding, she and Dinah literally clawed their way up the ladder to the higher deck. Breathless and soaked to the skin, Angela lay clutching the rail and began to pray in broken, earnest sobs. "Please, Lord! Save us! Don't let us die this way!"

"Too late," Dinah croaked out next to her. "Look! It's da raven, come to grab us in his great, deadly claws."

Indeed, viewed hazily through the wind-driven rain, the advancing object seemed to be a huge black bird skimming over the waves, its dark wings outspread. But as it drew nearer, Angela realized that the creature was actually the protruding figurehead of an approaching ship.

"Glory be!" she exclaimed, leaping to her feet and gripping the rail tightly with one hand as she waved frantically with the other. "Dinah! It's a ship, heading right for us. Quickly! Help me signal them, lest they pass by without seeing us."

"No!" Dinah whimpered. "It be a trick! Da Debil in disguise."

"Get up, you ninny!" Angela ordered, yanking at Dinah's shoulder. "Wave your arms and yell for all you're worth!"

Kyle Damien, captain of the *Raven*, an armed frigate pledged into service to the newly formed United States Navy for the duration of the war with Britain, wasn't at all surprised to encounter the floundering merchant ship in the midst of the storm. Nor were the three madly bobbing jolly boats filled to overflowing with British seamen any great shock. What did astonish and anger him was the discovery that these craven seadogs would abandon two helpless women to a watery grave in the middle of the Atlantic Ocean.

He'd just given the order to trim sail, ready to rescue the enemy sailors from their cramped crafts, when one of his men called down from the crow's nest, "Cap'n! Two ladies still aboard the merchant! Up on the bridge and sinkin' fast!"

Kyle instantly rescinded his previous command and issued a new one to his quartermaster. "Leave the English cowards to whatever the Fates hold in store for them! Head for the merchant ship. Haul alongside of her, as close as you dare."

"Aye, aye, Cap'n. What about the grappling lines?"

Kyle shook his head. "No. It would be too dangerous to tie up to her. She could drag us down with her. I'll swing over and board by line. Just hold the *Raven* as steady as you can."

Angela found herself holding her breath and praying mightily as the other ship drew nearer, for with every moment the quarterdeck upon which she stood was listing more precariously as the merchant ship surrendered to the relentless pull of the sea. Beside her, still on her knees, Dinah was fingering her juju and chanting what sounded suspiciously like some sort of African dirge. Not that Angela could blame her maid for her fright, for seen through the distorting sheets of rain, the approaching vessel looked most eerie, as if it might be a ghost ship emerging steadily from a wavering mist.

Finally, after what seemed an eternity, the two ships were but a fathom apart. Suddenly, from out of the cloud of sails on the other ship, a shadowy form appeared, swooping swiftly down from the skies like some huge bird of prey. Angela, her nerves frayed, joined Dinah in a startled shriek. Only at the last moment, just as he landed before her on the quarterdeck, did Angela realize that the flying figure was a man swinging on a rope—a very large man dressed all in black, his ebony hair plastered wetly to his head, his silver eyes glowing. Scarcely had he touched down when his hard, muscled arm wound about her waist, pulling her firmly against him.

"Put your arms around my neck and hold tight," he instructed her brusquely, his teeth flashing white in his sun-darkened face.

As Angela hesitated, taken aback by the man's American accent, Dinah cried out, "Don't do it, Miz Angie! He da Debil!"

At this, their would-be rescuer threw back his dark head and laughed. "Not quite, but not for lack of trying. Actually, I'm Captain Kyle Damien of the *Raven*, at your service, ladies. Now, I suggest we curtail the rest of the introductions until we're safely aboard my frigate."

"Damon?" Angela echoed faintly, her eyes growing wide with astonishment.

"Damien," he corrected shortly. As she continued to stare in stupefaction, as if incapable of movement on her own, Kyle wrapped Angela's limp arms around his neck and resumed his hold on her waist. Glancing down at her companion, he said, "Stay right here. I'll be back for you in a moment."

"No!" Dinah screeched, throwing herself at Angela and locking her arms around her mistress's legs. "Fight da Debil, Miz Angie! While ya still hab breath, ya gotta fight!"

"Oh, hell!" Kyle swore. "All right, ladies, if this is the way it's going to be, hang on tight. Both of you, or we'll all be shark bait."

With that, he launched the three of them into midair with a swift kick. In the next instant, they were soaring in a dizzying arc toward the deck of the *Raven*, with Angela clasped firmly to Kyle's broad chest and clutching his neck—while Dinah, screaming like a banshee, clung to Angela's legs with a terror-strengthened grip. They landed heavily, their less-than-graceful descent abruptly halted as Dinah's trailing posterior connected with the *Raven*'s starboard rail.

On a yowl of pain, Dinah released her hold and dropped to the deck. With the sudden absence of her weight, Angela and Kyle pitched forward, stumbled, and fell, still entwined. Though he tried to twist around so that he would be the one to take the brunt of their fall, it didn't work out that way. Instead, Kyle landed heavily atop the lady he'd just rescued, driving the air from her lungs in an audible whoosh.

Angela felt as if she'd been whacked in the chest with a ton of bricks. The oilcloth bag had swung around and the corners of her book were now poking painfully into her back, the drawstring nearly strangling her. For several seconds, the deck beneath her seemed to spin alarmingly, and when the world finally righted itself, Angela found herself lying beneath Captain Damien, their torsos pressed intimately together, and his legs resting boldly between hers. The heat in those smoky silver eyes was enough to steal her breath again.

"Are you all right?" he asked.

"I . . . I think so, if you could just get off of me."

He raised himself to his elbows, but no farther. On a gruff laugh, he drawled, "Actually, I rather enjoy having you for a pillow, albeit a soggy one." His gaze shifted to her chest, where her wet gown now revealed more than it concealed, then rose to lock with hers once more. His voice dipped to a low, seductive purr that sent shivers skating up Angela's spine. "Since I saved your life, don't I deserve to know your name?"

As if entranced, she replied on a shaky whisper, "Angela. Angela Aston, of Barbados."

An odd, stunned look crossed his face, his eyes searching hers as if seeking some answer beyond that which she'd offered. "Angela," he repeated somewhat vaguely, as if talking to himself. "Which originates from the word 'angel.' My God! Could it be that my old granny's prophecy that I would meet an angel is coming true, after all?" He shook his head, as if to dispel the thought from his mind. "No, not possible . . . or is it?"

"I'm no more an angel than you are the Devil," Angela assured him, pushing at his chest in an effort to dislodge him.

"Don't be too sure about that," he told her. "My grandmother was a Scot, and she had what they call 'the sight.' " At last, he took the hint and levered himself off her. He hauled her to her feet, where she wobbled dizzily before finding her footing.

"Dinah?" she called, turning to glimpse her servant, who was sitting on the rain-slick deck, gingerly rubbing her bruised bottom. "Are you badly injured?"

Dinah winced. "I don' think so, Miz Angie. But I won't be sittin' too good for a while."

"Your maid, I take it?" Damien commented, jerking his head in Dinah's direction. At Angela's affirmative nod, he chuckled. "I'd hazard her pride has taken a beating more than anything. At the moment, you both resemble near-drowned kittens."

Angela glowered at him. "How kind of you to bring it to our attention, Captain. Have you any other gems to impart?"

"Actually, I do. Since you are English and I'm an American, it would appear that we are enemies, compliments of our respective governments. Which makes you, Miss Aston, a prisoner of war—my prisoner, to be precise. Now, I shall have to consider what to do with you."

As she frowned up at him, she tugged at the restricting thong at her throat until she'd loosened it sufficiently to lift it over her head and clutch her precious package to her chest.

He eyed her and the parcel speculatively. "What

have we here? Clothing? Weapons, perhaps? Priceless family jewels?"

"A book," Angela retorted, clasping it possessively.

His brows cocked upward in disbelief. "A book? Good grief! Don't tell me I expended all that effort to save a bluestocking!"

Angela's spine stiffened, her midnight-blue eyes bright with indignation, the haughty posture only slightly less effective for the fact that her hair hung in soppy blond strands and her wet clothes clung to her slight frame like a second skin. "There is nothing wrong with a woman being able to read, sir. In fact, I consider it a most useful and enlightening skill, not to mention pleasurable."

"And what do you read that allots you such pleasure, my arrogant angel?" he queried, reaching out to snatch the bag from her arms before she could prevent it. Prior to opening the pack, he said, "Let me hazard a guess. Is it the Bible, perhaps?"

His wolfish gaze traversed the length of her, taking in her straggling blond hair, the form-fitting short-sleeved bodice of her clinging chemise-style dress with its Empire waist, the dainty bare toes peeping out from beneath the dripping hem. "I rather think not," he surmised with a smirk. "You are attired too fashionably, and too scantily, to lead me to believe that.

"Could you have absconded with the merchant ship's logbook, by some chance?" he ventured further. He gave a negative shake of his head. "Nay. That would prove much too boring for a young lady. The family archives, mayhap? But that, too, would likely be dull reading, wouldn't it?"

With a snap of his fingers, he declared triumphantly, "Ah, yes! I have it! This must be some fanciful romantic tale that has tugged at your tender heartstrings."

"What if it is?" she countered waspishly, making a hasty grab for her book. Kyle jerked it back out of reach, grinning like a cat with a mouthful of canary feathers. Then, to Angela's mortification, he drew the book from its waterproof covering and began to peruse it.

"Oh, please!" she cried out. "You'll get it wet! The pages will be ruined!"

After a quick look, he relented and handed the volume back to her. "Take it," he told her. "If the book means that much to you, I would not deprive you of it. However, you must share the tale with me soon. My Latin is a little rusty, but from what little I just gleaned, I am quite intrigued by the names of the characters in the story. Quite a coincidence, wouldn't you say, Miss Angela?" Those dark brows arched upward again in challenge, his silver eyes gleaming down at her. "Or is it fate, perchance?"

"Speaking of fate," she put in with cool disdain, "I wish to know what you plan to do with me, and with my maid. After all, we are but innocent victims in this war between England and America. Certainly, we have done you no ill, and should not have to pay for the crimes of others."

His grin widened, tinged with roguish delight. "Well, now. I could make you walk the plank, I suppose, or keelhaul the pair of you, or hang you from the yardarm," he listed smoothly. "Those measures always provide high entertainment for the crew, and they have so little amusement these days, poor fellows."

Angela's face paled, and she swallowed hastily before speaking up in a quavering voice. "Surely you can think of something more appropriate, something less drastic."

"Something more befitting a lady?" he crooned sardonically. At her wordless nod, he took a moment to consider her suggestion. After a pregnant pause, he said, "You say you're from Barbados? Would it be presumptuous of me to speculate that your family holds land there?"

"My father owns a sugarcane plantation," she admitted warily. "Why?"

"Given that, there is a chance we could ransom you back to your father for a fair price. You would gain your release, and my men and I would acquire a tidy profit, all in the same move. What say you, Angel? Does that seem a more reasonable scheme to you?"

"I suppose so," she replied. Nibbling nervously at her lower lip, she added hesitantly, "Though I do hope you don't intend to demand too much in exchange for me, lest my father decide I'm not worth the cost."

Kyle blinked in surprise. "Surely you jest. What father worth his salt would hesitate to pay his last penny to retrieve his own daughter?"

With a solemn look that told him she was completely serious, she offered tentatively, "One who considers her a burden to him and his new wife, and is none too pleased that his daughter is returning from England still unwed after he's spent a goodly sum toward that end. My ransom aside, I imagine our reunion will not be a joyous one, unless he's managed to arrange an advantageous marriage for me, which he threatened to do if I did not make a suitable match during my visit with Cousin Beatrice."

Dark brows drew together over cloudy silver

eyes. Advantageous to whom? he pondered silently, wondering why the thought of Angela wed to someone else should bother him. After all, they'd only just met, and it wasn't as if he actually believed his grandmother's puzzling predictions for his future. To do so would mean that he and Angela Aston had been destined to meet, to fall in love, and that was pure nonsense. Why, even his closest friends considered Kyle Damien a diabolic predator of the seas, more pirate than privateer. What angel would want such a devil for a mate?

"So much for your dire dreams," Angela commented to Dinah as the two women sat in their assigned cabin, huddled naked beneath coarse blankets while they waited for their clothing to dry. "The Devil turned out to be our savior, and the raven is nothing but his ship. If you aspire to be a great sorceress like your mother, then you'd better learn to interpret your visions more accurately."

"We'ze not out o' da woods yet, Miz Angie. 'Specially you," Dinah reminded with a smirk. "Your daddy gonna be hoppin' mad."

"Yes, and I presume he'll somehow make it seem as if it were all my fault," Angela agreed wearily. "He's never forgiven me for not being the son he wanted so badly, or Mother for dying in the attempt to deliver his sole male heir."

Dinah nodded. "Maybe your stepmama will birth him one soon and that will ease his temper."

Angela gave an inelegant snort. "If Miriam wasn't such a hateful witch, I'd feel sorry for her. As it is, I hope she gives him a dozen daughters and they all live unhappily ever after!"

"Speakin' o' which, I shore do hope dis Cap'n Demon don't take a notion to get under yore skirts, or da fat really gonna hit da flames! If you don' step foot on Barbados jus' as pure as da day ya left, we'ze both gonna wish we drowned on dat ship."

Angela gaped at Dinah in amazement. "Damon . . . Damien," she corrected automatically. "Moreover, how can you even entertain such a thought?" she countered shakily.

"Which? Drownin', or—"

"The other," Angela cut in. "For mercy's sake, Dinah, if he were planning something of that sort, he surely wouldn't have escorted us both to the same quarters. Besides, he'd have given some indication of interest, don't you think?"

"Gal, when it comes to some things, I swear you is dumb as dirt. Dat man was all but droolin' over ya! Fact is, if looks was lard, you'd both be lookin' like greased pigs, 'cause you was doin' yore own share o' gawkin'."

"Don't be ridiculous!" Angela snapped, thoroughly piqued that Dinah had noticed the way she'd stared at Kyle. But how could she have resisted doing so? The man had executed a daring rescue and saved her life, for mercy's sake. Moreover, he was absolutely fascinating! Tall, dashing, handsome—the embodiment of all her deepest, most secret fantasies come to life! Then, to have a name so similar to that of the hero in her beloved book. Why, it was downright eerie! Was it any wonder she'd been knocked off her pins from almost the instant she'd seen him? From the moment she'd gazed up into his sultry silver eyes and felt her heart lurch in her breast?

"Your imagination is playing tricks on you, Dinah," Angela insisted firmly.

"Maybe," Dinah allowed slyly. "An' maybe not. Time'll tell, and there's a whole lot o' ocean b'tween here an' home, lots o' time to fan da fire."

As if Dinah had conjured him up, Kyle walked into the cabin just as Angela was tying the ribbons of her still-damp chemise. Too late, she reached for her gown and held it up before her in an attempt to shield her scantily clad body from his avid gaze. Face flaming, she railed at him, "Sir! How dare you burst in here while I am dressing! You might have the courtesy to knock!"

One dark brow slanted upward. "And miss catching you in your underdrawers?" he drawled.

"Is there a reason for your rude intrusion, or did you simply mean to plague me with your lack of manners?"

He held forth a small bundle. "I thought you might need these, since most of your personal belongings are now lost."

Still clutching her dress to her breast, Angela motioned for Dinah to take the offered articles. The topmost object was a hairbrush. "Thank you, Captain," she muttered, clenching her teeth against the tide of humiliation which lashed at her.

He slanted a roguish grin at her. "Put that brush to good use, Angel. Not that you don't look fetching with your fair tresses in a wild tangle, but I'm curious to see what you look like when they're properly groomed." He paused, then added softly but firmly, "I expect you to dine with me tonight, in my cabin."

The captain's cabin, Angela soon learned, was the one next to hers and Dinah's. When, with some suspicion, she asked him why he'd located them so near, he explained bluntly that two lone women aboard a ship full of randy sailors were in danger, and he'd placed them in the abutting cabin to help insure their privacy and protection.

He brushed aside her contrite expression of appreciation, again quite frankly stating, "Though I would probably kill the first man who attempted to molest you, my decision is also based on sound business logic. I don't think your father, or any future spouse he's chosen for you, would pay much for soiled merchandise, so it's in everyone's best interest to keep you safe and sound until we make the exchange at Barbados."

Angela stiffened, her feminine pride stung. "I see. Well, whatever the reason, I am grateful that I and my maid will not have to fend off any unwanted advances from you or your crew."

He laughed, raised his glass to her in toast, and graced her with a wicked wink. "Don't discount me so easily," he replied smoothly. "After all, my lady angel, 'tis said that all is allowed in love and war, and to quote a famous fellow American sea captain, 'I have not yet begun to fight.' "

"Fight! Fight!" a strange voice suddenly piped up from an unlit corner of the room. Startled, Angela swung abruptly about, nearly toppling from her chair. Her hand clutched at her chest, her heart pounding, she peered into the dimness.

Again Kyle laughed, this time with no trace of mockery. "Don't be alarmed," he told her. "It's only Phantom."

"Phantom?" she echoed weakly.

"Aye. My pet raven. The ship's talisman."

"He . . . he talks?" she stammered, only now able to discern the bird's darker outline against the lighter wall. "Like a parrot?"

"His vocabulary is limited to a few words as yet," Kyle said, "but I'm hoping to teach him more." He held out a scrap of food and called to the bird,

"Come, Phantom. Show the lady what a fine fellow you are."

With a rustle of wings, Phantom hopped from his perch to the edge of the desk, daintily snatching the treat from Kyle's fingers. In the lamplight, his sleek feathers gleamed blue-black, his eyes shining like polished jet. Even his beak and feet were black, not a speck of another color showing anywhere, an austere appearance which sent a shudder down Angela's spine.

"He's quite . . . unusual," she offered lamely for lack of a more complimentary response.

The twinkle in Kyle's eyes told her he was aware of her aversion to his pet. "He suits me well, don't you think? Sets us apart from the more common pirates and their parrots."

"Pirates?" she croaked, swallowing her wine too hastily.

"More politely, the government refers to us as privateers, of course, but that is merely a white-washed term supported by the most flimsy legal authorization. It is very obliging of them, however, to render my chosen trade lawful in time of war."

"How . . . how convenient for you," she stammered, completely flustered. It was one thing to be captured by an enemy officer, a gentleman, and quite another to be told you were the prisoner of a pirate! A blackguard! Truly, it put an entirely new slant on the situation.

As he leaned forward to refill her wine goblet, Kyle's eyes laughed into hers. "Tell me about your book, Angel. I'm in a mood to be amused."

"You consider love amusing, then?" she countered daringly.

"Don't you?" he parried.

"Not particularly. I find it intriguing, adventurous, momentous, but I've never thought of it as droll."

"Ah, but you've only read about it, haven't you?" he remarked pointedly. "You've never actually experienced it . . . in the flesh, so to speak?"

Her color rose, painting her cheeks pink. "Have you?"

"Many times," he boasted.

She gave a haughty sniff. "I very much doubt that we are speaking of love in the same vein, Captain Damien. I am talking of the emotional feelings of the heart, while you undoubtedly refer solely to the . . . uh . . . physical aspects."

He nodded. "Touché. A point in your favor, my sweet. But do you really believe all that sugar-coated drivel someone has sprinkled upon a page for others to consume?"

"Yes. Not simply because someone has written a tale of love, but because I truly believe it exists."

"Do you also believe in magic?" he goaded. "Fairies and goblins, and such?"

She graced him with a shy smile that nearly stole his breath, so lovely was it to behold. "I used to," she admitted almost shyly. "Now I pray for more meaningful miracles."

"Such as?" he prompted.

"A husband who will cherish me, upon whom I can lavish my unstinting adoration. Children. A home of my own, filled with warmth and love."

"A simple enough request, from a woman's standpoint," he conceded. "But tell me about this book you find so fascinating that you sought to save it above all your other possessions."

"My reason was mostly sentimental," she allowed. "The book belonged to my mother, who died when I was a child. My Uncle Bram kept it for me."

"Then the story itself means nothing to you?"

She blushed again. "On the contrary, it's one of the most wonderful tales of romance I have ever read. An ancient legend passed down for centuries, it encompasses all one could hope for," she added. Her face turned soft and dreamy as she recounted the elements of the old legend. "Two star-crossed lovers, whose love triumphs over all odds. Intrigue. Greed. Jealousy. A test of honor and loyalty. Best of all, a happy ending for the two sweethearts."

"Angeline and Damon?" he questioned in a hushed tone, not wanting to break her reflective mood.

"Yes. Despite what others think, and all that should keep them apart, they are perfect for each other."

"As if fate had destined their paths to cross?"

"Exactly. One without the other would be incomplete. Lost. Unbearably lonely. But together they are whole, strong enough to surmount all barriers, incredibly happy, even in times of trouble."

"And so you wish for your own Damon, just as I have always wondered if I would meet my Angeline . . . my angel," he concluded gently. "Odd, is it not, that our two names so closely reflect those of your storybook lovers? One might say it's prophetic."

Their eyes met, and something wondrous passed between them. The air about them seemed suddenly charged with pulsating anticipation, as if some elusive discovery, some mystical truth, hovered between them, daring them to claim it.

"Are you my angel, I wonder?" he murmured softly.

"Are you my heart's hero?" she countered

breathlessly, trapped in the hypnotic glow of his silver gaze.

He shook his head and chuckled, breaking the spell which seemed to bind them both. "I fear not, my lady. Far be it from me to assume the role of a white knight when I am better suited to that of a dark warrior."

She gave a resigned sigh. "And I lack an angelic temperament, let alone wings or halo."

"There we have it then," he told her. "Far better that I deliver you into your father's keeping, collect my reward, and continue on my merry way." He reached for her hand, turned it palm upward, and planted a warm kiss in its center.

At the touch of his lips, Angela's heart doubled its rhythmic beat. Her breath caught in her throat, and her bones seemed to melt. A fiery tingle sizzled from her fingertips to her chest. She felt like singing. She felt like sobbing. Exhilarated and disillusioned all at the same time. He *was* the love she'd been waiting for, her shining knight. With tarnished armor perhaps, but still her beloved, her dearest desire. She knew it, knew him, in the deepest recesses of her heart and soul. Yet, little good it did her to recognize this, if he refused to acknowledge it as well, if he favored money over love.

Why? How could God be so cruel as to dangle all she craved before her, only to yank it out of her reach? To tempt and torment her with that which she so desired and could not have? To give her but a glimpse of happiness, only to deny it?

She swallowed her disappointment, her pride demanding that she not break down in front of Kyle. She gave a careless shrug, as if to say it was not that important a matter to her, and tugged her hand from his. "Oh, well, it was a lovely thought while it lasted. Now, if you will excuse me please, I would like to retire to my quarters. By now, Dinah with be in a fret."

"Imagining the worst, I suppose?"

She returned his mocking look with her own. "That would depend on one's perception of worst and best, wouldn't it, Captain Damien?" she replied shrewdly. "Good night, sir."

The days to follow were almost idyllic. After the storm, the seas became calm and sun-dappled, with a mild summer breeze to fill the sails. Each morning and afternoon, Kyle escorted Angela and Dinah on deck for a walk in the fresh air and sunlight. Each evening, Angela dined with him in his cabin. She came to treasure these stolen moments in his company. They talked of many things, and Angela learned, to her delight, that Kyle was well-read, though his interest in literature varied from hers, resulting in many a lively debate. He preferred history, and accounts of adventure and travel, while she leaned toward romance and poetry and tales of human nature. He did possess a rare English translation of the *Arabian Nights*, however, which she was dying to read, and which he readily offered to lend to her.

That evening, as she was preparing for bed, there came a knock on the door. Before either she or Dinah could ask who it was, or bid him to wait a moment until they could cover themselves, Kyle sauntered in with the promised book in hand and an impish twinkle in his eyes.

"Blast you, Kyle Damien!" she railed, yanking a sheet from the bed to cover her legs, which were bared beyond the trailing hem of the man's shirt she'd donned in lieu of a nightgown. "I told you to knock!"

"I did," he told her with an unrepentant grin. "My word, woman! I never thought I'd be envious of my shirt, but what you do to it, or in it, is positively provocative. I don't suppose you'd agree to let me entertain you in my bed tonight, rather than amuse yourself with this dull book," he tacked on hopefully.

Angela glared and grabbed the book from him. "Reading is much safer than dallying with you, Captain."

"But not half as much fun," he goaded.

"I'll simply have to take your word for that," she countered stiffly. "You'll excuse me if I assume you are not only pompous, but an outrageous braggart in the bargain."

He shrugged, gave her one last covetous look, and turned to leave. "Think what you like, but it's your loss."

"I'll live with it," she assured him with dry wit, though she was not nearly as calm as she appeared as she shut the door behind him. Her insides were all aquiver, her imagination already running wild as she pictured herself and Kyle in bed together—committing unmentionable acts of which she had only the foggiest notion. Shameful, tantalizing, sensual acts that, though yet a mystery to her, were ever so tempting, perhaps all the more because they remained such a secret.

If Kyle thought Angela appealing in his shirt, he nearly choked on his tongue when he arrived to take her for her walk the next morning. Again she was wearing one of his shirts, this time combined with a pair of his trousers which had shrunk beyond fitting him. The pants now hugged her hips faithfully, bagging only at the hem, where she'd rolled them up to avoid tripping.

"What . . . why aren't you wearing your dress?" he stammered.

"Because it needed laundering and is not yet dry," she informed him airily.

"Then you'll simply have to wait until it is. You're not appearing on deck dressed like that," he assured her.

"Why ever not?" she argued. "I'm fully covered, except for my feet, of course. And that merely because you can't provide me with footwear to fit."

"No. The men would take one look at you in those close-fitting trousers and I'd have a full-blown mutiny on my hands."

Hands propped on her hips, she stared him down. "For all your brash talk, you are naught but a prude, Kyle Damien. A dyed-in-the-wool prig!"

His heated gaze traversed her full feminine curves, so blatantly and alluringly revealed. "You tempt me to prove otherwise, but I'll not be baited so easily. Especially by a blushing maiden with a waspish tongue. Until you are properly attired, you'll remain in your cabin, with the door locked!"

With the knowledge that their time together was waning with every league the ship traversed toward the western horizon, Angela cherished each precious moment, hoarding memories to last through all the lonely years ahead. It broke her heart to realize that before long they would part company, and she would never see him again. Never gaze upon his handsome face, or see him smile, or witness that mischievous glitter in his eyes or watch them darken with open admiration and desire for her. Never again would she hear his deep, rumbling laugh, or listen to his teasing remarks, or relish the most innocent brush of his hand. For the rest of her life, she would be doomed to loneliness, resentful of any man who tried to take his place in her heart, and she would surely die a little more each day without him.

So she tried now to flood her heart and mind with treasured memories. She plagued him with questions about his ship, his adventures at sea, his home in America, his family, his favorite foods. He answered readily, asking only that she return the favor by relating details of her own life. This she did gladly, silently willing him to remember her when she was gone, to hold her memory in a special place in his heart forever.

During this exchange, Angela and Kyle discovered that they had more in common than either might have expected—small things, insignificant when taken separately, but which added to the delight of their mutual inventory of facts. Having been raised in the islands, Angela shared Kyle's love and respect for the sea, particularly the tropics, where the waters were warm and the breeze soft and flower-scented. Both were excellent swimmers, which was unique in itself since ladies rarely learned to swim, and neither did the majority of seamen, despite the fact that they spent a good portion of their lives traversing the oceans.

To Kyle's surprise, Angela proved to be a good sailor, not prone to mal de mer, which immediately raised his regard for her. Prolonged exposure to the August sun and salt air turned her honey-hued hair to a lighter flaxen, and her pale skin soon took on a golden glow. Rather than bemoan her darker skin, she seemed to consider it a natural consequence, not worth fussing over. Instead of avoiding the sun, she spent as much time as possible on deck, watching for dolphins and flying fish and thoroughly relishing the fair weather with which they were now blessed.

Kyle quickly came to admire Angela's quick intelligence, and would often draw her into a heated debate on a variety of topics ranging from literature to politics, merely to witness her avid arguments. For her part, Angela appreciated not only Kyle's sharp intellect, but his delightful, if slightly skewed, sense of humor. Within minutes, he could take her from serious discussion to hilarious laughter, and she adored him all the more for it.

During this serene interlude, Dinah was the one fly in the ointment. The woman determinedly held to her dislike and distrust of Kyle, continually casting him suspicious looks and grumbling to herself about devils and demons. She considered him a cross between Satan and a warlock, and insisted that Phantom was his sinister familiar. Though the raven wasn't Angela's pick of an ideal pet either, she had softened toward the bird somewhat since Kyle had taught him to say "Angel."

Angela's efforts to disabuse Dinah of her preposterous theories were futile. While Dinah mumbled and chanted, invoking various protective curses against the evil she believed threatened her and her mistress, Angela turned a blind eye to her maid's forbidden maneuvers, considering it better to ignore her than to lend credence to Dinah's foolishness—until the day Dinah got bold enough to creep up behind Kyle with a knife . . .

The day was perfect—the sea calm, the breeze mild, the sky blue. Angela and Kyle were sharing a private picnic on deck. Reclining beside him on the blanket, Angela was laughing as Kyle fed her bits of fruit from his hand and recited farcical verses of poetry, which he composed on the spot for her amusement. She glanced up just in time to see the sun glint off the sharp edge of the blade which Dinah was aiming at Kyle's back.

"No!" Angela shrieked, tugging at Kyle's shoulder, causing him to fall across her. Her flailing arm crashed into the wine bottle, toppling and breaking it. Wine ran like blood over the gently rolling deck as the glass shattered. "Dinah! Stop! Have you lost your mind?"

Kyle turned to see Dinah hovering over them, fear and frustration etched on her dark face. The knife hung from her hand limply, but Kyle was taking no chances. Lunging to his feet, his boots crushing the broken glass to slivers, he advanced on Dinah and yanked the weapon from her grip. "Would you repay my courtesy by stabbing me in the back, after I saved your worthless life?" he growled, towering menacingly over her now.

Dinah cringed away from him. "N-no! I only wanted to . . ."

"To do what?" Kyle bellowed. "If not to kill me?"

Obviously reluctant to tell him, but faced with his anger and the possible consequences, Dinah confessed, "I aimed to cut offen a lock o' yore hair."

Disconcerted, Kyle frowned at her. Angela was likewise puzzled. "What the bloody hell did you want my hair for?" he demanded to know.

Dinah shook her head, refusing to say more, but Angela suddenly had a good idea what was going on. She, too, sprang to her feet. "Oh, good grief, Dinah! It's for one of your asinine voodoo spells, isn't it?"

"I ain't sayin'."

"Voodoo?" Kyle echoed, nonplussed. "As in chicken bones and incantations? Black magic?"

"Precisely," Angela concurred with a nod. "Taboo, but practiced in the islands nonetheless, though no one takes it seriously but the slaves themselves."

"I'm aware of that. Native sorcery is practiced in the bayous around New Orleans, too, all very secretively, of course." He glared at Dinah. "So, what sort of magic were you planning to work on me, woman? You can confess now, or feel the bite of the lash on your back until you do."

Dinah's face, dark as it was, turned gray. "You'll whip me anyways, even iffen I does tell ya."

"That will depend largely on how lethal your spell was intended to be," Kyle responded. "Now spill the truth, and perhaps you'll save yourself much pain."

"I's makin' a hex doll what looks like ya," Dinah declared belligerently. "I was gonna stick pins in it and make ya sick 'nuff to leave off bewitchin' Miz Angela. Dat's all, jest sick some, not daid."

"Oh, dear Lord!" Angela exclaimed. "I can't believe you would actually stoop to such a thing, when Captain Damien has been nothing but considerate of our comfort."

"I can," Kyle grumbled. "She was trying to protect you, which is the only thing that has saved her miserable hide."

He called out to his master gunner, the only black man among his crew. "James! Confine this woman below deck. She will be your responsibility from this day forth. Do with her what you will, but I want her out of my sight and kept from making trouble for the duration of the voyage."

"Is that really necessary?" Angela queried with a

worried look as she watched James lead Dinah away.

"Don't worry. James won't harm her. I do suspect he'll divert her attention and energies to better use, however," he added with a sly grin. "Which is why I chose him for the task."

Angela gaped at him. "You mean he'll . . . they'll . . ."

Kyle tapped her sagging jaw shut with the tip of his finger. His eyes twinkled with devilment. "Aye. Haven't you noticed the way they've been ogling each other for the past week? They'll make the most of their time together, I'm sure. And I envy them that freedom, for 'tis exactly what I wish we could do. But you are a maiden lady, and I'm not quite the pillaging blackguard I seem."

The ardent desire on Angela's face and in her eyes mirrored his. Unconsciously, she took a yearning step toward him, her move aborted when her bare foot came down on a sharp sliver of glass.

No sooner did she cry out than Kyle swept her into his strong arms. "You've cut yourself."

"Only slightly, I think," she murmured, her face mere inches from his, her lips pouting for the feel of his upon them.

"Still, we must tend it immediately. Wounds fester quickly in this clime."

So saying, he carried her to his cabin, her head tucked securely against his shoulder, her long hair streaming like a golden wave across his arm. Placing her gently on his bed, right where he'd longed to have her since first rescuing her, Kyle forced himself to attend to matters at hand and quickly located the medicine kit.

Seating himself and laying her leg across his, he examined the small wound. "The glass is still there.

I'll have to extract it before we can bind it." His gaze caught hers, and he offered a smile of encouragement. "Stay still and be brave, my angel. This might hurt a bit."

With her foot cradled in his large hand, and his fingers lightly grazing the sensitive underside, Angela felt little more than a twinge when he pulled the tiny sliver free. Her concentration centered on the warmth emanating from his flesh to hers, on the peculiar tingling that zagged up her leg, causing her stomach to clench in delicious reaction. Even when he cleansed the wound, she scarcely noticed the pain. But when he placed his lips there, she thought she would expire with the thrill that danced through her bloodstream.

"All better now?" he inquired softly, teasingly.

Her eyes limpid with yearning, she managed to whisper a reply. "My foot is, but now I seem to have this awful ache all through me. Can you cure that, as well, Captain?"

No longer could he deny himself, or her, as her pretty plea shot straight to his heart. In the next instant, he was lying alongside her, drawing her into his embrace, their limbs entwined and his lips seeking hers. Lips meshed, tongues twined in eager exploration. Hands reached out in urgent quest, stroking, caressing, binding their bodies closer still. His fingers brushed over her breasts, making the crests stand proudly against the restricting cloth of her bodice. She arched into his touch in a silent bid for more, and sighed when he loosed the ties of her gown and bared her to his view, his adoring touch. His mouth suckled her, wrenching a moan from them both. At length, he forfeited the prize, pulling slightly away from her, his breathing heavy and his eyes shining like quicksilver.

She caught his dark head in her hands, twining her fingers into the onyx locks. "Don't stop," she implored weakly.

"We must," he told her, his voice hoarse with desire. "While it is still possible for me to do so."

"No. I want to know all there is to being a woman. With you, Kyle. Please."

"Once it's done, there will be no going back," he warned her. "I'll not let you go, for you'll belong to me, and no other, as long as we both shall live."

"Is that a proposal?" she whispered hopefully.

"Aye," he said, surprising himself as much as her. "We'll be wed as soon as we dock in New Orleans. I suppose that's the least I can do for the lady who saved me from her mad maid," he teased with a wry grin.

Her smile outshone his. "Dinah would not have dared kill you. Even had she truly tried, love has always been more powerful than any other magic, black or otherwise."

"Be sure, Angel. Be very certain what you want, for you'll be giving up your home and family and former allegiances in favor of mine."

"I'm sure, my love. Absolutely positive."

Angela could not recall ever being so deliriously happy. All her most treasured dreams were coming true. She was in love, and soon to be the bride of the most handsome, wonderful man on earth. She belonged to him—heart, body, and soul—and it felt so right! Even now, she could not fully fathom her tremendous good fortune. In just a few weeks' time, her entire world had turned topsy-turvy, all for the better. Just when she'd resigned herself to whatever fate her father might have in store for her, Kyle had charged onto the scene and rescued her, not just bodily, but emotionally. Her champion. Her dashing pirate, literally swooping down to sweep her off her feet. It was all so perfect. So marvelously romantic!

However, even at these dizzying heights, with passion and love so brilliant and new to them, there loomed a number of issues yet to be dealt with. First and foremost, there was this troublesome, ongoing war between England and the United States, and Kyle's participation in it. As dangerous as it was, and as much as Angela feared for his well-being, he was honor bound to see it through to the end. While she understood this, she despised the fact that he intended to deposit her safely in America and resume his seafaring activities without her. No sooner would they be wed than they'd be separated, for God knew how long, and she would be left waiting for him in a foreign land among strangers. Still, there was no other apparent solution, since Kyle had told her it was far too hazardous for her to continue to sail with him.

The *Raven* had already altered direction, bearing on a more westerly track for New Orleans rather than toward Barbados. Naturally, the crew had been informed of the alteration in plans, and the reason behind it. A few had grumbled good-naturedly about the loss of the ransom, but most accepted the change cheerfully, wishing their captain and his intended bride well, eager to set foot on American soil once more.

Just now, with the *Raven* skimming swiftly over tranquil, sun-kissed seas, the conflict between their native countries seemed distant, far removed from their daily lives. Angela wished it could remain so. But the war intruded sooner than she might have guessed. Three days after Angela's momentous decision to give herself so completely into Kyle's keeping, the *Raven* met up with a British warship and was immediately engaged in furious combat. Angela was summarily sent to her cabin and instructed to stay there, no matter what happened.

"Lock the door and don't let anyone but me or one of my officers inside," Kyle told her before delivering a brief, hard kiss to her lips and departing.

Men raced to their battle stations. Cannons roared and belched as volleys were swiftly exchanged. As commander, Kyle was in the thick of the battle, barking out orders to his crew, directing the fight, and defending his ship with all his vast expertise. Not one to allow the enemy an advantage for long, Kyle presently assumed the offensive. Shortly afterward, the British warship was boarded, rendering the cannons useless as men took up their pistols and swords for hand-to-hand combat. In such close conditions, the British proved no match for the superior fighting skills of the American pirates-turned-privateers, and victory soon went to the *Raven*.

Only then did Angela dare to approach Kyle. Once assured that he was not harmed, she asked what he intended to do with his captured warship and prisoners.

"Since the *Termagant* sustained minimal damage, I'll not scuttle her," he informed her. "The United States Navy has need of as many captured vessels as it can get, and this will make a nice addition to the fleet. If the navy doesn't want to buy her from me, I'll keep the ship for myself."

"And the crew?" she inquired, noting that many

men were already being transferred from the *Termagant* to the *Raven*.

"I'm offering refuge only to those men who were impressed into service to England against their will. The others will be set adrift in longboats to make their way to nearby islands. Why do you ask?"

"I was hoping you didn't mean to slay them, and also that I might send a letter to my father via their captain, advising him of my safety and future plans."

Kyle chuckled and shook his head at her feminine thinking and her undisguised relief that he was not going to kill her countrymen. "Make the missive short, Angel. I don't wish to tarry long, lest another British ship should happen along."

Within five minutes, Angela rushed back on deck, letter in hand. Kyle and the British captain were standing at the rail near the boarding ladder. A longboat was moored below, awaiting the last of the English seamen. She approached the British captain and held the note out. "Sir, if you would be so kind, once you are again amid your compatriots, to see that this letter is delivered to Gerald Aston on Barbados, I would greatly appreciate it."

The man glowered at her, drawing himself up stiffly. "I am not the postal service, nor do I deliver messages for my enemies or their traitorous harlots."

Taken aback, Angela could only stare at him in profound shock that one of her own countrymen would address her in such a foul manner. Quicker to recover, Kyle doubled his fist and planted it firmly in the captain's mouth. Under the powerful blow, the man crashed into the rail and went tumbling backward into the water below.

"Good riddance," Kyle pronounced gruffly. "So much for the reputed gentlemanly behavior of British officers."

Angela, peering over the rail at the floundering captain below, readily agreed. "I doubt one dunking will improve his manners all that much, but it was immensely satisfying to witness nonetheless. Thank you, Kyle."

Neither of them realized their peril until it was too late. Taking advantage of the commotion, and incensed that his captain had been struck by this American oaf, an English seaman produced a secreted pistol. Before anyone could prevent it, the man fired his weapon at Kyle, his aim thrown off only at the last second as a burly American crewman barreled into him. The shot went wide, striking a half-filled powder keg three feet from Kyle and Angela.

The explosion was instantaneous, the force immense. Kyle had a mere moment to throw his body over Angela's in a frantic attempt to protect her. Then the immediate area was filled with flying bits of debris, even as Kyle and Angela were lifted off their feet and catapulted into the air, only to arc inevitably toward the undulating surface of the ocean.

Angela hit the water with such force that for several precious seconds her entire body was stunned into immobility and she feared she might have broken her neck. Then, finally, her limbs responded to her brain's frenzied messages, and she stroked toward the beckoning surface, her lungs burning by the time she broke through to take great gasps of life-giving air.

Twisting about, she scanned the glittering waves, searching for Kyle. He'd hit the water near her, she was sure, for she'd felt the impact as an echo of her own. But where was he now? Why hadn't he risen yet? Then she spotted him, a dark shadow floating several feet below. He was face-down, not moving, simply bobbing with the current.

Angela didn't waste time calling out to him, or to anyone else. On a deep breath, she dived down after him, hooked her arm around his neck, and struggled upward, his limp weight hindering her efforts. By the time they'd surfaced, her air was gone. Bright spots danced before her eyes. Still she refused to give up. Shaking off her dizziness, she hauled her precious burden toward the boarding ladder. It took the last of her strength, but they made it, and she gratefully handed Kyle over to his waiting crewmen. Others helped her aboard, where she collapsed on deck, her muscles quivering from the strain.

Sitting in a sodden heap, she watched prayerfully as four sailors draped Kyle's inert body over the middle of a barrel and began rocking him to and fro. For long, heartrending minutes, nothing happened. Then, on a gurgling groan, water gushed from Kyle's mouth and he began to choke and finally to breathe.

As they turned him onto his back, Angela rushed to his side. There was a bloody gash near his left temple, and his face was ashen. He moaned and tried to raise his hand to the wound, but she caught his hand in hers. "Kyle? Darling, just lie still for a bit, until we can ascertain the extent of your injuries."

"Angel?" he rasped. "You're here? You're all right?"

"Yes, love, and so are you, thank goodness."

He opened his eyes then, blinked several times as if to clear his vision, and in a voice suddenly so devoid of emotion that it chilled the blood in Angela's veins, said, "I can't see."

Faithful to a fault, the crew took over running the ship, under the leadership of the quartermaster, second-in-command. Two sailors helped Kyle to his cabin, waited for any specific orders, and left him to Angela's care.

"It will be fine, darling," she assured him. "It must be that knock you took to your head. Once it's had time to heal, for the swelling to go down, perhaps your sight will return, as perfect as ever."

"And if it doesn't?" he inquired in a dull tone.

"Then we'll seek medical advice. Order special spectacles. Whatever is required to restore you to normal."

"You're whistling in the wind, Angela. Chances are, I'll never see again. Therefore," he added stiffly, "you'll forgive me if I renege on our engagement and send you back to Barbados to your family."

She gasped audibly. "You can't mean that!"

"Oh, but I do, my golden treasure. What kind of husband would I be to you like this? A millstone about your pretty neck, unable to earn a living or provide you with a decent home."

"No! I'll not allow you to send me away. You vowed to marry me, Kyle Damien, and that is precisely what you will do!"

"And have you pity me every day of my life? No, thank you."

"You won't need my pity if you continue to have so much for yourself," she informed him bluntly. "Moreover, I may even now be carrying your child within my womb, and I will not let you cast us aside. I belong to you, and you to me, and nothing this side of heaven is going to change that."

"You'll sing a different tune soon enough, I'll wager."

"Don't bet your boat on it."

"Ship," he corrected automatically.

"Speaking of which, I don't see why you can't use your remaining faculties and continue to run the *Raven*, with your crew's help, of course. After all, you do own it, and you do have your other senses to aid you."

He gave a mocking laugh. "Whoever heard of a blind captain?"

"So you'll be the first and set a precedent," she countered lightly, though her heart was aching for him and she wanted nothing more than to gather him in her arms and anoint him with the tears which ran steadily down her cheeks. "Surely your quartermaster can handle those tasks you cannot."

"For the most part," Kyle conceded. "But I am the only man aboard who can read. Who will chart our course and keep the log?"

"I will," she announced firmly. "I will be your eyes."

"Have you ever read a map before?"

"No, but I can read and write, and if you will explain the symbols to me, I'm sure I can do it. Please, Kyle. Let me try. Don't push me out of your life when I've just found you. I love you so dearly, it would surely kill me if you did."

He was silent so long, she was positive he would refuse. Then, on a deep sigh, he said, "All right. We'll give it a go. Your first assignment is to open the letter on my desk. The one addressed to the British captain we just set adrift. I have a sneaking suspicion it contains orders detailing important campaigns against American troops."

Somewhat reluctantly, wondering what she'd let herself in for, Angela did as he'd bid. Upon opening the letter, she found that the contents were, indeed, military plans. But how could she divulge this vital information without feeling like a traitor to her mother country? How could she betray friends and family and nation, and perhaps cause countless deaths?

"Well?" Kyle prompted. "Read it to me, Angela."

In the space of a few heartbeats, Angela was forced to make yet another major decision, weighing her loyalty to Kyle, who was soon to be her lawful husband and thus make his country hers as well, against her lifelong allegiance to England. Her fingers fluttered to her quivering stomach, and she imagined the new life which might be growing there. Her child, and Kyle's.

It struck her suddenly that simply being British, or of any other nationality, did not make one right, or just, or place one above others, though many people assumed it did and acted accordingly, with all the conceit and hateful pomposity the captain of the *Termagant* had displayed. Honor and justice came from the heart, and one's own convictions and principles.

"Angela?" Kyle queried, calling her back from her musings.

"How can I know that this information will not cause untold death and destruction once revealed?" she asked in turn.

"You can't, love," he answered softly, truthfully. "You can only hope it will help to shorten the war, and thus prevent more deaths in the long run."

Again she weighed her feelings, and found the

scales tipped toward Kyle's side. A particularly poignant section of her book came to mind, and she recalled the hero and heroine in a similar predicament. When seeking advice, they'd been told to follow their hearts, to be true to one another and to uphold their honor. She could do no less.

Slowly, distinctly, her voice calm and sure, Angela commenced to read.

Six months later, Angela waddled happily along the deck of the *Angel*, as Kyle had renamed the *Termagant*, her bulging stomach preceding her. She and her husband had just successfully completed a search for sunken treasure, and the hold of the ship was filled with gold coins, intricately engraved silver dinnerware, and mounds of glittering jewels, all reclaimed from shipwrecks which had lain undiscovered in hidden sandy shallows for decades. It had long been Kyle's dream to locate such rich remains, and now, with Angela beside him, he was realizing that wish. He was a fortunate man, and not a day passed that he did not thank God for his many blessings.

Half a year ago, he'd turned the *Raven* toward Barataria Bay, where he had delivered those secret British orders into the hands of his trusted friend, Jean Lafitte. Jean, in turn, had done his utmost to alert American officials of England's plans to attack New Orleans and other key sites. Finally, someone had taken Jean's warnings seriously, just in time to arm the city and win the Battle of New Orleans.

Miraculously, Kyle's sight had returned while he continued to recuperate on Jean's private island base. A second mutual friend, Dr. Charles de Beaumont, had prescribed rest, rejuvenating tonics, and copious amounts of affection, the last of which Angela had blissfully provided. Nature had done the rest, restoring Kyle's sight and nesting their babe in Angela's body.

Following the war, Kyle had forsworn piracy and begun his search for treasure, with Angela at his side. Now, as they stood together at the rail, watching the sun set in brilliant splendor over the gulf, he drew her tenderly to him, absently caressed her swollen belly, and commented, "The Sisters at the orphans' school will be pleased with our haul this time around. Just think of all the books they can purchase for their students with their share of the booty."

"You really don't mind donating a portion of our newfound wealth toward building libraries and schools and buying books, do you, love?" she inquired.

"Not when it brings you such pleasure, my angel," he assured her. "Besides, what good are riches if they're hoarded away or doled out in miserly fashion?"

"My sentiments precisely," she agreed contentedly, snuggling closer. The baby chose that moment to kick, and Angela smiled up at him, sharing the joy. "I'm glad we donated my book to the Library of Congress. Such a valuable manuscript shouldn't belong to just one person."

"Ah, yes, that ancient legend of yours. Romantic fluff! You took dastardly advantage of my forced convalescence, bombarding me with that tripe when you knew full well I couldn't fumble around fast enough to escape you," he teased.

She jabbed him gently in the ribs. "You know you enjoyed every word of it. When our baby is old enough to read I will have an English copy made of the book so I can give it to her."

"And I will give her a golden chest to keep it in, since it once brought me treasure."

Angela tipped her lips toward his. "Yes, the book taught me that the best treasures are those which cannot be bought. Truth. Honor. Love."

"Golden treasures, indeed," he whispered adoringly, just before his mouth claimed hers. "And the most priceless of all is love."

LOVING CHARITY

ELAINE BARBIERI

Loving Charity

She didn't like the looks of him . . .

Charity Bellewood stared at the tall, unsmiling stranger standing in the doorway of the Mother Lode Saloon. His broad expanse of shoulder, outlined against the lamplight of the dirt street beyond, sent her a mental step backward the moment before he entered and wound his way slowly through the maze of gaming tables toward the bar.

She had never seen the man before. She was certain of it, but there was something about him that was familiar, something about the self-possessed way he walked, the tilt of his head, and the set of his jaw that sent chills down her spine.

Nobody had to tell her that he was *dangerous*.

The raucous pounding of the Mother Lode's piano, barely heard over the din of shouted conversations, loud guffaws, and female shrieks of amusement, faded into the distance as Charity raised her chin in an instinctively defensive posture. She was somehow unable to look away as the stranger ordered a drink, then raised the shot glass to his lips and swallowed its contents in a gulp, without a flicker of change in expression.

Charity unconsciously acknowledged that a year or so earlier, before her father had stunned her mother and her by telling them he wanted to sell the family farm and join the trek west to the California goldfields, she might have considered the stranger a romantic figure. There was a sense of controlled power about the way he carried his superior height and breadth that set him apart from the mixed assortment of prospectors, fortune hunters, and weary idlers leaning against the makeshift bar beside him, and even under several days' growth of beard and the dust and grime of the trail, it was apparent at first glance that he was handsome. His features were strong, if somewhat irregular, and the thick, wavy hair touching his shoulders was as black as pitch. But it was his eyes that had brought all thought in her mind to a sudden halt—light eyes that had scanned the canvas-and-frame saloon, penetrating the blue cloud of tobacco smoke hanging over all with an assessing glance that was far from casual for all its brevity—light eyes that had not seen her standing in the rear despite the impact they made upon her.

But too much had happened in the course of the past year to color her view of the stranger with romanticism.

Charity raised her chin higher and straightened proud shoulders bared in a gaudy, second-hand gown that clung provocatively to her slender proportions. She was no longer the sheltered daughter of protective parents who had begun an exciting journey to the goldfields those many months ago. The gradual disillusionment of miles of incredible heat and physical exhaustion had introduced reality. The consistent shortages of food and water on the endless trek had revealed the shallowness of character behind many deceiving facades. The depletion of the stock and draft animals that had necessitated abandoning all but the most necessary of possessions on the wayside, had introduced fear and desperation. And the threat of Indian attack had laid souls bare.

It was the dreaded cholera, however, that had forced upon her a level of maturity far beyond her eighteen years. Miraculously spared its ravages, she had watched helplessly as the disease had taken her father and mother almost overnight. When she had stood at their shallow graves beside the trail, realizing she was truly alone for the first time in her life, romanticism had flown out the windows of her mind.

Romanticism returned only briefly now . . . to warm her heart when she needed it most . . . from the pages of *her book*.

Somehow unable to look away, Charity continued her perusal of the stranger. Since arriving in the goldfields as a "walker," walking beside what was left of their wagon train with nothing left but the clothes on her back, she had met many men like him. They were ruthless, determined men, with a singularity of purpose that inured them to all but the path they followed. None had been as handsome as this particular stranger. None had had the same arresting gaze, but all had conveyed the same message . . .

"He sure is good-lookin', ain't he?"

Charity turned toward the husky female voice at her shoulder. The blazing red hair of the woman standing there was natural, but the rosy color of her cheeks, the blue tinge to her eyelids, the dark color that thickened her lashes, and the brilliant scarlet of her smile were as artificial and colorfully drawn as her name. But Trixie LaFarge had a heart as big as the sumptuous bosom that swelled above her tight purple satin gown—and an intuitive eye that was unmatched.

Charity forced a smile. "I suppose . . ."

"Oh, come on. I saw you watchin' him!"

"He looks familiar."

"Honey." Trixie shook her head. "Take it from a woman who knows. There ain't many fellas who look like him."

Charity's forced smile grew strained. "He looks . . . dangerous."

Trixie gave an unladylike snort. "I'd say he is."

"I mean—"

"I know what you mean."

Charity paused in response. Trixie owned and operated the Mother Lode with experience earned in countless saloons, and Charity was well aware that Trixie's experience was not solely related to the business aspect of the trade.

When Charity did not respond, Trixie winked. "You're not alone in noticin' that big, handsome fella. Maybelle's been tryin' to get away from that hairy prospector she's with since the second that stranger walked through the door, and Winona is practically pantin'. So I'd say you're as normal as the rest, even if your duties here don't run along the same lines as theirs."

Charity maintained her silence. How could she respond? Were it not for Trixie, she could not truly say that she would not now be standing at the bar with the rest of the girls, supporting herself and earning enough to pay her way back to "civilization" the only way left to her.

A familiar piano chord struck for the third time, and Trixie gave an amused chuckle. "Honey, Charlie's been bangin' your chord on that piano for the last five minutes. If you make him wait much longer, he just might get disgusted and step up to the bar. There's no tellin' when he'll wander back to that piano stool then."

Charity glanced toward the heavily mustached piano player to find him staring at her with a fixed frown. How could she have been so distracted that she didn't hear Charlie's heavy-handed musical summons?

Trixie added offhandedly, "I had Pete make up a kind of stage for you." She gestured toward a rough wooden platform near the piano that had gone unnoticed by Charity. And at Charity's openmouthed surprise, she said, "Hell, you're the only *real* songbird in Sacramento City! Them croakers in the other saloons around here don't hold a candle to you. And them homesick fellas that push and shove in order to get a glimpse of you when you sing know that as well as I do. You're the biggest draw I have here!"

Charity was astounded. Trixie had actually had a stage built for her!

"When you're done singin' tonight, you can

stop back at my tent. That dress you're wearin' is startin' to look a little shabby. I got a couple of others in my trunk that I might as well get rid of, too. I'll never be able to stretch them over my hide again."

"Trixie . . ." Charity was at a loss for words. She had never met a more generous woman.

"Don't look at me like that. I ain't no Good Samaritan or nothin'. It's just good business. I could tell by the first note you sang when you came here lookin' for a job that you were goin' to be the best thing that ever happened to the Mother Lode. And you couldn't stand up and sing in front of *this* crowd in them rags you were wearin'. As far as limitin' your duties to entertainin' the customers *from afar,* well . . ." Trixie paused. "The truth is that you ain't experienced enough to survive the rabble that comes through here, and I don't intend losin' my star attraction. Besides, there's that little favor you're doin' for the girls . . ."

"But that has nothing to do with—"

"Honey, the other girls are doin' what they do best, and you're doin' what you do best. The truth is, if I had a voice like yours, you wouldn't see me standin' here stuffed into this purple dress tonight. I'd be the queen of the stage. You keep that in mind, hear? Now get movin'. Them grubby fellas are waitin'."

Charlie pounded out her chord again, and Charity turned toward him with a nod. Taking a deep breath, she stepped out into sight as a murmur moved across the crowd.

Cameron Monroe tilted back his head and tossed down another drink. He withheld a gasp as the amber liquid scorched all the way down to his stomach, then slapped his glass down on a bar that was no more than a rough plank stretched across several sawhorses. He glanced around him. Canvas walls, a dirt floor, the odor of perspiration mixed with heavy perfume, and the stifling heat of afternoon still lingering, the accommodations were primitive. Yet there was not a place to be had at the bar or the gaming tables, and there were so many bodies jammed between that there was hardly room to walk.

Sacramento City . . . Cam gave a short, sardonic snort. Situated as it was on the Sacramento River, it had become the commercial and transport center for the northern mining camps scattered along the tributaries. It had been nothing more than a few wooden shanties and canvas structures a year earlier and had gone from wilderness to thriving port in a matter of months. Now the sights and sounds of growth were everywhere. They were reflected in the endless pounding of hammers from dawn to dusk, in the shouts of wily entrepreneurs auctioning crates of merchandise stacked in the heavily pocked street, and in the music emanating from countless gambling saloons. Housing was at a premium, and buildings were being constructed of logs, canvas, sheet iron, bricks—everything and anything available. Countless ships lay tied up beneath the sycamore and cottonwood trees at the river's edge, appropriated as warehouses for the steady influx of merchandise when abandoned by crews who headed for the hills upon docking. Typical of the dozen or more boomtowns he had seen in the past year, Sacramento City was populated with gold-crazed men and money-hungry women who would sell their souls for the right price.

Cam gave a short, mirthless laugh at that thought. In looking around him, it appeared most of them already had.

Curious, Cam scanned the crowd again. With the exception of the crush within, the Mother Lode was little different from countless other saloons in countless other mining camps he had visited. But there was one critical difference about the Mother Lode that set it apart from the others. This was the place where his search would finally come to an end.

That thought stirring his heart to a slow pounding, Cam drew himself slowly erect. He slid his hand down to his hip, casually loosening his gun in its holster. It would be a mistake to stir suspicion by asking too many questions immediately after arriving. He knew the name and description of the woman he was looking for. Gypsy Clark was a tall woman in her early twenties who wasn't born to the fair hair she sported. She was also an experienced tart who was true to her man—whoever that man might be at the moment.

Cam's jaw tightened. Gypsy's current man of the moment was Billy Joe Holt.

Cam's light eyes grew cold. Billy Joe Holt was *his* man, too.

Uncertain of the exact moment when he realized that the clatter and roar of the Mother Lode had dimmed to a hush, that the frantic pace of the place had slowed almost to a stop, and that an air of expectancy had grown to sudden, almost palpable proportions, Cam raised his head to see the attention of the men directed toward the piano in the corner of the crowded canvas structure.

Cam restrained a gasp as a young woman stepped up into sight on a roughly constructed platform.

There was something about her . . . She didn't have the look of the other women, despite her tawdry gold satin dress trimmed with droopy black lace and dangling jets, and the black ostrich feather pinned to her upswept dark hair.

Cam inched his way closer as the potbellied fellow at the piano began the introductory chords of a song. She was very slim and she looked young, barely twenty. Her hair was dark, the color of ripe chestnuts. Her eyes were equally dark and trimmed with outlandishly thick lashes of an incredible length that was noticeable even at the distance between them. Her features were small and—damn the inconceivability of it—almost angelic!

Then she started to sing.

Cam hardly breathed. The young saloon girl's voice was sweet and clear. It carried with a gentle power, reaching highs and lows of perfection that struck tears to the eyes of the grimy, bewhiskered prospectors. The moment of total silence when she brought the final chorus to its conclusion was shattered by applause that erupted in a thundering, foot-stomping blast.

Hardened prospectors cried and shouted her name.

"I love you, Charity!"

"Sing us another!"

"You're an angel from heaven, Charity!"

"Sing 'Danny Boy!'"

"You're the gal of my dreams!"

"Sing us a hymn, Charity darlin'!"

"A hymn, Charity!"

"A hymn!"

The young woman called Charity leaned toward the heavily mustached fellow at the piano. The shouting stopped abruptly as the fellow struck another chord, then started to play, and the tarnished songbird began to sing:

Amazing Grace, how sweet the sound
That saved a wretch like me.
I once was lost, and now am found,
Was blind, but now I see . . .

The song trailed on from chorus to verse as the silence deepened. Glasses were gradually lowered back to the bar, betting at the tables slowed to a stop, and a grimy prospector in the back of the room sobbed aloud.

Cam looked around him in amazement. Grown men, publicly sniffing and crying as a tart with an innocent face hung them out and wrung them dry!

His own heart pounding, Cam felt the rise of sudden fury. Damn the witch! He had met spellbinders like her before—spellbinders who used their power over men and took men for all they could get, then calmly walked away.

Cam glanced around him again. Fools! Didn't they see? Wouldn't they ever learn that there was no innocence on the goldfields, most especially in the hearts of the women who inhabited them?

Cam's fury swelled. Well, he was one man this sweet Charity did not fool.

Drawing back, his gaze narrowed, Cam acknowledged a fact he could no longer deny.

But that didn't stop him from *wanting* her.

* * *

Charity closed her eyes briefly as the final notes of the hymn swelled around her. She remembered that she had found it almost inconceivable at first that these men, who minutes earlier had been engrossed in every manner of vice that the Mother Lode had to offer, would react with such boisterous approval of her song. It was a moment such as this that had soothed her anxieties at the situation into which fate had thrust her . . .

. . . and which confirmed in her mind the similarity to a situation an ancestor of hers had faced and written about in *her book*.

A familiar warmth rose within Charity. The book had been her mother's, and now it was hers. It had been in her family for more years than she could accurately calculate, passed down from mother to daughter. Her own grandmother, a most unusual woman, had given a copy of the book in a golden chest to each of her three daughters. It was a legend, a love story, and a legacy containing personal inscriptions from the women through whose hands the book had passed. It was the only thing she had managed to salvage from the devastating journey through the wilderness . . . and it was all she had left in the world.

One personal inscription in particular had called out to her in her desolation and uncertainty after arriving in Sacramento City. They were the words of Genevieve Betancourt, that ancestress who had lived centuries earlier. Genevieve had written that, after finding herself alone and without funds in a difficult, medieval world, she had supported herself by entertaining the nobility with her singing and lute playing. She became a great beauty and talent of her times and ended up marrying a nobleman who bested the king with the aid of *a book*.

Charity had always believed that she inherited both her love of reading and her singing ability from her beautiful ancestor, but the bond between her and the woman she knew only through her written words had grown stronger during her recent moments of deepest despair, until she had come to think of herself as a modern counterpart of her forebear.

Glimpsing herself in a nearby mirror as the applause began to fade, Charity could not help but be amused by her rambling thoughts. She was hardly the beauty her illustrious ancestor had been, and her faded finery held little to be admired. The men she entertained were a far cry from nobility, and the atmosphere could not possibly be more foreign from that of the royal court, but still . . .

"Sing another one, Charity!"

"Another hymn!"

Charity restrained a smile. No, she had sung her quota of hymns for the night. Trixie had given her strict orders. "Softening up" her customers was all right, but "makin' them downright repentant" was not.

"Sing 'Yankee Doodle!'"

" 'Oh, Susannah!' "

Charity allowed her smile full rein, then leaned toward the piano.

"Play 'Oh, Susannah,' Charlie."

Charlie grinned and struck up a lively introduction as Charity glanced around the saloon. She was unconsciously listening for her cue when her gaze was caught and held by the light eyes of the tall stranger. She felt her smile freeze when she saw contempt reflected there.

Contempt . . .

Suddenly aware that Charlie had started the introduction for the second time, Charity extricated her gaze from the stranger's stare and started to sing.

But the thought lingered that she had been right the first moment she had seen him.

He was *dangerous*.

Cam was not certain which had affected him more strongly—the unexpected linking of the singer's gaze with his, or its abrupt severance. But there were two things he knew for sure.

He wanted her.

And he would have her.

Applause was still ringing as Charity fled the smoky saloon and ducked out into the fresh air of night. Standing in a shaft of silver moonlight behind the canvas structure, she breathed deeply and attempted to settle her turbulent thoughts. Her performance had never been so well received, but she was deeply shaken. The stranger's stare had not lessened through the entire presentation, until she had begun to feel weakened under its assault.

Who was he?

What was he?

. . . And what did he want from her?

The sound of a step jerked Charity around with a gasp as the object of her anxiety appeared unexpectedly beside her. A soul-shaking tremor moved down her spine as he stood towering over her, his eyes so clear that they appeared an extension of the silver moonlight in which they stood. His voice was a stirring rumble when he spoke.

"You're very good at what you do, Charity."

A slow trembling began inside Charity. The heat of the man enveloped her. It drew her in. It stirred a longing that she could neither explain nor deny as she managed a soft reply.

"You liked my singing . . ."

"I said you're good at what you do." He paused. "I wasn't particularly referrin' to your voice."

Charity considered the unexpected response, confused. "I thought it safe to assume you meant my singing, since we're strangers otherwise."

The stranger's intense perusal deepened. "That's where you're wrong. You're no stranger to me."

Curiously recognizing that it was not physical threat she feared, Charity took a spontaneous step backward that was halted by his restraining touch on her arm.

"I think it's time I introduced myself. My name is Cam. I already know your name is Charity. I'd like to buy you a drink."

"I don't drink, Mr. . . . *Cam*."

His small smile was skeptical. "Then I'd like to invite you back to my table so we can become better acquainted while *I* drink."

"I don't mingle with the customers, Mr. . . . *Cam*."

The quivering within Charity deepened to shudders as the stranger moved closer.

"What *do* you do, darlin'?"

"I sing for the Mother Lode's customers."

Sliding his free arm around her unexpectedly, Cam cupped her nape with his palm, holding her fast as he drew her mouth up to his.

"Suppose I have other things in mind for us?"

Charity's reply was breathless. "I'd say you were going to be disappointed."

"Am I, Charity?" The warm lips so close to hers brushed her mouth with a lingering kiss that struck her momentarily defenseless. He prompted, "Am I?"

"Y-yes."

But Charity heard the feebleness of her reply, even as Cam drew her closer, as his arms closed around her and she—

"I think you heard her, fella."

Trixie's throaty interjection snapped Charity from her bemused lethargy as the buxom proprietress stepped out of the shadows. A smile on her painted face, the woman continued easily, "Like Charity told you, she don't have no duties here except to sing. You'd do better to find yourself another girl for what you have in mind. I know for a fact there are a few inside right now who would be downright anxious to spend a little time with you."

Charity felt the strong arm around her tighten the moment before a familiar blond woman stepped into sight behind Trixie, adding in a flirtatiously husky tone, "Trixie's right, handsome. My name's Gypsy, and I'm one of them girls who'd be happy to share a drink with you . . . and anything else you might be contemplating."

Charity felt the jolt that shook Cam when Gypsy spoke. Stunned when he released her abruptly, she watched him turn toward the saloon girl with a smile. She was equally stunned by the stab of an emotion she dared not name when he took Gypsy's arm, responding, "That might not be a bad idea after all."

Turning back toward Charity and Trixie as if in afterthought, the fellow tipped his hat, his parting words sardonic.

"Good evening, *ladies*."

Feeling strangely abandoned, Charity watched as the couple slipped back into the saloon. She was still staring when Trixie's well-meaning reprimand brought her back abruptly to the present.

"I saved your hide this time, Charity, honey, but I'm goin' to tell you now that I don't intend bein' your guardian angel when fellas like that one start sniffin' around. You gotta learn to say no with a little more force if you want to keep that kind away from you." Trixie paused, her gaze scrutinizing. "That's if you *want* to keep them away."

Regaining her voice, Charity managed, "Thanks, Trixie."

"Why do I get the feelin' you ain't exactly happy how things turned out?"

"Trixie . . ."

Trixie shrugged. "Whatever. From here on in, it's up to you."

In a moment, Trixie was gone, the import of her words lingering.

Why do I get the feelin' you ain't exactly happy how things turned out?

Charity turned back toward the safety of the canvas structure behind the Mother Lode where the saloon girls slept, hearing her own question in reply.

Yes, why?

* * *

"What do I need to know how to read for, anyway? I don't need to read about doin' things when I can just do them!"

Recognizing that Winona's agitation was spurred by frustration, Charity paused in response. She unconsciously stroked the cover of her treasured heirloom book. How could she explain to Winona, a pretty saloon girl who had reached the ripe age of twenty-one without the ability to read, that she simply could not imagine enduring such deprivation?

The reality that many of the girls in their communal sleeping tent could not read had come as a shock to Charity. She had noticed early on that several of them watched longingly on the occasions when she settled down to read her precious book. When they confided that they could not read, she had offered to teach them. She had gained eight pupils with that offer—eight who occasionally grew frustrated and angry at their ineptitude. She replied to Winona in the words inscribed in her book by her ancestor Genevieve Betancourt—words she would never forget.

"No man can taste and touch and feel all that life has to offer. But in a book . . . in a book, all things are possible. To read is to dream, to fly, to soar . . ."

Winona's eyes grew moist, bringing a moisture to Charity's eyes as well, as the discouraged saloon girl replied, "You . . . you ain't goin' to give up on me, are you, Charity?"

"No, never." Silently acknowledging that her heart wasn't quite in teaching that morning,

Charity continued softly, "But if you'd like to try practicing your reading a little longer and taking up where we left off tomorrow, that'll be fine."

Winona's bright smile flashed with relief. "Thanks, Charity."

Winona left the tent a few minutes later, anxious to escape the scene of her most recent academic tribulations, leaving Charity alone with her thoughts.

A tall male image returned to her mind unbidden, and Charity frowned. Cameron Monroe . . .

What was the matter with her? She wouldn't even know the man's full name, or the fact that he was in Sacramento City waiting to meet a partner due within a week or two, if Gypsy hadn't imparted that information when she had staggered back in the early hours of morning.

Charity sniffed, wondering what else Gypsy was able to tell her about Cameron Monroe . . . or if she'd want to hear it . . .

Charity glanced toward the tent's flapped opening to see a bit of cloudless blue sky and brilliant morning sunshine beyond. The previous night had been payday, and the girls had gone out early in an effort to avoid the heat of the day when they did their shopping. She knew they would come back with fripperies purchased at exorbitant prices. She also knew that one or two of them would actually come back with a book, eager to make use of lessons they pursued. She was pleased with their enthusiasm, but at present that satisfaction was far from her mind as Cameron Monroe loomed dark and mysterious once more.

Thinking of the man sent chills anew down Charity's spine. She remembered the warmth of his lips claiming hers with the promise of what was to come, the sensation of his strong fingers curled gently around her nape, the hard wall of his body tight against her. She—

No, she had to stop this!

Annoyed with her wandering thoughts, Charity drew herself to her feet beside her bed and replaced the book in its handmade chest. Cameron Monroe was the antithesis of the hero of the legend in her book, the character on whom she had based her concept of the perfect man. Rather than feeling an instant affinity that she was certain she would feel when she met the "right" man, she had felt instant adversity on meeting Cameron Monroe. Rather than feeling safe, she had felt threatened. Rather than feeling cherished, she had felt—

How had she felt?

Charity groaned.

She knew how she had felt. She didn't want to feel that way again . . . not with him . . . not with Cameron Monroe.

Frustration bringing a brief welling under her eyelids, Charity straightened her shoulders covered by the simple blue cotton dress she had purchased with the first money Trixie had paid her. She knew that it and another simple frock, which were the full extent of her daytime attire, did not match the appeal of the clothing the other girls wore. But she was not in competition with the other girls . . . was she? Not even Gypsy, who had turned Cameron Monroe's attentions from her so quickly that it had left her head spinning.

Charity swallowed the lump in her throat. Gypsy's intentions had been good. She thought she had done her a favor . . . and she had . . . hadn't she?

No.

Yes!

Maybe . . .

Oh, damn!

Grateful for the distraction Maybelle offered when she walked back into the tent at that moment, proudly displaying a book she had bought, Charity smiled. Feeling a hypocrite for speaking with a generosity she did not truly feel, she offered, "Do you want to try reading it now?"

Charity saw the gratitude in Maybelle's eyes as she handed her the book.

Certain she would never feel more unworthy of anyone's gratitude than she did then, Charity waited as Maybelle settled herself beside her and began to read.

It had been a damned long day.

Cam glanced up again at the clear blue sky as he sauntered along Sacramento City's dusty street, certain that he was either going mad or that the sun was really stuck in the same position that it had held for the last few hours.

His strong features drawn into lines of frustration, Cam drew the obvious conclusion. He *had* gone mad. He must have. What else could account for the excuses he had made to remain in town, hoping to catch a glimpse of Charity Bellewood's slim figure on the street when he knew he should be upriver, searching the nearest mining camp on the outside possibility that he would get lucky and find Billy Joe Holt without Gypsy's help?

Cam considered that thought, slipping his

hand down to again loosen his gun in his holster, a precaution that had become instinctive since the first day he had pinned on a star.

Cameron Monroe . . . a lawman. Who would've believed it? The son of the local drunk in a small Missouri town, he had run wild as a boy. He was always in trouble, but the town sheriff, Wilton Parker, had refused to give up on him. When Cam's father died, Sheriff Parker took the boy into his house and under his wing.

Sheriff Parker was the fairest man he had ever known, and the wisest. His daughter, Virginia, twenty years older than Cam, was the closest he had ever come to having a mother. He had learned a lot from both of them by the time he was eighteen, and although he had never admitted it to himself or them, he had loved them. But Sheriff Parker's good intentions and advice had not been successful in knocking the chip off his shoulder, and by the time he was eighteen years old, that chip had earned him few friends.

A familiar knot tightened in Cam's stomach as the story continued to unwind in his mind. About that time, he became infatuated with a local dance-hall girl despite Sheriff Parker's warnings about her. He had been so full of himself and so gullible that he had allowed her to use him to get information about a payroll to be shipped to the local bank. The dance-hall girl then passed that information to her boyfriend, who robbed the bank.

Wilt Parker was killed during the robbery.

Cam helped to track down the sheriff's killer and then watched the man hang, knowing that Wilt Parker's respect for the law was the only thing that had kept Cam from killing the man himself.

Cam freely admitted to himself now that guilt, and an effort to make retribution for the part he had unwittingly played in Sheriff Parker's death, had spurred his determination to become a lawman. He soon realized, however, that he had found his true vocation. He became as renowned for his doggedness in tracking down lawbreakers and bringing them to justice as he was for his lack of emotion in doing so.

As for the dance-hall girl who had used him, he supposed he owed her a debt of thanks, too, for teaching him the truth about women. He had never forgotten the lesson he had learned, and although he continued *loving* women, he never *liked* them nor trusted them—with Virginia Parker the only exception.

Ten years later, a widowed Virginia Parker was walking along a Missouri street when another bank robber emerged from a bank, guns blazing.

Virginia died in Cam's arms.

Billy Joe Holt was the man who killed her.

Cam had been tracking Billy Joe for two years. He had followed him all over Missouri and the surrounding states and then to St. Louis. When he discovered that Billy Joe had set off for the California goldfields, he put his badge in his pocket, knowing there *was* no law there. Feeling a deep, personal debt to the only woman who had ever shown him love, he had vowed to find Billy Joe and administer his own personal justice, knowing at that moment that he would never wear a badge again.

He had only recently discovered Billy Joe's

weakness for Gypsy Clark. Staying close to her, Cam now knew he would get the man sooner or later. So he had prowled the town, waiting for night to fall when he could visit the Mother Lode Saloon without being too obvious. He had found the baths first and soaked off the grime of the trail . . . then the laundry, where he had had his clothes washed . . . then the barbershop, where he had indulged himself with a haircut and a shave that was so sweet and close that he was still purring . . .

. . . and all the while he had had visions of a certain young woman purring under *his* touch . . .

Fighting the image of a heart-shaped face surrounded by hair the color of ripe chestnuts and dark eyes with lashes so long and thick that no artifice was needed to enhance them, Cam forced Gypsy Clark back to mind. The tall blonde had gone out of her way to be cooperative with him last night. She had started out by intimating that she had no inhibitions about sharing a bottle or a bed with him.

Cam shrugged. He hadn't wasted time being flattered. He knew Gypsy was merely attending to business. He had managed two positive accomplishments before the night ended. The first was to have won a roof over his head in a poker game, from a prospector who should have done less drinking and more thinking. The small cabin was a considerable prize in a place where most were sleeping in the open for lack of adequate accommodations. The second was in getting Gypsy to confide a few bits of information: namely, that she had a boyfriend who wasn't always on the right side of the law, that he was out prospecting for gold, and that he was coming back for her. She had added, of course, that her feelings for the boyfriend wouldn't get in the way of giving Cam a good time if he was interested.

Thanks . . . but no thanks.

Admittedly, he might have been interested under different circumstances, if he hadn't gotten his mind stuck on a little spellbinder who wasn't going to make it easy for him.

It annoyed him that he hadn't quite figured Charity Bellewood out. He had been surprised when Gypsy had told him that, aside from her duties in the saloon, Charity had started teaching a few of the girls to read from an old book that she treasured more than anything else.

A book . . .

It didn't make much sense, but he knew that, despite her complexities, Charity was no different from the rest. He had felt the inner heat of her when he had held her in his arms. His own response to her had been more powerful than any he had ever experienced, and he had known that despite her denials, she had wanted him as much as he wanted her. It frustrated him that he needed to stay close to Gypsy while his mind kept returning to the sweet warmth of Charity in his arms . . . the scent of her that had teased his senses, the—

Dammit!

Two years was a long time, and his tensions were high now that he was so close to catching up with Billy Joe at last. With each hour stretching longer than the last, he was in need of diversion. He supposed that was the reason the little spellbinder with the sweet voice and the big eyes had had such an effect on him.

Cam's jaw locked tight, dark brows knitting over the clear color of his eyes as he instinctively scanned the crowded street around him. While the little witch had haunted his dreams during the night past, he had made himself two solemn promises: that he would not leave Sacramento City before burning Charity Bellewood out of his system, and that he would not put the goldfields behind him until he put a bullet through Billy Joe Holt's heart.

Cam turned toward the nearest saloon that allowed him a view of the street. In the meantime, he would watch and wait, then make his appearance at the Mother Lode, where he would spend his time with Gypsy.

As for Charity . . .

Allowing that thought to remain unfinished, Cam entered the Sluice Saloon and approached the bar.

Just a few more hours . . .

Night had fallen and the Mother Lode was jammed to its canvas walls. Seated at a poker table with Gypsy hanging over his shoulder, her ample cleavage on full display, Cam pretended an interest in the game that he did not feel. He was growing more tense by the moment.

He had accomplished little since arriving an hour earlier, except to confirm that everything Gypsy had told him about her boyfriend taking off for the diggings was true, and that Charity was indeed teaching some of the saloon girls to read. The bartender had dropped a whispered warning that Billy Joe's provisions couldn't hold out much longer, that he would be back in Sacramento City soon and it might not be smart to get too close to Gypsy. Cam had nodded. The well-intentioned fellow would never know how happy he had been to hear those words.

It was just a matter of time . . .

. . . time that had been hanging heavily on his hands until the piano player struck a familiar, introductory chord.

Charity stepped up onto the stage, smiling at the shouts of welcome that greeted her. Waiting for Charlie to play the first few bars of her opening song, she looked around the crowded room. Her breath caught in her throat as her gaze met and held the light eyes she had unconsciously been seeking. Regaining her composure a moment later, she raised her voice in a haunting melody she had sung since childhood:

> *"Black is the color of my true love's hair,*
> *His looks are something wondrous fair,*
> *The purest eyes and the strongest hands,*
> *I love the ground on which he stands . . ."*

Charity felt the heat of Cam's gaze burn into her. The words of her song seemed to close the distance between them in the moment before he stood up abruptly, and with a short word to Gypsy, turned his back and walked out the door.

Thunderous applause still echoed as Charity slipped out into the moonlit darkness behind the Mother Lode. But the sound faded from her hearing as her mind returned to the image of Cameron Monroe's broad back as he had walked out the door. She could not understand it. Why did he despise her so? Why had he—

"Thinkin' about me, darlin'?"

Charity jumped with a start at the deep voice behind her. She swallowed, momentarily incapable of response as Cameron Monroe's handsome, shadowed face loomed above hers. His arms slid around her, drawing her toward him as he prompted huskily, "Were you, darlin'? Because I was thinkin' about you."

"No, I—"

His mouth touched hers, cutting off her words, and Charity's lips clung to his, despite herself. His kiss surged deeper, his tongue caressing hers, and a wild tumult washed over her as she leaned into the rock-hard strength of him. She had never felt like this before! In the space of a moment, uncertainty had changed to longing, and longing to wanting . . .

Charity was hardly conscious of her own softly uttered protest when Cam drew back with a whispered rasp. "Let's get out of here . . . now."

"No, I—"

"No, what?" Cam's pale eyes seemed to search her soul. "It's no use actin' with me, Charity. I'm not like those fellas inside who're satisfied to watch you walk in and out of their lives for the few minutes you stand on that stage. It wasn't meant to be that way between us, and you know it. You know it, darlin'."

Cam covered her mouth with his, taking her response deep inside him, eliminating her protest with a kiss that swept all thought from her mind except for the joy surging to life within her. Drawing back moments later, he whispered, "Come with me, Charity."

"But you and Gypsy—"

"There is no Gypsy . . . only you. There never has been." Cam's tone was deep with promise. "I'll make it good for you, darlin'. I promise you that. I'll make it sweeter than anythin' you've ever known."

"I can't."

"You can."

"I don't know you!"

"You know me, all right . . ."

Charity's bemused mind paused at Cam's unexpected response.

You know me, all right . . .

Gradual realization replaced Charity's bemusement. Yes, he was right . . .

Everything was suddenly acutely clear. She had sensed the danger emanating from Cameron Monroe the first time she had seen him, a danger she could not identify . . . but she recognized it now. The peril she had felt was in her instinctive, unconscious realization that this tall, intimidating man was the man she had been waiting for all her life—that her moment had come, and if she did not have the courage to seize it, she might lose him forever.

"Talk to me, Charity."

The moment was upon her.

"Charity . . ."

A coward would let it slip away . . .

"Will you come with me?"

But Charity had never been a coward.

She nodded.

Elation flared in Cam's eyes the moment before he slipped Charity to his side, curling his arm around her possessively, without a word, as he urged her through the shadows.

* * *

Flesh against flesh, heart against heart, Charity lay in Cam's hungry embrace. Soft murmurs of passion were the only sounds that broke the silence of the cabin as she exchanged kiss for kiss, caress for caress, wonder soaring. She had found the man of her own personal legend at last! She loved him. She wanted him. She—

Gasping as Cam slipped himself atop her, Charity quaked with a passion that shook Cam as well. His soft incoherent endearments echoed in her ears as he pressed himself deep within her, as she clutched him close, as he filled her with loving promise, ardor mounting to a rapture that erupted in sudden, breathtaking ecstasy unsurpassed.

Charity lay silent and fulfilled in the blissful afterglow of their joining, secure in her knowledge that it was as it was meant to be . . .

. . . and knowing that from this moment on, *her life was forever changed.*

Lying breathless upon Charity's intimate warmth, Cam clutched her close. His heart pounding in the aftermath of their loving, he reveled in the joy of her, knowing that this was what he had been waiting for from the first moment their eyes had met.

Cam drew Charity closer still, aware that the beauty of her was unlike any he had ever known . . .

. . . and knowing that despite it all, *nothing had really changed.*

The following days passed in a haze of loving exhilaration for Charity. She dismissed the concern of those around her, telling herself that

Cam's reluctance to talk about himself or the partner he was awaiting was unimportant—that the *present* would take care of the *future*. Cam's openly possessive manner toward her, his lingering touch, consoled her in her uncertainties and bespoke the true emotion they shared more clearly than the words he did not speak.

His reaction had been disheartening when she had told him about her book and the important part it played in her life, and about Genevieve Betancourt, declaring him the hero of her legend. She had been unprepared when he had snapped, "Don't go makin' me out to be somethin' I'm not, Charity."

But she had excused his response, telling herself the time would yet come, and the discussion had not been broached again.

And if she was occasionally pricked with unrest at the way she had seen Cam follow Gypsy covertly with his gaze, Charity ejected those thoughts as well.

Because she loved him.

The following days passed in silent tension for Cam. The joy he felt with Charity grew greater each day. He could not get enough of her. But he had learned the hard way, in a lesson that had cost his dearest friend his life, that however sincere saloon women appeared to be, they could not be trusted.

Forcing himself to concentrate on the mortal debt soon to be repaid, Cam was determined to use his new status in Charity's life to greatest advantage.

And if his heart reached out for Charity, despite the cautioning of his mind . . . he entertained no doubt which part of him would win out in the end.

Charity stood rigidly in the silence of Cam's cabin. Daylight had faded as Cam and she had indulged the newfound wonder between them. The beauty of those intimate moments had assuaged her concern at the growing tension she sensed within Cam. She had not expected what she had found when searching in his saddlebag for the soap he had mentioned before he stepped outside.

Charity's fingers curled around the metal star in her hand. She looked up slowly as Cam appeared in the doorway. Her bright world crumbling around her, she whispered, "This is yours, isn't it?"

The door clicked closed behind Cam.

"Yes."

"You're not waiting for your partner to come to Sacramento City."

"No."

"Everything you led me to believe about you is a lie."

Silence.

"Why didn't you tell me you're a lawman?"

"Because I'm not a lawman anymore." Becoming the dangerous stranger once more, Cam continued, "And because it's none of your concern."

The painful significance of Cam's words reverberated within Charity. "This has something to do with Gypsy, doesn't it?"

Silence.

"*Doesn't it?*"

Silence.

"It's her boyfriend, isn't it?" Charity's breath

caught in her throat. Suddenly, she knew.

"Oh, God . . . you're going to kill him!"

Beside her in a few, rapid steps, Cam wrenched the badge from her hand as Charity rasped, "Don't you realize that if you kill him, whatever your motive, you'll be a killer, too?"

"I said this is none of your concern!"

Charity stared up at Cam, incredulous. The question she had not dared ask earlier slipped from her lips.

"Do you love me, Cam?"

Cam's continued silence slashed at Charity's heart. A single tear trailed down her cheek as she whispered, "I can't say you didn't warn me. You told me not to make you out to be something you weren't. The only trouble is that I wasn't listening."

Charity squared her shoulders, her final words the most difficult she had ever spoken.

"Well, I'm listening now."

Charity disappeared into the evening shadows beyond the door as Cam stared after her, clutching the metal star tightly. The anguish in Charity's eyes had been almost more than he was able to bear.

Damn her! He had made love to Charity hoping to burn her from his heart, only to have her write her name so indelibly there that he knew he would never be free.

A warning bell sounded in Cam's mind.

No, he would not make the same mistake again! Nor would he allow his feelings to get in the way of a debt that could not go unpaid!

Suddenly realizing that Charity need only say a word to Gypsy to thwart his plans, Cam snatched up his gun. He took a moment to strap it around his hips, then started after her.

Her mind whirling, Charity walked quickly along the darkening street toward the Mother Lode. She had been a fool! The similarities she had seen between Cam and the hero of the legend in her book had been purely imagined. She had convinced herself that Cam and she were like the lost hearts of the legend that had discovered each other in the most unlikely of places because she had *wanted* to believe it was true. Cam had no true nobility at all. She was glad she found out about him before it was too late.

But it's already too late, a voice in her mind interjected mercilessly. *You love him*.

As that truth registered unchallenged, Charity felt tears well. Knowing there was only one thing she could do, Charity walked through the door of the Mother Lode. She needed to warn Gypsy quickly, before—

Charity's step came to an abrupt halt, the blood draining from her face as the man standing beside Gypsy at the bar turned toward the door.

No . . . no!

Her heart hammering, Charity started toward them at the same moment she sensed someone behind her. Turning to see Cam in the doorway, Charity did not see recognition register on Billy Joe Holt's face the second before he drew his gun in a lightning flash.

Gypsy's shout as she knocked Billy Joe's gun from his hand was followed by the startling crack of a gunshot gone wild, and a dizzying scramble as Cam thrust Charity to safety and raced past her.

A mad chase ensued . . . tables knocked to the ground . . . bottles and glasses flying . . . swinging oil lamps crashing against the canvas saloon walls as Cam pursued Billy Joe out the rear doorway.

Then . . .

. . . fire!

The frustration of two years' pursuit in his flying leap, Cam tackled the fleeing Billy Joe as he reached the tree line of the clearing and brought him to the ground. Wrestling the killer to his back, he pinned him down, dodging his flying fists as he pounded the man again and again. Blood spurted from Billy Joe's nose as Cam was about to deliver the final blow when—

The smell of smoke . . . the crackle of flames . . .

Cam turned to look behind him.

The Mother Lode was on fire!

Terror struck Cam. Charity was inside!

The man beneath him forgotten, Cam staggered to his feet and raced toward the blazing tent.

Swaying dazedly as she stood outside the flaming Mother Lode, Charity felt strong arms close suddenly around her. Snatched up tight against Cam's chest, she heard his gasping, incoherent words of relief, even as she struggled to withdraw from his embrace . . . Her voice rasped over the tumult around them.

"Did you kill him?"

"Charity . . ."

"*Did you*?"

His clear eyes appearing to freeze, Cam

dropped his hands to his sides.

The sudden gasp that went up from the crowd turned Charity toward the burning saloon as the sleeping quarters behind the Mother Lode, emptied of its occupants by the excitement, burst into flames. A gusting wind fanned the flames into an instant inferno as the spectators watched aghast.

Charity was gripped by a sudden, horrifying realization.

"My book!"

Her instinctive break toward the flaming tent was halted by Cam's rough grip on her arm as Charity shouted back at him, "Let me go! My grandmother's chest is in there! I can't lose it! It's all I have left!"

Cam's gaze held Charity's for long moments as myriad thoughts and hopes and dreams flowed between them in a fragmented rush of unspoken comprehension. Thrusting her suddenly backward to safety, Cam dashed into the burning structure in her stead.

Restrained by unrelenting hands as she attempted to follow him, Charity went suddenly still. Cam was risking his life for her . . . for her book . . .

Paralyzed with fear as seconds seemed to stretch into hours, as the flames billowed higher and the smoke thickened, as the structure's wooden frame creaked and swayed, fluttering in a wild dance in prelude to collapse, Charity held her breath.

Leaping out from the billowing smoke, Cam stumbled toward her, the chest which held her book in his hand. Her arms around him in a moment, Charity clutched Cam tight, prayers of thanksgiving flowing through her mind even as she covered his smoke-stained face with kisses.

Able to speak at last, she whispered, "I love you, Cam. I love you, no matter who you are or what you do. I love you."

"Your book . . ."

"I love you, Cam . . ."

"Charity, darlin'." His voice roughened from both smoke and emotion, Cam rasped, "I love you, too."

The chest in his hand forgotten, Cam clutched Charity tightly. The tender embrace that followed signified the important choices both had made that night—loving choices that would last a lifetime.

The gold of Charity's wedding band sparkled in the light of the oil lamp beside the bed while Cam and she lay, flesh and hearts joined. Outside the hotel room that was their belated honeymoon suite, the St. Louis street teemed with evening traffic as Charity lovingly traced the strong line of her husband's jaw with her fingertips.

An easy, intimate silence reigned between them as Charity thought back over the months recently passed. Billy Joe Holt had managed to escape in the confusion of the fire, but Cam caught up with him a week later. Cam's triumph was complete when he delivered Billy Joe back to face the law in St. Louis.

Cam was wearing his badge again . . . with honor.

. . . With honor comes glory . . .

That quote from her book, the book Cam had saved for her at the risk of his life, returned to Charity's mind with a triumph of its own.

Yes, Cam was truly the man of her personal legend . . . the man she would enter in her book when the time came for her to record the words that would sum up her life . . . and she loved him.

Brushing Cam's lips with hers, feeling a surge within, Charity had no regrets that she no longer sang at the Mother Lode, or anyplace like it. She now sang only for Cam's entertainment. But she had known from the first that she would never forget the joy on Winona's and Maybelle's faces when they read their first sentences. For that reason, she had formed a weekly class at a saloon nearby. She presently had seven eager students there . . .

. . . and every one of them was enthralled by the legend in her book.

Of course, Cam had protested at first when she told him about the class, but when he realized she was determined, well . . . Cam wanted what she wanted, if it made her happy. It was that way when someone loved.

That thought in mind, Charity scrutinized Cam's sober expression as he drew her closer, as he mumbled soft words of love that she would never tire of hearing, as he tasted her lips, then drank deeply from the fount of love there. She remembered the first time she saw him.

She hadn't liked the looks of him.

He had looked . . . *dangerous*.

And . . . he was.

SAVAGE FANTASY

CASSIE EDWARDS

Savage Fantasy

Tah-hay-chap-shoon-wee—Moon of Dropping Deer Horns

Wildflowers dotted the land in a tapestry of colors. It was a beautiful country, where the high hills were covered with lush, green grass and verdant trees.

Yvonne Armistead rested on her knees as she puttered in her flower garden. With gloves to protect her hands, she swept mounds of dirt around the roots of her rosebushes.

She smiled down at the snapdragons that were just revealing their faces to the sun. She shifted her gaze and sighed in pleasure. Her azaleas were the brightest pink this year that she had ever seen.

And the jonquils! They were so large and such a deep shade of yellow.

Yvonne wiped a bead of perspiration from her

brow and paused to savor the satisfaction she felt. She had been married to Silver Arrow for six years now, and she was completely content with her life as wife of the powerful Ottawa Indian chief.

The people of his village, who had welcomed her as one of them, were busy at their chores. The warriors who were not in council with her husband in the council house were out on the hunt. Some women worked in their vegetable gardens, planting seeds, while others sat outside their lodges preparing hides for various uses.

She gazed over at her own vegetable garden, glad that she already had her family's seeds in the ground. If she looked close enough, she could see the faintest of tiny sprouts shoving the dirt aside.

Later today, she planned to join the women in the larger fields, where corn, used by the whole village, would be planted.

But it was her flower garden that Yvonne cherished. It reminded her of many things, some sad, some happy. Her sad thoughts were of the times when the only money that her widowed mother could earn was from the sale of fresh flowers from their Saint Louis garden.

She chose to think of the happy times of her life, when her mother had remarried, and her flower garden was a source of joy rather than income. Her mother had brightened every nook and cranny of their large stone home in Saint Louis with flowers.

The sound of a horse and buggy approaching drew Yvonne's attention. She stood up. Shielding her eyes from the sun with a hand, she peered in the direction of the buggy.

Recognizing it, she smiled. It was her stepfather, who was a Methodist minister. Over the years he had taken the place of the father she'd lost. She adored him.

And everyone in the Ottawa village loved him, for he had given their children opportunities no other white man had ever offered. When Anthony had moved to the Ottawas' homeland of Wisconsin, he had not only brought himself and his family, but also plans to build a schoolhouse so that the Ottawa children could have the same book knowledge that white children had.

With assistance from the United States Government, the school had been built, and now it had been operating for seven years. Side by side with the white children of the community, the Ottawa children attended her father's school.

Yvonne and Silver Arrow's son, Black Crow, was among the children at the school today, as well as Yvonne's thirteen-year-old brother Stanley, and Silver Arrow's sister Rustling Leaves.

Smiling at Anthony as he drew closer in the carriage, Yvonne slipped off her gloves and thrust them into the pocket of her denim skirt.

When her father reined in the horse and buggy beside her, she walked briskly to the other side of the buggy and waited for him to step down to the ground.

The wind had picked up. It whisked Yvonne's long, flowing chestnut hair back from her shoulders. Dust particles stung her hazel eyes.

"Let's get inside quickly," Anthony said, his hat flying from his head. He looked heavenward and peered through his thick-lensed glasses at the clouds overhead. The beautiful day had turned suddenly dark, and lightning forked across the sky.

"I'll get your hat," Yvonne said, running after it as the wind tumbled it along the ground.

Anthony reached inside the back of his buggy and lifted a small, golden chest into his hands.

When Yvonne returned with his hat, they hurried into the longhouse where a fire in the large, stone fireplace greeted them. It cast its magical, golden light all around the room, revealing Yvonne's tasteful choice of plush armchairs arranged before the fire, and braided rugs made by her own hands on the wood floors. Flowers graced the tables, alongside kerosene lamps.

Farther still, where the kitchen was visible from the central room, a wild turkey roasting in the oven wafted its tantalizing aroma throughout the house.

Anthony spied a cherry pie sitting on his daughter's kitchen table and freshly baked bread cooling on a windowsill.

"I see you've been as busy as usual." Anthony chuckled as Yvonne laid his hat on a chair. Loving her deeply, he watched her rake her fingers through her long hair to untangle it. "I would ask for a piece of that pie, but, alas, I have a meeting soon at my church with the deacons."

"You can take the pie home with you, if you wish," Yvonne said, taking off her apron. Her eyes were on the small chest held between her father's hands. "I can bake another."

"My wife is home baking pies even now," Anthony said, seeing how Yvonne stared down at the chest.

Yvonne lifted her eyes to his. "What is in the chest?" she asked softly. "It looks vaguely familiar. Should I know what it is? And why you have brought it to me?"

"It was your mother's," Anthony said, his voice drawn with melancholy at the mention of his first wife, whom he'd adored, and whom he missed dearly. "I'm not sure if you have seen it before or not, for I am not even sure when it came into your mother's possession. She always meant for you to have it, Yvonne. But I was so upset by her death, and then our move to Wisconsin, I absolutely forgot about it."

"Did you bring it with you from Saint Louis?" Yvonne asked, taking the chest as Anthony gently placed it in her hands. She stared down at it. The handmade wooden chest had been intricately inlaid with gold, which gleamed bright in the firelight.

Yvonne gazed at it a moment longer, then questioned Anthony with her eyes. "Have you had it all this time since our move from Missouri?" she blurted out. "What is inside the chest? Why do I feel there is some mystery to your having it?"

Anthony shuffled his feet nervously. His gray eyes wavered. He leaned over, grabbed his hat, and placed it on his thick gray hair. "I really must be going," he said, turning to walk toward the door.

"Father, what is there about this chest that causes you to behave so . . . so . . . strangely?" Yvonne asked, her breath catching in her throat when he slipped a hand in his coat pocket and retrieved a tiny golden key.

"You will need this," he said thickly. "It unlocks the chest."

His eyes held hers as he handed her the key. "Yes, I guess I must tell you all about it," he said, sighing heavily.

He regretted having to bring up a sensitive subject. He knew Yvonne had struggled long and hard learning to read and had never succeeded. Even he had puzzled over her inability to master the skill. He was a scholar himself, and had never been able to understand her difficulty.

Because of her humiliation at not being able to read, Anthony had allowed her to quit school. He knew that, when she saw the book inside the chest, she would feel humiliated all over again.

Yet he had no choice but to tell her about the book, and implore her not to allow its presence in her life to make her feel inadequate. There were so many things she had mastered. Being unable to read was a small lack in comparison.

It wouldn't be fair to Yvonne to withhold something as precious as this from her—an heirloom which had been handed down through generations of her mother's family, a book, something which held her own mother's signature along with the personal annotations of the other daughters and mothers who had once had the beloved book in their possession.

It had been meant for Yvonne to own, and her daughter after her. It would have been wrong not to have brought it to her. In fact, he should have remembered it earlier. He never should have left Saint Louis without it.

Anthony removed his hat. "Yvonne, inside the chest is a book that belonged to your mother," he said, turning his hat nervously around between his fingers. "It is a copy of an ancient, treasured book, passed down from generation to generation, from mother to daughter, for centuries. Your mother told me the original book is in the Library of Congress. This copy was made for her when she was just a girl, but when she died, it was forgotten. The Smiths, who now live in our house in Saint Louis, found it and shipped it to me. It was delivered today."

"A . . . book?" Yvonne said hesitantly.

"Yes, a book, Yvonne," Anthony replied, his voice drawn. He was the only one who knew that she couldn't read. He had guarded the secret well for her, to hide her embarrassment.

"I see," she murmured, her fingers trembling as she held the chest, staring down at it.

"Your mother always kept the chest well hidden. In our Saint Louis home, she hid it in the attic. While renovating the home, the Smiths found the chest beneath some loose floorboards. They knew it had to be ours, since we were the only previous owners."

"I do recall seeing this once," Yvonne said, thinking back to the time she had come upon her mother reading the book. "It was before she married you."

Unable to read, Yvonne had crept away from her mother without asking her about it. She had never liked any reminders of her inability to read, especially in front of her mother, who was so skilled with book learning.

"Yes, your mother did have it before we were married," Anthony said as another rumble of thunder seemed to shake the ground.

He gazed out the window. "I must leave now," he said. "If I hurry, I might get to the church meeting without being soaked to the bone."

A smile quivered across Yvonne's lips. "Thank you for bringing this to me," she murmured. "Anything that belonged to my mother is precious to me, even . . . even . . . if I'll never be able to know what is written in the book."

"If you wish, I shall come from time to time and read it to you," Anthony said, reaching a hand to her cheek.

A quick panic filled her. "No, Father," she said,

her voice breaking. "I would never want to risk Silver Arrow finding you reading to me, when I should be able to read it myself. Silver Arrow doesn't know of my affliction. I have ways to hide that dark side of myself which I hate. At least I can write my name. Thank heavens you and mother were able to teach me that."

"Darling, darling," Anthony said thickly. "There is not one inch of you that can be described as dark. But I do understand how you feel, and I shan't cause you any more anxiety over this book. The main thing is that it is in your possession, where it should be."

"You are always so understanding," Yvonne said, following him to the door.

He gave her a quick kiss on her cheek, placed the hat on his head, and hurried through the blustery wind to his buggy.

Yvonne stood at the door and waved, then watched him ride away.

She turned and walked back inside the longhouse, slowly closing the door behind her.

She kept glancing toward the door, and then down at the chest. "Do I have time to open the chest to see the book before Silver Arrow comes home, or should I wait until later?" she whispered, anxious, yet in the same breath apprehensive, about seeing what had been so important to her ancestors.

One thing for certain, she didn't want Silver Arrow or her son to see the chest. Just as her mother had kept the chest hidden, so would she . . . but for different reasons!

Her urge to see the book sent her to her bedroom, where she would have time to shove the chest beneath her bed if she heard the door open when Silver Arrow arrived home. Their son, Black Crow, would not be home for hours, for the school day had only just begun a short while ago.

Swallowing hard, Yvonne rushed to her bedroom and closed the door behind her. The sky dark with the impending storm made it necessary for her to light a lamp.

She laid the chest on her embroidered, lace-trimmed bedspread and struck a match to the wick of a kerosene lamp on the table beside the bed.

After the flickering light flooded the walls and ceilings of the room, Yvonne sat down on the edge of the bed and rested the chest on her lap. Putting the key in place, she slowly turned the lock until she heard a low clicking sound.

"It's unlocked," she whispered, laying the key aside. "Now . . . to see the book."

A musty smell rushed from the chest as she slowly opened it, the small rusted hinges squeaking ominously. She sighed when she saw the beautiful book, where it lay on a bed of maroon crushed velvet.

From her first glance she knew that the treasured book was special and unique. Gilded in gold, it was exquisitely bound in doeskin.

Lifting the book into her hands, she squinted as she tried to decipher the letters that had been stamped in gold on the doeskin cover so many years ago, when her mother was just a girl.

Slowly she opened the book, taking care while doing it, for the pages were yellow with age. When she had the book all the way open, she gasped softly. Her mother's signature was inscribed on the inside page. Although she could not read, she knew her mother's signature.

Tears flowing from her eyes, Yvonne softly ran

her fingers over the faded ink. Touching the spot where her mother's pen had once rested was almost the same as having her there with her now.

And if Yvonne inhaled deeply enough, somewhere amidst the musty smell of the book was a faint fragrance of her mother's perfume. It smelled of lily of the valley, the perfume her stepfather had given her mother the first year of their marriage. Never, from that day forth, had her mother gone anywhere without the perfume dabbed behind her ears and on her wrists.

The sound of the door in the living room closing made Yvonne jump. It had to be Silver Arrow. Panic grabbed her as she glanced down at the book and then at the closed bedroom door. She must get the book hidden quickly!

Fearful that her secret might be uncovered, Yvonne hurriedly placed the book back inside its chest. Falling to her knees, she shoved the chest far beneath her bed, then rose quickly when the door opened. Silver Arrow stood looking questioningly at her.

"*Ki-mi-no-pi-maw-tis-noo?*" he asked. He stepped on into the room in his fringed buckskin attire. "Are you not well? Your face is flushed, yet beneath your eyes there is a strange paleness."

He swept his arms around Yvonne and drew her close to him. He gazed into her eyes as she looked meekly up at him. "My wife, there is something else about you that is different," he said. "You look guarded, as though you might be uneasy about something. Would you like to tell me what causes this?"

"I'm tired. That's all," she murmured, swallowing hard. "I guess I did too much this morning." She forced a laugh. "I not only baked a pie and a loaf of bread, but I also worked long hours in the garden."

"Did I not warn you against trying to put too much into one day?" Silver Arrow scolded. "And it is only midmorning." He gazed past her at the bed. "Were you in here to rest? Did I disturb your nap?"

Seeing his innocence, his gentle understanding and caring, Yvonne felt guilt rise inside her. She placed a gentle hand on his copper cheek, loving him so much her heart ached from the intensity of it.

Not only was he a man of wonderful compassion, but he was also handsome. His face was finely chiseled. His midnight-dark eyes were penetrating, as though they could look clean into a person's heart and soul. His coal-black hair hung to his waist, a band at his brow holding it in place.

Yvonne's gaze lowered, marveling anew at the width of his shoulders, the power of his bulging muscles.

He had swept her off her feet the very first time she had seen him. She had gloried in the moment she discovered that he had fallen just as deeply in love with her.

Theirs was a lasting love. And she never wanted to jeopardize it, or disappoint him.

She had never wanted to live the lie that she had been forced to live. But how could she explain to him that when she tried to read, she saw the letters backwards and out of order? Such letters as *d* and *b* were reversed. Something inside her mind kept her from sorting the letters of the alphabet out and placing them as they should be to form a word.

Even her very educated stepfather hadn't been able to discover the cause of her problem. If he couldn't, surely no one else could.

She had given up trying long ago.

And so now she had two secrets to keep from her beloved husband—her inability to read, and the book that she had inherited. The latter would be the harder to keep from him, for someday in the future she would be handing the special book down to their own daughter if they were blessed with one.

"No, you didn't disturb my rest," Yvonne said softly. "I . . . I . . . just came into my room to . . ."

Silver Arrow interrupted her as his gaze shifted to the vase of flowers on the bedside table. "You brought flowers to scent our room for our time together tonight," he said. He smiled slowly down at her. "What talents you have. You have such skill in gardening." He chuckled. "I am sure there are many more hidden talents that you have not told me about."

Yvonne paled. The conversation was coming too close to the secret that troubled her to the core of her being. She took him by the hand and walked him from the room. "My darling, how is the weather?" she asked, peering toward the window. "Do you think it will be too nasty for the spring celebration? I plan to cook many wonderful dishes before sunup tomorrow for the celebration."

Silver Arrow gave her a puzzled gaze, then shrugged off the thought that she seemed to be trying too hard to make conversation. He still saw something about her that troubled him. There was something different in her eyes today. He had seen her stepfather arrive while he was in council. Perhaps . . .

"Why was your stepfather here?" he asked, watching her expression.

Yvonne knew that his question was causing the

color to drain from her face, yet she could not help her reaction any more than she could help the fact that she could not read.

"He . . . he . . . just came to tell me that Black Crow was adjusting well to school," she said, wanting to bite her tongue as the lie slipped across her lips. She never liked to lie to anyone, especially her husband. But she knew now that lies were sometimes necessary, especially when the truth might cause a husband to lose respect for his wife.

"*Ni-wob*. It is good that Black Crow is doing well," Silver Arrow said. He went to the kitchen and pinched off a flake of piecrust. "But it was not necessary for him to come all this way just to tell us that." He turned to Yvonne, again questioning her with his eyes.

"Darling, look. The sun is out again! It's not going to storm after all. It's passed on over us," Yvonne said, ignoring his stare. She took the loaf of bread from the windowsill and wrapped it in a towel. "Tomorrow will be such fun, don't you think?"

Silver Arrow slowly nodded. "Yes, *ka-ye-ti*, truly so. The ceremony of spring will renew my people's faith for another summer," he said.

Yvonne gave him a slow stare, smiling sheepishly when she found him studying her as she never remembered him studying her before. Knowing that he had cause to question her, she lowered her eyes.

The weather had been beautiful for the long day of the Ottawas' spring celebration. Much food had been consumed and there had been many games and merriment.

Even now, as the sun was lowering in the sky,

Yvonne sat beside Silver Arrow on a raised platform covered with rich pelts. They were watching their son, Black Crow, as he played *paw-baw-da-way* with the other children. Yvonne had learned from her husband that *paw-baw-da-way* was a ball game the young braves played.

"The day has been good and you have had much time to relax while watching the children play their games, yet you look so tired," Silver Arrow said as he swept an arm around Yvonne's waist, to draw her close to his side.

His eyes moved over the beautifully beaded white doeskin dress she had worn for the celebration. It matched his own special white attire.

Yet no matter how much he wanted to look past the weary look in his wife's eyes, to see her total beauty, he could not. Ever since yesterday she had not been herself.

"Remember, darling, I *did* get up quite early today to prepare my share of the food for the celebration," Yvonne said, trying to hide her true feelings of despondency.

She was thrilled to have the special book that had belonged to so many women of her family, yet it had also brought the recollection of her dreadful inability!

She wanted to be as cheerful as she had been before yesterday, but it was impossible. She hid a lie beneath her bed, and by doing so, she felt as though she was betraying her beloved husband, who had always been nothing but good, gentle, and truthful to her!

"You have awakened early many mornings and prepared food for various celebrations of my people," Silver Arrow said, placing a gentle hand on her cheek, caressing her soft, silken flesh with his thumb. "Today is different. There is something wrong. Would you not feel better if you confided in your husband? Can you think of a time we kept secrets from one another? It is not a natural thing between us, my sweet wife."

"I'm sorry," Yvonne said, swallowing hard. She turned her eyes from him, fearing he would be able to see within her very soul and read her thoughts. "The celebration was wonderful this year, Silver Arrow. I love the ways of your people."

"You are one with us," Silver Arrow said, smiling at his son as Black Crow cast him a winning smile after having made another point for himself in the ball game.

Yvonne gazed at the large pole in the center of the village, which stood upright in the ground close to the large outdoor communal fire. She watched the fabric that hung from it flutter in the softness of the wind. She would never forget the first time she had seen the pole and had learned its meaning. Each spring the Ottawas gathered all the cast-off garments that had been worn during the winter. They strung them up on this long pole while they partook of a festival and jubilee to the Great Spirit.

These tattered bundles of old garments were a sacrifice to the Creator, *Kit-chi-manito*.

For many hours today the Ottawa people had danced around the pole, beating a consecrated drum and shaking sacred rattles made from the hard smooth shells of winter squash.

The instruments that had been used were very old and kept for that purpose only. They were accompanied by two musicians who sang, "The Great Spirit will look down upon us. The Great Spirit will have mercy on us . . ."

Though the ceremony had fascinated her in other years, today Yvonne's thoughts kept returning to the hidden book. She hated having to keep it secret from her husband. Yet how could she tell him? It would only be natural that he would ask her what the book was about. How could she tell him, when she could not read one line of the text?

Too troubled to sit still any longer while others were carefree and guiltless, Yvonne wrenched herself away from Silver Arrow and ran to their longhouse, where she flung herself across their bed, sobbing.

Stunned by her behavior, now certain that something was wrong, Silver Arrow rushed after Yvonne.

When he found her on the bed in tears, he lay down beside her and drew her to him. "My woman," he murmured, cradling her close. "Free your heart of whatever burden you are carrying by sharing it with your husband. Have I not always been understanding? Why would you think I would not be now?"

The book was so close, beneath this very bed on which her husband comforted her, that Yvonne's betrayal seemed twofold.

Yet still she could not find it in her heart to tell him. She did not want to appear ignorant in her husband's eyes. He had learned long ago how to read, even before the school was erected close to his village. Priests, traders, and past white friends had taught him. It was for certain that he could read as well as any white man.

"Just hold me," Yvonne whispered against his cheek. "Make love to me. While in your arms it is so easy to forget."

"Forget . . . what?" Silver Arrow persisted, framing her face between his hands, drawing her eyes to his. "What are you not telling me?"

"It is truly nothing," she said, blinking her eyes nervously under his close scrutiny. She thought quickly. "My time of month draws nigh. You know how my mood always changes with the moon."

Silver Arrow laughed, partly from relief that nothing so terribly wrong caused her strange behavior, and partly from recalling just how that time of the moon had always caused her to become somewhat of a stranger to him. He had often teased her about becoming a hellion who would snap at him without provocation when that time drew nigh.

"I should have guessed the cause," Silver Arrow said, brushing a soft kiss across her lips. "Your moods *do* change with the moon. But this time, you are more softly emotional than glinty-eyed."

"Glinty-eyed?" Yvonne said, raising an eyebrow at the way he described her. "Do I look and act so bad during my monthly? If so, I am sorry."

"I would not be able to say that you look or behave as gentle as a butterfly," Silver Arrow said, chuckling. He rose from the bed and closed the door, then undressed as his body grew warm with passion. "Seems it is best I love you now, my woman, for perhaps tomorrow night my monthly enemy will keep me from it."

"The children," Yvonne said, glancing toward the door.

"Rustling Leaves and Black Crow have learned that when our door is closed, it locks in our privacy," Silver Arrow said, bending to slip off his moccasins.

Yvonne's eyes widened as she watched him removing his moccasins. With him bent so low, he just might see the chest beneath the bed!

She slipped off the bed quickly and began seductively removing her clothes, which she knew would draw his undivided attention.

She relaxed by degrees when she realized that her ploy had worked. Unclothed, he stood close beside her, his passion-filled eyes watching each and every one of her movements.

Yvonne was glad that, for the moment, there would be no more questions. The way her husband was looking at her melted her insides with need. Her need, her want, *his* need, *his* want, took precedence over everything else.

Silver Arrow reached out for Yvonne and gathered her into his arms and led her down onto the bed. He knelt over her as his lips found hers, warm and quivering. His mouth then brushed her cheeks and ears. He tenderly kissed her eyelids.

"I love you so," she whispered.

"You are my everything," Silver Arrow whispered against her lips, then covered her mouth with a meltingly hot kiss.

Yvonne's breath quickened with yearning as he filled her with his heat. She closed her eyes and reveled in ecstasy as their bodies strained and moved rhythmically together. All that she was aware of now was being with him, her golden knight. She was floating, thrilling, soaring. The web of magic was weaving between them, drawing them together as though they were one breath, one heartbeat.

Yvonne twined her arms around his neck, breathless as they continued making love. She sucked in a wild breath of pleasure as his lips swept over a breast, brushing it with a feathery kiss.

A delicious languor stole over Yvonne as rapture totally overwhelmed her.

Silver Arrow moaned as ecstasy leapt through him. Hot, silver bolts of lightning were zigzagging their way through his veins.

And when they floated down from their shared cloud of paradise, lying side by side, only then did Yvonne once again think about what lay so close beneath them on the floor. Tomorrow she would take the book far into the forest. She would study the words. Perhaps if she tried hard enough she could glean the sense of the book so that, if she showed it to her husband, she would be able to answer his questions.

"Again you are pensive," Silver Arrow said as he turned on his side to face Yvonne. He stroked her silken flesh with a hand, running his fingers over the gentle curve of a thigh. "If only it were possible to wish the coming days away so that you would not have to battle the moods that plague you."

"My darling," Yvonne murmured, running her fingers gently over his sinewed shoulders. She laughed softly. "I promise to be better. I shall smile and laugh my own moods away."

He filled his arms with her and held her. "Ah, but if it were that easy," he said, chuckling.

She closed her eyes and sighed as they shared ecstasy's moments again.

After the children had left for school, and Silver Arrow had left for the trading post to do his weekly trading, Yvonne put her plan into motion. Carrying the book, she went far into the forest where she knew she would not be disturbed, not even by her husband should he return from the trading post earlier than usual. To find her place of solitude, she chose the route exactly opposite that which her husband had traveled today.

The scene from the top of the hill where she sat on a blanket was rapturous. The wooded slopes, the meadows of wildflowers, and the rippling river below her took her breath away.

But she had not come to enjoy the view. Yvonne's fingers trembled as she opened to the yellowed pages. She took the time to gaze again upon her beloved mother's signature.

"Mother," she whispered, brushing her fingers across the signature. "If only you were here with me now to read this to me. I know that you read it time and again in the privacy of your bedroom. Why didn't you read it to me then? I would at least know the story enough to tell my husband and child!"

Not wanting to spoil any of the pages with her teardrops, she flicked the tears from her eyes with trembling fingers.

Slowly she studied the words, going from one to the other. She soon became frustrated as she always had in the past when she had tried to read. She still could not make sense of anything on the page.

"What have we here?"

A voice behind Yvonne, deep and mocking, caused her spine to stiffen. She gently laid the book aside on the ground and rose slowly to her feet.

Fear gripping her insides, she turned and stared at the interloper.

She backed slowly away. The man's face was darkly bearded, and his eyes were almost as round as coins, yet bottomless in their empty gray coloring.

Yvonne's gaze swept quickly over the man. His

clothes were soiled and smelled of dried perspiration. One side of his jaw was puffed out like a chipmunk's and a stream of chewing tobacco trickled from the corner of his lips as he slowly shifted it inside his mouth. He held a rifle aimed directly at her middle, his leering, crooked smile almost as threatening as his firearm.

"I wouldn't go much farther, ma'am," the man said, chuckling beneath his breath. "You just might fall over the edge of that cliff. I wouldn't want that. You would lose your value."

Filled with a quick panic, Yvonne turned with a start and gasped when she saw how close she had come to falling over the edge.

She turned again.

Now standing her ground, she turned fearful eyes back to the man. "What do you want of me?" she asked, her voice guarded. "What value could I be to you? Who *are* you? Where did you come from?"

"My, oh, my, ain't you jest full of questions?" the man said, taking a slow step toward her. "There ain't no need for me to answer them 'cept to give you a name to call me by. Just call me Owl—you know, as in bird, as in big eyes?" He laughed again, then spit a long stream of tobacco from between his lips. "Come with me, ma'am. I've got plans for you, and your savage husband."

"What could you possibly want with me . . . and . . . Silver Arrow?" Yvonne said, gasping when he grabbed her arm and shoved her ahead of him. Her insides tightened when she felt the barrel of his rifle nudge her in the back.

"Don't ask no more questions," Owl said. "I'll let you in on my plan after I get you tied up in my cabin."

"Your . . . cabin . . . ?" Yvonne said, giving him a quick glance over her shoulder. "I don't remember seeing any cabin."

"Now maybe that's 'cause I built it so safely hidden 'midst a grove of cottonwood trees away from the snoopin' eyes of your savage husband," he said, chuckling. "It ain't far."

"My husband isn't a savage," Yvonne defended, then cried out with pain when she stubbed her toe on a tree root.

"Watch your step now," Owl said. "Cain't hand you back over to your savage with bruises all over you or he might think I placed them there."

She paused and steadied herself. "Then you mean me no harm?" she asked softly. "You are going to eventually set me free?"

"If your savage cooperates," Owl said, shrugging nonchalantly. He spat over his shoulder. "If he does as I asks him, you'll be as free as a bird."

He took a quick step toward her and gave her another shove. "But not until I get what I'm after," he growled. "Hurry along. You see that cabin up ahead? Head straight for it."

"Why are you doing this?" Yvonne asked, her heart pounding harder the closer she came to the isolated cabin. Once inside, she would be at the crazed man's mercy.

A sudden hope filled her when she saw a piece of cloth tied to a low limb of a sassafras tree. She knew that cloth tied in such a way was how Indians left an offering to the spirits. It made her feel better to know this wasn't an altogether isolated area. The spirit offering was proof of that.

"I'm sure you've heard tell of your husband's grandfather's gold," Owl said, giving her a crooked smile as she sent another quick, alarmed look over her shoulder. "Yes, I see that you have. Well, ma'am, I intend to trade you for some of that gold, *if* your savage cooperates, that is."

"Many have tried to find ways to get at the buried gold and none have succeeded," Yvonne said, a chill racing up and down her spine as she recalled her husband's determination not to give in to past threats.

Many years ago, the neighboring bands of Ottawa Indians had brought their gold coins to Silver Arrow's grandfather for safekeeping. His grandfather had hidden the gold. It seemed now that everyone was hearing about it.

"Have you been used as ransom before?" Owl snickered.

"No, but—" Yvonne stammered.

"Then there's your answer," Owl said, giving her a shove through the open door of the cabin. "I'm the smartest of them all for having thought up a certain way to get my hands on the gold. Your savage will gladly hand it over to me to get you back in his bed."

Yvonne scarcely breathed as she looked around the shadowy interior of the cabin. Except for a table and one chair, it was devoid of furniture. And it smelled of fresh lumber. That had to mean that Owl had only recently built it.

"Sit down on that chair over yonder," Owl said, using the barrel of his rifle to motion toward it.

Knowing that she had no other choice, Yvonne did as she was told. She flinched when a wasp darted out of the shadows and buzzed wildly about her head.

"Damn you. Scat," Owl said, waving off the wasp.

He grabbed a length of rope from another dark

space. "Now sit still while I tie your hands and feet, or by damn, I'll grab up my rifle so quick and shoot you, you won't have time to think about escapin' my clutches," he warned.

Knowing that he meant business, Yvonne anxiously nodded. Trembling, she placed her wrists together. Tears spilled from her eyes while she watched him tie the rope around her wrists, and then her ankles.

Then something else came to her which momentarily made her breath catch. "The book!" she cried, eyes wide. "Oh, no, my book! I can't let anything happen to it! How could I have forgotten it?" She glared at him. "You are the cause. You and your schemes made me forget it."

"What book are you talkin' 'bout?" Owl said, stepping away from her and idly scratching his brow. Then his eyes widened in remembrance. "The book you were reading when I came up behind you? Is that what you're fussin' about?"

"Reading?" Yvonne said, the very word causing her insides to ache. She swallowed hard. "Yes, uh, yes. The book I was reading."

"Why do I get the feeling you are more concerned about that book than you are your very own hide?" he asked, leaning his face into hers. "What is it about that book? Tell me."

"It is very valuable to me," she blurted out. "Please, oh, please go and get it for me."

"Hmm," Owl said, kneading his chin contemplatively. "If it's that important to you, I must at least go and fetch it so I can see for myself why."

"Thank you, sir. Oh, thank you," Yvonne said, sighing heavily.

"*Sir* she calls me!" Owl said, laughing boisterously as he left the cabin.

Yvonne held her breath until he returned. When she saw him with the book, she let out a breath of relief. At least she had done one thing right today. She had convinced him to retrieve the precious family keepsake.

Now to see what he would do with it!

Owl held the book to the light of the door and leafed through the pages. Then he stopped and read some of the passages to himself.

Yvonne watched his expression, seeing a sudden amused glint in his eyes.

"A love story," he said, sending her a quick, teasing smile. "This ain't nothin' but a damn love story between characters with the strangest names I've ever seen. Damon? Angeline?" He held his head back in a fit of laughter, then sobered as he laid the book aside on the table.

He went and leaned over Yvonne, bracing himself with his hands on the arms of the chair. "And so you sneak away into the woods to read love stories, do you?" he taunted. "Well, ma'am, if you need more romance in your life than what your savage is givin' you, I can oblige. Ma'am, I can give you a true lovin'."

The thought so repelled Yvonne she visibly shuddered. "You dare not touch me in that way," she hissed out. "When Silver Arrow catches up with you, he'll hang you!"

A love story, she thought to herself; now at least she knew what the book was about!

"Don't worry yourself about it," Owl said, taking a step away from her. He yanked a piece of paper from his rear pocket. "I don't have time for such pleasures as you. I've more important things to see to while your husband is at the trading post."

Yvonne gasped as she realized that Owl knew so

much about both her and Silver Arrow's activities.

"Yes, ma'am," Owl said, as though he had read her mind. "I've been watchin' you for days, hopin' to get the chance to catch you alone. I've been watchin' your savage's daily activities. I knew where he'd be today. And by gum, lo and behold, even you. You served yourself to me today on a silver platter, wouldn't you say?"

"What are you going to do now?" Yvonne asked, working with the rope, trying to get it free at her wrists.

"I'm going to deliver this note, then see if your savage cooperates," Owl said. His laughter trailed after him as he left the cabin.

Yvonne twisted and yanked on the ropes until her wrists were raw. She watched the sun slipping slowly toward the midpoint in the sky, and then its slow descent.

"Silver Arrow . . ." she whispered.

She stared at the book, wondering if she would be the last of her family to have it. Surely this evil man would kill her once he got what he was after. He would probably burn the book, laughing while watching it go up in flames!

"Will Silver Arrow part with his gold . . . ?" she whispered.

She felt guilty for having put her husband in the position of having to choose, and a sob caught in her throat.

Silver Arrow had made a good trade today and done it more quickly than usual; he was anxious to return home to his wife. This morning she had seemed even more moody than yesterday. He knew why and had come home early to see if there was anything he could do to lift her spirits. He was going to suggest taking a long walk in the woods, where they could breathe in the sweet scents of the forest flowers, and the fresh fragrance of the leaves in the trees.

Yes, he would cheer her up, one way or the other!

When he stepped inside his longhouse and didn't find her in the living room or kitchen, he gazed toward the bedroom door, which was ajar. Expecting to find her there, perhaps taking a nap, he walked lightly toward it, his moccasined steps making no more sound than a panther's.

When he opened the bedroom door and didn't find her there, he raised an eyebrow.

"Her garden?" he whispered, smiling as he envisioned her puttering amidst her flowers, a flower herself in her loveliness.

But something captured his attention. When he saw a small chest lying open on the floor beside the bed, he gazed questioningly at it for a moment, then knelt down and picked it up.

Studying the chest, he turned it slowly from side to side. "Where did this come from?" he whispered to himself. "Why did she not show it to me?"

Something else caught his eye. A small gold key, which lay in the folds of the bedspread on the bed. He reached for it and placed it in the lock of the chest. "They go together," he murmured.

He thought long and hard, then laid the chest and key aside.

"I must find her," he said, his jaw tightening. "Something is amiss here. I must find answers."

He ran outside and checked the garden.

She wasn't there.

He asked around, whether or not anyone had seen her.

None had.

He checked his horses. They were all accounted for in his corral.

Yvonne's buggy rested beneath a tree where she always left it when not using it.

"Her father must have come for her," Silver Arrow said, swinging into his saddle.

He rode in a hard gallop until he reached her father's cabin.

His hopes were dashed when he found no one there.

He then rode to Anthony's church, where it was normal for the minister to be in the study, preparing his Sunday sermon.

Silver Arrow strolled into the study without knocking. Anthony sat behind his desk, his Bible opened to a particular scripture. He looked up at Silver Arrow, startled by his sudden appearance.

"Have you seen my wife?" Silver Arrow asked, his heart racing when he saw that she wasn't there.

"No, I haven't," Anthony said, rising slowly from behind his desk. "Silver Arrow, why do you ask? Isn't she home?"

"*Kau*, no," Silver Arrow said, kneading his brow. "I cannot find her anywhere."

A thought came to Silver Arrow. The chest. The key. And Anthony's visit the day before yesterday. "Anthony, you came the day before yesterday to see Yvonne," he said. "Did you possibly bring her a chest?"

Anthony's eyes wavered. "Why would you ask?" he said warily.

"Today when I was looking for her, I found a small chest on the floor of our bedroom," Silver Arrow blurted out. "I have never seen the chest. Did you bring it to her?"

Anthony felt torn—between his daughter, who had chosen not to confide in her husband about the book and her inability to read it, and a true friend, Silver Arrow. And he was not even sure if the book had anything to do with Yvonne's disappearance.

Unless she had taken it with her somewhere in private . . .

He hurriedly explained everything to Silver Arrow.

Silver Arrow's lips parted in surprise, not so much at Yvonne not being able to read, but because she had chosen to hide her mother's book from him.

"Please try to understand her feelings," Anthony pleaded. "She has always felt so inadequate because of her inability to read."

"With me, she should never feel inadequate about anything," Silver Arrow said. He turned on a heel and rushed back to his horse, quickly mounting it.

When he returned home, he found a note tacked to his front door—a ransom note. The note told him where to leave a bag of his grandfather's gold, and that soon after, in the gold's place, he would find his wife, unharmed.

Growling as rage filled him, he tore the note in shreds.

Never giving in to threats, and knowing every inch of this land, he gathered many of his warriors and explained to them about the ransom note.

"Fan out!" he shouted as they came to him on their horses. "Comb every inch of this land! Find . . . my . . . wife!"

When the sun was dipping low in the sky, Silver Arrow and several of his warriors found the cabin.

He gave them instructions in sign language since it was the quietest way to communicate. One by one they slid from their saddles.

Rifles clutched in their hands, they crept stealthily toward the cabin.

When they reached it, and no one fired at them, Silver Arrow ran inside.

"Silver Arrow!" Yvonne cried, a sob of joy lodging in her throat. "How did you know?"

"Do you think any white man can outthink and outdo this red man?" he growled as he laid his rifle aside. He slipped his knife from a sheath at his side and sliced the ropes away from his wife's ankles and wrists.

He then drew her into his arms. Over her shoulder he saw the book on the table. He stiffened at the sight.

But he had no time to question her about it now. Gunfire broke out outside the cabin. A shriek of pain filled the air, and then there was silence.

Yvonne went with Silver Arrow to the door and looked outside. "He's dead," she said, staring at Owl, who lay sprawled on the ground, blood seeping from a chest wound, warriors standing over him.

"He was an ignorant man who did not know well the art of planning that which would have placed gold in his pocket," Silver Arrow said, his teeth flashing white as he smiled confidently.

Then he reached for the book. He held it out before him for Yvonne to see. "Your father told me about the book, and . . . and . . . other things," he said, his voice drawn. "My woman, why would you not trust my love enough to confide in me about all things?"

"It was not that I didn't trust your love enough,"

Yvonne said, swallowing back another choking sob. "It was because I . . . I . . . was so ashamed about not being able to read. I have so often felt not good enough for you. You have mastered the art of not only speaking English, but also reading. How could I feel otherwise?"

"Because of my deep love for you," he said, laying the book aside. He embraced her. "My wife, you do not need to have knowledge of reading. I love you for what you are. You are my everything. Have I not told you that enough times for you to believe me?"

"I so want to believe that," she murmured, clinging.

"If reading is so important to you, *I* shall teach you," Silver Arrow said, his hands framing her face. "Together we shall read the book that was your mother's. Will that make you happy?"

"Father tried often to teach me and I . . . I . . ." Yvonne stopped, grimacing at the thought of Silver Arrow trying and failing, and her feeling doubly foolish.

"Your father tried when you were younger," Silver Arrow said. "This is *na-go*, now. You are older. You *will* learn, but only if you will allow me to teach you."

He placed a soft hand on her cheek. "And did you not quickly learn the art of speaking my language as well as my own people speak it?" he asked.

Yvonne battled feelings inside herself, but knew, in the end, that she must give him the chance or lose a part of him that she might never regain. "*Ae*, yes, I did learn your language well and even how to write it," she said, recalling the ease with which she had done that.

"Then, my wife, I know that you will now be able to learn how to read the words of *your* people," Silver Arrow said determinedly.

"Oh, Silver Arrow, I hope that you are right," Yvonne said, sighing. "I would love for you to teach me how to read. I have wished to know for so long, not only for the knowledge that one gets from books, but also the pleasure. Do you truly think you can teach me?"

"If you have the same faith in yourself that *I* have in you, *ae*, you will read," he said.

He held her close. "Your father says the book is a love story," he said, chuckling. "Will that not make reading it together much more pleasurable?"

"I doubt that it will teach us anything more than we already know," she said, giggling, trying her best to make light of the situation, while deep inside she dreaded these next few days and weeks . . . perhaps even *months*, while she might look like a clumsy fool in the eyes of her beloved husband!

The days passed into weeks. Each day there was a special time set aside when Silver Arrow and Yvonne sat before the fire in their longhouse, the wonderful book shared between them.

Word by word, sentence by sentence, Yvonne learned how to put the letters together to finally form words she had never been able to decipher before.

She beamed as she mastered one page of reading, and then another.

And the story was so romantic, it made their lovemaking even more special each night. In a sense they *became* Damon and Angeline, the hero and heroine of the wonderfully romantic saga.

Then when the last page was conquered, and

Yvonne realized that she could finally say that she had read one complete book, she felt as if she were glowing from the pride of it.

She gazed at Silver Arrow. "But why now?" she asked as she clutched the book in her hands. "Why was I able to learn how to read now, but never in the past?"

"Because, my wife, your life is as you wish it to be now, sweet and full of peace, with no worries plaguing you which before clouded your thoughts," he said softly. "When you were just a child you were thrown into a world where survival each day was more important than reading."

"Yes, when I stood with my mother on the street corners in Saint Louis selling flowers," she murmured, the remembrance so vivid it was as though she were that child of yesterday now.

"Then came your mother's death," Silver Arrow said. "I need not bring more painful memories into your heart. But you see, do you not, how it was that you had many things that made learning difficult for you?"

"*Ae*, so much of my past is steeped in sadness," she said, swallowing hard.

She turned to him and smiled. "But now I am surely the happiest woman on the earth," she murmured. "For I have *you*, my darling."

He took the book and placed it inside the chest, then lifted her on his lap and held her close. "There is one other thing that may have made learning easier now than in the past," he said, laughing huskily. "It was your husband teaching you."

"Yes, my husband," Yvonne said, snuggling closer to him. "Sweet darling, the book has brought so much into our lives."

She gazed over at it; then she looked with wavering eyes at Silver Arrow. "Darling, we have no daughter to pass it on to. Only . . . a . . . son . . ."

Silver Arrow laughed throatily. He swept her up into his arms and carried her to their bed. "My wife, shall we begin now making that daughter?" he said huskily.

"*Ae*, yes, oh, yes," she whispered, closing her eyes with rapture when he covered her lips with a warm, quivering kiss.

HIDDEN TREASURES

PENELOPE NERI

Hidden Treasures

I

1865

"You're late tonight, Megs."

Sorry," Meg murmured as she stumbled across the street to meet him. Flashing him a grateful smile, she wearily took the arm he offered, explaining, "Mr. Thomas wouldn't let none of us—"

"Any of us."

"—*Any* of us leave till the order was done. Sixteen hours I put in today. But it was worth it!" Her tired, grubby face lit up. She was suddenly so beautiful she made his throat constrict. "Oh, Rob, I sewed *four* coats t'day! *Four!* That's an extra half crown for us, come Friday!"

For Meg's sake, Rob forced a smile, though it never quite reached his dark blue eyes. "Well done,

Meg! We'll be rich as Croesus someday, just see if we won't!" *But not this way*, he vowed silently. Not with Meg working fifteen hours a day in conditions unfit for a dog, let alone a girl of sixteen. He wouldn't have it. There *had* to be a way to get her out of this wretched life—out of this teeming city!

He was still scowling as they passed beneath a gaslight; its jets hissing. He'd not talked Meg into fleeing the workhouse with him two years ago so that she could her kill herself slaving in a tailor's sweatshop! He wanted better for her than that, by God. Aye, much better.

The small hand tucked trustingly in his squeezed a little tighter as they passed the public houses, darkened factories, and tommy shops that lined the cobblestoned streets in this run-down part of London Town.

The tarts were out in force tonight, he saw, boldly strutting along the pavement. They had bedraggled plumes tucked into hennaed hair and frowsy boas slung about their shoulders. Their cheeks were reddened with rouge, their eyes bright with gin, but they had lost all claims to prettiness long ago. Instead, they looked weary, hard, and desperate.

"Well, I'll be beggared! If it i'nt Mr. Rob Betancourt, Esquire! How's about it, love?" The tart grinned as she sidled up to him and bumped his leg with her scrawny hip. "Fancy a tumble, do yer? Just two copper pennies and I'm all yours, ducks. They don't call me Tuppence Tilly for nothing!"

Rob grinned. "Thanks, Tilly, but . . . no."

Tilly sighed and fluttered her soot-blackened lashes. "You're a 'eartless sod, you are, Rob. A handsome cove, but 'eartless nonetheless!"

"It's part of my charm." He smiled. "Maybe next week?"

"In a pig's eye, lover! That's what you always say."

Tilly's raucous laughter followed the pair as they moved on.

"I hate this street," Meg murmured, more to herself than to Rob. She pulled her shawl closer about her shoulders as they passed the open door of a public house. Loud female laughter and coarse male voices billowed out on the cool night air. The odors of beefsteak and onions, unwashed bodies and ale accompanied them. A roaring drunk cut loose with a sea chantey. Others joined in with the rousing chorus:

"Heave-ho, and *up* she rises, early in the mornin' . . ."

"It's all right, Meg. We're almost home," Rob reassured her, slipping his arm around her waist. Her trembling and the frail warmth of her slender body through the thin serge dress made his throat grow dry. He swallowed and drew his hand away as if scalded. Truth was, of late it had grown harder and harder to be just a protector to Meg. Left alone at an early age, he had been forced by the rigors of both orphanage and workhouse to grow up very quickly. The innocent boy he had surely been had vanished without a trace. He was nineteen in years, but far older in terms of experience. He was a grown man doing a man's heavy labor—and a man needed a woman.

"Evenin', Meg."

The voice that came out of the shadows of the alley made Rob freeze in his tracks. His grip over Meg's hand tightened. His free hand clenched.

"I'm lookin' for a new gel, Meg, lass. Interested, are you?"

Feeling Rob tense with anger at her side, Meg returned the comforting pressure of his hand. "No, thank you, Mr. Devlin. I have more than enough work."

"Pity, that. There's good money in whoring for a lively gel. Easy money, too! Beats sewing coats from dawn t' dusk fer a lousy half a crown, it does." Stepping out into the light that spilled from the doorway of the Sailors' Return, Devlin winked slyly at her. "How's about it?"

Meg flushed. "I said no, Mr. Devlin. And I meant it," she said with quiet conviction, then dragged a furious Rob after her down the poorly lit street. She could tell he wanted to punch Devlin's nose, but she wasn't about to have him get hurt, not today. Today was special.

A half hour later, they reached the abandoned, crumbling match factory overlooking the oily Thames that they called home. The fog was rolling in off the river, obscuring the moon, lending the sounds of foghorn and whistle a disembodied quality. In the cellars two floors below the factory, which—thanks to seepage from the river—were always six inches deep in stagnant water, water rats scurried and squeaked. Big as cats and vicious, besides, they terrified Meg.

Rob built a fire in the empty hearth of what had once been the factory owner's office, while Meg carefully scraped the two potatoes that were their supper. As soon as the water was steaming, she dropped potato chunks into the kettle Rob had hung over the flames.

"Here," he said gruffly. "Happy birthday!"

Meg's eyes filled with tears when she saw what

Rob had drawn from inside his shirt. A small piece of salted beef. An onion. Two turnips. A half loaf of bread. "Oh, Rob, we'll have a feast! Thank you!"

While Meg happily put together a meager stew from the bits and pieces he'd swiped from Covent Garden and Smithfield Markets, Rob went to his hiding place.

The sharp odor of sulfur matches still hung on the cold, damp air as he removed some loose bricks from a wall. Taking a quick look about him, he lifted aside several pieces of brown wrapping paper, covered with his scribblings, and carefully withdrew a rectangular object wrapped in grimy sackcloth. Replacing the bricks, he carefully carried it back to the fire and Meg.

"All this and the story, too?" she asked. Her green eyes shining, Meg gestured at the fire and at the simmering kettle hanging over it. The stew was giving off a savory aroma that made her belly grumble.

His own growled in answer. He'd had nothing but a bit of bread-and-scrape since dawn, although he'd spent ten backbreaking hours loading and unloading cargoes from the ships moored in the Pool that day. Still, he counted himself lucky to have found work, however arduous. There were many who didn't.

In response to Meg's comment, he nodded. "I'll read to you tonight. It will be your birthday treat. But you have to work harder to improve your reading, starting tomorrow, Meg," he cautioned sternly. "You'll need to know how to read, write, and cipher if you want to make something of yourself someday. You can't be a—a lady-in-waiting to Her Majesty, or a duchess, say, unless you can read."

Meg giggled at the idea of being wed to a duke or becoming one of Queen Victoria's ladies. Rob was so silly sometimes, but she did enjoy his funning. "I will. I promised, didn't I? It's just that . . . sometimes I'm so tired after working all day. Oh, Rob, this is the best birthday I ever had!" she declared blissfully, settling back to listen.

Sitting cross-legged before the fire, Rob carefully unwrapped the book. It was all he had left of his mother, Suzanne Betancourt, other than his memories. Consequently, it was his most precious possession.

Bound in well-worn calfskin, the book's spine was leafed with gold. Its pages boasted illuminated letters of fanciful design. Ivy vines that curled around a graceful letter S. Wild roses peeping out from behind a letter R. The romantic tale of valiant Damon and his beautiful Angeline had been penned many centuries ago, his mother had told him. Years later, the original work had been lovingly copied in graceful, flowing script by a woman named Genevieve Betancourt, his mother's distant ancestor. The inscription said that Genevieve had done this so that her children and those who came after her could benefit from the wisdom, beauty, and inspiration contained within the book's pages. Just as he had surely done, after his mother's death of consumption when he was seven had left him all alone in the world.

After they had downed their sorry supper, he read to Meg until her eyelids grew heavy and she was stifling sleepy yawns.

. . . Then it was that Damon understood the truth: that with honor comes glory, and through sacrifice, love reaches its noblest expression!

Removing his helm, Damon raised his broadsword aloft and gripped its shining blade. On the cross formed by the weapon's jeweled hilt, he swore before God to uphold honor, and to sacrifice his own life, if it would save his beloved Angeline.

As his last words died away, Rob softly closed the book. He glanced across at Meg. She had fallen asleep, he saw. A smile curved her lips as she dreamed of knights in shining armor who rescued fair damsels in distress, of warmth and security, good food and soft feather beds. In short, of all he could not give her.

The flickering firelight cast patterns of shadow and light over Meg's pale face, gilding a brown curl. Dark lashes fluttered on rosy cheeks, like tawny butterflies stretching velvety wings. How lovely she was, he thought as he drew his own threadbare blanket over her. Too lovely to die here, in the stinking stews of London, like a delicate flower denied the sunlight.

"I love you, Meg," he murmured. A lump formed in his throat as he knelt down and gently kissed her brow. "Happy birthday, sweetheart."

. . . Through sacrifice, love reaches its noblest expression.

Damon's words seemed to echo through his dreams that night.

II

After he saw Meg safely to the sweatshop the following morning, Rob left the stews. Hitching a ride on a wagon bound for the produce markets, then clinging to the rear of a post coach, he made his way across London to Chancery Lane and the plush offices of Messrs. Doyle and Blenkenship, Solicitors.

Drawing a deep breath, he squared his shoulders, whipped off his battered cap, and marched inside the spacious oak-paneled chambers with as much confidence as he could muster.

"What do you want?" one of the office boys rudely demanded. Flicking an imaginary speck of lint from the lapels of his fine tweed overcoat, he looked down his nose at Rob in his flat cap and threadbare brown jacket and moleskin breeches as if he smelled something foul.

"I have a matter to discuss with Mr. Doyle, sir. Be so kind as to tell him I am here."

" 'Be so kind' is it? La-de-da! Just hark at you!" the boy crowed scornfully. "Doyle 'ud have my guts for garters, he would, so scarper! We don't want your sort hanging about the premises."

A muscle twitched in Rob's temple. His jaw hardened. "I'm not leaving until I've spoken with your employer. It's a matter of some urgency," he added, glowering at the copyclerk, who was peering at him over his gold-rimmed spectacles. "What about Mr. Blenkenship?"

"Old Blenkenship's dead as a doornail," the boy said with relish. "And Dicky Doyle's in court, trying a case. A hangin' offense," he added darkly, drawing a finger across his throat.

"When will Mr. Doyle be back?"

"Lord knows!" the boy came back with every evidence of glee. "Could be soon. Could be later. *Much* later."

Rob met the office boy's scornful eyes without flinching. "I'll wait."

Taking a seat in the outer office, he settled down to do just that, the precious book—still carefully wrapped in sackcloth—balanced upon his knees.

On the wall above him, a large round clock sedately ticked off the passing seconds, then minutes, then hours . . .

"Good night, Betty. See yer tomorrow. 'Bye, Meg."

"'Bye, Sal." With a jaunty wave, Meg left the sweatshop, drawing her knitted shawl up over her light brown hair with a worried frown as she crossed the darkened street. There was no sign of Rob. She looked up and down Taylor Lane, but with the exception of Betty, scurrying homeward like a mouse, and a black cat slinking along the gutters, the street was deserted. Where could he be? she wondered as she set off alone. He'd never been so late before.

There was still no sign of Rob by the time she reached the Sailors' Rest. A pair of coarse laborers came barreling out of the tavern, cursing good-naturedly. When they saw her, they exchanged sly grins, then stepped into her path.

"Oi! Oi! What have we here, then? You're a pretty piece, ain't you, lovie? Come on, ducks. Give us a kiss!"

Head down, Meg tried to step around the pair, but one man tugged the ends of her shawl, so that she was jerked this way and that. The other man tweaked her hair. They both brayed like donkeys, enjoying their childish games.

"Please let me pass!" She batted the lout's hand away.

"What's your hurry, my gel? Meeting your sweetheart, are you? Give old Bill a kiss before ye go, eh, lovie?"

"Stop it! Please, I—"

"Leave the gel alone. Damn your eyes!" Devlin, dressed in a greatcoat and bowler, stepped from the pitch-black alley that ran alongside the public house. He was smoking a fat cigar, and the gold watch chain looped across the front of his waistcoat winked dully in the gaslight.

"Er, good evenin', Mr. Devlin, sir. And a fine evenin' it's turned out to be, too. We—er—we didn't know the little chit was one o' your gels, sir, honest we didn't!"

As the pimp strolled toward them, the pair showed their heels and beat a hasty retreat, leaving Meg quite alone with Devlin.

"Thank you, Mr. Devlin," she muttered, trying to step past him. She was brought up short against a solid, immovable chest.

Devlin's hand closed around her upper arm and squeezed. His stubby fingers brushed her breast. With eyes like cold, wet stones in a pitted face, he idly traced its budding curve, then wet his lips. "You don't have t' live 'round here, my lass," he purred. Her flesh crawled. "I could give ye fine clothes, tasty victuals—everything a pretty gel could ask for. You've only to crook your little finger!"

"I already have everything a girl could ask for," she flared hotly, shrugging off Devlin's foul fingers. "I have Rob."

"That young cock?" He snorted in disgust. "Ha! That's a good 'un!"

"Aye. More than good enough for me," she agreed. "Good evening, Mr. Devlin!"

She ran the rest of the way, her worn boots beating a loud tattoo on the pavement as she braved the foggy streets, the water rats, and the darkened stairwell of the match factory to reach home.

She was short of breath and her hands were still

trembling uncontrollably as she tried to light the fire. Try as she might to put it from her mind, her skin prickled when she remembered Devlin's coarse hand cupping her bosom, touching her in ways that no one had ever dared to touch her before. Nausea filled her throat.

The sorry scraps of kindling had almost caught when the door was flung open and Rob all but fell inside. The draft blew out the match gripped in her fingers.

"You're here!" he exclaimed. Relief flooded his white face, yet his gentian eyes were still shadowed with fear. "I went by the shop but you'd gone. I was worried about you, Meg," he added in a gentler tone. His eyes narrowed as he took in her waxy pallor, her wounded expression. "Megs? What's wrong? What happened?"

"N-nothing," she lied brightly, reluctant to worry him on her account. "Nothing at all. Really."

"You're fibbing, Megs. You can't look me in the eye, can you?" he insisted, plucking the matches from her frozen fingers and lighting the fire himself. Carefully he fed the tiny flame with straw, then curly wood shavings, until it had caught the dry boxwood. When the fire was crackling merrily, he began chafing her icy hands between his own to warm them. "Out with it, love. What really happened?"

She bit her lip. She could never tell Rob what Devlin had done. He'd be so angry, he'd want to kill him, she knew—and Rob might get hurt, instead. She couldn't risk that. "It was just Devlin."

"Devlin!" Rob's face turned dark with anger, as she'd known it would. "What did that bas—what did he do?"

"He didn't *do* anything. He just stopped me and

said—oh, what he always says! That I should be one of his girls. You know Devlin—or should, by now."

Rob scowled as he stared into the yellow heart of the fire. Aye, he knew all right. And there was more to it than Meg was letting on. He'd bet money on it—if he had any. It had taken more than words from that slimy Devlin to drain the roses from her cheeks. "Well, you won't have to worry about Devlin or his sort bothering you ever again, Megs," he said without looking at her. "See, you're leaving this bloody stew. First thing tomorrow!"

"We are?" Her pretty face lit up. "Where are we going? To the country? Oh, I do hope it's to the country." Her eyes took on a dreamy light. "Somewhere far, far from London, with green hills and pretty flowers and tall trees, instead of smoke and chimneys and—" She broke off, belatedly realizing what Rob had said. Or rather, what he hadn't said. "You did mean that we're *both* leaving, didn't you?" She held her breath as she awaited his answer. It was a long time in coming.

"Noo," he said heavily, standing and moving away from her. "I meant you. Just . . . you."

Her heart started a frantic hammering against her ribs. It felt as if a little sparrow had been trapped inside her and was frantically beating its wings against its cage to escape. "*Why?* Why aren't you coming with me, Rob? I—I don't want to leave, not without you." Crossing the shabby room, she lifted huge green eyes, brimming with tears, to his. Placing slender fingers over his arm, she whispered, "I love you, Rob!"

I love you, Rob! The words sang inside him. For a moment . . . one golden second . . . he let them sing. Let them soar and swell and fill his heart to bursting . . . before he cut her out of his life forever.

"Love?" He snorted. "What do you know about love, Meg? What you call love is nothing more than gratitude! You're grateful that I've kept you from starving—that I've protected you from the likes of Devlin these past years—that's all. But starting tomorrow, you won't need me anymore. You'll have your grandfather to take care of you."

"My grandfather?" Her tawny brows rose. She frowned. "But I have no grandfather—leastwise, none that I know of." Her voice cracked with apprehension. "What have you done, Rob? And where were you today? Tell me!" Not working on the docks, she'd be willing to bet. But what terrible thing had he done that made his dear, handsome face so very stern and closed tonight? Fear clenched its cold fist in the pit of her belly, for his eyes would not meet her own.

"We're to meet your grandfather tomorrow morning. Ten o'clock sharp at the offices of Messrs. Doyle and Blenkenship, Solicitors," Rob said dully, still without answering her questions. Drawing a knife from his belt, he sawed the stale remains of yesterday's loaf into two thick slabs. These he toasted over the fire on the end of a rusty fork. When they were nicely browned, he spread each slice with tasty beef drippings, skimmed from the top of the leftover stew. "Here. Eat this, while I tell you what you must do and say."

When he had finished, Meg stared at him in openmouthed horror. Her appetite had flown. Her supper was forgotten.

"But those are lies, Rob! We both know I'm not Meg Betancourt, nor Margaret Betancourt. I'm just plain Meg. And as for my mother being Suzanne Betancourt—well! I don't recall ever *having* a mother, let alone knowing her name! Betancourt is *your* name, Rob, *your* family—just like the book is yours. You can't just—just give them away." A sudden thought dawned. Her heart began to thunder, roaring in her ears. "Rob?"

"Aye?" he growled. "What now?"

"Where is the book?"

His jaw hardened. "Safe, never fear. It's back where it belongs, at last."

She swallowed, feeling sick to her stomach. "You gave it to the solicitors, didn't you?" she whispered. "To send to that—that man."

"To Alexander Betancourt. Aye. To *your grandfather,* Lord Betancourt. I had to give him some proof that you were his granddaughter, didn't I?"

She sprang to her feet and began pacing to and fro. "He's no relative of mine, I tell yer! He's your grandfather. And I want no part of this, Rob! How could you give the book away—you *loved* that book. You lived your life by it! Well, you've done it all for nothing, love, 'cause I won't leave you. I won't!"

"Oh, yes, you will, my girl!" Rob said sternly, shaking his finger at her. He looked very dark and tall—almost frightening as he drew himself up to his full height. She believed he'd like to shake her until her teeth rattled. "It's all settled, so there. You'll go. And do you know why? Because I've had enough of playing your bloody nursemaid—that's why! And more than enough of *you*."

Heartsick, he saw the color drain from her cheeks, from her lips, and died a little himself as she whispered, "What did you say?"

"You heard me," he said coldly, cruelly. "Did it never occur to you that I might want to be well rid of *you?* That I might wish to live my own life in my own way, without a stupid girl tagging after me like a—like a shadow? Without you, I could make something of myself! Be somebody!"

"You don't mean that. Tell me you don't!" she cried, the words wrenched from her. Her face was the color of wax in the firelight. Her green eyes were wounded, dark with pain and betrayal.

"I could say it, aye—but it'd be a lie."

A great shudder ran through her. "I thought . . . I hoped . . . that you loved me, too, Rob."

"Well, you were wrong," he came back brutally.

Mortification flamed in Meg's cheeks. Tears clogged her throat like leaves trapped in a water-spout. "I'm sorry to have been such a burden to you all these years, then. You should have told me before, Rob, and saved yourself the bother."

Mustering all the dignity she could summon, Meg regally turned away, walking stiff-legged to the straw-filled potato sack that was her bed. Her face expressionless, she unlaced her boots, tugged them off, then lay down, her face turned to the brick wall. Grief choked her, bottling the agony deep inside her.

In the distance, Big Ben solemnly chimed the hour. To Meg and Rob, both wrapped in silent misery, its chimes sounded like a death knell.

III

Betancourt, Devonshire, five years later

Meg set the *Monthly Magazine* aside and sighed. For the past two years, the periodical had been publishing moving, thought-provoking essays and short stories by a new writer who called himself

The Observer. Like those of the popular author Charles Dickens, who had recently passed away, The Observer's engaging working-class characters and humble settings never failed to remind her of her life with Rob, and of the wonderful book he had inherited from his mother.

With the wisdom that comes with hindsight, she realized now that Rob—lacking a father and mother to guide him—had lived by the principles and ideals found within the book's pages. He had also used the endearing romance of Damon and Angeline as a primer to encourage her to read, in the hopes that someday she might better herself. He would have been pleased to know that she was passing the precious gift of reading on to others. Since the spring, she had been teaching the children in the nearby village to read and cipher—and loving every moment of it!

With a rustle of rose taffeta skirts, Meg stood and went to the tall arched windows. Draped in green velvet and lace, they overlooked the park, the dolphin fountain, the shingled drive, and the Italian gardens of Betancourt, Lord Alexander's estate.

As she lifted the lace curtain aside, she saw His Lordship cantering his dappled-gray hunter up the driveway to the house. He lifted a gloved hand to her in salute as he rode past, a distinguished, silver-haired old gentleman dressed in black riding coat, fawn breeches, and polished black boots. Smiling, she waved back. He looked younger, happier, than when they had first met five years ago, she thought. It pleased her to think that she was, in some small part, responsible for the transformation.

"Miss Margaret?"

"Yes, Kitty?" She turned to the doorway, where a uniformed maid stood, hands clasped before her, demurely awaiting her reply. "What is it?"

"The carriage has been brought around for you, miss."

"Very good. Tell Dick I'll be out shortly. Oh, and Kitty?"

"Yes, miss?"

"Thank you."

"You're quite welcome, I'm sure, Miss Margaret," Kitty responded, smiling shyly as she bobbed her young mistress a curtsy.

Meg was well aware that the staff of Betancourt, Lord Alexander's country estate in the heart of Devon—a county that was "far, far from London, with green hills and pretty flowers and tall trees, instead of smoke and chimneys"—considered her a "rum," or strange, one. She wondered what the below-stairs inhabitants of Lord Alec's townhouse in London's Regent Street had thought of the uncouth little hoyden their master had brought home five years ago, then introduced as his beloved daughter's long-lost child?

There had been an oil painting of Lady Suzanne, a black-haired, blue-eyed beauty, hanging over the marble mantel of the townhouse's elegantly appointed drawing room. One morning just a few weeks after her arrival, she had found her new guardian gazing up at the portrait with a faraway expression, his hands clasped behind him.

"This portrait is of my darling Suzanne. Your mama," His Lordship had observed softly. "When she joined the angels in heaven, she left us both desolate, did she not, my dear?" He sighed. "I often wonder where I went wrong. Why could she not bring herself to tell me that she was carrying that wastrel's child!" Betancourt's dark blue eyes—eyes that reminded Meg painfully of Rob's—had grown moist. "While I certainly did not approve of—of *him*, I loved Suzanne far too much to ever turn my back on her, or her infant!"

Tenderhearted and unable to bear the anguish in his expression, she had hesitantly touched his elbow and murmured, "Please don't cry, sir. Rob always said that his mother was too proud to admit she'd made a mistake when her young man left her. It's not your fault, sir!" She had added gently, "Miss Suzanne feared the scandal her—her unmarried condition would stir up, you see?"

Betancourt's brow had creased. "Who told you this? Who is this Rob you speak of?" he'd demanded hoarsely.

"The lad wot—the lad who brought me to you, my lord. Rob Betancourt," she'd whispered, frightened by the intensity of His Lordship's voice, his eyes. "Your—your grandson."

"What!"

Breaking down, she had confessed everything to His Lordship, ending tearfully, "And it's all as Rob promised, sir. You've been very kind t'me, Lord Betancourt! But . . ." Her lower lip had quivered and her eyes had filled with tears as she added huskily, "But without Rob, none of it matters a farthing t'me! I'd rather share a—a tater or a bit of bread with Rob than stuff meself on pheasant and pudding without him!" With a sob, she had promptly burst into tears.

Stunned, the peer had handed her a monogrammed kerchief and gingerly patted her shoulders, muttering, "There, there, child. Don't take on so. There's a good girl." When she had recovered some of her composure, he had gently drawn the entire story from her, word by hiccuping word.

"Oh, sir, I beg you. Take me back to the match factory," she'd implored him when her story was done, lifting a lovely, tear-streaked face to his. "I have to find Rob. I simply have to! I love him! I can't bear it without him!"

And so they had gone back to the East End together, determined to find Rob, only to learn that he had vanished soon after Meg went away.

"Rob? Why, he scarpered, love," Tuppence Tilly had told Meg, with a saucy wink for the distinguished toff at Meg's elbow. "Ran off right after he blacked both of Devlin's eyes, he did. Blooming wonderful, it was, too! You should have seen it."

"He didn't tell you where he was going, Tilly?"

"Nah, love, not a blooming word. Cripes, Meg, just look at you, ducks! Why, I ain't never seen such fine feathers, I ain't! Set you up in a fancy place, did he, the old lecher?" she'd asked in a loud whisper, nodding at Lord Betancourt.

"On the contrary. His Lordship has been very proper and kind to me," she had insisted primly, giving Tilly a scowl. "But I'm back here now. To stay."

"Hrrrmph. That's where you're wrong, my dear," Betancourt had disagreed, taking her firmly by the elbow. "In fact, I believe it's high time we returned home." He'd nodded at Tilly and tipped his hat as he pressed a gold sovereign into her hand. "Good day, madam."

Meg had been stunned when His Lordship handed her up into his black-lacquered carriage with the matched pair—a rare sight in the East End.

"But, sir—milord!—I lied to you," she'd stammered, squirming with guilt as the coach rumbled down the narrow streets, heading for the spacious, tree-lined thoroughfare of Regent Street. "I—don't deserve to—"

"I'll decide what you deserve, Margaret, my dear. Please indulge me in this matter, if you would. I'm a rich, selfish old man, but also a very *lonely* one. It's been too blessed long since Betancourt rang with a young woman's laughter. Margaret—Meg," he'd added huskily, "I would be honored if you'd let me take care of you." Seeing suspicion and indignation fill her eyes, he'd added hastily, "Er, in a very proper sense, of course! I would like to be your guardian, my dear. I cannot allow you to suffer my Suzanne's sad end. Nor shall I rest until I have found my grandson, and brought him home."

And so, Uncle Alec, as she had chosen to call him, had become her legal guardian and more—oh, so much more!—since then. Against all odds, they had grown fond of each other over the years, too. It was as if she were truly his beloved granddaughter, rather than his ward. For his part, Betancourt had delighted in spoiling her.

Seamstresses had come to the house to fit her for dresses and gowns of silk, taffeta, and satin, trimmed with pearls and lace. Milliners had created outrageous, beautiful hats of felt, straw, or silk, just for her. Best of all, a steady stream of tutors had come to the house each week to instruct her in grammar, botany, geography, and history, while others had taught her music, elocution, and dancing.

In short, she had acquired the education, polish, and accomplishments society would expect of Lord Betancourt's ward.

Yes, thanks to His Lordship's generosity, she had

lacked for nothing these past five years, except the one thing she wanted. *Rob*.

Wiser and more worldly now, she realized that Rob had undoubtedly been so cruel to make it easier for her to leave him. Her heart ached anew whenever she remembered their cold parting in the solicitors' office that morning; the stiff-necked pride that had kept her from throwing her arms about his dear neck and kissing him farewell, as she'd ached to do.

"The book's yours now, Meg. Mind you keep up with your reading," he'd told her huskily, feeding his cap through his hands.

But she had not even deigned to look at him. Lord, no. She could not! It had hurt too much.

"Here, lad. Here's five guineas for your trouble," Lord Betancourt had offered generously, drawing a crisp bank note from his inner pocket.

"No, thank you, sir," Rob had refused. He'd proudly squared his jaw and scowled at the silver-haired aristocrat.

Meg had been amazed that the two men could not see themselves in each other in that moment. Though one was old, the other young, the resemblance was striking, like reflections in a mirror. But, alas, they had not.

"As you will, then," Betancourt had murmured, nodding in understanding. A proud man himself, he respected pride and honor in others, regardless of their station in life, she later discovered. "Come along—er—Meg."

When she meekly turned to follow His Lordship out to his carriage, she'd seen that Rob had gone, leaving without another sound. She would have doubted he'd been there at all, were it not for the void he'd left in her heart.

Remembering that day, she swallowed, tears smarting behind her eyes.

He had wanted better for her than long days spent in the horrid sweatshop; eighteen men and women shut up for six days a week, working hours at a time in an airless room that measured a cramped nine by fifteen feet. She had sewn coats until her fingers bled and her eyes streamed, she recalled. Both rain and snow had found their way through the leaking roof in winter, while in the summer, she'd felt as if she were being boiled alive in an airless prison. He had wanted a better home for her than the squalid, damp match factory, too, with its water rats and other vermin, and the stink of the river filling her nose day and night.

And he had found a way out for her. Had loved her so deeply, so selflessly, he'd sacrificed his beloved book—and his only link with his mother's family—for her sake.

". . . Through sacrifice, love reaches its noblest expression."

Surely the noble Damon had not loved his Angeline so very dearly?

IV

"You look simply enchanting tonight, my dear!" Alexander Betancourt exclaimed on Christmas Eve of that same year.

He and Meg were greeting their last guests in the paneled hallway of Betancourt, where suits of polished medieval armor stood stiffly at attention in gloomy corners, lances or swords raised to do battle at the drop of a hat. The hollow knights stood guard over busts of Beethoven and Shakespeare, and over stern Betancourt ancestors whose portraits scowled down on them from the upper gallery.

"The red velvet makes you glow," Betancourt added.

"Thank you, kind sir, but it's the season that makes me glow," she denied gaily, blushing with pleasure. She went up on tiptoe to kiss his cheek. "I do so love Christmas!"

"So do I, by Jove!" Betancourt agreed. "It's a time for making wishes and having them all come true, is it not? Tell me. What is your Christmas wish this year, my dear?"

"Now, now, Uncle. If I tell, it won't come true," she teased gaily. By his smile, she suspected her guardian knew very well what it was she wished for. It was always the same wish. One that for five long years had gone unfulfilled: to find Rob. "Now, I really must go in and see to our guests."

Blowing him a kiss, she left him for the ballroom, a poised, graceful beauty gowned in crimson velvet. Rubies and garnets, a gift from her guardian, blazed at her throat and ears. Jeweled hairpins sparkled like drops of burgundy wine tucked into her elegant chignon, while her slender arms were encased in white kid gloves with a great many buttons.

Glittering chandeliers blazed above her, and fragrant wreaths of evergreens and holly hung from the wainscoting, spicing the air with the scent of pine and bayberry. Like fireflies, the flames of a hundred tiny candles decorated the lofty green fir by the fireplace. Their light winked off crystal teardrops, gold-foil bows, tiny gilded fans, and other shiny ornaments.

After ensuring that the platters on the groaning buffet tables had been refilled, Meg moved among her uncle's guests, pausing to converse with each one.

"Rev. Chapman, how good of you to join us . . ."

"Why, Miss McBride, what a pleasure to see you again. Merry Christmas!"

"Good evening, Your Grace. My guardian and I were delighted you could attend this evening."

"Nonsense! The pleasure is mine, child. I wouldn't dream of missing Alec's Christmas ball! You look charming this evening," gushed a matronly dowager attired in yards of fringed dark blue material that looked suspiciously like window drapery. She kissed Meg's cheek. "Tell me. Does the sparkle in those pretty eyes have anything to do with our guest of honor?"

"Guest of honor?"

"Why, yes, dear girl. I was given to understand that The Observer would be here this evening." Seeing Meg's startled expression, she explained, "You know, the author of those marvelous stories in the *Monthly Magazine?"*

"I'm very familiar with the gentleman's writings, of course," she admitted. "But I had no idea Uncle Alec had invited him to our ball." She frowned. She had written and posted the invitations herself, and had recognized all of the names on the guest list from past Christmas balls. Was The Observer someone she already knew?

"Oh, drat it all. Do tell me I haven't spoiled your Christmas surprise, Alexander," the Duchess of Norfolk implored as Lord Betancourt, splendid in evening attire, appeared at Meg's elbow. The duchess tapped His Lordship's chest with her closed fan. "I would feel quite terribly wretched if that were so."

"Then prepare to feel quite terribly wretched, Hypatia," Betancourt told her ruthlessly, grinning. "I was about to tell my ward that the fellow would be putting in an appearance tonight when you let my secret slip. She's quite an admirer of his, are you not, Meg?"

"Very much so, yes," she admitted, delighted at the prospect of meeting the writer whose works she enjoyed. Like Dickens, The Observer's writing had done much to stir up the social conscience of British society, resulting in several badly needed reforms that protected the rights of children. Going up on tiptoe, she kissed Alexander Betancourt's cheek. "Thank you for inviting him, Uncle Alec. You're a dear man, and so very kind to me."

"I know," Alec came back, his sapphire eyes twinkling. "Now, then. Would you care to dance with a dear old man?"

"Certainly not!" she came back pertly. "However, I'd be delighted to dance with *you*, sir!"

Laughing, he swept her into a waltz.

It was almost midnight before the guest of honor arrived. Meg was first aware of The Observer's arrival when an excited murmur ran through the gathering. The scattering of polite applause gradually built in volume until the orchestra ceased its playing and the dancers stopped dancing.

The gathering parted like the Red Sea to applaud the tall, dark-haired man in evening dress who strode between them to Alexander Betancourt.

In a moment that seemed frozen in time, Meg took note of the man's wavy dark hair . . . his handsome features . . . his sensual sapphire eyes under stormy brows . . . his broad shoulders. The breath caught in her throat. Her heart skipped a beat. The Observer was none other than *Rob!* The lanky, boyish good looks she remembered had been translated into the tall, powerful physique and chiseled features of a striking man!

Feeling her gaze upon him, Rob halted. And, as if only the two of them were in the vast ballroom, he smiled for her alone. It was a smile that filled her heart to bursting.

"Merry Christmas, Megs."

With a sob of joy, Meg flew across the parquet floor, burying Rob in a flurry of frothy petticoats and crinolines as she flung herself into his open arms.

V

She leaned back against him, shivering in delight as Rob buried his face in her hair, then pressed hungry lips to her throat, her bared shoulders, her mouth in turn.

"Cold, my love?" he asked at length, turning her to face him.

Smiling, she shook her head.

With Lord Betancourt's permission, they had escaped the crowded ballroom and the curious scrutiny of his guests for the privacy of the veranda. It overlooked the Italian gardens, which were bathed in the milky light of a wintry full moon.

Snow had been falling since late that afternoon. The box hedges, the cypress trees, and the lichened statuary were powdered in white flakes. The light of several Japanese lanterns reflected in the snow as a rainbow of pastels. But it was neither the snow nor the wintry air that had made her shiver. Dear Lord, no! And judging by the wicked grin that quirked his lips, Rob knew it, too.

"No? Then why do you shiver, my love?" he asked softly. The laughter fled his eyes as he looked down at her. Now they burned with desire, with love. His handsome face was very serious and stern as he raised her chin with the tip of his finger, forcing her to look up at him. "I've spent five years mourning you, Meg. Five long, empty years, pouring my heart into my words, into my stories, never once imagining I'd ever see you again, let alone be with you like this. My writing not only kept me sane—it brought you back to me again."

She laughed, giddy with delight. "Just as teaching the village children to read preserved my sanity! I've shared Suzanne's book with them, Rob. *Your* book. You should see how their little faces light up with the magic of its words, the wonder of discovering new worlds within its pages!"

"It is a romantic tale," he agreed.

"Damon and Angeline's tale is much more than a romantic story. It is the wings on which inspiration and imagination soar! It imparts the message that dreams really can come true. And that if two people love each other, together they can triumph over the greatest adversity. I understand now what you were trying to give me, Rob."

"Oh? And what was that, my love?" he asked tenderly, smiling down at her. Her green eyes shone like emeralds in the moonlight. Tousled tendrils of golden-brown hair wove a shimmering halo about her face.

"A golden key with which to unlock all the secrets of the world. A priceless treasure that I would not trade for a sultan's ransom. The ability to *read!*"

He chuckled. "I gave a ragged little guttersnipe into Lord Betancourt's—my grandfather's—care. She has grown into a beautiful, radiant woman. And despite my fears, a *wise* one!" He caressed her cheek. "I've always loved you, Megs. Can you ever forgive me for the things I said to hurt you?"

"There is nothing to forgive. I think I always knew, in my heart, why you'd said those things. It was what Damon would have done to save his Angeline, was it not?"

He nodded. "I knew I had to let you go, to keep you safe from the likes of Devlin. '*Through sacrifice, love reaches its noblest expression,*' " he quoted. "Remember? But, dear God, giving you up nearly destroyed me! Never again, Megs," he swore. "I'll never let you go again. I swear it!" Cupping her chin, he crushed his mouth over hers, then framed her face between his hands to deepen his searing kiss. "Dearest Meg—will you marry me?" he asked at length.

To his surprise, his proposal made her stiffen in his arms. "Marry you? But you are the grandson of an earl, Robert! While I—"

"While you are the woman I love. That's all that matters, Meg."

"—while I am an orphan, with no knowledge of my pedigree," she countered as if he had not spoken. Her voice broke. Pulling free of his arms, she went to the stone balustrade. She stared blindly at the gardens below, frozen in a web of sparkling white hoarfrost. Her fingers curled into fists. "I know nothing of my mother or father. I could be—I could be the daughter of an unfortunate, a prostitute like Tuppence Tilly!"

"I know everything I need to know about you, darling. That you're a fine, honorable person. The woman who loves me as deeply, truly, as I love her."

It was true. She had loved him for so long that loving him had become a part of her. He was as vital to her as the air she breathed, or the heart that beat within her breast.

Other men, finding themselves in Rob's predicament, would have offered her a discreet townhouse, pretty clothes, and a few blissful hours of his company each month. An offer she would, of course, have refused, however tempting, for she would be no man's mistress. But to offer her marriage? She sighed. It was quite out of the question. Heirs to a peerage did not marry commoners of doubtful bloodlines! Rob would realize how absurd the idea of marriage was, once he'd thought it through, coolly and calmly.

"Meg? Answer me! Will you marry me?" he asked a second time.

"No, Robert. I regret I must refuse," she whispered, her head held high.

Then, picking up her skirts, she twisted from his arms and fled.

VI

It was the second week of the New Year. The Christmas holidays over, Meg returned to her pupils on a frosty Monday morning in January, determined to forget her misery in teaching. It had always helped in the past.

Today, however, it did not. She felt restless, melancholy, unable to concentrate. Abandoning all attempts at teaching phonetics or sums to fidgety children ranging from five years to twelve, she told her pupils to put away their slates and primers. Instead, she added a log to the fire and read to them, choosing yet another chapter from Rob's precious book.

She had just concluded a particularly enthralling episode when little Nan—usually a shy, quiet child—suddenly jumped to her feet, upsetting her inkwell.

An indigo blot spreading across her ruffled white pinafore, she ran to the small schoolhouse window. Scratching a hole in the feathery frost there, she pointed excitedly. "Look, miss! A knight! Just like the one in the story!" she cried. Her thin face was wreathed in a smile, her brown pigtails jiggling excitedly as she peeked through the hole.

"It cannot be a knight, Nan dear," Meg gently corrected her pupil, going to the door and throwing it open. A gust of frigid air rushed in, setting the flames on the wide hearth to dancing. "Knights belong to the medi—ev—*oh!*"

She fell silent, stunned speechless by what she saw before her. Her eyes widened. Her jaw dropped, for little Nan was right!

A knight, armored in shining silver, sat his horse before the little stone schoolhouse. Scarlet plumes fluttered from his visored helmet, while a long, pointed lance was held stiffly at his side. He was mounted upon a huge, dappled-gray hunter caparisoned in crimson and gold. The valiant steed snorted and proudly tossed its mane as it pranced about the village square.

She blinked, for it was as if the warrior had materialized from another time. Or . . . from the very pages of the book.

As the children crowded about her, giggling and

exclaiming over the magnificent figure, the knight raised a hand to lift his visor, revealing a glimpse of Rob's darkly handsome face.

"Hear ye, good people of Betancourt!" he declared in a deep, ringing voice. "Let it be known throughout the kingdom that on this, the twelfth of January, in the year of Our Lord eighteen hundred and seventy-one, the valiant knight, Sir Robin of Pen-and-Inkton—having been refused the hand of the lady Meg—did herewith take the beauteous lady as his prisoner and carry her off to his tower!"

"Eeh! He means you, he does, miss!" one of the village boys exclaimed, scratching his head and grinning.

"Hurrah! Hurrah!" the children cheered.

"You're utterly mad, Rob!" she accused primly, blushing yet unable to keep from laughing as she added, "Or else you are quite drunk, sir!"

"On the contrary, damosel. I am stone cold sober, relatively sane, deeply in love—and desperate!" With that, he cast the lance aside and kneed the gray hunter toward her. Before she could guess his intent, he leaned stiffly from the saddle and swept her up before him.

The children jumped up and down, laughing and clapping their hands in delight as the gallant knight urged his steed into a brisk canter that carried their teacher away from the school, down the rutted village high street, toward Betancourt.

"School's out!" cried one lad, winding his muffler about his throat. "Come on, lads. Let's go home!"

One enterprising fellow began ringing the school handbell, setting up a loud, plangent clanging that was sure to bring folk running from the village to see what was going on.

"Rob, let me go! What will people think? And the

children! I cannot desert them like this!" she wailed, laughing nonetheless. "Lessons are not done for the day!"

"They are now! And if it's truly freedom you crave, then you shall have it. But remember, freedom has its price, fair lady," Rob said sternly.

"Indeed it does," she agreed with equal solemnity, yet her heart beat a little faster. "Name yours, pray, brave sir."

"Your hand, fair damosel—and all the rest of you!—in marriage. Or else . . ."

"Or else what?"

He grinned wickedly. "Or else I shall carry you off to my tower, and force you to live with me there—in sin!" he vowed with every evidence of relish. "Either way, I will have you, Megs!" he swore. There was steel in his voice, determination in his eyes. "The choice, fair lady, is yours."

She laughed as he drew the helmet from his head, turning in the saddle to reach up and rumple his black hair. Truth was, her melancholy and restlessness had lifted the very moment she saw him. Right or wrong, she knew in her heart that she could never be happy without him. She loved him with all her heart, just as he, thank God, loved her.

"Then what can I do, sir knight," she asked softly, "but accept?"

Angeline would have done no less.

Meg Betancourt stretched languorously, coming awake like a sleepy, contented kitten. It was morning—her first morning as Rob's bride. The first day of their honeymoon, and of their wonderful new life together.

From below, in the snowy, tree-lined thoroughfare that fronted Lord Betancourt's townhouse, she could hear the barrow boys, muffin men, and dairymaids of London singing the praises of their wares:

"Ho, buttered muffins! Ho, hot muffins! Will you buy, sirs? Will you try, sirs? Ho, hot muffins!"

"Milk—ooo! Fresh milk today-ooo! Milk-ooo!"

"Good morning, my sweet. Did the vendors wake you?"

She shook her head, lazily rolling over to find Rob propped up on his elbow, watching her. She smiled and tenderly touched his cheek. His broad shoulders and torso were bare and corded with muscle, a legacy of loading cargo on the London docks. Firelight played over his body, dispelling the cold, wintry light of dawn that pierced the lacy draperies. Just looking at him, remembering what had passed between them the night before, had the power to stir her senses.

"I don't mind their cries at all," she said in answer to his question. However, the rising pink blush in her cheeks hinted that her thoughts were elsewhere. "In fact, I enjoy hearing them."

"I wonder what else you enjoy, my darling bride," he murmured, grinning. One by one and very slowly, he unfastened the countless little ribbons that closed the front of her nightgown, to bare her breasts. He kissed them, making his tongue dance over her skin like wildfire.

Her head fell back, baring her throat to his lips. His mouth grazed the hollow at its base where her pulse beat wildly. "Meg. My darling Meg!" he whispered, his voice thick and whiskey dark. "Sweet Lord, how I love you!" Sliding up the length of her soft curves, he covered her with his hard body.

She shuddered as he began to move, the feeling of helpless, unbearable longing sweeping over her, as it had last night, when he made love to her for the very first time. As it would do in all the wonderful years yet to come.

His book—*their* book—had torn them apart, then brought them wonderfully, beautifully together, as man and wife.

And together they would remain, Meg vowed much later as she lay in Rob's arms, whether the future brought sickness or good health, riches or poverty, good times or bad. A naughty smile curved her lips as she cuddled closer to Rob. And then, one day, God willing, it would be their children's turn to benefit from the book's hidden treasures.

All *twelve* of them!

WINDS OF CHANGE

JANELLE TAYLOR

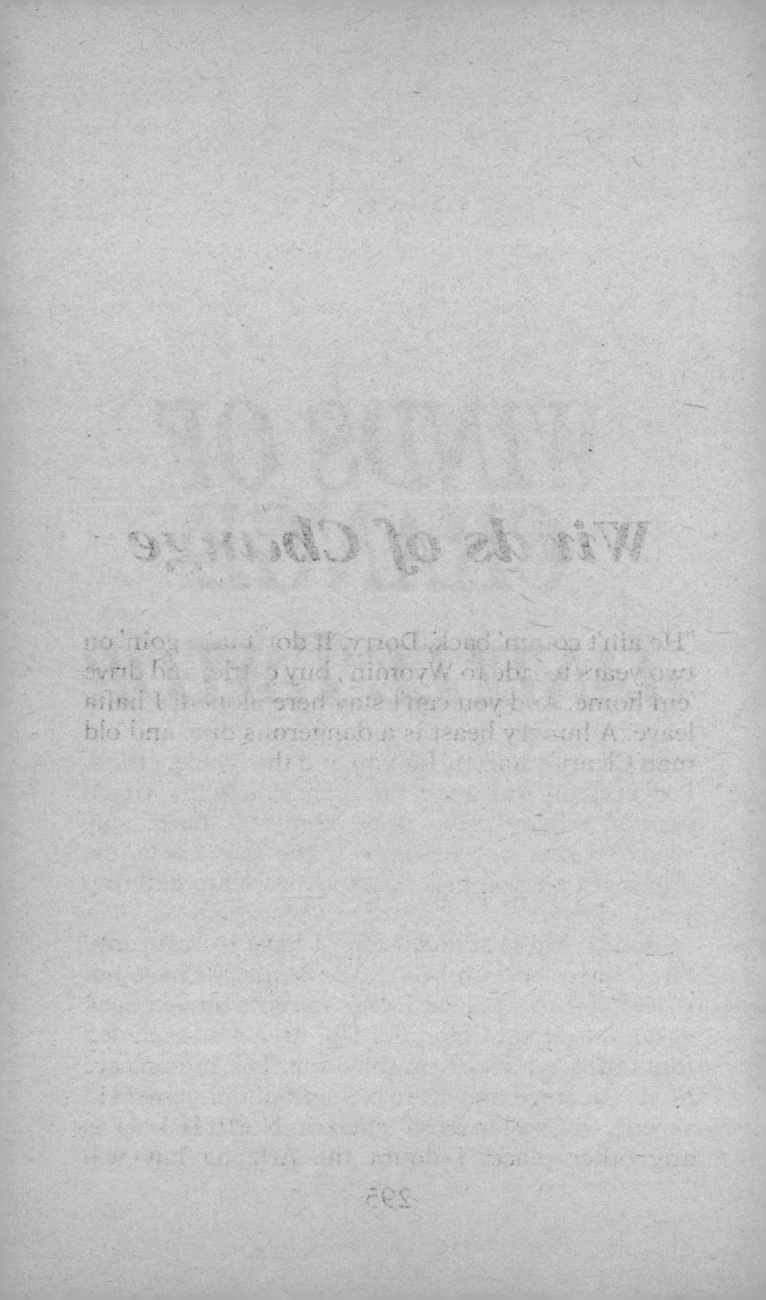

Winds of Change

"He ain't comin' back, Dorry. It don't take goin' on two years to ride to Wyomin', buy cattle, and drive 'em home. And you can't stay here alone if I hafta leave. A hungry beast is a dangerous one, and old man Cleary's starvin' for you and this place. I think I covered my trail good, but there's no tellin' what'll happen when spring thaw comes. I hafta stay ready to ride like lightnin' if the law tracks me down. If I go, you hafta go, too, or Cleary will trap you."

"John's my husband, Luke; I have to wait until I'm told for certain he's dead. Besides, I have nowhere else to go since John's parents moved back east after we left Colorado. This area is so secluded that outlaws haven't troubled me. The Indians are no threat since they were brought under control in seventy-six, so I'm as safe here in North Dakota as any other place. I doubt the Arizona law will search for you this far away, and with your help, William Cleary will never get his greedy paws on me or my land. You will stay until John returns or news of his death arrives, won't you?"

"And let him call me out for . . . livin' with his wife for three months? Watch him step in and claim the only woman I love and want?"

Dorry Sims blushed as she caught his meaning. "You know I love you, Luke, but a future together is impossible unless things change for both of us; we've known and accepted that dark reality from the beginning. I vowed to be John's wife 'until death do us part,' and I have no proof he's dead. I don't know how long I should or will wait for news, but eighteen months isn't enough. And you, you might have to flee for your life at any moment. I wish we could marry and make this ranch ours, have children, have a wonderful life together."

"I didn't mean to put them tears in your eyes, woman. They're as pretty and blue as Texas flowers. I just can't abide knowin' somethin' could happen to me and you'd be left alone to fight Cleary and who knows what other dangers."

"I've survived plenty in the past, my love. I sometimes think someone watches over me. When my family was killed by those Indians, I was with John's folks in town. I've outlasted blizzards, hunger, injuries, and more since I've been here alone. I know how to shoot, ride, ranch, farm, and do whatever's needed to survive here. But my survival won't mean anything unless I have someone to inherit my family's legacy, my book. I want that person to be our child, Luke. Maybe that's wrong and wicked of me, but I can't help but feel that way. My grandma gave each of her children a copy of the book and a chest to keep it in, and it's been part of our family ever since. When I hold the book, it gives me strength, courage, hope, and joy. It isn't just a legend, a made-up story, Luke; it's true; I know it's true; Mama said so."

"A book can't protect you from guns and bullets and knives and greed. If I'm killed or captured, I can't neither. But Cleary ain't gonna give up on gettin' you and this land till he's lyin' facedown in dirt. You ain't forgettin' he came over at Christmas and tried to buy you out if you wouldn't marry him. He's been makin' cow eyes at you ever since John left. He told you months ago he'd get news about John, but he won't tell you nothin' till it suits his needs. You can bet he ain't pleased you plan to hire a helper come spring; he'll do his darnedest to make sure you don't get none. If I kill him to protect you, I'm in worse trouble. I'm bettin' he knows John's dead, 'cause he did the shootin', or had it done. He'd kill me, too, if he knowed I was here." Luke wished he hadn't made that last remark, though it was true. "You got good grass, a lotta trees, and plenty of water—mighty temptin' to any man, specially with you comin' along with 'em."

Dorry gazed into dark brown eyes that were filled with bittersweet emotion. She noticed how black hair fell over his forehead whenever he lowered his square chin. Luke James was tall and strong, over six feet of hard muscles. He was rugged and handsome, and he'd stolen her heart and wits within days of meeting him. She had trusted him from the start and hired him to help her battle her landgrabbing neighbor. But her missing husband stood between them, as well as a crime Luke swore he hadn't committed.

"Whatcha thinkin' about so long and deep?"

"How we met and why you came here. Are you

sure there's nothing we can do to clear your name? If John's dead, we could—"

"Don't go dreamin', Dorry. My neck still itches from that rope's tickle. One more minute and I'da been ready for a dirt blanket to cover me. That posse woulda stolen my last breath if that knot hadna been tied wrong. The minute it came loose and my boots hit the ground, I was in them woods and hidin'. Plenty of times they almost caught up with me to finish the job."

"But you didn't murder your partner for his share of that gold claim, and a posse has no right to play judge and jury. If you, we, went back—"

"We can't, Dorry. It was my gun they found, and two men said I did it. I don't know how the murderin' snake got my pistol or why those cowpokes lied, but the law believes I done it and wouldn't hear nothin' I said to the contrary. If I go back, I'm a dead man. If you went, you'd be in the fire with me. I run for seven months with bounty hunters eatin' my dust before I came here. Like I told you, I was headin' for Canada to hide out when I stumbled onto this place. It was lucky Henderson showed me that newspaper sayin' I would hang soon as I was caught, or I wouldn'a knowed the law was after me."

The redhead didn't want to remind Luke that he couldn't read ten months ago, so he didn't really know what that newspaper story had said. He had only R. T. Henderson's word about what was printed, and Henderson owned the claim next to Luke's. He might have had his own reasons for wanting Luke to run and desert his claim. "We can't settle any of our problems tonight," Dorry said, "so let's go back to your lessons. You're learning fast, Luke. By spring thaw, you'll be reading and writing as well as I do."

"You're a good teacher, Dorry; I'm obliged to you for helpin' me. My pa shoulda sent me to school when I was a kid. Nobody wants to be dumb."

"You were never dumb, Luke, just uneducated; and we're changing that fast. You've already learned your letters and numbers. Besides, we're helping each other. It's a good bargain since I don't have money for wages."

"Food, trust, and a bunk is plenty of pay for me."

Dorry didn't mention his many speaking errors; those instructions would come later, if they had a *later*. She pushed aside that dread for tonight. "Even if you have to share that bunk with a filly?" she teased.

Luke's brown gaze fused with her merry blue one. During his thirty years, he'd never enjoyed a woman's company more than Dorry's. He'd never loved a woman more than Dorry Sims, unless it was his mother. His gaze drifted over her ivory complexion and beautiful features; then he let it journey over her flaming curls. Her smile was sunshine bright. She was everything a man could desire, in and out of a bunk or a bedroll. If only he could lay claim to her, it would be worth losing his gold strike in Arizona.

Wind whistled around the small house and a wolf howled in the distance, but Dorry ignored both sounds. The ones that she noticed were the crackling of a cozy fire and their uneven breathing. "If you keep looking at me like that, cowboy, lessons will be forgotten."

Luke grinned, rubbed his shaved jawline, and said, "Winter's mighty long and cold in these parts, so we got plenty of time to school me good."

The desperado's husky tone and playful expression caused her to grow warm. "Are you asking me something, Mr. James?"

He reached his hand across the table and captured hers. His fingers stroked her flesh as he murmured, "I was just thinkin' it's time to turn in. I'll work twice as hard at sunup to finish this lesson."

Her love's peril and possible departure at any hour pressed down on Dorry like a heavy weight. What she needed were his comforting arms and kisses. "Bank the fire while I take the coffeepot off the stove and douse the lanterns. We have to shovel the stables tomorrow, so a good night's sleep will help. We'll leave our things here and finish after breakfast."

As Luke did his chore, Dorry kept glancing at his broad back and ebony hair. He was risking his life and freedom by staying with her this winter, and she was more than grateful. The first time he had made love to her on Christmas night had been glorious, like nothing she had experienced with John. Luke was gentle and caring, and her satisfaction was as important to him as his own; not so with John, who never considered her feelings in bed. They hadn't planned to break her marital vows, but love and passion had stolen their wits and control. Love, yes, they were in love, ill-fated love. Perhaps one day their fortune would change.

Luke James was honest and dependable. He was a proud man, but he was allowing her to teach him to read and write. When she'd discovered he couldn't do either, she had convinced him to let her teach him by pointing out how that knowledge could save his life one day and would prevent anyone from taking advantage of him. Every time they sat down to do his lessons, she made certain her words, looks, and actions never discouraged or embarrassed him. John would never have let a woman help him in this manner. Perhaps it was terrible of her, but she hadn't missed her husband since Luke James arrived and stole her heart. She didn't want John Sims's death, only that he never return.

Although John had courted her for over a year in Colorado, she had married him in a moment of weakness while suffering over her family's loss. With all possessions and kin gone and the area too dangerous for her to stay alone, John and his family had convinced her to wed him. Within a month, John had packed them up and moved them to North Dakota. Three months later, her husband had taken their money and left on a cattle-buying trip. When he didn't return by winter, she assumed bad weather or an injury had delayed him, though he hadn't sent any word. Spring, summer, fall, and another winter had arrived but not her husband, nor an explanatory message. Surely he was dead and she was a widow. But what if she started a new life and John returned? How long should she wait for him or for news?

Luke stood and stretched. He'd never been one to do so much sitting and lazing around, but it felt good with her. He had taken to this existence with ease and speed and didn't want to lose it or the woman he'd come to love. She was teaching him more than to read and write; she was teaching him joy and confidence and sharing. Except for his mining partner and a few friends in Arizona, he had been a loner. He hadn't thought about becoming a husband, a rancher, or a father. He hadn't thought about having others depend on him for happiness and survival. He had lived from day to day until Dorry entered his life and changed him.

What he had discovered here with her was all he wanted in life now, and it was too late to stake his claim. "Fire's safe. You ready for bed?"

Dorry walked to him and leaned against his firm body. His arms banded her and held her tight. Could something that felt so wonderful be wrong? She lifted her head and locked her gaze to his before their lips meshed. As always, her senses whirled and her body blazed. When their mouths parted for a minute, she whispered, "I'll love you forever, no matter what happens."

Luke lifted Dorry and carried her to the bed they now shared as if it were theirs. He laid her there and gazed at her for a moment before extinguishing the last lantern, undressing, and joining her. . . .

After breakfast, Luke helped her clear the table. While she washed the dishes and pans, he dried them and put them away, familiar now with everything in the house. He enjoyed doing any and every chore with her, and she enjoyed his assistance. He savored her smiles, laughter, and talk. He hated the thought of ever leaving her side, but the law might force him to take that dreaded action one day, any day. This lovely mountain setting was secluded and distant, but those bounty hunters had been persistent. He was lucky he had managed to elude them so many times, but how long would that luck hold out?

He gazed around the small cabin, seeing Dorry's touch wherever he looked. It was well built to keep in heat and to keep out the Dakota winter. It had been built near a grove of hardwoods that sheltered it from brisk winds and heavy snows. John's uncle had chosen a perfect site and carved out a nice place before old age and bad health forced him to sell and move back east with his kin. John had been lucky to get it at such a bargain price, and luckier still to get Dorry. Would he, Luke pondered, be just as lucky one day?

He looked out a window, where outside shutters had been opened earlier. Adjoining barns were nearby for doing chores even in the worst weather. A covered walk led from the house to the barns. Dorry had built it herself last summer, and had lined the exterior with delimbed logs to prevent snowdrifts from closing it off during blizzards. There was a well to supply water when the stream froze, as it often did for long periods. In every direction, the cabin was surrounded by forest, so firewood was no problem. The area John's uncle had farmed was fertile, and grass was plentiful and lush in season to feed the cattle John had intended to raise. The Missouri River was only a few miles southward, so transporting crops or stock to market wouldn't be difficult. Luke wished this were his wife, his home, his land, his future, if he had a future. He wouldn't if the Arizona law discovered his location. Yet he couldn't leave Dorry alone, not with Cleary so hot for her and her land.

"Ready to finish our lesson before it warms up enough to do outside chores?" she asked.

"Ready and willin', teacher," he replied with a grin as he joined her at the table, where books, a slate, and chalk awaited him.

Bundled up against the biting cold, Luke and Dorry went out to break up the ice in the water trough so the animals could drink: their horses, two milk cows, and three steers too young to market. He fetched a tool similar to a large hammer and returned to the corral. Dorry watched him slam it into the hard surface several times and send chips of ice flying in all directions. He labored until the frozen barrier yielded to his superior strength and efforts. He flipped large hunks to the white ground; then he and Dorry made several trips with buckets to fill it halfway with water from the nearby well.

"It'll freeze again tonight, so we'll have to repeat this every morning," she said. "You've made us enough room to add what the stock needs for today. At least we haven't gotten that blizzard yet, but it's been threatening to come for a week. I recognize the signs by now."

"Never been this far north. Didn't know about this kind of weather."

"After you've been here awhile, you'll learn the signs, too, and get used to the cold."

He stole a glance at her as he murmured, "I hope so."

Dorry gazed around at the lovely valley and cloudy sky as she checked the weather's clues and talked. Upon her arrival in the spring of seventy-six, the meadow had been adorned with colorful wildflowers and verdant grass. The valley, foothills, and mountains had been green with pine, spruce, birch, oak, elder, willow, and aspen. During her two autumns, she had watched the hardwood leaves turn to blazing shades, then fall to the ground, leaving the branches bare and ready for their cloaks of white. Now, only the green of pine, spruce, and a few others could be seen through blankets of snow and ice. It was cold this time of year and this far north, but the coldest and worst weather—in her opinion—would come in February. This year she longed for that to happen, so she would be shut in with Luke.

Dorry knew her cheeks were as red and her nose as numb as Luke's were. Both wore gloves and layers of garments, but the cold and wind still seemed to find little places to sneak in to attack one's body. Beneath those gloves, her hands felt stiff and frozen, and she was certain his were too. She shuddered and blinked as northern gusts from Canada dipped into the valley and tugged at her clothes. Whenever they talked or breathed, wispy smoke left their warm mouths and quickly vanished.

"I'll turn out the steers and horses to do some walkin' and stretchin'," Luke said. "Snow's not too deep for them to move around a mite. I'll leave the milk cows till you're done with them."

While he did so, Dorry gathered eggs, but left the chickens penned up because the cold weather and snow were too harsh and deep for their feet. She tossed feed on the coop floor and gave them fresh water. She fastened the gate, used cleansing snow to scrape clean her boots, and trudged back to the house. She placed the basket on the table and lifted a milk pail, not wanting to risk carrying too much while she traversed the frozen and often slippery ground.

Dorry went to the barn. Luke had climbed the ladder into the loft and opened a small door; he was tossing down hay for the stock to eat. She closed and bolted the door to keep out blasts of icy wind. She talked softly to the animals as she placed a short stool near a cow's back legs. She hated to remove her gloves, but she had to do so for a proper grip on the cow's teats. She kept speaking in a mellow tone as she worked as fast as her rapidly stiffening fingers allowed.

When she finished, she moved the pail out of

danger of a spill while she readied the second cow. After she finished with it, Dorry put away the stool, replaced her gloves, and let the two cows out to roam. When Luke joined her, she told him they could wait until tomorrow to shovel the animals' stalls.

Luke carried the bucket of milk to the house with great care, as Dorry followed. When they were safely back inside, with doors locked, the desperado set the milk pail beside the egg basket on the kitchen table.

Dorry removed her coat and scarf, then hung them on their peg. She pulled off her gloves and stuffed them into her coat pocket before changing from damp and dirty work boots into clean and warm house shoes. Luke did much the same, using John's boots and garments, since he'd left his campsite too quickly to collect his belongings. If not for the gold nuggets in his pocket, he would have been forced to steal food, a pistol, and clothes after his escape. He was glad he hadn't been compelled to break the law, even if he was a hunted man.

Dorry walked to the fire to warm and loosen her fingers. Luke joined her there. As he and the heat worked on her hands and body, she relaxed and savored their stolen moments together.

At least for a while, he would distract her from her constant worries. Later, there was milk to be churned into butter. Animals to be tended. Fires to be fed. Cleaning to be done. Warming water to wash clothes and then iron. She also had mending and sewing to do, which would take up more time. Time she wanted to spend with Luke.

He eyed her flaming locks, mussed from the scarf she'd worn while doing chores in the near freezing weather. As if she sensed what held his attention, her fingers tried to straighten her hair, but he grasped them between his larger ones to finish warming them. "You look beautiful. I could stare at you all day, woman."

She returned his smile and caressed his chilled cheek. "So could I."

"Stare at me all day?" he teased, eliciting merry laughter. He rested his cheek atop her head, his ebony hair a striking contrast to her fiery tresses. She had come into his life and changed it, had changed him, both for the better, for the best. *Almost*, his mind challenged. If only they could live where they would be blissfully happy and safe.

Dorry leaned back and looked into his face. She stroked his jawline, darkening with stubble since his shave last evening. He was so handsome and his gaze so entreating that it always stole her breath when she watched and touched him. How lucky she was to have met this special man; she would be luckier still if she were given a fresh start with him. As her fingers brushed over his parted lips, she said, "I wish a blizzard would lock you in with me forever and no one would trespass on our land."

Luke captured the mischievous fingers and pressed kisses to their tips. He wanted to lift her in his arms, carry her to the bed, and make love to her again. Even if he did, it wouldn't be enough. He desired her more often than food, water, or air. But he could not ignore the danger surrounding them; he should stay on guard during the daylight. "So do I."

Two days later, Luke said he was going to hunt before the threatened snowstorm arrived. While he was gone, Dorry busied herself with chores.

By late afternoon, she was concerned when Luke hadn't returned. She went to each window in turn and stared outside. Snow-burdened limbs displayed icicles of various sizes. White flakes were falling and getting thicker by the hour on the already covered ground. She heard wind whistle through the valley and saw it shake trees near the house. She heard wolves howling, but they usually remained in the forest. A growing haze allowed little light to brighten the surroundings, so visibility was limited. As dusk approached, the dimness increased.

Dorry felt anxious. She prayed an accident hadn't befallen her lover, because he'd be helpless against bad weather and wild animals. It was too late to saddle her horse and go search for him; darkness and snow soon would conceal his trail. He hadn't even mentioned which direction he was taking when he left this morning. All she could do was wait and worry and pray.

Then she heard the sounds of his horse's ragged breathing and trudging hooves. She rushed to the door and opened it. She almost slipped on the porch ice as she hurried to the corner to peer toward the barn. Luke was putting away his horse after laying several rabbits on the frozen earth. She shivered and her teeth chattered, but she refused to go inside until she saw him. She watched Luke retrieve the rabbits and join her.

"Get inside, woman; it's freezin' out here. Porch's slippery as grease; you could fall and break a leg." Luke grasped her arm and guided her into the house, then bolted the door. He released his snug hold to place the rabbits on the work counter. "These shutters should be closed by now. I'll go tend them. You get by that fire and get warmed."

Luke rounded the house as he closed exterior shutters to keep out the cold. Afterward, he bolted the door and the inside shutters before he removed his coat, gloves, and wool scarf. As he took off each one, Dorry hung them on sturdy wooden pegs and stuffed the gloves in a coat pocket. He tried to do the task himself, but she insisted on helping, making it impossible to conceal the clue that she soon discovered.

"What's this?" Dorry asked as her finger toyed with a hole in the sleeve of the jacket. She fused her alarmed gaze to his lowered one as she added, "Don't tell me a limb snagged it. I know a bullet hole when I see one. What happened out there? What took you so long to come home?"

"Some hunter probably mistook me for a buck."

"Did you fire a shot to let him know he was wrong?"

"Yep, right over his head and he took off like a scared rabbit."

"It was one of William Cleary's men, wasn't it? He was shooting at you on purpose. Cleary knows you're here, doesn't he?"

"Don't go gettin' worked up, Dorry. I'm safe. No wounds. We don't know he was aimin' for me and we don't know if Cleary's seen me around. I've hidden ever' time he came to see you, and my horse ain't in sight."

She sensed he was worried about the landgrabber getting bold. "You don't believe that for a minute and neither do I. You're in danger."

"I've been in danger for almost a year, woman. One more threat don't mean much to me. I won't let Cleary harm us. I can shoot better 'n all his men put in a stack. So can you. 'Sides, he can't do nothin' in this storm."

"Even so, we'd better stay alert. Supper's ready, and I'm sure you are, too. Let's get you warm and fed, then talk. I'll mend your jacket later. Hot coffee sound tempting while you unstiffen those muscles?"

"Sure does. Maybe we can do some readin'," he suggested with hopes it would distract her from this new trouble. "I'll keep us safe."

Dorry knew he would try, but his prowess and confidence might not be enough against a determined man like William Cleary. Bill hadn't wanted or needed to harm her, not yet. But it was different for her lover and protector. Whatever it took, she had to keep Luke James safe and alive.

Two weeks later, Luke insisted on going hunting again. "We need fresh meat, woman. We can't eat salted-and-dried meat any longer. We can't live off of eggs and biscuits and gravy. And we can't butcher them steers or cook them hens; you'll need 'em later. We can't be prisoners here, Dorry. Cleary ain't tried nothin', so maybe that shootin' was an accident."

"And maybe he's just letting us get confident before he strikes again. I don't trust him, Luke. Please don't go. We can eat anything until it's safe."

"When will it be safe to hunt, Dorry? Winter's the hardest time to hunt if your prey is a man. Spring thaw's gonna help him more 'n us. A big buck or mule deer would give us plenty of meat for a while."

"I should go with you. Cleary's men won't—"

"Who'll guard your home? If it's gone, you'd hafta change your mind about leavin' or marryin' him; ever thought of it that way?"

Dorry was shocked and panicked. "He wouldn't dare burn me out!"

"Wouldn't he to get what he wants? Stay here. Stay armed."

"I can't argue with your words, Luke. Be extra careful."

"I will. Dorry . . ."

She noted the expression in his brown eyes and the way he ruffled his sable hair. "What is it?"

"Leave if you hafta, but don't marry that snake for any reason."

"I promise I won't. Maybe I should sell to him and leave with you."

"I wish you could. But it ain't safe, and I can't make you hunted like me. Long as that reward's on my head, bounty hunters'll be lookin' for me. I can't let you catch a stray bullet with my name on it. Maybe in a few years I can return from Canada and we can . . . if John don't come back."

"Perhaps I should go to Bismarck and ask the authorities to get me facts. I could if you'd stay with the animals; then we'd know for sure."

"I can't make that promise. If the law or them flesh hunters came, I'd hafta take off. We'll talk later; light's awastin'. See you by dark."

After midday, Dorry Sims was stunned to see William Cleary riding up to her house. He was alone. He was grinning and whistling and gazing about the land he craved. She wondered if he knew Luke was gone. She donned her coat, gloves, and scarf to meet him outside, since she didn't want to invite him—neighbor or not—into her home. Besides, she fretted, clues to Luke's presence were lying around and might be noticed.

The gray-haired man dismounted and joined Dorry at the steps. His piercing slate eyes made a slow journey over her body and settled on her face. "Good morning, Miss Dorry. I wanted to see if there was anything you needed or wanted before I send my men downriver for supplies."

She wondered why he persisted in addressing her as "miss" when she was a married woman. To hurry his visit and to avoid more problems, she didn't correct him this time. "Good morning, Mr. Cleary. That's very kind of you, but I have all I need."

"Surely those supplies I brought you at Christmas have run low by now. It's no bother and I won't charge you. John can settle up with me when he returns. Have you heard from him yet?"

Dorry refused to break their locked gazes and expose any weakness or fear before this man. "No."

"Perhaps we'll have a reply to my query about him by spring thaw."

"I hope so. I'm sure something important is delaying him."

The fifty-year-old rancher lazed against a porch post. "I fear it's more than difficult business or a minor accident, Miss Dorry, to keep him away this long. If such were true, he would have sent word to halt your worries. I wish you would come to my ranch and remain there until he or word arrives. The boys will guard your place and tend your animals."

"That's a kind offer, sir, but I—"

"If your husband has met his fate, my dear lady, my offer to purchase your property still stands. However, my offer of marriage is the one I hope you'll accept. I've been a widower much too long. I can take care of you and provide for all your needs if you'll marry me."

Dorry frowned at him. "It isn't proper to propose to a married woman, sir. I've—"

"It's less proper for one to be living here with a stranger, Miss Dorry. I'm sure John would be upset to learn that fact. Surely you didn't hire a drifter; that's unwise and dangerous."

"How do you know I have a hired man?"

"Our properties aren't that far apart, my dear lady. I and the boys have seen him around doing chores and hunting."

"What were any of you doing on my land?"

"Does that mean strangers are welcome but neighbors are not?"

"Of course not, but it sounds more like spying to me."

"Concern for your safety and comfort, Dorry dear, nothing more. I had hoped he wouldn't stay long but I can see he has. My advice is to tell him it's time to move on."

"I appreciate your . . . concern but I'm perfectly safe."

"I hope you remain so. If anything frightens you, please come to me. My boys will encourage him to move on if he gives you trouble. Now, are you certain, with two mouths to feed, you need no supplies?"

"Nothing, sir, but thank you."

"I'll check on you again in a few weeks. Good-bye, Dorry. Remember, I'm close by if you need or want anything."

"Thank you again, sir, but it isn't necessary."

"Please, dear lady, don't call me sir. Bill, please."

"Good-bye, Bill," she complied to be rid of him. She didn't like the way his ravenous gaze feasted on her from head to foot. She didn't like his slick talk. She didn't like or trust him.

"Until I see you again." William Cleary mounted, smiled, nodded his head, and left, again whistling a merry tune.

Dorry watched his departure until he was out of sight. He knew from spying that Luke was there! He had known for a long time! Perhaps his visit was an alibi for—Her fair complexion paled even more as she worried that Cleary's men might be ambushing her lover even now. She rushed inside and changed into better clothing for her task: breeches, wool shirt, heavy boots, wool socks, longjohns, her thickest coat, wool scarf and hat, and leather riding gloves.

Using caution on the slippery ground, Dorry hurried to the corral to put away the stock. Ice crunched under her boots and she glanced at the familiar haze over the landscape, which told her the heavens were making fresh snow. In response to her urgent proddings, the three steers ambled into a large stall they shared. The two milk cows were in separate ones. She made certain they had water and hay, in case the weather prevented her from coming to tend them later. She knew the chickens were fine so it wasn't necessary to check on them. After saddling her horse, she walked him from the barn and bolted it against cold and predators. She mounted, checked her weapons, and headed out to search for Luke James.

The sun was out today, so the ice and snow were melting a little, only to freeze again in the bitter cold. When she exhaled, her breath came forth in smoke puffs. She heard the suction her mare's hooves made with each step. She saw the trail Luke had taken, because his tracks were distinct holes in the crusty snow. She prayed once more for his safety.

Time passed and she didn't catch up with Luke; nor did she find him dead. She shivered and her teeth chattered. The sun had vanished behind ominous clouds. The temperature was dropping rapidly. She had to get home and out of this frigid air before darkness came. If Luke failed to return tonight, she decided, she'd search again at dawn.

The ground was freezing again and she heard the crunch of the snow beneath her mount's hooves. The wind was frigid and numbing. It took her longer to return by backtracking than she had imagined, but she finally made it. She dismounted, unsaddled her horse, and put away her gear. Before going inside, she checked on her animals. Her footsteps and labored breathing were loud in the almost eerie silence of the sheltered valley. She sighed with relief when she was inside, with the doors and shutters locked. She leaned against the wall, closed her eyes, and was thankful to be home safe. She only wished Luke were here with her.

Dorry reminded herself that the weather was unpredictable this month and travel over snow-covered landscape was hazardous and slow. She also reminded herself how skilled and smart Luke was. Still, she fretted. What if she'd spent her last night in his arms? In his life? What if Cleary's men or bounty hunters had killed him? What if she never saw him again? No, she must not think that awful way! Her ancestor had not given up in the face of despair; the book her mother had passed on to her said so. Her ancestor had found a way to surmount impossible odds, so she must do the same. Nothing and no one would be allowed to destroy her; she must remain strong, proud, hopeful, and cunning.

It wasn't long before Dorry heard noises. She rushed to the door, pressed her ear to it, and strained to listen. She dared not open it and allow possible peril to enter. She couldn't unlatch shutters and peer out because the exterior ones were fastened. Time passed as she wondered who or what was out there. She squealed and jumped when somebody knocked on the door.

"It's me, Dorry!"

Dorry unbolted the door and opened it. She flung herself against him and hugged him. "I was so scared and worried," she murmured.

Luke embraced her for a minute before he backed them inside, closed the door with his foot, and replied in a hoarse voice, "I'm fine, woman. I shot a nice buck and hung him out of any wolf's or bear's reach. He'll freeze fast and stay fresh. Sorry it took so long. I had to discourage some wolves from stealin' him while I was skinnin' and guttin' him."

"Was there any trouble?" she asked as she helped him out of his jacket and hung it on the peg.

He grinned and teased, "I just told you what happened."

"I meant, with Cleary's men. He came by today," she began and related the incident, her panic, and her actions.

Luke removed his gloves, hat, and scarf. "I told you to stay put, woman. That was dangerous. Game seems low for some crazy reason, and those wolves and bears are gettin' hungry and bold. Might be best if we stay close to the house and keep the critters penned up awhile. In a few weeks, game should return."

Dorry followed him to the chair before the fire, where he sat down to doff his wet boots. "Do you think they'll try to break into the barns?"

"Might try, but those barns are sturdy. Your animals are safe. But I'll check for any weak spots tomorrow. Repair any I find."

Dorry set the boots on the hearth to dry and faced him. "What are we going to do about Cleary?"

"Nothing we can do yet. That tells me why I felt eyes on me all day. Figured it was those wolves, but I guess it was more like the two-legged kind. They didn't try nothin'. See, no new holes."

"Don't joke about something serious, Luke. He tried to appear calm and polite, but I could sense evil coming from him. I don't want you to leave, but if you must go to stay safe, please do."

The desperado pulled her into his lap. "You tired of me already?"

Dorry cuddled against his hard chest and stroked his icy cheek. "You know I'm not and never will be. I love you and need you. I—"

"No more sad talk, woman." His lips roamed her face, a soft terrain he had learned well since their meeting in early October of last year. His fingers wandered into her red tresses and warmed themselves. She was a perfect fit in his arms and life. He loved her and wanted her with all of his being. It pained him to know how short time was for them. When April came, he had to leave, leave so she'd be safe from the men pursuing him. Yet, how could he leave her in peril? If only he could prove his innocence . . .

Dorry unbuttoned his shirt and pressed kisses to his chest. She wound sable hairs around her fingers and made tiny curls. She peeled the garment off his broad shoulders with his assistance. She spread kisses on the bronze surface, tanned deep from years of working shirtless beneath countless desert suns, so dark that even months of winter hadn't faded it much. She trailed her fingers over that firm territory and reveled in exploration. He was sleek and hard and smooth. Touching him aroused her to a desire hotter than the flames in the fireplace. She removed her dress and tossed it on the floor; numerous nights in his arms had erased her modesty just as she erased the slate after their writing lessons.

Accepting the heady inducement, Luke rose with her in his arms and walked to the bed. There, he removed her chemise and undergarments, then discarded the rest of his clothes. He gazed into her expressive blue eyes and said, "I love you, Dorry Sims, and I need you, too." He covered their naked bodies with the quilt she had made and covered her parted lips with his. Supper could wait; this was the nourishment he needed . . .

March tenth came, and so did William Cleary. Luke was out hunting again. A glorious month had passed since her neighbor had shown his wrinkled face at her home—weeks of relaxing, sharing passion, reading and writing lessons, and peace. Dorry hated for their reprieve to end as she went to see what the gray-haired man wanted.

"Lovely day, Miss Dorry. Spring will be here soon. You're looking as lovely and sunny as always."

"I still don't need any supplies, Mr. Cleary, but thanks for coming—"

"That isn't why I came, Dorry dear. The man I

hired to search for John brought me news of him yesterday."

Dorry trembled. "John's alive? Your man found him?"

"Found him, yes. Alive, I'm afraid not."

Dorry knew Bill was watching her reaction closely. She tried to retain an unreadable expression. "How? Where? Are you certain it's John?"

"I hate to be the bearer of sad news, but I thought it best if it came from a good friend. It appears poor John was robbed and slain by bandits on the trail to Wyoming. Evidence was found of his . . . unfortunate demise. I believe these possessions are his. Am I correct?"

Dorry accepted the bundle and sat on the porch to untie it, as if her shaky legs would not have supported her weight much longer. She found a belt buckle with John's initials, one she recognized. There was a torn and faded letter addressed to her from John, which she would try to read later. There was a handkerchief from his mother with his initials on it, which she didn't recall him taking along. "They're John's. Is this all your man found?"

"Of course his horse, saddle, money, and other belongings were stolen by those wicked culprits. My detective had his remains buried."

"That was very kind of him and of you." The evidence was undeniable: John Sims was dead. She was a free woman. Yet the proof appeared to be in better condition than it should if exposed to weather for twenty months. It was also convenient and suspicious, Dorry thought, that all three items had John's name or initials on them. "I'll send John's family the bad news. I appreciate you going to so much trouble and expense to verify this for me."

"As you can see, you are a widow now. I think it would be wise if you accepted my proposal and we married as soon as possible."

Dorry's head jerked up and she gaped at him. "Marry? I can't marry you, Mr. Cleary."

"Why not?"

"I don't love you."

"In time, I'm sure your feelings for me will change. It's the perfect and only solution to both of our needs. You can't manage this place by yourself. You have no money for support, and being alone is dangerous."

"I'm not alone; I have a hired man. I'm sure he can help me earn my living by farming as John's uncle did." Dorry witnessed the narrowing of Cleary's gaze. He was standing stiff and straight, and his jawline was taut. His fake smile had vanished.

"Perhaps I should give you two weeks to grieve and reconsider my purchase offer and proposal of marriage. One or the other will be in your best interest, my dear. Accidents do happen, Dorry. Look what happened to poor John when least expected. I would hate for you to be left alone if anything similar happened to your employee. A lady like you certainly should not continue to live with a common drifter; that isn't wise or safe. I'm sure you'll make the right decision during the next two weeks."

Dorry grasped the meaning behind his frigid words: Luke would die if she didn't agree to his proposal. She thought it smart to pretend she didn't understand. "I'll think about all you've said, sir. Right now, if you don't mind, I'd like to be alone to mourn my lost husband. Good-bye."

Dorry stood and entered the house. She locked the door and leaned against it. She heard Cleary depart without further trouble, no doubt licking his thin lips in anticipated victory. She walked to the table, sat down, and placed the bundle on it. She was sorry John Sims was dead, murdered. In his own way, he had tried to be a good husband.

It wasn't right for William Cleary to get away with John's murder or to take her land. Yet what could she do? She couldn't summon the authorities and endanger Luke's life, and she had no evidence to prove Cleary was a criminal. How could justice prevail for John, Luke, and herself?

Dorry took the biscuits from the oven and set them on the table. "You can come eat, Luke," she said as she poured their coffee.

Luke came in and eyed the deer she had sprinkled with spices and roasted for hours; its aroma caused his mouth to water. Fragrant coffee gave off steam to say it was too hot to drink. Green beans and corn from canning jars did the same, and the catshead biscuits released wispy white warnings to grasp them with caution.

"I'll be glad to get my garden planted soon," Dorry said. "I'm more than ready for fresh vegetables. I noticed some wildflowers coming up this morning."

"We haven't finished our talk, Dorry. Don't saddle another horse before this one's been ridden."

"There's nothing more to discuss. We've gone over this problem every day and night for two weeks since that snake hissed his warning. I'm going to offer him a compromise tomorrow; my deadline is up at sunset."

"He'll never accept your terms."

"I'll give him no choice. Either he buys me out but lets me continue to live here or I'll fight him to the death. This is my home."

"He's dangerous and cunning, woman. Don't stay here. Sell to him, Dorry, and move into Cross Corners to wait for me. I'll return in a few years."

"The only way I'll sell out is to leave with you. We could use the money to begin a new life in Canada. I'm free, Luke. John is dead for certain."

"But I'm not free, Dorry. I can't put your life in danger. Wait for me."

"I will, but I'm waiting here."

"If Cleary refuses your terms, will you do as I ask? Please."

"Yes, I'll yield that far, for you, for us." *For our baby. I can't tell you about our child or you won't leave and be safe from the Arizona law, those bounty hunters, and that wicked neighbor of mine. But I have to stay here where we belong: this land is ours. I'll kill Cleary before he steals it.*

"You will?"

Dorry fibbed, "Yes. By tomorrow night, we'll have our answer."

As Luke watched her, Dorry headed her mare toward Cleary's ranch. It wasn't too far and she was skilled with weapons, so she'd be safe. The only difficulty had been in persuading Luke to let her go alone.

Dorry eyed the scenery during her journey. It was a wild and rugged land, but beautiful and challenging. Birds sang to announce the coming of spring soon. Squirrels and rabbits scampered about in search of food. Leaves were returning to bare hardwood limbs. Daring wildflowers were showing their stems and a few, their colorful faces. The world around her was being reborn; various colors mingled with splotches of green from pines that towered above the other trees. The sun beamed and the sky was clear. There was still a slight chill in the air, but her jacket warded it off. She had come to love it here and could not bring herself to allow a criminal to take anything more from her. She rode forward, determined to prevail.

"You heard me right, Luke. William Cleary is dead, killed by a grizzly two days ago. There is justice, if not by the law's hand, then by God's. He is no longer a threat to me; I'm free of his wicked greed. After he died, his men emptied his office and house of money, took the supplies, and left. Only the housekeeper is there, and she's planning to leave shortly. She says there's nothing to stop me from claiming the place myself if I want it. Cleary has no kin to challenge me. When you get back, we'll have all the land we need to start our ranch. I'll be waiting for your return, my love."

"I wish I could stay, Dorry, but it's more important than ever for me to get going."

She noticed he put a "g" on "going" and smiled at his progress. Her lessons had worked; he would be better able to take care of himself now that he could read and write. "I'm so proud of you, Luke James; you've learned so much here. You can send me letters from Canada and use a fake name. I can write back and tell you all the news. Are you sure there isn't something we can do to prove your innocence? We are having a run of good luck lately."

The desperado ruffled his black hair and smiled. "That's just what I'm going to do. I won't be in Canada. I'm going back to Arizona to clear my name. Read this for yourself." Luke fetched the ragged clipping he had carried for months. "Remember that article Henderson read to me, the one that said I'd be hanged if I was caught? I saved it all this while, but today was the first time I could actually read it for myself."

Dorry unfolded the paper and read it. She looked at Luke in confusion. "I don't understand. What does this article have to do with your trouble? It doesn't even mention you or the murder."

"I know. If only I'd showed it to you months ago, I would have realized that a lot sooner." His brown gaze narrowed as anger flooded him anew. "Henderson lied. He tricked me."

"But what about that posse and those bounty hunters who chased you?" Dorry asked.

"I'm betting they were men hired by him to get rid of me so he could take over my gold strike."

"Since this story isn't about you as Henderson claimed, maybe you're not wanted by the Arizona law. Or maybe you can prove he framed you."

"That's what I'm hoping. Henderson and those fake lawmen are the ones who said there were two witnesses against me. Since I didn't murder my partner, either there are no alleged witnesses or they're lying, maybe hired by Henderson. I'm going downriver to Bismarck and telegraph the Arizona authorities. That's the only way we'll ever know the truth. With Cleary gone, you'll be safe here alone."

"Do it, Luke. It means so much to us. If it was just a trick, you don't have to leave, ever."

"If it was just a trick, I can get back my claim. It's a rich one, Dorry."

"If you aren't being hunted by the law, do you want to return to Arizona?"

"I don't know; never thought I could. We can think on that later."

* * *

Dorry stood on the riverbank and watched the flatboat Luke had waved down until it was out of sight. For two days, they had talked and loved and done chores together. They had written a telegram her lover was going to send to check out his fate. They had written a second one to send if the reply revealed that Henderson had lied. She didn't know how long it would require for a response to come, and Luke was going to wait for it. If by some horrible twist of fate he was convincingly framed, he'd have to leave for Canada immediately after seeing her, since the telegram would expose his general location and would coax lawmen or bounty hunters to head this way.

While he was gone, Dorry decided, she would keep herself busy and distracted with spring tasks. She didn't know what she would do or say if an innocent Luke wanted to return to Arizona instead of remaining in North Dakota. Yes, she did know, because there was a child growing inside of her to consider. That was news she would reveal upon his return.

On April tenth at dusk, the raven-haired man rode into sight as Dorry finished evening chores. She hurried to the barn and awaited him there, her gaze glued to him. Her joyful heart sang, *He's home safe*! She laughed as he bent over and lifted her onto the saddle with him, as if he could get to her faster that way than if he dismounted first.

Luke hugged her and responded to the heady kiss she placed on his lips. All else was forgotten as he fed his starving senses. After many kisses and embraces, his adoring gaze examined her. "You look good enough to eat for supper. Lordy, I've missed you. Been any trouble while I was gone?"

She stared into his chocolate-colored eyes and read the truth of his words. "None, if loneliness and worry don't count as problems."

Luke shared laughter and exchanged smiles with her. "I love you, Dorry Sims. I don't know what woulda become of me if I hadna met you."

"The same is true for me, Luke James. I love you and missed you. Tell me the news before I burst with curiosity. What happened?"

"Henderson's greed and evil have done him in. He did near the same thing to another man, after he thought he was rid of me; he used those men with stolen badges to try to scare him off. His bite was too big that time, 'cause the man's brother is a real lawman who didn't take to having his brother accused of murder or being framed. Henderson was tricked, caught, and hanged. Law never even knew about my partner being murdered and them saying I done it. Fact is, Dorry Sims, there aren't any charges against me, and that claim's still mine. I can return and work her or I can sell her."

"It's over? You're free? You don't have to run or hide anymore?" She watched her lover nod his head after each question.

"From where I'm sitting, we're both free," Luke said with a wink.

"What does that mean?"

"Means you can marry me if you're willing. I'm doing the asking."

"Where would you want to live, here or in Arizona?"

Luke played with a red curl. "Does that change your answer?"

"No, my answer is yes. I love you and want to marry you and I'll live wherever you choose."

"I think this is the best place of the two. We'll be wanting young'uns, and a mining camp ain't no place to raise them. You changed my whole life, Dorry. You're like some magic wind that blew away my troubles. Now that you've taught me to read 'n write, nobody can trick me again. Looks like our future's as bright and pretty as that smile of yours."

She hugged him and warmed from head to foot. For now, she wanted the attention to remain on just the two of them. Later tonight or tomorrow, she would share news about their baby, news he was ready to hear. "Why don't we go inside and have a better reunion before supper?"

"Suits me more than fine, woman."

After his horse was tended and they were walking to the house, Luke murmured in awe, "Never thought I was running to a wife, kids, and home of my own instead of away from trouble and death. Fate gave me a nice but scary shove. I'm a mighty lucky man, Dorry, mighty lucky."

"So am I, just as my ancestors were."

"Maybe I should read that book of yours and learn all your secrets."

"You will, my husband to be. But for now, reading can wait."

Luke James agreed, and soon they were making passionate love. . . .

ANNABELLE'S LEGACY

DIANA PALMER

Annabelle's Legacy

The high rose hedge next door was the first thing Annabelle noticed when she followed the hefty moving men her parents had hired into the huge Victorian mansion on Main Street. El Paso was very far away from her beloved St. Louis, of the green fields and wide rivers. She missed the greenery already, because West Texas was dry and brown and she had been told that the rivers never ran the year around. Instead of the graceful homes and manicured lawns she was accustomed to, she found mesquite with its prickly thorns, and prickly pear cactus, which was even worse.

"Annabelle, don't dawdle, dear," her mother called from the window of the front room. "Help me decide where to put the bookcases."

Annabelle lifted her long skirts and went up the few remaining steps, careful not to show anything but her shoes. The moving men weren't looking, but one must be vigilant, she thought.

Her mother was standing in the middle of the

room, fanning herself with a colorful cardboard fan that had *The Last Supper* painted on one side and a funeral home advertisement on the other. "Dear, dear, how hot it is here in the summer!" she moaned. "Annabelle, we shall fry."

"Perhaps not," her daughter said with a smile. Like herself, her mother was small and blond with pale green eyes. All the Monroe women looked like that, her father had once remarked of her mother and her aunts. She took after that side of the family, rather than her father's, who were Colemans. In almost direct contrast, the Coleman men were tall and dark. Her father's hair was still dark brown, although he was approaching his forty-fifth year. His sideburns and beard and mustache had streaks of silver, which gave him a regal dignity. "It will be a new experience," she added. "We must try to be happy here, for Papa's sake."

Her mother sighed. "Yes, I know. Poor Edwin, he did not wish to take this appointment, but it was difficult for him to refuse. He has only just been given this position with the Texas and Pacific Railway, and of course he must be here to oversee his duties. I think there will be much socializing. That should make our stay here bearable, at least."

Annabelle grimaced. She hated social gatherings. She much preferred her beloved books to the sort of people her parents kept company with.

Absently she glanced toward the house next door. It was older than this nice one they were to live in, rather unique in its design. It was made of rock and it had a neat, small yard with rosebushes everywhere. She was immediately captivated by it, and she wondered who lived there.

"Do you know anything of the house next door?" Annabelle asked one of the movers.

"Yes, ma'am," he said, wiping sweat from his brow with a brawny arm. "John Torrance lives there. Wouldn't bother him if I was you. He hates people. Cussed a man out just this week, in fact, for asking him to write some answers down for a census. Threw him off the place, he did. He's one tough customer, miss."

"Is he an elderly man, then?"

The mover chuckled. "Nope. But he's got a temper that acts like it took years to cultivate."

"Does he have a family? Is he married?"

The mover shook his head and started to lift the heavy chair again. "Not likely that a woman would go near him. He shocks folks, when they first see him—" A loud voice inquired as to his whereabouts. "I'm coming, Ned!" He excused himself and went on down the hall.

Annabelle was intrigued by their mysterious neighbor. She and her father and mother and two young sisters, Rose and Jane, settled in, and she found time to sit and read near a gap in the rose hedge in the garden the yardman cared for so lovingly, on a bench under a big mesquite tree with long, feathery green fronds.

She had a special book, an heirloom that her mother treasured, and which she had given to Annabelle when she was just eighteen. Her mother had told her that there were several copies of the book. Annabelle had once seen the original manuscript written by a monk in the Middle Ages in Europe, in Latin, of course. It had been donated almost a century ago to the Library of Congress. At that time Annabelle's great-great-grandmother had given a copy of the book to each of her three daughters. One of those copies had been passed down to her through her own grandmother, Charity Monroe.

Annabelle had first seen the original during a memorable visit to the nation's capital. Her loving hands had trembled as they traced the colorful Latin script. The delicate pages were illuminated, and it was just as well that it was in Latin, for the English of the Middle Ages when it had been written would have been very nearly unreadable in 1900. Its language would have been more akin to the style of *Beowulf* than to the language of Shakespeare. The Latin had not proved difficult, as almost every university student in America studied it, along with Greek. Annabelle had been tutored in Latin, and it was a thrill beyond words to actually read something so old, so priceless, to hold the original book, with its illuminated capital letters: broadswords for the T's and kite-shaped shields for the V's and fiery dragons for the S's.

Her own copy of the book resided in a handmade wooden chest, inlaid with gold. She loved to sit and read it while she yearned to find the wondrous love that the book spoke of. Her fingers would trace the leather binding and her eyes would caress the pages. There were inscriptions in it that ran through generations of women, many in almost incomprehensible Old English, all undoubtedly in quest of the magical feeling called love. One inscription written in the time of Elizabeth I—by one of her ladies!—read, ". . . with honour comes glorie." It was that inscription which had fired Annabelle's imagination and made her thirst for so noble a love that it inspired a great work of literature. And she was not the only one whom it inspired. Her sisters, Rose and Jane, who were still in grammar school, loved to curl up in the porch swing or the bench in the backyard, one on each side of her, to listen as she read from the special book.

It wasn't long after their arrival that she became aware of noises in the brush near where she sat each afternoon reading to the girls, after the noon meal. At first it was distant. Then, slowly, day by day, the noise came closer.

One day, when she sent the girls back inside, she lifted the skirts of her lacy white dress and followed the noise, moving quickly around the crepe myrtle bushes before her unknown audience could get away.

The man she confronted caused her heart to still in her breast. He was tall, very dark, with narrowed eyes the color of peridots. His hair was black as coal dust. He was wearing respectable clothing, a good cotton shirt and tie with cord trousers and a lightweight jacket. But it was his face that would haunt her. She winced when she first saw it, and the man flinched.

"I beg your pardon," he said gruffly. "I was trimming my roses. I did not mean to intrude."

She saw, then, the shears in his left hand. She wondered if her heartbeat, so wild and fluttery, would cause her to faint. The whalebone corset was restricting her breath in the heat and she could feel her lungs straining for air.

"Will you faint, then?" he demanded with a sarcastic smile. "Plenty before you have taken that avenue of escape."

She straightened, pale but resolved. "You must be Mr. Torrance," she said, extending a small hand. "I am Annabelle Coleman. I have just moved here with my mother and father and two young sisters. My father is an executive with the Texas and Pacific Railway."

He ignored her extended hand. The thick white scars down his cheek seemed to grow as his face tautened. He wore no beard to hide them, nor did he look embarrassed or ashamed. But he said nothing.

"What happened to your face, Mr. Torrance?" she asked gently, with concern, not pity.

He blinked. It was an approach that had never been made toward him before. He hesitated.

"If the question offends, I will withdraw it," she added in a conciliatory tone.

"It does not offend. Not when you ask," he said quietly. "I was in Mexico helping to hunt down insurrectionists. Yaquis caught me and another recruit out on the desert."

"Yaquis?" She waited, because the word was unfamiliar.

"You might call them Indians. They were desperate men. They thought I was working for the *Federales*, so they gave me a going-over. The man with me died."

It was a blunt remark, and it presented a vivid picture of what he must have endured.

"This is only what shows," he added, touching the scarred cheek. He laughed coldly.

She bit her lower lip. "It was a knife, was it not?" she said. "It must have hurt terribly. I am sorry, Mr. Torrance, if I have brought back unpleasant memories for you with my silly questions."

He waved the inference away with a big, tanned hand. His eyes narrowed as they searched hers. "You aren't afraid of me."

She smiled. "Should I be? You grow the most magnificent roses, Mr. Torrance. I have admired them, and your house, ever since we moved here."

The cold eyes twinkled. "You like flowers, Miss . . . ?"

"Coleman. And, yes, I like them very much."

He studied her, from the topknot of blond hair that ballooned into a halo around her oval face to her soft green eyes, so much darker than his own. The high lace collar at her neck fluttered, as if her pulse was racing. The lace at her breast was rising and falling quickly, too, but he had enough gentlemanly instincts not to lower his eyes indiscreetly.

"You are very young, Miss Coleman," he remarked finally.

"Twenty, sir," she replied. "Hardly so young."

"When you are thirty-six, you will not think so."

"At that time, I shall be in my prime," she answered pertly, and smiled.

He lifted the shears. "I must get back to my work."

"Have you lived here long?"

"Longer than I ever meant to," he said. "My brother was an invalid. I came to live with him after . . ." He paused. "He died a few months later and left me the house. I stayed."

"Are you a native Texan?"

He nodded. "But you, I think, are not."

"We are from St. Louis."

"Northerners."

"You need not make us sound like a curse," she returned with mock hauteur. Her green eyes twinkled. "We are good people and neither nosy nor noisy. You will find that we make excellent neighbors, except that we are all inclined to talk too much."

He laughed. The sound shocked his own ears. It

had been such a long time since anyone had made him want to laugh.

"There, you look much less ferocious when you are not scowling at people."

He shook his head. "You are too familiar, Miss Coleman. Your parents would not approve. I am no fitting companion for a child of your years."

"I shall say who is a fitting companion," she returned, but she glanced back at the house for a flutter of window curtains, just the same. "If you are trimming your roses at the same hour tomorrow, you might let me introduce you to my sisters."

He averted his gaze. "And shock them, too?"

"It was a momentary shock," she replied. "You expect people to be horrified by you, but once you speak, one forgets that you are scarred."

"By God!" he snapped, irritated.

"Sir!" she exclaimed, shocked that a gentleman would use such language in front of a lady. Outbursts of that sort in a lady's presence, like cursing, were against every convention known to society.

He let out an angry breath. "Very well, excuse me. I must go."

"Then good day, Mr. Torrance."

He inclined his head and turned to walk away. She noticed then that he limped, and her face contorted. The scars on his face were the only ones that showed. She could have wept for him, but she sensed that such a man would abhor pity. So her features were carefully schooled when he suddenly looked back, as she expected him to. He saw no trace of pity in her steady gaze. He laughed mirthlessly at his mistaken certainty that there would be, and continued painfully on his way.

Annabelle wandered back into the house, wondering how long it had been since his terrible experience and if he would ever be able to walk naturally again. The scars on his face were white and thick, which must denote age. New wounds, such as the cut on her hand from a mishandled knife, were red and raw-looking. She had one old scar, which was white and thick like his. But hers was from a fall at the school she had attended in St. Louis. His were from a much more terrifying source.

She walked into the parlor, and her parents looked up expectantly.

"The girls said that you spoke to that recluse next door," her father said solemnly. "This is not proper behavior, to be seen alone with a man of his sort."

"His sort?" she asked innocently.

"He is a rogue," her father related. "I have heard of Mr. Torrance in the town. He was one of that vicious breed of Texas Rangers. They say that he has killed men, my dear."

"If he was a lawman, that is not surprising. Grandpa Monroe was a lawman, too," she reminded him, hiding her momentary shock. She had not thought of Mr. Torrance as a killer of men, and she did not like to. She smiled at her father. "He is a good man. I feel it. He adores roses. He grows them."

He shifted. "Hardly an occupation for a rowdy border outlaw," he muttered.

"He is not an outlaw."

"You must not contradict your father," her mother said firmly.

"If he were correct, I would not," Annabelle said, and grinned at her father.

"I am a poor father," he muttered. "I spoil you, Annabelle."

"You both do," she agreed. "He is a bitter, hurt

man," she added. "A good Christian does not turn away from those who are lost sheep," she reminded them.

Her father muttered something about some sheep faring better as mutton, but he didn't insist that she stop speaking to their neighbor. He knew that it would do no good. Annabelle was as stubborn as he was. And trying to save the lost souls of society was, as his daughter said, every good Christian's duty.

"Do take care not to be alone with him, Annabelle," her mother cautioned. "One does not expect gentlemanly conduct of such a man. I would not have your reputation endangered for all the world."

"Nor would I, Mama," she assured her parent.

"Is he an outlaw, Anna?" Rose asked excitedly.

"Perhaps he's a robber, like that Cassidy man," Jane seconded.

"He was a peace officer," she countered. "A Texas Ranger."

"Oh! Oh!" Rose exclaimed. "How very exciting! Does he have a gun? Do you think he might show it to us?"

"Rose, shame on you!" her mother exclaimed. "You are reading far too many dime novels. Those are not true. Surely you know that it is only fiction!"

"Where there is smoke, there is often fire," Annabelle replied. She grinned at her mother. "Remember Grandpa's stories about desperadoes and lawmen with their guns blazing, shooting it out in a hail of smoking gunfire?"

Her mother flushed. "For shame, Annabelle! I always believed he made most of those stories up."

But Annabelle wasn't fooled. She knew that her

mother had loved her papa's tales of the Wild West as much as her children did. Annabelle went out to the backyard with her sisters and her precious book, hoping that her desperado would be there. The violence of his former job she pushed to the back of her mind.

Every day she read aloud, and every day he listened. She knew, and he knew, that pruning the roses was only a pretense. She wondered why, if he enjoyed hearing this story so much, he didn't read books himself. He was a curious man. She introduced him to Jane and Rose, but he was withdrawn and quickly excused himself. After that, she kept her distance.

He fascinated her, though. She noticed that when he left his house, which was rarely, he always rode the horse that he kept at the local livery. He never drove a carriage or a buggy.

One day, when she finished reading to the girls, she clutched the book to her breast and went around the hedge to ask him why.

"What business is my mode of travel to you?" he asked, but not unkindly.

"I am curious."

"My mother was killed in a buggy wreck," he replied simply. "I never ride in one if I can help it."

"Some horses never adapt to pulling buggies," she began.

"I know that, now," he returned.

She smiled ruefully. "I'm sorry."

He searched her face with slow, strange eyes. "How is it that your parents allow you to speak, alone, with a stranger? Are they not concerned that I might mean you harm?"

She lowered her eyes so that he couldn't read too

much in them. "They are good parents. They trust me."

"They do not know me," he reminded her.

"They do, after a fashion," she replied. "You are spoken of by people."

"Gossiped about," he flashed irritably.

"That, too. You keep to yourself. People in communities always talk about those who avoid the company of their fellows."

He shrugged. "I have no interest in socializing."

She remembered the census taker he'd thrown out, and the way he listened when she read from her book. She eyed him with curiosity, hesitant to frame a question she would have to ask one day.

He glanced down at the book in her hands. "What is that book you read from?" he asked abruptly.

"It is a copy of an heirloom," she told him, "handed down in my family from mother to daughter for generations. The original, which is in the Library of Congress, is written in Latin. It is so old that no one alive remembers its origin, although certainly it came from Europe. Legend says that it was written by a monk. Certainly it's a story to inspire reverence."

"The way you read it is invigorating."

"Thank you." She smiled. "Do you have a favorite book, Mr. Torrance?"

His face closed up. "No."

"Not even the Bible?"

His jaw tautened. He didn't answer.

She stepped closer to him. "Mr. Torrance," she said gently, "you cannot read, can you?"

He gave her a furious glare, turned on his heel, and stormed back toward his house. She grimaced, disgusted with herself. She should not have blurted it out like that. She should have waited, led up to it. Now she had insulted him and he would not come near her again. Oh, her wicked tongue!

She went back into her own house with a morose expression, prompting her mother to ask what had caused it.

She lifted her eyes to her mother's, smiled wistfully, and replied, "It is the part I have reached in my book," she lied glibly. "It is so sad."

"Ah, but there is a happy ending." Her mother, having read the book many times, knew. "Do not let the obstacles impede you, my dear. True love must pass through a difficult course or it is not worthy of the name. Nothing worthwhile is ever achieved without struggle and risk."

The words were an adage, but Annabelle realized that she had expected her friendship with John Torrance to progress easily, without risk. It could not. He was a bitter man, and a proud one. If he truly could not read and write, he would not want to admit it, especially to a woman who was a stranger to him. She had imposed on him, rushed him. It would take time to bring him around. But if she could, perhaps she could help him.

How sad that a man could achieve such an age and not know how to read. It was such a waste. Why, what would life be without the joy of exploring another human being through the pages of a book? So many authors had become friends to Annabelle through their words, reaching across the centuries sometimes to find her eyes and her heart and her mind. What a treasure of history was contained in those black markings on white paper. Oh, she must teach Mr. Torrance, somehow, to read. He had no idea what worlds she could present to him, if he could.

She read to the girls for the next few days in the garden, but there was no more rustling on the other side of the hedge. The house next door stood silent.

Annabelle began to despair, because she could hardly walk up on his porch and demand that he speak to her. But now that she had some inkling of the reason for his bad temper and his reclusiveness, she had to help him. If only he would come back! She would be more patient; she would bide her time until she could win his trust.

When it looked as though he had given up listening to her sessions with her sister, one day she heard again the sharp snip of the shears on the other side of the hedge. She had to fight sudden tears, because it was certainly the answer to a prayer.

"Annabelle, do you hear . . . ?" Jane began excitedly.

Annabelle put a finger to her lips, also cautioning Rose, whose eyes were like saucers as she tried to add her comments to her sister's.

"What an exciting book this is," Rose said instead. "I never tire of hearing you read it, Anna."

"Nor do I," Jane added. "Do continue."

And Annabelle did, slowly, enunciating every word. The shears were silent for the duration of the story. Then they began again, more animatedly.

This time, though, Annabelle didn't go around the hedge to find the gardener. She continued on to the house with her sisters. For several days afterward, she read the book until, finally, she finished it.

"What a delightful tale," Jane sighed. "Is such a love possible, do you think, Annabelle? Can a man and a woman care so much for each other that they would risk everything to be together?"

"I think that it is possible," Annabelle said carefully. "I have never been in love. But one day, I shall. And so shall you. Now scoot! Mama will be expecting you to help with the new quilt."

"I hate quilting," Rose muttered.

"Me too," Jane agreed.

They continued on to the house, still complaining. Annabelle lingered on the bench, hesitating. She listened for a step, and wondered if he had gone back inside after all.

But a minute later there was a rustle, and he came around the hedge, his shears in his hand. He looked out of sorts.

"Have you always known that I was there?" he asked, nodding toward the hedge.

"Yes," she said simply. She gnawed on her lower lip. "I am sorry to have made you uncomfortable when I spoke to you last. I am sometimes impetuous. I say things that I should not."

He waved it away. "I have been a victim of the written word most of my life. Both my parents were illiterate. I was too busy on our ranch to go to school. I never learned to read and write. Now, it is becoming an embarrassment to me. The census taker insisted that I fill out his form, without bothering to ask if I could read it."

"And that was why you threw him out?"

He chuckled. "I see that my reputation has spread."

"Indeed." She clutched the book closer.

"I have enjoyed hearing you read from that book," he said after a minute. "Is that what it really says, or do you change it as you read it?"

"Oh, no, I read it exactly as it was written so

many years ago." Her hands tightened around the book. "This is a translation, of course, and there may be minor differences. But the story is just the same." She hesitated, peering up at him. "When I read the Bible, I learn about the people and places that existed when our Lord walked the earth. When I look at a book of poetry and prose, I hear words that some writer thought up centuries ago. It is . . . it is like communicating with people who are long dead. Their thoughts, their dreams, their goals, their heartaches are all there on the paper for me to see and think about and experience." Her eyes gleamed with excitement as she spoke earnestly to him. "I can see into the past through the pages of this book," she said, tracing its leather binding to the tiny brass latch that held it together. "I can hear the thoughts of some of the most famous thinkers and dreamers who ever walked the earth."

"I could . . . do that, if I could read?" he asked.

"Oh, yes. And more than that, you could write down what you think and feel. And perhaps in a hundred years, someone might read what you had written and know what sort of person you were, where you lived, what you thought and felt."

He began to smile. "It sounds like magic."

"It is," she said fervently. "It is!"

He hesitated, glancing from his shears up to her flushed face. "Miss Coleman . . . could you . . . teach me . . . to read and write?"

"I believe so," she said. She smiled. "Oh, yes, I believe so, Mr. Torrance, if you would like me to!"

He nodded. He glanced toward her house and grimaced. "I would not like my . . . lack of education to become common knowledge. Of course, your family would have to know, otherwise they would not approve."

"I know that."

"And we must not be alone," he emphasized.

She flushed. "Sir!"

"I do not mean to sound forward. But for the sake of your reputation," he insisted, "your sisters must accompany you if you come to my house."

"I am certain that they would be delighted."

He wasn't. But he wanted to be able to read a book. She made it sound like the end of the rainbow. "Then will you speak to your parents, or do you wish me to?"

"Let me," she pleaded. "It will be easier."

He agreed. "Then . . . you will let me know?"

"As soon as possible. Tomorrow?"

"Tomorrow." He moved jerkily back around the hedge, limping more than usual. She watched him go with a peculiar sense of pleasure. It was the beginning of something. Time would tell what the something was.

She spoke with her parents that very evening, prepared for a stand-up fight, if that was what it took.

But, surprisingly, her father was astonished at what she told him.

"The poor chap!" her father exclaimed, putting down the paper he was reading. "Annabelle, what a handicap he must suffer in his business dealings."

"Indeed, Father," she said. "I am encouraged that he could admit to such a lack of knowledge. I have the time, you know, and I was best friends with Matilda Hawkins in St. Louis, who was a schoolteacher. I observed, and even helped with her charges when she taught primary school. I am certain that I know how to teach reading."

"In that case, I have no objection. But you must not go to his home alone . . ."

"Rose and Jane can come with me," she said, grinning.

Her father nodded. "Very well. And not at night."

"Certainly not," she agreed.

Her mother, who had been an interested but passive listener, nodded. "I am encouraged by your interest in this poor man, Annabelle. Perhaps we were wrong to judge him so harshly on first appearances."

"And perhaps we were not," Mr. Coleman said carefully. "All the same, it will help him to better himself if he is able to read and write."

That seemed to be the end of the matter. Delighted at having gotten her way, Annabelle went to her room and sprawled on the canopied bed with lace dripping from its high ceiling and, pencil and paper in hand, began to outline a course of study.

A week later, her daily meetings with John Torrance, with her sisters, were beginning to show promise. Impatient at first with his slow pace, Torrance had finally accepted that these lessons would not lead to immediate literacy. He stopped complaining at the snail's pace and began to work hard at tracing each letter of the alphabet until he knew them on sight. From there, they progressed to sounding out the vowels. By the second week, they were ready to begin with simple text from the primer.

He read each word carefully, pausing to ask what it meant. Annabelle was the soul of patience, not rushing him, not demeaning him when he forgot the occasional letter or had to have a vowel sounded out for him.

When he could read a whole sentence without help, the brilliance of his smile was startling.

"I never knew it would be fun," he remarked.

"But of course it is," she replied gently. "And this is only the beginning, Mr. Torrance."

"Indeed," Jane said, catching the enthusiasm of the adults. "Why, you can read about other countries and other people, like the Indians."

He pursed his lips and his eyes twinkled. "Which Indians?"

Jane paused. "I do not understand."

"Which tribe?" he persisted.

"Oh, tribe! You mean like the Comanches and the Apaches."

"Very good. Now, do you know how to recognize one from the other?"

"No. Do you?" she asked excitedly.

He did, and took a minute to describe the feathered headbands and the long-feathered headdresses worn by the Comanche warriors and chiefs as opposed to the cloth bands worn by the Apaches.

Not only the mode of dress was different, so was the language and the way they lived. Plains Indians lived in tepees, tall circular tents covered by hides, while Apaches built small round wickiups of wood and grass.

"Even the arrows are different, and the arrowheads bound to them with sinew or rawhide," he continued. "Back in the old days, you could tell not only which tribe made a certain arrow, but which warrior within a tribe made it."

"That's swell, Mr. Torrance!" Rose enthused. "My, you do know a lot about Indians!"

He smiled coolly. "I do, indeed, Miss Rose."

Annabelle thought it prudent to change the subject, which she did, pointing out that time was running away and they still had much ground to cover in this lesson.

Later, the girls walked ahead to the hedge while Annabelle dawdled behind with John Torrance.

"I'm sorry if Jane embarrassed you with her questions," she said.

"I wasn't embarrassed," he replied. "I like talking about the few subjects that I'm not ignorant about."

She blushed. "If I have made you feel uncomfortable—"

"Don't be absurd," he said curtly. "It is only that I feel ignorant when I see how well-read you are. I know a great deal about Indians and Mexicans and guns. I know very little of polite society."

"I think your parlor manners are extremely well developed," she replied, smiling as she remembered how meticulously he had served them tea, despite the age and condition of his teapot and cups; they were clean, if not expensive.

She glanced at him, fascinated all over again by his elegancc of carriage. He was a tall man, but unlike many tall men, he didn't walk stooped over to diminish his height. His back was arrow straight, and his jutting chin was always held up. He had a way of looking at people that would have intimidated a lawbreaker. He didn't blink or avert his eyes. He looked straight at people, and there was honesty in his level gaze. Even on such short acquaintance, Annabelle would have trusted him with her life. It surprised her that he made such a strong impression. Certainly, she told herself, it was because he was an apt pupil.

They paused at the row of hedge bushes, where the path led to her front porch. The gas lamps were on inside, and light spilled out of the long windows onto the green grass and the front porch. Where Annabelle stood with her student, however, it was pleasantly dark.

"Next week we shall try something harder," she promised.

"Not this weekend?"

"I always go to town with my family on Saturdays, and there is church on Sunday."

"I see."

"You are not a churchgoer," she guessed.

He made an awkward movement with his shoulders. "I never was. But that doesn't mean I don't believe in God. A man who's seen the things and suffered the things I have must believe in Him or go mad. Now, more than ever, I am convinced of a guiding hand in life."

She smiled, delighted. "One day you might consider going to church."

"With this face?" he asked mockingly. "The ladies of the congregation would exit screaming through every door of the building."

She went close to him and laid a gentle hand on his arm. It was surprisingly strong and muscular, warm under her cool fingers. She heard the stark intake of his breath, and a thrill went through her.

"You are not so hideous as you seem to think," she told him. "You are a brave and good man."

He stilled. "You take risks," he said.

His voice sounded strained, and she noticed a tension in his posture that had not been there before.

"I do not understand," she faltered.

He laughed sardonically. "No?" His lean hands

caught her firmly by the upper arms and brought her against him. While her mind worked frantically at solutions, he bent, and she felt the brief, hard pressure of his mouth against her soft, untouched lips.

She gasped aloud, but she didn't strike him or speak when he drew back a breath. In fact, she hung there, more fascinated than ever, frozen in time by the unexpected action, which was not at all unpleasant.

His fingers contracted, bruising her arms. "You do not recoil," he murmured deeply. "Am I truly not repugnant, or are you merely curious about this? Have you not been kissed before?"

Her mind managed to curl around one of the questions. "I have not," she whispered. She stood very still in his grasp, afraid that he might withdraw if she moved. Her book spoke of a kiss, but she had never known what one was, not really. This might be the only time she would have to find out. "Mr. Torrance," she continued in a hushed tone, trying to see his lean face in the dim light, "would you . . . could you . . . do it again . . . please?"

His chest rose and fell both visibly and audibly. This was outrageous behavior, and he should be ashamed of himself. She was very young and he knew better. But the lure of her soft lips was more than he could resist.

He bent again, to her secret delight, and she kept her eyes open. She could barely make out his eyes. They closed and she saw his thick eyelashes as his lips touched hers again. But this time, there was a difference. His lips lingered, brushed and lifted, traced and teased until he made her feel curious sensations that centered in her breasts and her belly. She felt her breath catch and as he continued the tender assault, her body began to tense and tingle all over.

Instinctively, she stepped closer to him, finding that his hands eagerly approved this familiarity. Indeed, they encouraged it, sliding around her to close around her shoulders and waist and urge her body even nearer his own.

This was magic, indeed, she thought dizzily. She could actually feel his legs touching her through her skirt, his chest crushing her breasts above her corset! She made a soft sound, and her arms reached up to curve around his neck.

His lips lifted once more. She felt the uneven tenor of his warm, coffee-scented breath and she stood on tiptoe, dazed, hungry.

"Miss Coleman," he said in a faint, choked tone, "this is becoming . . ."

What it was becoming never made it past his throat, because her mouth pushed upward against his and his arms contracted, lifting her so that her body fit exactly against his own. He shuddered with pleasure and gave himself up to the sacrifice of her warm mouth.

A long moment later, he forced himself to release her. He was shivering with need. It had been so long, so very long, since he had known a woman's touch. He moved back from her, afraid that she might be offended.

"How . . . sweet," she whispered brokenly. "How very, very sweet! I have read about it, you know, but the reality is . . . devastating!"

"And dangerous," he replied curtly. "This should not have happened. You must go home at once."

She was surprised. "You did not like it?" she asked hesitantly. She wished that she could see his face. "I am sorry. I thought . . . good night, Mr. Torrance!"

She whirled and ran, tears in her eyes. She had been too forward. She had offended him. He hated her!

He had her by the arm before she made it to the porch. He turned her gently, and mopped her face with a pristine white handkerchief.

"You have much to learn about men," he said with black humor. "And I should not be the one to teach you. Suffice it to say that some pleasures are too sweet to remain innocent, and let it go at that. You must not take things so much to heart."

"I thought that you hated me. You have said before that I am too forward," she said, subdued.

"What just happened was not solely your doing," he replied. "If you recall, it was I who started it. I have no regrets, and I hope that you do not. But it must not happen again. We are pupil and instructor. That is all we can ever be to one another."

She listened to him with dismay and had a sudden, terrifying thought. "Are you . . . married?"

"No!"

She relaxed a little.

"Nor do I cver intend to be," he said firmly. "Make no mistake about this. I will take another month or so to heal completely, and then I will return to my job, to the Texas Ranger post in Alpine."

"But . . . but you are in such poor condition!"

"I have seen Rangers in worse condition return to the job," he mused. "We are a tough bunch."

She thought of what he had endured, and what he might yet have to endure, and she was horrified. She could find nothing to say to him.

"You will find a young man," he said, made uncomfortable by her silence.

She still could not speak. She finally found her voice as she heard her father and mother through the open parlor window. "I will see you on Monday, Mr. Torrance. Good evening, and thank you for the tea."

He made a rough sound under his breath as she turned and walked composedly to the porch and into her house. He went back home in a vicious temper. He hoped that she would give up on him now that he had told her what his plans were for the future. He had no right to subject such a young, well-bred woman to the sort of life he led. She was not fit for it. But that one taste of her lips had been sweet. It would last him all his life, he thought as he closed and locked his own front door. Yes, it would last him until he went down into the dark, with her name on his lips.

Unaware of his thoughts, Annabelle muttered until she fell asleep, with tears on her pillow. There would be no younger man in her life, she thought miserably, because she was in love with a scarred, embittered Texas Ranger who did not want her. For the first time, she loathed her heirloom book. It was a lie, she told herself as she closed her eyes. There was no such thing as true love or glory. It was a pretty myth to read to children, who still had their illusions. After tonight, she was certain that hers were gone forever.

But, oh, the pleasure of his arms and his hard mouth on hers would last her until she was an old woman, she mused. And even then, she would still see his beloved face and hear his deep drawl and be in love all over again.

* * *

The weekend dragged by. Annabelle pretended not to notice the lights going on and off next door. She followed her usual routine with her parents, and after the second Sunday service in the evening, she prepared for bed without any real enthusiasm. Tomorrow was Monday, and she had no idea if she would even be welcome at the house next door.

She opened the chest that contained her precious book and touched it lovingly. If only, she thought, if only it were more than a sweet fiction. She wanted nothing more than to share the hard, dangerous life of their neighbor. She would ask nothing, need nothing, if she only had his love. She closed the chest and put it away. Time would tell, she thought. If it was destined, then she would certainly share his fate. If not, then all the hoping and wishing and dreaming in the world would not transport her one step nearer him.

She gathered her primer and paper and pencils the next afternoon and, with Jane and Rose in tow, started determinedly next door.

But when she knocked, there was no answer. The curtains were all drawn. There was no sound from within. She noticed a fresh bottle of milk beside the door, but it was a day old and unrefrigerated. Out of an icebox, it was certainly spoiled.

"Where is he, do you suppose?" Jane asked.

"He must be away," Annabelle replied loudly. In fact, he was probably hiding on the other side of the door to avoid her. He was making it obvious that he didn't want to see her. "Let us return home, girls," she added, her voice raised.

But instead of leaving, she motioned the girls next door and winked at them. Curious but unprotesting, they took the primer and paper from her outstretched hands and quickly went away.

She put her ear to the door and listened. Sure enough, there was a voice inside. But it was not Torrance's voice. Her heart stopped as she heard it.

"Your posse just took to its heels, Torrance," a rough voice said, laughing unpleasantly. "Too bad. You won't be spared, now. I figured you'd be easy game after the Yaquis cut you up, and so you were. In the old days, I'd never have got the drop on you. Now you're going to pay for shooting my brothers. When the 4:30 train rolls through town and blows its whistle, I'm going to ease a .45 slug right through your hard head, and by the time the train is gone, so will I be, right out the open back window. They probably won't find you for days!"

Horrified, Annabelle put a hand to her throbbing heart. She must act, but how? Her father was not at home. There were no men close by except old Mr. James, who could not even hold a pistol in his arthritic hands. Annabelle had no gun.

Her eyes searched frantically for a weapon, and found one easy to hand. It was a big hoe, the one he used to weed his roses. Now, how to save him?

The man inside had said that the back window was open. The windows were very low in this house, and without screens. She dashed around back, keeping low, and discovered the kitchen window raised.

Carefully, heart pounding, she eased off her shoes, and in her stocking feet she climbed through the window. Thank God she had been something of a tomboy back home, and not the proper lady her mother had wanted! She reached down for the hoe and pulled it carefully inside.

Then she made her way, ever so cautiously, down the wide hall to the front room, where she caught a glimpse of John Torrance sitting in a straight chair while a short, wizened man leveled a huge pistol at his chest. Heavens, how would she ever sneak up on the man?

As she stood there, undecided, Torrance's head turned. She never knew if it had been a sound that his sharp ears had picked up, or an instinctive knowledge that she was nearby. Whatever the reason, he saw her. The expression on his face at that moment would haunt her as long as she lived. There was astonishment, delight, joy, and then a sort of horror.

Without giving any indication that his quick glance had found anything out of the ordinary, he lifted his chin and looked at the gunman. "Go ahead," he challenged. "If you're going to kill me, do it right now. Pull the trigger, damn you! You coward, you fool, shoot!"

Annabelle's heart stopped in her chest. She realized immediately what he meant to do. He was going to force the man to kill him so that she wouldn't put herself at risk on his behalf. It was a sacrifice of unspeakable proportions. And she knew at once why he had done it. She knew that he loved her.

From anguish, she felt transported to almost ethereal joy. Did he not realize that she would have no life without him? If he were to die, then so would she. Her jaw tautened and she began to look around the room for a better weapon than the one in her hand.

Torrance, having failed at his gamble, saw the gunman laugh.

"Oh, no, you're not going to trick me into doing anything hasty," he told Torrance. "The train will come any minute. Then I'll do the deed. I'm not going to risk getting caught. It's too bad you weren't on your guard, isn't it?"

Torrance forced himself to remain calm, although he stood right now to lose the thing he loved most in the world, and it wasn't his own life. "It's a pity I didn't have time to get to the loaded shotgun I keep in the corner near the pantry," he agreed. He had no idea if Annabelle could even shoot a gun, but if she could find it and threaten the outlaw with it, that might be enough. If only the man didn't take the risk of trying to shoot her. Dear God, keep her safe!

Annabelle heard the admonition, and with a faint sigh of something akin to relief, she tiptoed to the corner of the dining room where the pantry was and found the shotgun. It was incredibly heavy. But she knew how to use one; her Grandpa Monroe had taught her.

With determination, she hefted the weapon and tiptoed back to the doorway. The gunman was looking at his watch, paying no particular attention to anything except the time. Sure enough, in the distance, the sound of the train's whistle could now be heard. Any minute it would chug into town and that awful pistol would fire, and her John would be dead!

She saw John's body tauten and knew that he was aware of her presence. She didn't look at him. She leveled the shotgun at the gunman.

"Drop it right now!" she yelled, and cocked the shotgun.

The gunman flinched as if she'd struck him. The watch fell from his hand and the gun jerked in anticipation of his next action.

"Don't do it!" Torrance yelled at the gunman. "She's won awards with that shotgun!"

The remark startled the gunman into indecision, and before he could gather his thoughts, Torrance dived for him.

It was over in seconds. Torrance had wrestled the pistol away from him and laid the barrel across his forehead with a sickening thud. The man sprawled unconscious.

Torrance got to his feet and turned. His face was paper white, his eyes terrifying. "Are you all right?" he asked hoarsely.

She was shaking. "No!" she burst out, tears stinging her eyes. "I've never been so afraid in all my life."

He burst out laughing. After that brave show, she'd suddenly become witless. He took the shotgun out of her tense hands, released the trigger gently so as not to discharge the weapon, and put it aside.

She flew into his arms, pressing as close as she could get, her voice breaking as she let all her fears past her tight throat.

He gathered her close and bent to kiss her with such tenderness that she did cry. She clung to him, a second skin, part of him.

"Oh, you shall have to marry me now," she whispered at his hard mouth. "I can be your backup man and carry something smaller and less intimidating, and I shall help you catch outlaws. See? Now I am experienced!"

Her laughing eyes defeated him. He touched her face with a lean hand that trembled. "I can give you so little," he began heavily.

"That is not true," she replied softly. "You love me."

His cheeks went ruddy. "You sound very sure of yourself."

"You would have let him kill you to spare me any risk," she said, humbled by the memory. "But do you not know that there would be no life for me without you?"

That stunned him. "You love me?"

"Oh, yes," she said, and slid closer to him, clinging contentedly. "Terribly!"

His hands smoothed up and down her back absently. He reviewed all the obstacles in his mind, but he couldn't find one that really mattered. Age, upbringing, none of it could stand against the love they shared.

"I shall ask your father for your hand in marriage," he said quietly. "But I fear that he will not give it."

"Then we shall elope in the dead of night and live in sin until we can find a circuit preacher!"

He laughed out loud. "Annabelle!"

"He will agree," she promised. "My father loves me. He will want nothing more than my happiness." She traced his scarred cheek with a loving hand. "All the long years I read my wonderful book, I hoped that I would one day find the sort of life it spoke about. I never dreamed that it would be so sweet, or that I would discover it in such a violent way."

He sighed contentedly. "You can read it to our children," he said, smiling. "And perhaps they, too, will find the miracle we have found."

She reached up to kiss him. "Of that, I have no doubt."

Her family was horrified at the risk they had both taken, but no one objected to Annabelle marrying her Texas Ranger. He did return to his job in Alpine, and she went with him, an excited and rapturously happy new bride. And in time, after years of happiness and the birth of two sons, Annabelle had a daughter. She was the delight of her parents and the worst nightmare of her two brothers, but she completed the family circle. She grew into a beautiful young woman and, when she was eighteen, Annabelle's literary legacy was once again passed from mother to daughter. And a new chapter of love began.

KINDRED HEARTS

LORI COPELAND

Kindred Hearts

California, 1967

The knock sounded at the door. Ted groaned and rolled over to sit up on the side of the bed. "Like, man, it can't be morning yet!"

" 'Fraid so," Ginny murmured, pulling the blanket closer around her chin.

"Tuesday?"

Nodding, she opened her eyes slowly, trying to focus. A ray of sun came through the window, striking a prism that slowly turned at the end of a string, sending brilliant colors dancing along the peeling wallpaper. Though twelve people lived in the house, Ben was the only one with an alarm clock, and he had taken the responsibility of waking them on his way down to the kitchen for breakfast.

"It's Tuesday," she said.

"Crap. Seven columns of copy to fill before six."

Ted's habit of numbering his days by the number of columns he had to fill for a local newspaper where he and Ben worked was annoying. She didn't remember when he'd started doing that.

Making a snorting sound, he padded toward the connecting bathroom. Three other rooms shared the one down the hall.

"Another day," he mumbled, the clank of old water pipes muffling his words.

Ginny knew his philosophy by heart. "Turtle," as Ted was nicknamed by the commune, was intent on dropping out of society, returning to what he termed the true basis of culture, back to the beginning.

Back to the land, to fundamental living, growing one's own food, making do with as little of society's trappings as possible.

It was hard to believe she had been with Turtle almost three years now. When they met in Boston, he was on the five-year plan, working his way through college with reduced class hours. She was attending on a scholarship.

After graduation she took a job with an insurance office until she could find a teaching position, but Ted decided they should move on, go somewhere he could find more meaningful work. Knowing how unhappy he was with his part-time position as a clerk in a car rental agency, she agreed.

She listened for hours as he expounded on the state of the nation, a country whose institutions, from the family down, he said, had lost a vital, unifying vision. This, he declared, was the prime reason he wasn't about to support that crumbling framework with an empty commitment to marriage.

Ginny was beginning to wonder about his particular turn of the phrase "empty commitment." Did he actually believe marriage was an empty commitment, or was it that he did not believe in commitment at all? When she finally confronted him, he seemed shocked that she would doubt his commitment to *her*. *Civilization* had screwed up! It had clearly made a wrong turn, and he wasn't about to be part of a society that couldn't tell the difference.

So they moved on. She found a job the second day they were in Ohio. The teacher's assistant position offered minimal pay, but it helped assuage her need to be in the classroom. It also bought groceries and put gas in the ancient VW tank.

She filled her spare hours with books she found in the school library. She read novels, newspapers, anything. Friends teased her about being the only person they knew who looked forward to reading the ancient magazines in doctors' offices and laundromats. They were right. She had been known to read the back of cereal boxes for lack of anything better to peruse. Books, and the adventures she found there, opened new, exciting worlds to her.

They were in Ohio only three months when Ted became bored with his job as a security guard. He had heard about the Land of Opportunity, the Haight-Ashbury district in San Francisco, so they moved on again.

It took six days to reach the West Coast. They were a funny sight, these two young hippies, wearing white tunics, baggy pants, sandals, headbands, and love beads, driving a battered VW painted the colors of the rainbow.

It struck her as ironic that they followed almost the same trail as pioneers had taken a century earlier, and for the same reason.

Freedom. Freedom from oppression. The freedom to be who they wanted, what they wanted, how they wanted. It all seemed so right.

If they chose to let their hair grow long, they could, and did. If they wanted to wear jeans with holes in the knees, who was to say they couldn't? Certainly not a society that had sold out to materialism.

Peace. Love. Happiness. These were the things that counted.

In the beginning, Ginny believed the theory as much as Ted. She had seen what society had done to her father. He became a workaholic, a slave to materialism, always working longer, harder. She saw the effect loneliness had on her mother. When her parents finally divorced during her freshman year, she vowed not to let that happen to her.

When she met Ted at a campus coffee shop and discovered his opinion on the life-consuming monster that urban America had become, she fell hopelessly in love. She would never marry a man like her father. Ted's aversion to owning things, his dedication to having only the necessities for sustenance, his Spartan lifestyle, his free spirit, fascinated her. His dream was to teach, spend his summers traveling, owning only what could be packed and moved in thirty minutes. She was twenty-one, he nineteen. Both brimmed with idealism.

"I'm outta here," Ted said, pulling on a faded green T-shirt and shrugging into a linen jacket that was a leftover from his college days.

"Better take a tie," she murmured.

Groaning, he stuffed one into his pocket and slammed the door as he left. She knew he would wear the offensive accessory only when forced by the day editor.

Trouble was already brewing.

In the last couple of weeks she had recognized the signs of restlessness, signs that meant he was about to move on again.

She tried to ignore them, hoping that just once he would conform to regulations, but in her heart, she knew it would be only a few days until he decided he couldn't cope with the confining lifestyle of a newspaper writer. He was an excellent conversationalist, but the discipline of putting facts on paper was more than he was willing to accept.

Getting to her feet, she fought back the queasiness that had plagued her the past week. She closed her eyes, and the room tilted as she made her way into the bathroom.

"Ginny Girl? You ready?"

"Ready," Ginny called back, pulling on a pair of worn jeans. Shoving her arms into the sleeves of an oversize shirt, she fumbled with the buttons as she met Regina at the door.

"Turtle split?" Regina handed her an apple while biting into her own.

Ginny nodded. "Ten minutes ago." She had struck up an immediate friendship with Regina. The outspoken eighteen year old with a penchant for red-and-white-checked gingham, and her man, Smitty, had moved into the room across the hall the week after Ted rented the house.

On impulse, Ginny had asked Regina to give her supervisor her name, and two days later she landed a decent-paying job on the same plant assembly line. They rode the bus to work together every morning since.

Smitty had a summer job with the park board, but Regina confided that once summer ended, they would be moving on.

"Still think he's gonna chuck it all?" Regina asked.

"I could almost guess the day."

"Like, you going with him?"

Ginny knew that Smitty and Regina lived together for convenience. She and Turtle were different; at least she believed that love was the driving element in their relationship. "I don't want to move again."

Regina laughed. "Careful . . . you're beginning to sound like Establishment."

Ginny managed a smile, recalling that Regina could barely read above a fifth-grade level. She had begun skipping school at twelve and left home at fifteen. Thumbing rides, she made her way west until she met Smitty two years ago. Barely eighteen, she was far more worldly than Ginny.

Frowning, Regina glanced at her watch. "Jeez, look at the time! Old man Harris'll have a cat if we're late."

Tossing a worn paperback book and a sandwich into her bag, Ginny slung the strap over her shoulder and followed Regina out the door.

The commune's stabilizing force was the first person she saw that evening when she returned from work.

"Hi, Ben."

"Hey, Ginny."

Ginny tried to ignore her accelerating pulse. Ben Sanders was part of the family. There was no reason for her to feel any differently about him from any other man who lived in the house, but she did. There was something special about Ben; she just hadn't figured out what yet.

Ben's warm, friendly eyes swept over her as she self-consciously smoothed escaping wisps of hair off her face. Glad to see that dinner was almost ready, she reached for a glass beside her plate.

"Turtle," she groaned, "you were supposed to bring ice. The juice is warm."

"I got more on my mind than ice," Turtle growled from his place at the table. Ginny grimly surveyed his linen jacket, which was carelessly wadded in the seat of a chair.

Ben grinned. "She's giving you the evil eye, Turtle. Better go back for the ice."

Turtle grumbled something disparaging.

Ben was wearing a stylish red tie, khaki pants, and a navy jacket this afternoon. His thick black hair, longer than Turtle's, was neatly tied back in a ponytail. Ginny couldn't remember ever seeing him rumpled. He was the one who made sure the communal kitchen was neat, and supervised the performance of duties.

He collected the rent, and paid bills from the kitty to which each resident contributed. A local reporter, he focused his columns on community interests. Ginny knew he wrote in a journal every night, and she longed to know what he wrote, but never had the nerve to ask.

Summoning a friendly smile, she turned to Turtle. "How was your day?"

Turtle muttered an obscenity, and she noticed Ben's disapproving glance. Ben didn't use vulgar language, just as he didn't use drugs or alcohol. He kept to himself, and was the only one in the house without a roommate—male or female. She admired his calm assurance and his sense of order.

Ben was twenty-eight, a graduate of USC. He had been at the newspaper a year. Other than that, she knew nothing about him.

"It's the damn Establishment again," Turtle said, heading toward the bathroom.

As the door slammed, Ginny released a breath she hadn't realized she was holding.

Ben glanced at the closed bathroom door, then back to her. "Don't mind him. He's had a rough day."

Nodding, Ginny reached for a bottle of warm juice and went to her room.

Her bouts of morning sickness were more noticeable now. To her, not to Turtle. He was unusually self-absorbed these days. She found herself looking forward to seeing Ben in the kitchen when she came home nights. He was there Tuesday afternoon, along with a surly Turtle.

"Hi."

Turtle managed a curt greeting.

"Hi," Ben said, smiling. "How's it going?"

"Not bad, how about you?"

"Not bad. Got a raise."

"Congratulations."

"Big deal." Turtle took a swig out of a bottle. "Fifty measly cents more an hour."

"Getting a raise is a big deal." Ginny's eyes silently shared the occasion with Ben.

Turtle shoved back from the table and disappeared into the bathroom, slamming the door behind him.

Kicking off her shoes, Ginny moved to the old refrigerator. "Something bothering him?"

"A memo came down from the brass today." Ben broke spaghetti into a pan of boiling water. "The staff's been ordered to cut their hair to collar length."

Ginny studied Ben's earnest face, taking in the deep-set green eyes beneath straight brows, aquiline nose, and full lips that found it easy to smile.

"Is he going to do it?"

He shrugged.

"Are you?"

"Sure, why not? It's only hair. Letting it grow is just easier—I'm not trying to make any kind of statement."

Ginny smiled, tilting her head to one side. "You're not like the others."

His leisurely smile gave her inner peace. "Neither are you."

She lifted her shoulders briefly. "The Establishment may call us hippies, but we nonconformists are conforming more than we would if we'd stayed in what society calls the norm." She laughed, her hand coming up to cover her lips. She was babbling. "I suppose some would say by marching to our own drummer, we've only joined a different parade."

He glanced up, his eyes glinting with respect.

"What about you?" she asked.

"Me? I guess I'm right in there somewhere between the tubas and trombones."

Ginny leaned against the counter, studying him. "No, I don't think so. You don't follow anyone."

His gaze encompassed her again, and it seemed he was going to say more, but Turtle emerged from the bathroom and they both looked away.

Drawing a deep breath, Ginny asked, "What are you going to do about your hair?"

"Nothing," Turtle said, his mouth set in a stubborn line. "If they don't like my hair, they can fire me. We'll take the severance and clear out." His face flushed with anger. "Who are they to tell me what clothes I can wear and what hair length is 'acceptable?' They can't make me conform to their rules! My personal choice is my right!"

"Every company has its policy," Ginny quietly reminded him. "Like it or not, there are always going to be rules."

"Yeah, well hear this. I'm not gonna be anybody's lackey!"

Ben calmly poured sauce over the spaghetti.

Turtle was wound up now. "They sit up there in their three-piece Brooks Brothers suits with their dollar shoeshines and fifteen-dollar haircuts and buffed nails and hand down edicts like God to Moses on the mountain. Well, Turtle Bond is not buying into it."

Ben took the salad out of the refrigerator and set it on the table. "Dinner's ready. I think I'll eat later."

Ginny watched him leave, sorry he had to witness this scene.

Ben's friendly knock woke them the next morning.

"Wednesday?"

"Wednesday," Ginny murmured into her pillow, wishing she didn't have to get up.

If she could just lie very still for a while, the dizziness and nausea would pass. But it wasn't to be. The moment Turtle left, she headed straight for the bathroom and threw up.

"When are you gonna tell him?" Regina challenged from the open doorway.

"Soon," she managed, splashing cool water on her face.

"How far along?"

"Two months, I think."

"Seen a doctor?"

"Not yet."

"Free clinic six blocks down." Regina's earnest brown eyes searched Ginny's pale features. "If you're thinking about getting rid of it—"

"No! No," Ginny repeated more calmly. "I would never do that." The thought had never entered her mind. She would keep the baby, regardless of Turtle's reaction when she told him.

Regina shrugged. "Didn't think so, but I had to ask. If you need anything, let me know, okay?"

"Okay."

"Promise?"

"Promise."

"A rug rat." Regina flashed a smile. "Far out!"

Somehow Ginny made it through the day. She worked on autopilot, her thoughts straying to Turtle and whether he would be fired today, and if he was, what would he do? What would she do? She didn't want to move again. She had to tell him she was pregnant, but she was afraid of his response. They had never spoken of children.

When the quitting bell rang at five, she still struggled with her dilemma.

Ben was just climbing the stairs when Ginny got home. His hair was cut in a stylish, becoming manner. It gave him a neat, professional look she found incredibly attractive.

Pausing on the lower landing, he waited for her, his hand resting on the railing.

"Hi."

Ginny's grin was wide as she paused beside the staircase. "I like it."

"Do you?" He ran his hand self-consciously through his newly shorn locks. "I feel bald."

"It looks wonderful. Sort of savoir faire."

He grinned, color staining his cheeks. "Thanks."

"Catch you later, Gin." Regina brushed by Ben, calling hello as she skipped on up the stairs.

"Yeah, see you," Ginny said absently. "I never realized how curly . . ."

She stopped, feeling a little out of line. "Honestly, Ben, it looks wonderful."

"Well, it passed inspection at work."

She sobered. "What about Turtle?"

Ben looked uncomfortable. "You'd better ask him."

Ginny closed her eyes sickly.

"Look," he said softly. "Turtle believes in what he's doing."

"I know." So had she, once not so long ago.

"What will you do . . ."

"If he's fired? I don't know. He'll want to move on."

"Is that what you want to do?"

A door opened upstairs and Turtle came out. Coming down the stairs, he mumbled, "Runnin' low on smokes. Back in a minute."

Ginny viewed his long hair with a sinking heart. "Turtle . . . your hair . . . you didn't . . ."

"Get off my back, Ginny! I don't need you telling me what to do!" He stormed past her.

She clamped her mouth shut, looking at Ben, embarrassed again, as Turtle slammed out the door.

"It's my night to cook," she murmured, quickly turning away.

Ben trailed her into the kitchen. "What's on the menu?"

"Chicken and salad. I found some nice produce at the market." The air was strained. She was embarrassed not only for herself but for Turtle. When had he become so radical? When had he turned so rude?

"Need some help?"

Normally, she would refuse, but tonight she welcomed the company. "Thanks, Ben. I'd love some help."

After dinner, Ben was scraping the plates into a garbage pail while she ran soapy water into the sink. Turtle had not returned.

The subject they'd carefully avoided was suddenly there. "What will happen to Turtle?"

Ben didn't immediately answer.

She glanced at him.

"I'm not sure. The company memo was explicit about dress code."

"Maybe you could talk to him?" Cutting his hair seemed a small concession to keep the peace, and he and Ben were friends.

"I'd rather stay out of it." The lid on the garbage can slammed closed. "You talk to him."

"He doesn't listen to me." She realized he hadn't in a long time. They were pulling in opposite directions, changing, growing apart. It frightened her. She turned, her eyes searching Ben's plaintively. "Ben, I don't know what's happening between Turtle and me. I'm confused . . ."

Laying the dishcloth aside, Ben draped a friendly arm around her shoulders. "Come on, Confused. There's something I want to show you."

They climbed the long stairway, arm in arm.

"Where are we going?"

"You'll see."

Outside, a clap of thunder warned of an approaching storm. Rain would be a welcome respite to the unusually oppressive heat. Occasional flashes of lightning lit the hallway as they made their way toward the attic.

"We're going to the attic?" Ginny asked.

"Yes, my innocent beauty." Ben attempted a sinister Boris Karloff tone. "Would the lovely lady care to see my etchings?"

She laughed at the bad impersonation. "You're weird."

He leaned over and sucked her throat in an equally bad vampire imitation.

The old attic was dark and musty. Rain splattered noisily overhead on the leaky roof.

Leading her to a far corner windowsill, Ben showed her a bird nest filled with four tiny blue eggs.

"Ohhh," she cooed. "How did the mother bird get in here?"

"With all the broken windows it wouldn't be hard."

Ginny started to touch one of the eggs when he stopped her. "Don't touch it. The mother won't come back."

She smiled. "That's really not true. Birds actually have a very poor sense of smell. One time, I nurtured three robin eggs for weeks and the mother never abandoned her babies."

"Really? I'd always heard they wouldn't come back."

The attic was littered with boxes and old furniture. For the next hour they sorted through old trunks, modeling old clothes, leafing through abandoned picture albums, sharing the lives of complete strangers.

"Look at this!" Ben reached into the recess of an old wooden chest with tarnished fittings and came up with a book. The leather binding was cracked and fragile.

Ginny peered over his shoulder. "What is it?" It appeared to be a novel, or perhaps a biography of sorts.

"I'm not sure. Some kind of old book." He leafed through the yellowed pages. "Very old, in fact. I wonder if the owner knows it's up here?"

Her love of books intervened. "I'll take it to my room for safekeeping. When you pay the rent on the first, you can return it to the landlord."

"Good idea."

"Why would someone leave their family pictures behind?" Ginny mused as she turned her attention to a worn photograph album.

"It seems the landlord is careless with his personal effects," Ben reflected. They both had a good laugh at the outdated styles in the faded snapshots. "Where's your family, Ginny?"

"Michigan."

"You come from a big family?"

"No, just Mom and Dad and one brother. Mom and Dad divorced a few years ago."

"Tough break."

"Yeah. How about you?"

"Four sisters." He winced playfully. "Big, happy family."

"You're lucky."

Their eyes met as the rain pattered gently down on the eaves. "Yeah, I'm beginning to realize that."

They wrapped themselves in the serenity of the

old attic, talking, sharing memories past and present.

As Ginny fell asleep that night, she realized she and Turtle had never talked about anything other than his disappointments.

The old adage "Time flies when you're having fun" flashed through her mind on the morning of their third anniversary.

Fun wasn't what she'd had in mind when she committed to Turtle. Love had been the driving force. Love, respect, sharing the same values. What had changed?

Her hand rested on her still flat stomach. Had the baby already made a difference in her life? In their life together? What would happen when it was born? She restlessly rolled to her side and tried to go back to sleep.

When Ben knocked, she was still awake.

"What happened at the newspaper yesterday?" she murmured as Turtle's feet hit the floor.

"Haven't you heard? I've got until five on Monday to cut my hair."

Closing her eyes, she struggled against her queasy stomach. "Are you going to do it?"

"Hell, no," he said, pulling a pair of jeans out of the dresser. "Crap. One of my black socks is missing."

"In the third drawer."

"Hell, Ginny, can't you do a simple thing like pair up socks?"

"Sorry."

Sinking down on the side of the bed, he jerked his footwear on.

"If they're going to fire you—"

"If I knuckle under to their demands, then I've

lost more than just a battle," he grumbled. "Someone's got to stand up for individual choice. I wasn't punched out like one of those little washers on your assembly line. I'm a human being, with full freedom of choice. That includes the way I dress, not just the right to bear arms or free speech. Hell, free speech is what their business is all about, and here they're trying to tell me how to dress! How hypocritical can they get?"

A headache bloomed in Ginny's right temple, and she was relieved when he left the room minutes later.

Getting up slowly, she walked to the window to watch the two male forms stride down the sidewalk, Ben's solid frame straight and tall beside Turtle's slighter build and perpetually hunched shoulders.

Turtle was still ranting, gesturing emphatically, while Ben patiently listened, his hands shoved into his trouser pockets.

"Ready to go?"

Ginny turned at the sound of Regina's voice, then caught the breakfast roll her friend tossed her way.

"You got to eat. For the kid," Regina admonished, sending a pint carton of milk flying in her direction.

Ginny smiled. "Thanks, Mom."

"You okay?"

"Yeah," she said, balancing the roll and milk in one hand as she stuffed a couple of books into her bag with the other.

"I don't believe you."

"I'll be fine—as soon as I throw up." She managed a wan smile.

As they rode the bus to work, Ginny pulled out

a book and opened it to a marked place. Lately she'd begun to read the classics again, enjoying the familiar tone of Dickens. Regina peeked over her shoulder and frowned at the small type.

"You should be a professor or something," she said, scooting down in the seat, balancing her knees against the back of the seat in front of her.

"I was an elementary-education major in college."

"Ever teach?"

"Just as an assistant, once."

"It figures. Then how come you're like, you know, not one?"

"A teacher? Never enough time. Before I could get established, we always moved."

"What was Turtle doing when you met?"

You mean back when he had dreams and aspirations? she thought. "Oh, he wanted his own business; then he talked about teaching philosophy."

"Figures. He's always spoutin' some kind of drivel. Sorry," Regina added, sending Ginny a sheepish glance. "I know he's your old man, but sometimes I wonder how you—" She paused. "Seems like he never runs out of words."

"He's always been good with words," Ginny admitted, remembering how he'd fired up campus demonstrations with his spirited rhetoric.

They reached their stop and left the bus.

Ginny thought the hours would never pass. By the end of the day, she was exhausted. Turtle was already home when she got there.

"Hi," she said, dumping her bag in the corner. "How was your day?"

"Well, listen to little Miss Homemaker," he goaded, popping the top off a long-neck bottle.

"Things didn't go well?" she presumed.

He ignored her.

"I'll go down and help with dinner."

He still didn't answer, and she left him nursing his drink.

Ben was cooking again. He slid pork chops into the oven to broil as she walked into the kitchen.

"Hi," she said, picking up a stack of plates to set on the table. "I thought it was Twig's turn to cook tonight."

"Hi," he returned. "It is, but he's not here, and I'm hungry."

They worked in companionable silence for a few minutes.

"I'm almost afraid to ask," she finally ventured.

"Fire away."

"What happened at work today?"

He straightened, tossing aside the towel that had been slung over his shoulder. "Better ask Turtle."

She should, but she wouldn't. "I'm asking you."

His eyebrows lifted.

"Sorry, I know you don't want to be involved in this." She knew she was being unfair, but she wanted Ben's opinion of the day's events.

"Well, there was a petition circulating, protesting what's happening to Turtle. I took it to the executive editor." He picked up the towel again. "Nick's a liberal who left his last position because he had the courage to stand up for his convictions, and we thought, well, he'd be the most likely to present Turtle's case."

She studied his profile, waiting.

"And?"

"Nick's got a family and a mortgage now, and—"

"And he wouldn't present the petition," she guessed.

"No, he did it. But the publisher exploded. He's so firm on the matter that Turtle was given the choice: cut the hair, or resign."

"Nick put his own job in jeopardy? He can't afford to do that!"

Ben's gaze met hers steadily. "No, he can't, Ginny."

"So Turtle had to resign."

"Not yet," Ben said. "He has a day or two to reconsider."

She turned away. "A couple of days won't make any difference. He won't resign; he'd rather be fired. It would mean more to his cause."

"You never know."

But she did know. She knew only too well.

Ginny went upstairs immediately after dinner. Turtle followed a short time later.

"Are you ready to talk about what happened today?" she asked, jerking her nightgown over her head.

"Head honcho sent another message down from the mountain," he said, stretching out on the bed.

"And?"

"I'm gonna do what he wants."

She turned around, surprised. "You are?"

"Yep. I'm gonna cut my hair." He grinned. "And I'm gonna leave the residue piled in the middle of his desk."

Her heart sank. "What?"

"I'm gonna give him what he wants. My hair on a platter."

"Ted—"

His eyes dared her to stop him. "That's it, Ginny. I'm sticking to my beliefs, or I'm a bigger hypocrite than he is."

Picking up the scissors, Turtle snipped at his hair until he had a sizable handful. The remainder fell into a jagged line at his chin. Cramming the clippings into a legal-size envelope, he left it lying on the table for morning.

Ginny went to bed.

Turtle was in a foul mood when she opened the door to their room the next afternoon. Dropping her bag on a chair, she opened a bottle of juice, then sank into a chair opposite him.

He took a long swallow from a bottle. "Mr. Publisher didn't appreciate my submission."

"He fired you." It was a statement, not a question.

He chuckled. "Let's just say there was a great storm on the mountain."

Getting up, she moved to the window. "How much money do we have?"

"Enough to get us to Morningside Ranch."

"Morningside?"

"Yeah. This guy named Lou Gottlieb opened a thirty-acre ranch in Sonoma County. I hear it's a place where we can live like we want. 'Experimentally,' *Time* magazine calls it. A good place for the 'technologically unemployable,' which means me." He lifted his bottle in a silent salute. "To us, babe."

"Who is this Gottlieb?"

"Gottlieb? A dropout jazz musician." Turtle leaned forward, excitement lighting his eyes. "He's a modern-day prophet of the Open Land Movement. He renounced ownership of the land. Says it should be open for everyone to use. It sounds exactly like what we're looking for. We'll leave first thing in the morning. I've already told Ben to find somebody to take our room."

Her hand crept to her stomach as she silently stared out the window.

"It'll be good, Ginny," he coaxed. "We'll have our own land, raise our own food. It'll be good."

Ben didn't knock the next morning, but Regina stopped by as usual.

"Ready?"

"In a minute." Ginny approached Turtle. "I have to go in and give my resignation," she told him quietly.

Turtle was shoving things into his duffel bag. "You don't owe them anything. Get packed—"

"I owe them the courtesy of resigning in person." Before he could stop her, she turned and left with Regina.

"You going with him?" Regina hurried to keep up with her.

"Yes."

"Because of the baby?"

"Yes."

"It ain't any of my business, but you know Turtle's a rolling stone."

"I know, but maybe this time—"

"You're a dreamer," Regina said, a smile softening her words. "But I hope you get what you want anyway."

They parted, Regina going to the line and Ginny heading toward the personnel office.

Three days later they arrived at Morningside Ranch. A sea of tents, wrecked cars, and plastic-covered huts stretched across the horizon. Ginny's heart sank. This wasn't what she expected, but Turtle's energy seemed to rise another notch as he stepped out of the VW.

"Who do I have to see?" he asked a passing man

dressed in dingy jeans and a limp vest with a bandanna around his head.

A thumb gestured to a large tent in the center. "In there, man."

By evening, they had their own tent. Ginny fell asleep on a sleeping bag Turtle bought at an army surplus store that day. As she unpacked the next morning, she discovered the book Ben had found in the attic. Somehow it had been packed along with her other belongings.

Handling the fragile binding carefully, she realized she would have to mail it to Ben. Thumbing through the worn pages, she noticed that former owners had jotted down random thoughts about the book. Ginny wished she had more time to explore the writings, but that would have to wait. She tucked the book into the large bag she carried for safeguarding.

Two weeks passed. Turtle didn't seem inclined to look for work, insisting they had enough money to last if they were careful. When she suggested she find a job, he got angry and they argued.

A shouting match erupted when she was no longer able to hide her morning sickness.

"You're pregnant? Well, *hell*." He ran his hand through his shaggy hair. "Man, this *stinks*."

"Turtle, it's a child! Our child!"

"Yeah—a kid. That's *all* we need."

"If we settle down, it'll be all right. We can find a place, a house. A job. Maybe I could teach, after the baby . . ."

There were ways to make it work. When had he become so inflexible?

He whirled on her. "The whole point of coming here was to defy the Establishment. Here you're talking about all the trappings of a society that's gone crazy over 'things.' "

"I'm not talking about 'things,' " she argued. "But a baby needs a home. A nice solid house without two hundred strangers traipsing about all hours of the day and night."

Now that she'd started, she couldn't stop.

"Have you taken a good look at what's going on around here? This isn't the kind of life we visualized!" They had wanted less in order to have more. They had neither.

"What do you want, Ginny? I don't know anymore!"

"I don't know either, but not this—we have—"

"Freedom," he said, bending so his face was level with hers. "Freedom to be who and what we want."

"Someone else's freedom extends only to the point of intruding on my freedom, and if I'm not comfortable with what's happening here, if I don't feel I can live my life as I want, then I have no freedom."

"Rhetoric," he muttered, straightening. "Middle-class rhetoric."

His comment stung. Turning, she left the tent in frustration.

She sought refuge in the town's library, relishing the cool air-conditioning and the quiet. There were riches on the shelves and she wandered through them, picking books at random, finally settling at a long table with a current newsmagazine. She didn't return to Morningside until the library closed at seven. Turtle gave no sign of noticing her absence. He was sound asleep, snoring, when she entered the tent and silently changed into her gown.

The next week a letter arrived from Ben. "The baby birds have flown," he wrote. "I thought of you, wishing you were here to see them make their grand entrance into the world."

Smiling through a veil of tears, she folded the letter and hid it. Turtle wouldn't understand a thing about birds.

Unaccustomed to inactivity, Ginny began going into town first thing in the morning and staying all day. She considered getting a job, but knew her pregnancy would preclude employment. Then she saw the classified ad in the newspaper.

"Vintage cottage. Perfect starter home. Needs work."

The listed price was much lower than she'd ever imagined. A spurt of excitement prompted her to phone the real-estate agent to ask if the house was still available. To her surprise, it was.

As she drove to the real-estate office, her thoughts bounced between being positive the house was a dump—that it had to be or it would have already been bought—to wondering how in the world she'd pay for it, if it was suitable.

It dawned on her she'd made a decision without realizing it. If the house was structurally sound, and Turtle would move there, then there was hope for them. But if he refused to leave Morningside, and if she could by some miracle manage to purchase the house, then she would make a home there for her child on her own. There was her grandmother's inheritance fund—she could always use that.

It would take a miracle to make it all fall into place—more than a miracle—but she had a strong urge to try.

The house was a tiny two-bedroom cottage with crabgrass overtaking the lawn. It needed paint, and the screen door hung lopsidedly on a broken hinge. The floor creaked, and the real-estate agent seemed to talk very fast so she wouldn't notice its problems, but she adored the place. It felt like a real home.

The odor of age permeated the musty-smelling interior.

"It's a steal," the agent vowed, hugging her expensive suede skirt to her legs to avoid brushing against a grimy windowsill.

"Can I go upstairs?" Ginny asked.

"Upstairs?"

"Yes. I saw a dormer window, so there must be a room up there, perhaps a bedroom, or a writing room?"

"You're a writer?"

"No," Ginny said, the words springing to her lips. "I'm a teacher."

"Oh, how nice! Well, go right on up. Poke around all you like. I'll check the listing for precise details."

Ginny found the attic stairs without difficulty and was glad for the few minutes to herself. The carpeted steps muffled her footsteps as she climbed them. The door opened effortlessly when she pushed at it.

Sunlight filtered through a broken window, dust motes floating through the air. The attic was floored, and half the shortened walls were paneled as if someone had once thought of finishing the space. She turned in a slow circle, trying to picture a desk and bookshelves.

Hands clasped on her forearms, she walked to the window, staring down on the row of orange daylilies fringing the property line below. She tried to picture Turtle, the baby, and herself living here. No matter how hard she tried, Turtle didn't fit the picture. Ben's face kept popping into her mind instead.

Ben, her heart whispered.

Reaching for her bag, she removed the old book. Aged, the faded leather had faint gold letters stamped on it, but she could not make out the title.

With trembling fingers she touched it, absorbing the texture of the bound cover. Her fingers absently slipped over the edge and opened it.

Words, evocative and poetic, beckoned her: "For the scent of her was like a field of flowers, the taste of her flesh was honey and life."

She turned another page, and another. Her eyes were drawn to a notation at the end of the book.

With honor came glory!
Burgundy Mountjoy, Countess of Devon, 1602
Elizabeth M, 1803

There were other entries, too, and other names. Some were just a few words, others several paragraphs:

Flowers open their petals and give pleasure to the eye, as does this book give pleasure to the soul.
Yvonne Armistead, 1851

A daughter's search for happiness through the eyes and heart of her mother.
Little Flower, 1870

The agent's voice drifted up the stairwell. "Are you about finished up there? I hate to rush you, but it is late—"

"Jus—just a moment," Ginny called. Shoving the book back into the bag, she looped the strap over her shoulder.

"Well, what do you think?" the agent chirped. "Isn't it lovely?"

"I'd like my . . . husband"—she winced at the lie—"to see it. I'll be in touch," she promised.

She drove slowly back to Morningside. She would never be able to explain to Turtle about the book, or the house. Her earlier courage faded.

That night, as she lay sleepless, she thought about the book and the strange notes written after the story.

Words. She was a teacher. It was all she'd ever wanted to be. Ever since she was a child in school and the magic of words had been revealed to her by a teacher, she'd had a love of reading.

From the time she was able to sound out syllables, she'd immersed herself in anything written. It wasn't until the fourth grade that she realized some people couldn't read. Even as a child, the revelation was horrifying.

A shy little girl had joined the class and when the teacher asked her to read a passage from a book they were reading aloud, they'd waited in silence while she struggled through the simplest of phrases. Painful embarrassment had flooded the child's face with scarlet and tears had slipped down her cheeks.

The teacher had been sympathetic. She put her arms around the little girl and took the book from her hands. And then, in a gentle voice, she explained that not everyone was as lucky as the other children in the class. Not everyone had the advantage of a school system that knew the importance of learning to read.

She continued, explaining that there were even adults who could not read, for one reason or another. She explained their struggle through life because they were unable to read employment applications, street signs, menus. And then she asked the class's help in teaching the new student the joy of reading.

They took turns during lunch hours, and for those who could, after school, reading, pointing out words, pronouncing words, listening as the little girl struggled, then slowly began to discover for herself the adventures between the covers of books. It was then that Ginny's love of teaching had begun to bud. Dick and Jane gave way over the years to "The Gift of the Magi." She discovered Dickens and *Jane Eyre*, and then Fitzgerald and Hemingway. Her thirst was never quenched; with each "The End" she eagerly searched for a new beginning.

Throughout her life, Ginny turned to books for the answers to her problems, for passages that would help guide her life; in times of trouble she read and found peace. Books had helped her through many choices.

But at that moment, she had run out of choices. For the first time, she acknowledged to herself her fear of being alone with the baby.

She had made mistakes before, but her choices were limited now that she was responsible for another life. *You have no choice*, she reminded herself, *until the baby is born and you can work again.*

The next morning she drove into town and found a quiet place in a small park and once again opened the book. After reading awhile, she rested her head on the back of the bench, closing her eyes.

The story seemed to have been written expressly for her.

The Quest
You alone decide your Destiny.
At the crossroads, choose wisely.
One path is cursed, the other blessed.
Life is a double-edged sword.
You have free will to carve out the rock!
Will you rise or fall, succeed or fail,
Taste ambrosia or bitter aloes?
To find the key, ask what is neverending, everlasting;
What is noble and sacred, selfless and eternal?
The answer is Love.
Love is the greatest power on earth.
Pass on the gift of Love.
With Honor Comes Glory!

She, too, was at a crossroad. But was there honor in her life with Turtle? She knew he would scoff at the very word.

When she had finished reading, she recalled one of the notes at the end of the story.

Search for the truth, and find the treasure.
Angela Damien, 1815

Was she searching for the truth? Did her unsettled feelings mean more than unhappiness at having to live in a tent? More than her reluctance to admit she had grown, and Turtle hadn't?

She stared across the park at two children running in the sunlight, kicking a red ball. Soon her own child would be running in the sun, laughing at simple delights. And what would she be doing?

The sun was setting by the time she started back to Morningside. She drove slowly, thinking, somehow reluctant to face Turtle tonight.

Turtle wasn't at the tent when she arrived. She set out the food she'd bought at a market near the park. She'd gone to look out the tent opening to see if she could locate him when the wail of sirens sounded through the encampment.

At first everyone seemed frozen in place; then heads swiveled toward the line of police cars descending on the ranch. Several people sprang to life, diving into their tents for safety.

A swarm of officers piled out of the cars. Their leader sent someone after Lou, the owner of the ranch. There was a lot of shouting, confusion.

Women screamed, men cursed, children cried. Chaos reigned.

It was several minutes before the owner arrived and was served a search warrant.

The officers spread out and began going through the tents. Each time one of them emerged with a paper folder or some other item in his hand, someone was handcuffed and escorted to a waiting patrol car.

Ginny stepped away from the tent in search of Turtle. He had nothing illegal, but humiliation bloomed on her cheeks.

It was late before the officers climbed back into the patrol cars, pulled into a tight circle, and drove back down the lane, leaving a cloud of dust in the air.

It was another hour before an angry Turtle entered the tent.

Ginny lay on her bedroll, staring at the ceiling of her tent, the book lying open on her stomach.

"Damn fuzz!" he said, beginning to stuff his

clothes into his duffel bag. "Did you see that?"

She didn't bother to answer; he didn't expect one.

"The apes. They closed the ranch." He shoved clothes into paper sacks. "The neighbors—with their two point five children, picket fence, and pedigreed dog—complained about the noise. The straights said they were sick of hippies livin' in their midst." He paused, looking at her. "Can you believe it? They told Lou he could have only fifteen guests at a time. Who are they to tell us what to do? We're outta here. Get your stuff together."

A cold chill snaked up her spine. "Where to this time?"

"To Holiday. Twenty or so of us are leaving in the morning."

Holiday. Ginny recalled the name. Yet another typical community of dropouts.

By the time they reached Holiday and established their place for the night, she had seen enough to know that Holiday was no different from Morningside.

Residents had gravitated there after growing tired of California smog, freeways, and harassment. Their free lifestyle was criticized constantly by the media.

Ginny listened to the complaints with half an ear, wanting nothing more than to lie down and sleep.

Finally she climbed into the VW and opened the book that she kept with her at all times.

The pages now opened easily at her touch. It was as if she were not choosing the pages to read, but the book was choosing the pages for her.

The words in the book stirred her soul. The beautiful story touched her heart and made her realize that something was missing from her life. She'd never felt so alone as she did right now. She could feel her love for Turtle evaporating, fleeing, and she didn't know how to stop it.

They were never alone anymore. If he was in the tent, there was usually someone with him. He was always drafting dissertations against the lifestyle he was intent on eradicating. At times she wondered if anyone but Turtle and his friends cared any longer about what they were doing.

She fell asleep, grateful for the respite.

With morning came the challenge of finding a permanent place to pitch their tent. Turtle had little time for such mundane things, so the task fell to Ginny.

Increasingly, she found herself missing Ben. She longed to feel the comfort of his friendly arm around her neck, to hear his gentle voice.

The women at Holiday were much like those at Morningside. All were adamant about their decision to drop out of society. Ginny grew increasingly restless in their company, wishing for something with meaning for her.

While Turtle mingled, Ginny sought a quiet place where she could read the book. Those times were the only periods of peace she experienced, and she found herself growing more and more hungry for the words that calmed her soul.

They'd been at Holiday less than a month. She awakened from an afternoon nap and was standing in the tent doorway trying to locate Turtle to tell him she was driving into town for supplies, when she saw Ben striding toward her.

She could hardly believe her eyes. "Ben?"

"Ginny!" He broke into a run, heading straight for her.

Surprise mingled with joy sent her racing toward him, and when she threw herself into his arms she wanted to cry.

"I can't believe you're here!" She held on to him like a buoy in rough water. "What *are* you doing here?"

"I'm doing a story on Holiday." They clung together tightly. "You look wonderful!"

"You do too!"

His hair was neatly cut, and his crisp jeans and dark blazer made him look very journalistic.

"Couldn't you have written the article from the house?" she asked.

He appeared as reluctant to relinquish his hold on her as she on him. "You've caught me. I volunteered to come up here."

When a crowd began gathering, they finally broke the embrace. Looping her arm through his, she walked him in the direction of her tent.

"Well, it should make an interesting story. Things are changing. I see the movement getting more . . . intense. Militant almost."

He didn't respond for a moment. When he did, his tone was solemn. "Are you all right?"

She felt herself caught up in his concerned gaze.

"I'm fine. Just fine."

"Feeling all right?"

Her breath caught.

"Regina told you."

His mouth curved in a smile. "Yeah, she mentioned it. But I'd already guessed. You looked . . . different. There's a special glow about you—and your tummy's bulging a little."

She looked down, amazed at his perception. "You noticed?"

He grinned. "I noticed."

She marveled at that. She lived with Turtle. He was the baby's father, and he hadn't noticed.

She gazed up at him. "How long are you staying?"

"A few days. Talk to a few people, see how things go. How's Turtle?"

"Oh, you know . . . the same." Her face brightened. "Are you staying here?" She didn't dare hope that he would be.

"No, in town. A small motel."

"What?" she teased. "Not roughing it?"

He grinned. "I can make my point and still sleep in a decent bed and take a shower and shave every day."

That sounded wonderful. The communal showers were inadequate, and she found herself getting up earlier and earlier to be first in line.

"Let's go get a sandwich in town, Ginny."

She was startled by his impulsiveness.

"Sure," she said, suddenly hungry for news of Regina and, she had to admit, Ben himself.

They went to a small Italian restaurant filled with wonderful aromas and people who laughed and talked in quiet tones. The food was delicious, and she was so full when they finished that she had to undo a button on her slacks.

But more than that, she felt full of the wonder of talking about something besides society and its ills. She couldn't remember the last time she'd been so happy.

Later, as he stopped his rental car outside the gate of the ranch, Ben turned toward her in the seat.

"What are you going to do, Ginny?"

"What do you mean?"

"You know what I mean. This life isn't for you.

You don't want to raise a child here."

"Right now I . . . Turtle is the child's father, Ben."

"A father's more than a moment of passion, Ginny."

She sucked in a deep breath, blinking back tears that suddenly threatened.

He drew her to him gently. "Aww . . . I'm sorry. I didn't mean to make you cry."

"You didn't," she lied. "I'm just tired." Drawing away, she pushed open the car door and slipped out. "Oh, Ben . . . remember that old book we found in the attic?"

"Yes?"

"Somehow it got mixed in with my things." She wanted to keep it so badly, to have something to hang on to, but she knew she shouldn't. "You need to return it to its owner."

"All right."

She got out of the car.

"Ginny."

"Yes."

"Think about what I said."

"Sure." As if she would be able to think of anything else.

As she threaded her way through the maze of tents and open bedrolls, she *knew* what she wanted. She just wasn't sure she'd have the conviction to go through with it.

Turtle hung around after the evening meal. He was writing on a Big Chief tablet with a stub of a pencil, and she found herself studying him as if he were a stranger.

His hair fell well over his shoulders, his beard was scruffy. He was thinner, his shoulders decidedly rounded. Where was the strong, visionary young man she fell in love with three years ago?

He had changed not only physically but in values. They were both so different from when they'd started out together. Or were they? Had he changed? Or had she?

"Turtle?"

"Hmmm?" He kept writing.

"Ben is here."

"I heard."

"Don't you want to see him?"

"You did, didn't you?"

"Yes."

"Then what's the problem?"

"Turtle, we need to talk."

"Not now, Ginny."

She waited until he finished whatever it was he was writing. When he reached for another notebook, her tone stopped him.

"We need to talk."

"All right," he said, his impatience showing. "What is it?"

Now that the moment was here, she wasn't sure how to begin. Her eyes traveled to her bag, where she kept the book.

"Spit it out, Ginny. I'm busy."

"It's about the baby," she blurted, immediately realizing the timing was wrong.

He glanced up. "What baby?"

"*Our* baby."

His face went blank. "What about it?"

"A baby, Turtle. We're having a *baby*. Doesn't that mean anything to you?"

He stared at her as if he didn't comprehend what she was saying.

"I know . . . the other women will help you."

Now it was she who didn't comprehend.

"What?"

"When it's time. The other women will help you."

She was stunned. "Is that all you have to say? We're having a child, Turtle, a tiny human life to guide, direct, to teach right from wrong, good from evil."

"Whatever." He went back to what he was doing.

She stared at him, all remaining hopes for their future dashed. "Is that all you have to say?"

"Ginny, I'm busy. What is it you want me to say? You know I'm not ready for a kid. You should have been more careful."

"What do I want you to say?" she repeated numbly. "I want you to say that you're happy. I—I want to make plans. We're out of money. You need a job. I want a home for—"

He shoved himself upright. "We're here at Holiday because society doesn't recognize or accept our lifestyle, and now you're wanting to buy into it? How many kids do you see running around here? Two dozen? Three? They're all healthy, happy, free. Just like our kid will be. *Chill out. Hell,* I'm going to Skeet's tent. Maybe I can get some privacy there."

Ginny stared at the tent opening long after he'd gone. One central thought kept going through her mind. Turtle wasn't going to have a child; she was. To him, the child would be community property.

She fell asleep with her hand resting against her rounding belly. The child inside her was the future, and she would cherish and love it.

* * *

The next morning, Turtle was arrested for harassing people on the street and spent twenty-four hours in jail.

When he returned to Holiday, he was hailed as a conquering hero. If there had been any lingering doubt for Ginny, it was gone now. She knew where her future lay, and with whom.

"Get packed. We're outta here," Turtle ordered, striding into the tent that night.

Coincidentally, she was already packing.

"The coast is saturated. We're heading back east where we won't be persecuted for our beliefs."

Neatly folding a blouse, she placed it into the brown paper bag that served as her luggage.

"Everybody's sick of what's going on. Ice is going to Taos. Mertz and Bird are moving on to Wheeler Ranch near Bodega Bay. But the Oz family is moving back east. They've got some land back there."

Taking a deep breath, Ginny answered, "I'm not going." *Search for the truth and find the treasure. Angela Damien, 1815.*

Turtle wasn't listening. "We'll travel with the Ozes. It'll be cheaper that way. Work along the way when we need—"

"I'm not going."

He glanced up. "What?"

"I'm not going." She felt suddenly strong, decisive, protective.

Motherly.

"What are you talking about?"

"I'm not going. I'm going to buy a cottage, maybe a dog—certainly a white picket fence—and raise my baby."

"You're selling out!" Disbelief mixed with anger singed his voice.

"No, I'm trying to find some honor in my life. I can't live like this; I want more for our child. *I* want more for myself than this."

Shaking his head in disbelief, he was clearly sickened. "You've changed."

"Yes, I have. Thank you for noticing."

Disgusted, he turned away. "It's your choice. But don't expect to come running back when you wake up and discover you're one of 'them' now."

No *Please, Ginny, I love you*. No *It's our child, so maybe I should make some changes in my life, too.* Just *It's your choice.*

Simple.

The values she held could be taught to her child—the values of independence, of courage, of thinking for himself and dealing with people with fairness and honesty—whether she was 'dropped out' or living in harmony with the Establishment.

Life had rules; it always had, and it always would.

"I'm sorry." Her eyes met his. "I hope you find what you're searching for, Turtle."

He picked up his notebooks and stalked through the tent opening.

Oddly, Ginny felt no anger. Turtle had sold out to a cause that was not even clear to him. In his struggle to avoid the society he so vehemently hated, he had found a new demon that demanded its own regimen. For the first time in a long time, she felt at peace.

Ben.

She needed to share her revelation with Ben. When she went in search of him, one of the band told her he had left an hour earlier.

Devastated, she returned to her empty tent. He had not only forgotten the book; he hadn't even said good-bye.

The following morning she packed the remainder of her personal articles along with the book into a duffel bag and started down the lane that led away from Holiday Ranch.

The sun felt good on her face, and she breathed deeply of the early morning air. The baby fluttered inside her womb and she smiled. "I'm gonna make some humdinger blunders, baby," she confessed aloud, patting her stomach. "But we'll learn together."

She'd gone less than a mile when she heard a car approach from behind. Perhaps she could thumb a ride. She turned.

The car slowed, and Ben leaned out the window, his gaze on the duffel bag she had slung over her shoulder.

"Need a ride?"

Her heart nearly burst at the sight of him. "It seems I do."

"Need a husband?"

She smiled, love glistening through her tears. "Looks like I might need one of those, too."

His tone was husky. "Get in."

Resting her hand on the car door, she leaned forward and met his waiting kiss.

"If you're looking for a father for your child," he breathed against her lips, "I'm volunteering for that, too."

"You're hired."

"Just like that?"

No, not just like that, she thought. She'd known

for a long time he was destined to be a larger part of her life.

The book had made her see that. She had searched for the truth and found the treasure.

And together, she and Ben would teach it to another.

TO LOVE AGAIN

MADELINE BAKER

To Love Again

I

Angela Wagner grimaced as she shut the book. Ever-lasting love, she thought bitterly. There was no such thing. Not in this life. Not on this earth. No man could be trusted. Her father had left her and her mother for another woman. Her brother had left her to fend for herself after her mother passed away. Even Roger, who had sworn he would love her forever, had proven to be nothing but a liar. His betrayal hurt worst of all. She had given him her heart, her virginity, and her life's savings, and he had skipped town with all three.

Angie threw the book across the room. There was no fool like an old fool, she mused, and she, herself, was proof of that! Sheriff Howard had told her just yesterday that he had learned that Roger Highland was a rogue of the worst sort, preying on unsuspecting women, sweet-talking them into bed and out of their life savings.

Angie had refused to believe a word of it until Howard had thrust an official-looking piece of paper under her nose, letting her read about Roger for herself. Roger Highland was a professional con man, all right, wanted in fourteen states.

Angie had lifted her chin and fought back her tears as she bid the sheriff a good day, silently berating herself for being such an easy mark. She had heard of men like Roger, men who preyed on the weak, the unsuspecting. She had always pitied the poor, weak-willed women who had been fleeced out of everything they owned by a handsome face and pretty words. It shamed her to acknowledge that she was no better than those women, to admit that Roger Highland had played her for a fool. Worst of all, soon the whole town would know.

Angie groaned softly. Quincy, North Dakota, was a small, close-knit town. There were no secrets in Quincy, at least not for long.

A crude oath escaped Angie's lips as she stood up and went to the mirror. Thirty years old, she thought with a shake of her head. Thirty years dumb! She should have known better than to believe that a man seven years her junior would be attracted to a plain Jane like her.

Angie frowned at her reflection. She wondered how Roger had kept a straight face when he was whispering all that rubbish in her ears, raving about her bonny face and golden hair and sea-green eyes. No doubt he had been laughing all the while to think that an old maid would believe such malarkey. And yet, who needed to hear those things more than an old maid, even if they weren't true?

Never again, she vowed. Never again would she let her head be turned by some sweet-talking man. Never!

Returning to the living room, she scowled at the book lying on the floor. It was a copy of an old, old book that had been given to her by her mother. A book that had been handed down from generation to generation for countless years.

The original manuscript was in the Library of Congress, but copies had been made. Angie's mother had told her that more than a century ago, one of her ancestors, another Angela, had made three copies so that she could pass one to each of her daughters.

Feeling guilty for having handled such a cherished book in such a manner, Angie stooped and picked it up from the floor. Odd to think that the story of Damon and Angeline had lasted for hundreds of years. Supposedly it was unlike anything she had ever read. The author had painted a beautiful story, not with colors, but with words. Magical words that had carried Angie to another time and place.

Others who had read the book in previous ages had added their own thoughts to the end, so that it was no longer the story of one man and one woman, but a love story that spanned a thousand years.

One woman had written "Great risks reap great rewards," at the end of the story. The words "With honor came glory" had been penned by another.

Angela frowned again. Love had brought her neither rewards nor glory, she thought bitterly, only a broken heart and an empty bank account. How would she ever face the people she knew when they learned how easily she had been duped?

She could hear the townspeople now, laughing behind their hands, making jokes.

She stared at the book in her hands. It had fallen open and she found herself reading aloud:

"For the scent of her was like a field of flowers, the taste of her flesh was honey and life . . ."

Roger had whispered words like that, sweet lying words that had blinded her to what he really was. Flowery words that had made her believe that she, too, could enjoy the kind of loving relationship that Damon and Angeline had shared.

With a strangled sob, Angie slammed the book shut. She was tempted to toss the thing in the trash, but something stayed her hand. Instead, she placed it on the bookshelf.

Keeping her mind carefully blank, she took a shower, slipped on her nightgown, braided her hair, brushed her teeth.

But she could not bring herself to sleep in her bed. The same bed where Roger Highland had seduced her. She knew then she would never sleep in that bed again. Tomorrow she would get rid of the darn thing.

If only she could dispose of her shameful memories as easily!

II

Angie woke with the dawn, stiff from spending the night on the sofa. She dressed quickly, then went into the kitchen to fix breakfast, only to find she had no appetite.

Sipping black coffee, she knew she couldn't go to work, couldn't face her coworkers, her customers. She knew everyone in Quincy, and everyone knew her. By now they would all know that Roger had left town, alone. There would be no wedding in the spring. She supposed she should be grateful he hadn't left her standing at the altar, but she didn't feel grateful.

Angie poured herself a second cup of coffee. She hadn't taken a vacation in years, but now was definitely the time. Some might call it cowardly to run away, but she didn't care. She needed some time alone, time to sort her thoughts. Time to come to grips with the fact that she was probably never going to marry, never going to be swept off her feet by a handsome knight on a white horse.

Before she could change her mind or lose her nerve, she called the bank and told Mr. Black she was taking a month off. Then she packed her bags and left town, headed for the small cabin in the mountains that her Grandmother James had left her. It had been in her mother's family ever since Dorry and Luke James had established a thriving ranch on the land a century before.

Angie hadn't been there in years. It was a good thing she hadn't mentioned the place to Roger, she thought with a grimace, or he probably would have taken that with him, too!

There had been many changes in the little town of Cross Corners since she'd been there last. Her family had once owned most of the land around it, including the big cattle ranch that occupied several hundred acres adjacent to the cabin. The ranch had been sold again recently, and the new owners had turned the place into a dude ranch. She had passed several groups of would-be cowboys riding across the countryside as she drove up the long, winding dirt road that led to the cabin.

She felt a sense of freedom when she pulled into the front yard. The cabin looked just as she remembered it. A weathered dwelling made of logs, it sat in a small clearing surrounded by hardwood trees, wildflowers, and berry bushes gone wild. The old barn nearby looked as if it was about to fall down.

Grabbing her suitcase, she locked the car, then made her way to the front door. Slipping the key into the lock, she gave the door a shove, then stepped inside.

A fine layer of dust covered everything. Lacy gray cobwebs hung from the corners of the ceiling. Instead of filling her with dismay, it gave her a sense of purpose.

She spent the next two hours cleaning house. She swept the floors and dusted the furniture. She uncovered the dark brown leather sofa, the matching easy chair. She washed the dust from the kitchen sink, polished the stove, plugged in the ancient refrigerator.

She put clean sheets on the bed and towels in the bathroom, hung her clothes in the small closet. She washed out the bathroom sink, scrubbed the small, claw-foot bathtub.

That done, she bathed and changed her clothes, donning a pair of comfortable sweatpants and a pair of Reeboks. She ran a brush through her hair, then wound it into a tight knot at her nape.

Going back into the kitchen, she sat down at

the table. Blowing a lock of hair from her forehead, she sat down and wrote out a grocery list.

She felt better than she had in days as she drove to the store. For the next four weeks, she would hide out in the cabin and lick her wounds. She would resign herself to the fact that she was never going to get married.

"Just remember," she muttered, "a woman without a man is like a fish without a bicycle."

She didn't need a man. She had a good job, a nice apartment. When her vacation was over, she'd go back home and get on with her life. Lots of single women lived full, rewarding lives, and so would she.

Dakota Sanders leaned against the outer wall of the tobacco shop, an unlit cigarette dangling from his lips as he watched a bevy of curvy young women parade up and down the boardwalk. They were all guests at the ranch, pretty young things who rarely thought about anything more serious than what to wear.

But they were a comic sight in their skintight jeans and frilly shirts. It always amazed him, what city folk thought of as Western wear. Most amusing of all were their boots. Red boots with pointy toes and spiked heels. Blue boots with fancy silver trim. Purple suede boots. The cowboys of old would have laughed themselves silly if they could see these dudes.

Dakota shook his head as he glanced at his watch. The girls wouldn't be ready to go for another hour at least, time enough to buy a carton of cigarettes and then go have a cold one over at Olson's.

Pushing away from the wall, he was about to

step into the tobacco shop when a sudden clatter followed by a soft oath caught his attention.

Glancing over his shoulder, he saw a woman standing in front of the grocery store. She had two sacks of groceries balanced in the crook of one arm, and held what was left of a torn brown paper bag in her right hand. Her mouth was set in a grim line as she frowned at the cans and boxes scattered at her feet.

"Let me help you," Dakota offered.

"It isn't necessary." She dropped the torn sack and took a firmer hold on the other two bags.

"My pleasure, ma'am," Dakota insisted.

Angie stared at him as he quickly picked up her groceries. He was tall and lean, with broad shoulders and sun-bronzed skin. Faded blue jeans hugged unbelievably long, muscular legs. Thick black hair fell past the collar of his denim shirt. The sleeves had been cut off, exposing muscular arms browned by the sun. He was the most outrageously handsome man she had ever seen. Next to him, Roger Highland looked like a wimp.

Dakota stood up, her groceries gathered in his arms. "Where are you parked, ma'am?"

"Over there." He had the most beautiful brown eyes she had ever seen. With an effort, she tore her gaze from his. "The green Camry."

With a nod, he followed her to the car, dumped the cans and boxes into the backseat after she opened the door.

"Thank you, Mr. . . ." She couldn't stop staring at him. Lean and rugged, he looked every inch a cowboy, from the crown of his black Stetson hat to the soles of his scuffed leather boots.

"Sanders. Dakota Sanders."

"Yes, well, thanks again," she said stiffly. "I appreciate your help."

Dakota watched as she slid behind the wheel and drove down the street. Who was she? he wondered. Not a guest at the ranch, that was for sure. None of the would-be cowgirls ever ran around with their hair skinned back and their faces makeup free, nor would any of them have been caught dead wearing those baggy black sweatpants. No, the girls who came to the dude ranch preferred tight-fitting white denim shorts that showed off their long, well-tanned legs, and low-cut midriff tops that flaunted their ample breasts and flat bellies.

With a shrug, he walked back to the tobacco shop. There were too many pretty girls waiting back at the ranch to worry about one tight-lipped, dowdy woman.

He swore under his breath. She'd had the prettiest green eyes he had ever seen. The prettiest, and the saddest.

He tried to put her out of his mind, but he was still thinking about her when he drove the guests back to the ranch late that afternoon.

Angie bolted upright in bed as another shaft of lightning slashed the skies. Thunder rumbled overhead, sounding as though it would come right through the roof. Rain pelted the bedroom window, pounding relentlessly against the glass like angry watery fists.

"Just my luck," she muttered, clutching the covers to her chin. "A second Flood, and I'm all alone."

Knowing she was never going to get back to sleep, Angie slid out of bed, drew on a thick terrycloth robe and a pair of furry blue slippers, and padded into the kitchen. She flicked the light switch on, but nothing happened.

Great, she thought, the power's out.

She rummaged through the cupboards until she found a candle and some matches. Lighting the candle, she placed it on the kitchen counter, then poured some milk in a pan and put it on the stove. A cup of hot chocolate was just what she needed.

Moving to the kitchen window, she stared out into the storm while she waited for the milk to heat. She had always loved storms, and this one was a doozy. The sound of the rain filled her ears. Lightning scorched the skies. A brisk wind blew through the trees, bending them to its will.

A quick flash of lightning lit up the sky, revealing a man slumped over the withers of a horse. Angie gasped and drew back, adrenaline pumping through her veins. No man in his right mind would be out riding on a night like this . . .

Suddenly aware of how alone she was, Angie closed the curtains, then stood there, one hand pressed over her racing heart. Had he seen her? Did he know she was alone?

A hissing sound sent her to the stove. The milk was boiling. After removing the pan from the burner, she went back to the window and peered into the darkness.

She could barely make out the shape of a horse standing in the driveway, its back to the wind, its head lowered. Where was the man?

Opening a drawer, she withdrew a butcher knife,

quietly cursing the fact that she didn't have a phone. Or a gun.

Standing with her back to the wall, she waited. And listened. But all she heard was the steady sound of the rain.

Minutes ticked by. Clutching the knife, she risked a glance out the window again. The horse was standing as before, and then, as a sheet of lightning lit up the sky, she saw the man lying beside the horse.

He was hurt. She didn't know how she knew that, but she did.

She watched him for several moments, and when he didn't move, she ran out the back door, her slippers squishing in the mud.

He was lying facedown. "Mister?" She shook his shoulder. "Mister?"

A low groan escaped his lips.

"Can you stand up? I can't carry you."

He grunted softly.

Taking that for assent, Angie grabbed him by the arm and gave a tug. The man struggled to his feet. Dropping the knife, Angie placed one of his arms around her shoulders, slid one of her arms around his waist, and started toward the house. He staggered along beside her, his weight heavy as he leaned against her.

She was soaked to the skin by the time she got him into the kitchen.

Angie guided him to a chair and he sagged into it, his head lolling forward.

She didn't have to ask where he was hurt. Blood was dripping down his left hand. Gently, she removed his sheepskin jacket, noting a jagged rip in the jacket's heavy material. His left shirtsleeve was torn and soaked with blood.

Angie knelt before him. Unbuttoning his shirt, she eased it off his shoulders, down his right arm, and then, very slowly, off his left. Blood welled from a long, shallow gash along his forearm.

"I'll change clothes and take you to the hospital," Angie said.

"Can't," he said, sounding groggy. "The bridge is out."

Angie stared at him as the full implication of his words struck home. Any doctoring necessary would have to be done here, now.

He looked up at her through pain-filled eyes. "Think you can handle it?"

"Me?" Her stomach churned at the very thought.

"I don't see anyone else."

She stared at the blood that covered his arm, sickened by the sight of it. "I can't. I never . . ." She looked up at him. "It looks as if it might need stitches."

He shook his head. "I don't think so. Just wash it out and bandage it up tight." He offered her a reassuring grin. "Nothing to it."

Angie took a deep breath. "All right."

She lit several candles, placing a couple on the table, another in the bedroom, one in the bathroom. She found a clean cloth, some disinfectant, a roll of gauze, and some tape, then returned to the kitchen.

Once cleaned, the wound wasn't as bad as she'd thought. She washed it thoroughly, applied several butterfly bandages to hold the edges together, then wound several layers of gauze around his arm and taped it in place.

She was congratulating herself on a job well done when she saw the blood in his hair.

"Your head's bleeding!" she exclaimed.

"It is?" He looked up at her, his gaze unsteady. "Where?"

He winced as she parted his hair, looking for the source of the blood. She found a long, shallow gash behind his right ear.

Angie grimaced as she found a clean cloth and washed the blood from his hair and scalp. Fortunately, it didn't look as though it would require any stitching either, but . . .

"You might have a concussion," she remarked. She gazed into his eyes, trying to decide if his pupils looked dilated. Trying to remember if that was a good sign or not.

She taped a bandage over the gash, then washed her hands. "You need to get out of those wet pants."

He nodded and began to unfasten his jeans.

"Wait!" Angie said. "Let's get you into the bedroom. You can undress in there, then get into bed."

He didn't argue. With a sigh, she helped him to his feet and down the hall to the bedroom. He was swaying unsteadily by the time they reached her room. His face was pale, his brow sheened with perspiration.

Wishing she had stayed home, Angie backed him up against the wall; then, with her eyes carefully averted, she unfastened his jeans and pulled them off.

If he wanted his briefs off, he'd have to do that himself, she mused as she helped him into bed and drew the covers over him.

He was asleep as soon as his head touched the pillow.

Angie stared at him for a moment. He looked

vaguely familiar, and then she realized where she had seen him before.

He was the cowboy who had helped her in town that afternoon.

III

Dakota squeezed his eyes shut, trying to ignore the voice that was pestering him to wake up.

"Mr. Sanders? Mr. Sanders, wake up."

With a low groan, he opened his eyes. Squinting against the flickering candlelight, he stared at the woman kneeling beside the bed. "What d'ye want?"

"Do you know who you are?"

He looked at her as if she'd lost her mind. "Of course I know who I am. Who the hell are you?"

"Do you know where you are?"

"Your bed?" he remarked wryly.

"I'm serious. What's your name?"

"Dakota."

"Do you have a headache?"

"No."

"Do you feel sick to your stomach?"

"No. Listen. I'm fine. Just tired."

Angie stood up. He knew where he was and he seemed coherent enough, so he probably didn't have a concussion.

"Sorry I woke you," she said, folding her arms. "Go back to sleep."

Dakota stared up at her. He recognized her now, the woman from town. Amazing, he thought, how different she looked wearing a long blue robe. A wealth of wavy sun-colored hair cascaded over her shoulders. Her lashes were long and dark, her lips full and slightly pouty. But she still held herself as rigid as a fence post; there was no softness in her expression, no compassion or welcome in her eyes. And he was man enough, and hurting enough, to want both.

"Sorry to put you out, ma'am," he said, sitting up. "I'll be going now."

"Don't be silly!" she exclaimed. "You can't go out in this storm."

"I can, and I will."

"But . . ."

He swung his legs over the side of the bed, grunting softly as the movement set his head to pounding. He closed his eyes for a moment, then lifted his head to meet her gaze. "I make it a point never to stay where I'm not wanted, ma'am."

"I wish you'd stop calling me that," she snapped. "It makes me feel as if I'm eighty years old!"

He stared at her, one brow raised, the corner of his mouth turned down. "Sorry." He stood up, clutching the bedpost as the room began to sway around him.

Angie rushed forward and grabbed his arm. "Get back into that bed before you collapse."

"Yes, ma'am," he murmured, sinking down on the mattress. And then he offered her a wry grin. "Sorry, it just slipped out."

Lips compressed, Angie drew the covers up to his chin. She was turning away from the bed when his hand caught hers. His palm was callused, his fingers long and strong. The touch of his hand went through her like lightning.

"What are you doing?" she exclaimed.

"I just wanted to thank you for looking after me," he murmured, perplexed by the electricity that had arced between them the moment his fingers closed around hers.

Angie studied the hand imprisoning hers. It was big and brown, crisscrossed with tiny white scars. She was alarmed by the shivers of pleasure that washed through her as his grip tightened. "Let me go."

He released her hand immediately, his expression curious. "I didn't mean to scare you."

"Don't be ridiculous. You didn't scare me. I just don't like being touched."

"Sorry."

Angie stared down at him, irritated that she found him attractive, that looking at him made her feel all warm and gooey inside. Would she never learn!

With a sigh of disgust, she turned on her heel and left the room.

Dakota stared after her, wondering what her problem was. Wondering why he cared. He wasn't unaware of the effect he usually had on women, though he was at a loss to explain it. He wasn't any better looking than any other man, but from the time he'd turned fifteen, women had flocked to him. He'd had his pick of girls, first in school, then on the rodeo circuit, and now at the ranch.

But this woman looked at him as if he were some kind of vermin.

Dakota laughed softly. Maybe it was to keep him humble. Still, there was something about her, something that made him want to see her smile, make her laugh.

He fell asleep with that thought in mind.

* * *

Angie staggered into the kitchen and put the coffeepot on. It had been a long night. She had checked on the man sleeping in her bed several times during the night. Dakota Sanders.

She shook his image from her mind as she went to the window to look out.

"What the . . ." She shook her head, unable to believe her eyes. The man's horse was still standing out in the yard. Its back turned to the wind, it was contentedly cropping the weeds alongside the driveway, oblivious to the rain. She could see the butcher knife lying in the mud, where she'd left it.

A sound behind her drew her attention and she whirled around to see Dakota standing in the doorway. He wore rumpled jeans and held a blanket around his shoulders.

"Coffee smells good," he said. "Think I could have a cup?"

"Of course," Angie said, drawing her robe more firmly around her. "Sit down."

She took two mugs from the cupboard, filled them both, then handed him one. "Your horse is outside."

"I'd best go look after her."

"I don't think you should go out. Just tell me what to do."

"You know about horses?"

"No."

"I'll take care of her." He rose carefully to his feet and made his way back into the bedroom.

He emerged a few minutes later. "Thanks," he said, gesturing at the shirt Angie had washed and mended for him.

"You're welcome."

He studied her a moment before he shrugged into his jacket and went outside.

Determined to put Dakota Sanders from her mind, she turned to preparing breakfast, only to find herself wondering if he liked waffles.

"What difference does it make?" she muttered to herself. "I like them, and I'm doing the cooking!"

She fried some bacon, set the table with butter and jelly and syrup, refilled his coffee cup.

He was back fifteen minutes later. "This yours?" he asked.

Angie looked at the knife in his hand and nodded.

Wordlessly, he dropped the knife into the sink.

She offered him a towel to dry off with, then stood there, unable to look away, as he towel-dried his long black hair.

She looked away when his gaze met hers. "Breakfast is ready. I hope you like waffles."

"My favorite." He wadded up the towel and placed it on the counter before taking a place at the table. "Looks good," he remarked.

"Thank you." She sat down at the far end of the table and turned her attention to her breakfast, refusing to look up, refusing to meet his gaze even though she knew he was watching her.

Silence stretched between them. Awkward. Palpable. She thought of his hands, so big and brown, and wondered what they would feel like against her skin.

"You never told me your name."

"What?"

"Your name," he repeated. "You never told me what it is."

"Angela Wagner."

"Pleased to meet you, Angela."

"You may call me Miss Wagner."

He quirked an eyebrow at her. "Are you going to be staying here long?"

"A month."

He nodded, as if that pleased him, though she couldn't imagine why he would care one way or the other. "Maybe I could teach you how to ride."

"I don't think so."

"You might like it."

"I said no."

"Is it just me," Dakota asked, "or do you dislike everyone?"

"I don't dislike you, Mr. Sanders. I came up here to be . . ." She let her words trail off. As much as she wanted him to be gone, she couldn't bring herself to be rude.

"To be alone?" he guessed, finishing the thought for her.

"Yes."

He nodded, and she had the uneasy feeling that he knew she was running away, and why. "Just let me finish my coffee, and I'll be on my way."

"You're welcome to stay until it stops raining," Angie said, trying to force some enthusiasm into her tone.

"I think I'd better go. They'll be wondering what happened to me."

"What were you doing out in the storm last night, anyway?"

"One of our guests got thrown from her horse. She made it back to the ranch on foot, but the horse didn't come back. I was looking for her horse."

"Did you find it?"

"Yeah," Dakota replied tersely. He didn't add that he'd found the horse at the bottom of a ravine with a broken leg and had to destroy the animal. "I was on my way back to the ranch when lightning hit a tree alongside the trail. Spooked my horse and she went down. I landed pretty hard." Swallowing the last of the coffee, he stood up. "Good-bye, Miss Wagner."

Angie gazed up at him, her heart pounding erratically. He was leaving. She had expected to feel relieved; instead, she felt an unexplainable sense of loss. "Good-bye."

He looked at her for a long moment, then crossed the room. She refused to watch him leave, refused to admit that the house felt cold and empty without him.

Angie didn't know what had possessed her to bring the book with her, but after doing the breakfast dishes, she curled up on the sofa and began to read it again, drawn, against her will, into the story of Damon and Angeline, a haunting tale of lost love, of two hearts and souls striving to be together in spite of the evil forces determined to keep them apart.

To be embraced deep within her sweet fire, a part of her, was anguish and ecstasy, she read, *like dying just to live again. To love, to soar, to reach the glory of heaven upon the very earth . . .*

"Hogwash!" Angie muttered, but she didn't stop reading, and as the story unfolded, she found herself envisioning Dakota as Damon, and herself as Angeline. Even their names were similar, she realized.

What if there was such a thing as true love? Damon and Angeline had been real people, she believed, a man and a woman who had overcome adversity to be together. At the end of the book, Genevieve Betancourt had written that great risks often reaped great rewards.

Angie frowned. She had vowed never to risk her heart again, but what if, in refusing to try again, she missed out on her chance to know the kind of love Damon had shared with Angeline . . .

"Rubbish," she muttered. "You're just feeling maudlin because you're lonely . . ."

Lonely for Dakota?

The words, unspoken, echoed in the far recesses of her mind.

But that was ridiculous. She didn't even know the man. She told herself she wouldn't think of him again, but, try as she might, she could not put Dakota Sanders out of her mind. He invaded her every waking thought, and that night he slipped into her dreams, whispering words of love in her ear . . . words that sounded suspiciously like the words Damon had spoken to Angeline . . .

IV

The sound of a horse whinnying brought Angie to the kitchen window the following afternoon. Peering out, she saw Dakota swinging down from the saddle, found herself smiling as she watched him stride up to the back door. Dressed in a pair of faded Levi's, a blue denim shirt, worn boots, and a black cowboy hat, he looked good enough to eat.

The thought brought a flush to her cheeks. She was still blushing when she opened the door.

"Afternoon, Angie." His smile was bright enough to heat the whole state. "I thought you might have changed your mind about learning to ride."

"I haven't."

His dark brown eyes held her gaze as he stepped from the saddle, the reins loosely held in one hand. "Are you sure?" he drawled softly.

"Yes," Angie said, though her voice lacked its former conviction. "I'm sure."

"Come out with me, Angie."

The words, the way he said her name, made her shiver with pleasure. "Why? Why would you want to spend time with me?"

"Why?" He looked at her as if she were none too bright. "I'd like to get to know you better." He smiled at her again, a megawatt smile that warmed his eyes and made her heart flutter. "I'd like to make you smile."

"I smile all the time," she retorted defensively.

His gaze caressed her. "Then I'd like to see you smile just for me." He lifted his free hand, let his knuckles slide down her cheek. "Come out with me, Angie," he said again. "Please?"

She meant to say no. Instead, she nodded. "Just let me get my jacket."

"That's it," Dakota said, smiling his approval. "You're doing fine. Just ease up on the reins a little. Misty's a good trail horse. You can trust her."

Angie nodded. Three weeks had passed since her first horseback-riding lesson. She didn't know how Dakota explained his absences from the ranch, but gradually, the time they spent together stretched from an hour to two, and then three.

Angie had grown to love riding more than she had ever thought possible. Dakota had told her she had a natural seat and light hands, and she had been enormously pleased by the compliments, after he had explained them to her.

Riding wasn't nearly as difficult as she had thought it would be. There was something restful about riding through the timbered hills, with the blue sky above and Dakota at her side. Dakota. She slid a glance at him, wishing she knew more about him, but afraid to ask, afraid to read too much into their daily rides, afraid to let herself admit that she cared for him. Afraid to hope that he cared for her.

They'd been riding about an hour when they paused to rest the horses. Dakota lifted Angie from Misty's back, then offered her a cold drink pulled from one of his saddlebags.

"You ever been married, Angie?"

"No," she said, startled. It was the first time he had asked her such a personal question. "Have you?"

"Yeah," he admitted. "Once. For about ten minutes."

"Ten minutes?"

Dakota nodded. "She was a buckle bunny . . ."

"A what?"

"A girl who follows the rodeo. Kind of a cowboy groupie. Anyway, she was pretty and I was drunk and one thing led to another. Next thing I knew, she was beating on my trailer door, crying that she was pregnant and we had to get married." He shrugged ruefully. "Couple months later, she had a miscarriage. That's when she told me the baby wasn't mine."

"Did you love her?"

"I thought I did at the time. But now . . . I guess

it was just a bad case of lust." He took a long drink, then crushed the can in his hand. "Why aren't you married, Angie? Pretty girl like you, I'd think the men would be beating down your door."

Angie could feel the heat climbing into her cheeks again and she lowered her gaze.

"Someone hurt you, didn't he?"

"Does it show that much?" she asked sharply.

"Yeah. But you know what they say: nothing ventured, nothing gained."

"You mean, it's better to have loved and lost than never to have loved at all, and all that crap?" she asked in disgust.

"Something like that. I read something in a book once that sort of stayed with me, something about it being better to reach for the moon and settle for the stars than to make do with a handful of earth."

Angie looked up sharply, her eyes narrowing. "Where did you read that?"

"I told you, in a book."

"What book?"

"I don't remember the title. It belonged to my mother. Why?"

"Never mind," she said, her mind reeling with the knowledge that he had read *the book*. She remembered those lines all too well, remembered thinking that only fools reached for the moon.

"Who hurt you, Angie?" Dakota asked softly. "Who put out the light in your eyes and made you build that wall around your heart?"

"I don't want to talk about it."

"All right." He took the empty can from her hand and shoved it into his saddlebag, along with his own. He didn't understand his feelings for this woman, couldn't explain how he knew her so well, but he did. She was hurting, hurting deep inside, and for some reason he couldn't define, he wanted to erase the hurt from her eyes and make her smile again.

He wanted to kiss her . . .

Angie's eyes widened as Dakota moved toward her. Surely he didn't mean to kiss her, she thought, yet even then his arms were circling her waist, drawing her up against him as his mouth slanted over hers.

Honey and fire filled her veins, butterflies dipped and swayed in her stomach. Her eyelids fluttered down, her knees went weak, and she swayed against him, her lips opening to his, drinking him in.

She had never known such bliss, such pleasure, such an overwhelming urge to share her innermost thoughts and dreams. His hands moved over her back, her shoulders, then cupped her breasts, and she leaned into him, wanting him as she had never wanted anything in her whole life.

"Angie." Her name was a low groan in his throat as he drew her body against his, letting her feel his strength, his need. "Angie, do you know how beautiful you are, how good you taste?" he murmured, nuzzling the curve of her throat. "Do you have any idea what holding you does to me?"

He sank to the grass, carrying her down with him, until they were lying side by side, their bodies straining to be closer.

Never, she thought as his tongue teased hers, never before had she felt like this, not even with Roger. . . . Images of Roger Highland flashed through her mind, cooling her desire: Roger, telling her she was the prettiest woman he had ever known; Roger, telling her one lie after another until she was so caught up in the web of his words that she handed him her life savings, apologizing because it wasn't more!

With a sob, she wrenched herself out of Dakota's arms and sat up, her arms wrapped around her knees. "Why?" she exclaimed. "Why are you doing this? I don't understand."

Dakota sat up, frowning. "What's to understand? It's a beautiful day. You're a beautiful woman." He shrugged. "I thought that we . . ."

"How old are you?"

"Twenty-six," he replied, obviously puzzled by the question. "Why?"

"I'm older than you."

"So?"

"So I think it's time we went back."

"Is that what you really want?"

"Yes."

"Talk to me, Angie."

"Leave me alone!"

"I want to," he said, "but I can't."

Slowly, he reached for her again.

"Don't," she whispered. "Please don't."

"Trust me, Angie." His words were softly spoken as he drew her into his arms. "I won't hurt you."

"That's what Roger said, and it was a lie. Everything he said was a lie!"

"Roger? Is he the one who hurt you?"

She refused to meet his eyes. Instead, she stared straight ahead, her gaze fixed on Dakota's shirt pocket. "He said I was beautiful, too. He told me that he loved me, that he'd never hurt me, that he'd be mine forever. He wined me and he dined me and he . . ."

She drew in a long, shuddering breath. "And then he sweet-talked me out of my virginity and five thousand dollars."

"Angie." There was a wealth of compassion in his voice as he put his finger beneath her chin and forced her to look up at him. "I'm sorry, Angie. I'm sorry he hurt you."

Two large tears rolled down her cheeks. "Let me go, Dakota. Please let me go."

"You can't quit living just because life throws you a curve," he said quietly. "You make adjustments and go on."

"Are you speaking from experience?"

He nodded. "I grew up in California, but for as long as I can remember, all I wanted to do was rodeo. I never thought of doing anything else. I was gonna be the best there ever was, and then I was gonna take my winnings and buy my own ranch. It was my goal, my dream, and I almost made it to the top."

"What happened?" she asked, her own hurt momentarily forgotten.

"I drew a rank bronc at the semifinals in Amarillo. Damn horse threw me, then stomped on me pretty bad. I was in the hospital for six months, and when I got out, my rodeo days were over. It was a hard thing for me to accept, but . . ." He shrugged. "When I got tired of feeling sorry for myself, I went to work for Tom. It's not the life I dreamed of, but I can still rope and I can still ride, and I'm grateful for that."

"I'm glad things worked out for you," Angie said, pushing him away, "but, personally, I just don't feel grateful for the way my life has turned out."

Anger flared in Dakota's eyes, and then he hauled her up against him and kissed her hard.

She was breathless when he let her go.

"Enjoy your solitude, Angela," he said curtly, and before she could think or speak, he had mounted his horse and ridden away.

Angie stared after him, her lips still tingling from his kisses, afraid she had just made the worst mistake of her life.

V

Dakota rode at the head of a group of tourists, his thoughts turned inward as he tried to sort out his feelings for Angela Wagner. There was no reason why he should even be thinking of her. He hardly knew the woman. It was blatantly obvious she had just come out of a bad relationship, and just as obvious that she wasn't looking to start a new one. She had a hang-up about the fact that he was a few years younger than she was. If he was smart, he would just forget about her.

Thing was, sometimes he just wasn't as smart as he ought to be. He couldn't forget the awareness that vibrated between them whenever they touched, nor could he forget the rush of desire he'd felt when he kissed her. And yet there was more to it than just lust. He knew what that felt like, and what he felt for Angie was as far from mere lust as the sun from the moon.

Maybe it was just the fact that she didn't seem to like him that caused his interest. Maybe it was just his male ego refusing to take no for an answer. And maybe not . . .

He swore softly. He couldn't explain his attraction any more than he could ignore it.

Suddenly anxious to see her again, he headed back toward the ranch, cutting the trail ride short by a good thirty minutes.

In his quarters, he changed his shirt and combed his hair, then ran an assessing hand over his jaw, debating whether he needed a shave. He decided against it because he didn't want to take the time.

Five minutes later, he was riding for the old James place.

Angie wandered through the house, looking for something to do, but she'd already cleaned the house to within an inch of its life. She'd watered the plants, changed the sheets on the bed, fed the squirrels, filled the bird feeder. The dishes had been washed and put away, and it was only three o'clock.

She knew now why she liked living in town, why she worked six days a week. What did people in the country do with themselves?

With a sigh, she grabbed the book and went out to sit on the narrow front porch. Maybe within the pages of this ancient story she could find the answer to her own unrest.

She thumbed through the pages, her gaze settling on a sentence that seemed to stand out: "Dreams lie in books, and knowledge also . . ."

Dreams . . . she had always dreamed of finding a man who would love and cherish her, who would respect her, who would love her for who she was, who would allow her to be herself. She wanted a home of her own, a half-dozen children, a man to grow old beside her. She wanted to be able to write a short legacy of her own in the back of the book.

Closing her eyes, she imagined what she would write, but nothing earth-shattering came to mind.

She was hovering on the brink of sleep when the sound of hoofbeats roused her. Opening her eyes, she saw Dakota riding up the trail toward her.

He sat tall and straight in the saddle, his black hat pushed back on his head, his broad shoulders filling the dark blue cotton shirt. Her heart quickened at the sight of him; the butterflies that had been sleeping in her belly fluttered to life as she recalled the kiss they had shared. She hardly knew the man, yet she was drawn to him in ways she had never been drawn to anyone else.

He swung out of the saddle with lithe grace, vaulted the porch steps, plucked her out of the chair, and kissed her.

Blood really did boil, Angie thought, dazed, as his lips worked their magic on hers. Flooded with heat, she swayed against him, her legs suddenly weak.

She whimpered in protest when he took his mouth from hers.

"Be quiet," he admonished, and swinging her into his arms, he carried her into the house, down the narrow hall, into her bedroom.

"We belong together, Angie. I know it. I can feel it." He lowered her feet to the floor, looped his arms around her waist. "Search your heart. You know it's true."

She shook her head, drawing her hurt around her like a shield. "No. We don't even know each other."

His gaze burned into hers. "You know me," he said quietly. "You've always known me. I'm the happiness you've been looking for, the other half of your heart."

"How can you say that!" Needing to put some space between them, she stepped out of his embrace and folded her arms over her chest in a defensive gesture. She couldn't think clearly when he was standing so close to her, couldn't think of anything but how right it felt to be in his arms. "We hardly know each other."

"That's not true."

"You're too young for me. People will talk. They'll say I robbed the cradle."

"Do you really care what other people think?"

She nodded, then shook her head. "No, but what will *you* think in a few years? I couldn't bear it if you started looking at younger women."

"Dammit, Angie. You make it sound as if there're forty years between us instead of four."

"Sometimes I feel as if there are."

She felt the sting of tears behind her eyes, and she shook her head, hating the weakness that made her want to cry, hating Roger Highland for the pain he had caused her, for making her afraid to try again.

"Angie, you've got to trust me."

"I want to," she said, "but I think I'd rather spend the rest of my life alone than be hurt like that again."

"Angie, I can't promise that I won't ever hurt you. I'm only human. I'll make mistakes. Big ones sometimes. But I'll never betray you. I'll never leave you. I swear it."

Great risks often reap great rewards . . . Genevieve's words rang out loud and clear in the back of Angie's mind.

"I love you, Angie," Dakota said fervently. "I'll live for you and die for you, but first you've got to trust in me, in us."

"How can you love me? We hardly know each other," she said again.

"We have the rest of our lives to get acquainted," he promised. "Take a chance, Angie. Say you'll marry me, or I swear, I'll follow you till the end of your days."

She wanted to, oh, how she wanted to, and yet

she couldn't say the words. She stared up at him, mute, miserable.

Dakota took a deep breath. "All right," he said wearily. "We'll end it now. Just tell me you don't love me and I'll never bother you again."

And then he kissed her with all the love in his heart, kissed her out of her clothes and onto the mattress, kissed her until there was nothing in all the world but the two of them.

He whispered her name, telling her that he loved her, as he kissed away every doubt and every fear, kissed away her shyness so that her hands boldly explored the broad shoulders she so admired.

Her fingertips glided over his chest and over his strong, flat belly, marveling at the sheer beauty of the man. She gazed into the depths of his eyes—dark brown eyes that blazed with desire, warm brown eyes that spoke silent, endearing words of love.

And then he was touching her, teaching her that there was more to intimacy than the touch of passion-heated flesh against flesh, that it was a joining of heart and soul and spirit, a coming together that was stronger than yearning, more lasting than desire.

She felt a soul-deep sense of rightness as their bodies merged and became one. *Great risks reap great rewards . . . With honor came glory . . .* In the hazy recesses of her mind, she heard the words that wise women of earlier times had written in the book.

All true, she mused, but with love also came peace of spirit, a melding of two souls, and an implacable certainty that with love, all things were possible.

To be a part of him was to be a part of life itself

. . . Angeline's words settled into Angie's heart, and she knew that, for some unexplainable reason, fate was offering her the love of a lifetime, the same unconditional love that Angeline had shared with Damon, the same timeless love that Genevieve had shared with Lord Robert.

His hand cupped her cheek. "Tell me," he urged. "Tell me you love me, that you'll marry me."

She smiled at Dakota, her heart brimming with joy, as she reached out with every fiber of her being to embrace the love that Dakota offered her.

"I love you," she whispered fervently, "and I'll marry you."

She knew then what she would write in the book. Nothing earth-shattering. Just a simple phrase that wise women had known since time began: With love, all things are possible.

A Message From Liz Smith

How fortunate you are to be able to read and enjoy this entertaining book. Do you know how many adults in this country can't do that simply because they can't read? Over 40 million adult Americans.

The challenges of adult literacy are great and the problems don't lend themselves to easy solutions or convenient categories. Adults who can't read and write come from diverse economic, geographic, and cultural backgrounds. What they share is the desire but the inability to participate in the simplest daily pleasures, like reading the newspaper or reading a story to their children.

And in their struggle to learn to read and write, what adult literacy students also share is a willingness to experience growth in all its pain and possibilities, and a deep motivation to make their lives happier. In a word, courage.

As one older man said, "I waited all these years to do something about it because of the fear."

Luckily there is hope through a wonderful organization that helps these deserving adults turn their lives around – Literacy Volunteers of New York City. The really exciting news is that this established, respected not-for-profit organization is going national with an expanded mission and a new name – Literacy Partners.

In order to help more adults learn to read and write, Literacy Partners will work with other educational organizations across the country to provide excellence in training and in teaching adults to read.

Our inspiring vision is to create a national community of learning composed of eager, motivated students, dedicated volunteer tutors, and outstanding professionals.

As chair of Literacy Partners, I am proud of the work we have done in the past and enthusiastic about our plans for the future. We are grateful to Dorchester Publishing Co., Inc. for caring so deeply about our students' journey to literacy through the publication of this book.

One of our students best expressed the impact of our programs when she wrote, "I don't want my girls to grow up like I did, not being able to read or write. I want them to learn everything positive they can learn. Because I feel if you know how to read and write, there is nothing in this world that you cannot do."

Sincerely,
Liz Smith

For more information on Literacy Partners and its programs, please write or phone:

Literacy Partners
30 East 33rd Street
New York, NY 10016
Phone (212) 725-9200
FAX (212) 725-0414

Special Thanks To:

Offset Paperback Mfgs., Inc.
Creative Label, Inc.
Assel Studios LTD.
ICD/Hearst Corporation
Kathryn Falk
Stone Consolidated Paper Sales Corp.

Madeline Baker
Mary Balogh
Elaine Barbieri
Lori Copeland
Cassie Edwards
Heather Graham
Catherine Hart
Virginia Henley
Penelope Neri
Diana Palmer
Janelle Taylor

ALL PROFITS
FROM
LOVE'S LEGACY
WILL BENEFIT
THE
LITERACY
PARTNERS,
AN
ORGANIZATION
PROMOTING
READING
AMONG ADULTS.